LIKE A BEE TO HONEY

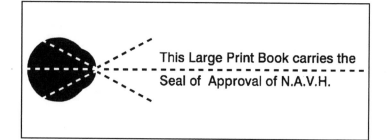

This Large Print Book carries the
Seal of Approval of N.A.V.H.

LIKE A BEE TO HONEY

JENNIFER BECKSTRAND

KENNEBEC LARGE PRINT
A part of Gale, Cengage Learning

GALE
CENGAGE Learning

Farmington Hills, Mich • San Francisco • New York • Waterville, Maine
Meriden, Conn • Mason, Ohio • Chicago

GALE
CENGAGE Learning®

LIBRARY OF CONGRESS CATALOGING-IN-PUBLICATION DATA

Names: Beckstrand, Jennifer, author.
Title: Like a bee to honey / by Jennifer Beckstrand.
Description: Large print edition. | Waterville, Maine : Kennebec Large Print, 2017.
| Series: The Honeybee sisters | Series: Kennebec Large Print superior collection
Identifiers: LCCN 2016046988| ISBN 9781410495037 (softcover) | ISBN 1410495035
(softcover)
Subjects: LCSH: Amish—Fiction. | Sisters—Fiction. | Bee culture—Fiction. | Large
type books. | GSAFD: Christian fiction.
Classification: LCC PS3602.E3323 L55 2017 | DDC 813/.6—dc23
LC record available at https://lccn.loc.gov/2016046988

Published in 2017 by arrangement with Zebra Books, an imprint of
Kensington Publishing Corp.

Printed in the United States of America
1 2 3 4 5 6 7 21 20 19 18 17

LIKE A BEE TO HONEY

CHAPTER ONE

Josiah Yoder's heart pounded so hard, they could probably hear it in the next county, and it made him kind of disgusted with himself. He'd been to the Honeybee *schwesters'* farm at least a dozen times. The mere thought of possibly, maybe, hopefully seeing Rose Christner shouldn't make him feel as if he were going to have a heart attack.

Just because he had been completely and hopelessly in love with Rose for four long years didn't mean he couldn't be perfectly calm when he saw her. He had never managed to be perfectly calm before, but surely he could muster his levelheadedness today. He'd scare Rose away if he drove onto her farm jumpy and agitated like a spooked horse.

His chicken heart only beat faster as his open-air buggy passed the sign on the road that stood at the entrance to the Christners' property. BEWARE THE HONEYBEES, it said. Every time he saw that sign, his pulse raced out of control — not because he was especially afraid of honeybees, but because Rose had painted that sign herself. With her own two hands. It was almost as if she were standing there at the entrance to their property greeting him with a smile and a wave.

Almost. It was almost like that.

The sign had Rose's touch all over it. She'd painted red roses and bright yellow daisies, pastel tulips and spiky dandelions. Bees and butterflies frolicked among the flowers — kind of like the ones making a home in his gut at this very minute.

His heart knocked into his ribs like a sledgehammer and smashed all the butterflies in his stomach.

Oy, anyhow. He was hopeless.

No matter how *ferhoodled,* he was determined not to mess things up with Rose — not when he had already made a connection with her. And by "connection," he meant that she didn't cower like a nervous bunny rabbit when he said hello.

With a light tug on the reins, Josiah guided his horse, Max, onto the small wooden bridge that marked the entrance to the Honeybee *schwesters'* property. He caught his breath and nearly choked. Rose and her sisters, Lily and Poppy, were but thirty feet away tending to their beehives. Each of them wore one of those beekeeper hats with netting draped over the top, plus a long-sleeved jacket and jeans tucked into long stockings. The outfits weren't strictly Amish, but the sisters couldn't wear Plain dresses while tending the bees or they'd be stung for sure and certain. Josiah pinned his gaze to the shortest of the three beekeepers. Rose looked pretty no matter what she wore.

All three sisters turned to see who was coming over their bridge and waved to him, even Rose. Surely his heart couldn't beat any faster.

He raised his arm and waved back but tried not to look too eager. Eagerness tended to make Rose nervous. Once, after a fellowship supper, Josiah had watched Benji Kauffman follow Rose around like a lost puppy looking for a scrap of food. Benji was persistent and wouldn't leave her alone until Rose had planted herself firmly between her sisters for the rest of the day and Poppy had given Benji a very dirty look. Benji had slouched home as if he were going to his own funeral.

Josiah's gut clenched. He couldn't make any mistakes. He'd been to enough funerals to last a lifetime.

The sisters turned back to their hives. He slumped his shoulders. All he needed to do was deliver his little bag to the house. He had no *gute* excuse for talking to Rose whatsoever.

He realized he had an iron grip on the reins when Max veered onto the grass and started trampling dandelions. Josiah quickly pulled the horse up and pointed him in the right direction. Rose would be unhappy if the dandelions got trampled and so would her *aendi* Bitsy.

He guided Max to the end of the lane, where the Honeybee sisters' house stood to his right and their red barn with the pink door stood to his left. Josiah, with his friends Dan and Luke, had come in the middle of the night a few weeks ago to paint that door. In the dark, they hadn't been able to get the color quite right. It had turned out a lovely shade of rose-petal pink.

A ragged-looking black-and-white cat sat on its haunches not three feet from Josiah's buggy, guarding the farm from intruders. The cat scowled at Josiah as if daring him to set foot on their property. Josiah raised his eyebrows. That cat looked mean enough to halt a whole herd of charging bulls. He didn't know if it would be wiser to ignore him or run away as fast as he could.

Rose probably wouldn't like it either way.

Rose had barely noticed him. She probably wouldn't even know.

He climbed from the buggy and stuffed his hand in his pocket to make sure the bag was still there. If he wanted to talk to Rose, he'd have to make his own chances, like Luke Bontrager was always telling him. Luke said Josiah was as slow as a turtle. Would it hurt to pick up the pace?

Even though he was risking a finger or two, Josiah bent down and reached out to smooth his hand along the ragged cat's head, partly to impress Rose with his love for animals and partly to make peace so the cat wouldn't bite off his arm.

The cat bared his teeth and hissed as if he were trying to set Josiah on fire. Wanting to keep both of the hands he had, Josiah pulled away and glanced in Rose's direction. He'd have to impress her some other way. She didn't need to witness his failure with a cat.

When he stood up straight and tried to walk away, the cat threw himself at Josiah and hooked his claws into one of his trousers legs. *"Ach!"* Josiah said, as the cat's sharp claws pierced his ankle. The animal was trying to kill him.

The warning at the front of the property

hadn't said anything about cats.

They should probably add that to the sign as soon as possible.

CHAPTER TWO

Gasping in pain, Josiah tried to shake the cat gently from his leg. Rose had a tender heart for all living creatures. She would be unhappy if he kicked out and sent the cat flying.

The cat didn't budge.

Josiah reached down and tried to wrench it away from his leg without taking several chunks of flesh with him, but the cat's claws were buried deep, as if he were holding on for dear life. An orange-marmalade ball of fur bounded across the lawn and started climbing Josiah's other leg. This one was a cute little kitten with sharp, not-so-cute claws that made Josiah flinch when they punctured his leg.

The kitty making its way up Josiah's trousers would surely fall if Josiah made any sudden movements, and the ugly black cat had decided to park on Josiah's foot with its claws firmly embedded in Josiah's shin.

Another cat, milky white and elegant, sauntered across the lawn and planted itself at Josiah's feet. She rolled onto her back and looked up at Josiah with a mixture of disdain and indignation, as if she had a plan to make Josiah very sorry for intruding.

Either the cats were trying to keep him from escaping or they were overjoyed to see him. He couldn't imagine they were overjoyed. He barely knew any of them.

The Honeybee *schwesters* were a good twenty yards off, so he couldn't hear what they said to each other, but at least they had noticed he was in trouble. Poppy nudged Rose and gestured toward him with her smoker. Rose hesitated, then stepped away from the hives and removed her long canvas gloves and beekeeper's hat to reveal her golden hair tied up with a light pink scarf and her cheeks tinted an appealing shade of peaches and cream.

His heart did a flip, three somersaults, four push-ups, several cartwheels, and a double back handspring.

Rose Christner was coming to his rescue.

His mouth went dry as he thought of about a million things he wanted to say to her, and — *oh sis yuscht* — he had suddenly lost the power of speech.

She glanced at him and gave him a tenta-

14

tive half smile before turning her attention to the cats. "Billy Idol, Leonard Nimoy, you naughty, naughty kitties." She knelt on the ground and carefully detached the orange kitten's claws from Josiah's trousers. He'd made it all the way up to Josiah's knee.

"He's a *gute* climber," Josiah said, trying to sound cheerful and meek, but not too eager, all at the same time. Mostly, he sounded gravelly, like he'd swallowed a cup of rocks for breakfast.

Rose nuzzled the kitten's soft head against her cheek. "I hope she didn't hurt you. Leonard Nimoy is just learning her manners, and Billy Idol is a bad influence."

"No harm done," he said, wishing she'd turn her gaze to him and give him a glimpse of those eyes that were as blue as ice on Lake Michigan. "Is the kitten a female?"

She finally looked at him. He tried to act like nothing important had just happened, even though his head spun like a washing machine in a tornado.

"*Jah,*" she said, looking away as soon as their eyes met. "Aunt Bitsy named her Leonard Nimoy after a movie star, but she's a girl." Rose set Leonard Nimoy on the grass and shook her finger when the kitten tried to scale Josiah's leg again. "*Nae,* Leonard Nimoy. Leave Josiah be."

Josiah liked the way she talked to the cats, as if they were adorable and she loved them with all her heart, but there was nothing adorable about the black-and-white cat still clinging to his trousers. Rose smoothed her hand over the cat's blotchy fur. "Billy Idol, there's no need to attack people. You're being a very bad example to Leonard Nimoy."

"Billy Idol?"

A cautious smile flitted across Rose's face. "Aunt Bitsy named all our cats."

She gently but firmly pried Billy Idol from Josiah's other leg. The cat snarled as Rose wrapped her arms around him and cuddled him like a newborn *buplie.*

One of Billy Idol's ears was split down the middle, and his right eye only opened halfway. His nose was also scarred, and his coat looked as if he'd been in a few catfights in which fur had literally been flying. His upper lip was permanently lifted into a sneer by a scar that ran down the side of his mouth.

"I'm sorry if they hurt you," Rose said. She secured Billy Idol in one arm and scooped up the white cat, which was still rolling around in the grass, with the other hand. "Farrah Fawcett isn't usually so friendly."

Friendly? If this was friendly, he had no

desire to see hostile.

"I don't mind," Josiah said. "I'm not sure why all three of your cats suddenly took a liking to me." Or how he could get Rose to do the same.

Her lips twitched with uncertainty. "Well, you are a very nice boy."

Really? She thought he was a very nice boy? He cleared his throat in an attempt to keep his voice from betraying his elation. "You're the one who's nice. My sister can't stop talking about that chocolate cake you baked for her family." He threw caution to the wind and sat cross-legged next to her in the grass. Surely she wouldn't mind if he sat beside her instead of towering over her.

Rose tensed and clutched Billy Idol and Farrah Fawcett closer.

Josiah's heart sank. *Nae.* She didn't like that better at all.

To his added horror, all three cats chose that moment to resume their attack. Either they were incredibly protective of Rose, or it just wasn't Josiah's day. Leonard, the girl kitten, catapulted herself toward Josiah and gave his forearm four deep scratches trying to catch herself. Billy Idol struggled out of Rose's arms and practically vaulted into Josiah's lap, where he sunk his tiny teeth into Josiah's pocket. Farrah Fawcett also

17

jumped onto Josiah's lap and dug her claws into his leg. Josiah shouted in surprise and leaped to his feet, making all three cats tumble like balls of yarn off an Amish *mammi*'s lap.

"Ach, du lieva!" Rose said.

Not only had he sat too close to Rose without her permission, but he had also unintentionally upset her beloved cats. He might never be allowed on the farm again.

Rose pursed her lips, and her blue eyes turned dark with distress. She scooped Leonard Nimoy into her arms. "Are you all right?"

Josiah paused for a second until he realized Rose was talking to him and not the kitten. He swiped his hand across his forearm, hopefully erasing any evidence that Leonard Nimoy had drawn blood. He didn't want Rose to worry. "I'm sorry. I didn't mean for them to fall like that."

She seemed more concerned for his feelings than her own. "Please don't worry. Cats always land on their feet." They both looked down at Billy Idol. He was rolling around in the grass. "I don't know why they went crazy like that."

Poppy and Lily, Rose's always-protective sisters, must have recognized that Josiah had tangled himself into some sort of impossible knot. They set down their smokers, took off their hats and gloves, and were at Rose's side in less time than it would have taken Billy Idol to sink his teeth into Josiah's neck.

Poppy's unruly hair was tied up in a royal-blue scarf, and she wore a thick cast on her right hand. She'd broken her hand a week ago punching an *Englischer* in the mouth — an *Englischer* named Griff Simons who had tried to give Rose a kiss.

Lily wore a bright yellow scarf with a white zip-up jacket. They stood on either side of Rose and eyed Josiah as if he were a horse at auction. "It's *gute* to see you, Josiah," Lily said. She even acted like she meant it.

Poppy folded her arms and cocked an eyebrow while amusement and annoyance made an uneasy truce on her face. "Need some help, Josiah?"

Of course he needed help. Rose was nervous, the cats had gone crazy, and he had several puncture wounds in his legs — not to mention the blood that was slowly dripping down his arm courtesy of Leonard Nimoy. He quickly slid his arm behind his back.

It would be best if he went away and tried again tomorrow. Was there a nice, nonthreatening activity he could do with Rose? Would she like sitting next to him on the porch while he read from the dictionary?

Nae. She got anxious when he got too close.

"I'm wonderful sorry about disturbing you," he said, pulling the drawstring bag from his pocket and handing it to Poppy. "Luke asked me to bring this to you. He said you need it for a recipe."

Poppy put the bag to her nose and rolled her eyes. "That boy!" she said, but there was affection behind her aggravated tone. Luke Bontrager drove her crazy, but she was still madly in love with him. "Doesn't he know what basil is?"

Lily grinned while keeping her eyes glued to Josiah's face. "He's better with tools."

"It isn't basil?" Josiah asked.

Poppy closed the bag and looped the drawstring around her finger. "It's catnip. No wonder the cats are so interested."

Lily and Poppy shared a look that Josiah knew wasn't meant for him to see. "Maybe Luke is smarter than we think," Lily said.

Poppy winked at Lily. "The smartest."

Lily's expression was one of pure, unsympathetic pity. "He sent you into the lion's den with a pocketful of catnip. No wonder the cats attacked."

"I'm sorry about my thick-headed fiancé," Poppy said, not acting sorry at all.

Josiah wasn't sure what to think. The catnip had attracted the cats, and the cats had attracted Rose. He'd actually had a conversation with Rose Christner because of Luke's catnip.

And that had probably been Luke's intent all along.

Luke thought Josiah was slower than cold tar on a frosty morning when it came to courting Rose. Perhaps Luke was trying to speed things up.

Josiah didn't know whether to be offended or grateful that Luke had stuck his nose into Josiah's business. He'd have a few wounds, that was certain, but Rose had said more to him in that one conversation than she had in almost four years combined. He wanted to give Luke a big hug. And then punch him.

He wiped a grin off his face. With friends like Luke, who needed a meddling *mammi*?

Rose gasped. "You're bleeding."

Oy, anyhow. He should have left his hand behind his back so Rose wouldn't be upset. He studied the smear of blood on his forearm. *Ach.* He probably had a *gute*-sized spot of blood on the back of his shirt from trying to hide his injured arm.

21

"It's nothing," he said, giving Rose the most reassuring smile he could muster. "Doesn't even hurt."

Poppy glanced sideways at Rose. "Josiah, you should put some ointment on that. It looks like it really hurts, and I'd hate to see you get an infection." Josiah had never seen such consideration from Poppy before. She was more likely to tell him to go rub some dirt in it.

"*Jah*. It looks very bad," Rose said, her eyes alight with sympathy. Rose wrapped her fingers around Poppy's wrist. "Will you go help him wash it out? I would feel terrible if it got infected."

Poppy waved her substantial cast in the air. "I've only got one good hand."

"It's not that bad," Josiah said. "I'll rinse it in the hose when I get home." He'd have to be tricky and leave without turning his back on them. Rose would probably faint if she saw the blood on the back of his shirt.

Rose's lips drooped. "I'm sure it hurts something wonderful. You need special ointment." She looked at Lily. "Can you take Josiah into the house and bandage it up?"

Lily was already strolling the other way, smiling like Billy Idol with a mouth full of mouse. "I've got to get back to the bees."

Rose glanced at Josiah and nibbled on her

bottom lip as the tiny lines around her eyes crinkled with worry. "It was Leonard Nimoy's fault. We should see that Josiah is taken care of."

Poppy waved the bag of catnip in Farrah Fawcett's direction. "I'll take care of the cat problem." She scooped some catnip from the little bag, crumbled it in her hand like dry bread, and let it fall to the ground as she walked away. All three cats followed her. Billy Idol meowed and carried on as if she were dragging him by the tail.

Josiah frowned to himself. Didn't Rose's *schwesters* see how unsettled she was? Couldn't one of them sacrifice two minutes of her time to take him into the house and slap a Band-Aid on his arm? Rose would feel better if he had a Band-Aid.

Rose fingered a strand of hair at the nape of her neck. He did his best not to be distracted by the graceful curve of her fingers or her hair the color of white clover honey.

Josiah took a handkerchief out of his pocket and swiped it across the scratch. He grimaced. The attempt to wipe it away smeared the blood across his arm and made it look ten times worse. "I'll go straight home and wash this out with soap. It's not deep."

Rose eyed him as if he might bite her. How was he ever going to convince her to love him when he saw nothing but uncertainty in her eyes? He swallowed the lump of despair in his throat and took two steps backward. "It was wonderful-*gute* to see you, Rose. *Denki* for saving me from the cats."

"Will you be able to work the fields today?"

He nodded. "I'll be sure to wrap it up."

The troubled, vulnerable look on Rose's face made him ache to gather her in his arms and reassure her that she could be certain of him, that things weren't as bad as she seemed to think they were. But something told him that ambushing Rose wouldn't be a *gute* idea. Not a *gute* idea at all. He couldn't prove his love if she ran away.

Rose pressed her lips into a determined line. "*Cum* into the house. I will wrap it up for you." She was too tenderhearted to let anyone suffer. Though fear often paralyzed her, she would brave a whole roomful of strangers if someone needed her help. It was one of the things Josiah loved about her.

Spending even three more minutes in Rose's company sounded *wunderbarr,* but knowing how uncomfortable she was, he would be selfish indeed if he took advantage of her kindness. "I don't want to be a bother."

She lowered her eyes. "Please come into the house. I'll feel better knowing someone saw to it."

"Rose," Josiah said. He paused long enough for Rose to lift her gaze to his face. "What will make you happy?"

"What do you mean?"

"Would you be happier taking care of my scratch or having me out of your hair?"

She cracked a smile. "You're not in my hair."

He returned her smile with an uncertain one of his own. "I don't want to be a pest, and I want you to be happy."

She started playing with that strand of hair again. "What I feel doesn't matter."

"It's what matters most to me."

That seemed to trouble her more than anything. She swaddled both arms around her waist. "It's better if we just do what *you* want. If you do what I want, then it's my fault if you're unhappy about it."

He smiled to prove to her he didn't care either way. He cared deeply, but she wouldn't see that from him. "Maybe it is my fault if you're unhappy. I can be very pushy. Your cats were right to try to scare me off your farm."

Rose's lips curled slightly. "Would you like to come in, or would you rather I stay out of *your* hair?"

He took off his hat and ran his fingers through his hair, cropped short, courtesy of his nephew. "I don't have enough hair to answer that question."

Her smile bloomed like roses in late spring.

His heart swelled until his chest felt crowded. "Although you have cleverly tried to change the subject, I'm going to walk to my buggy — backward so you don't see the big spot of blood on my shirt. If you want me to come into the house, stop me now. Otherwise, I'll climb in my buggy and go. No hard feelings either way." He made the gesture of buttoning his lips together and took four steps backward.

She glued her gaze to his, and he could see the choices struggle with each other on her face. "I'd feel better if you came in the house," she finally said.

He stopped short and smiled with his whole body. "Me too."

She smiled back and motioned toward the house. He let her lead the way up the porch steps. A tiny dead mouse lay on the welcome mat. Rose shuddered but pasted a pleasant look on her face. "Billy Idol is such a dear cat. He's always leaving presents for us. He has taken care of our mouse problem, but Aunt Bitsy isn't happy about the dead mice. She keeps threatening to give Billy Idol away."

"She'll never have to know about this one," Josiah said, picking up the mat and shaking it so the mouse tumbled into the dirt to the side of the house off the porch.

"Denki," she said, not meeting his eye but smiling anyway.

He opened the front door for her and followed her into the house, where the heavenly smell of freshly baked bread met them.

"It smells delicious in here," Josiah said.

Rose's Aunt Bitsy stood at the butcher-block island, straining at the lid of a jar of pickles, and Josiah grew more agitated than he already was. According to Lily's fiancé, Dan Kanagy, Bitsy did not like boys in the house, even if it was for something as harmless as a Band-Aid. She owned a shotgun, and she wasn't afraid to point it at people.

Bitsy wasn't old. She couldn't have been more than fifty or so, but she seemed to have a permanent frown on her face and it looked as if the worry line between her eyebrows had been ironed into place. Even though she wasn't elderly, she had salt-and-

27

pepper gray hair that she often tinted pastel colors. Today, her hair was a light shade of green. With her kelly-green dress, she looked a little like a houseplant.

Bitsy narrowed her eyes when Josiah followed Rose into the house. "Josiah Yoder," she said. His name sounded like a grunt when she said it. "I'm glad you're here."

Josiah nearly choked on his surprise. "You are?"

"Well, not really glad. I don't want you to get the notion that I'm happy to see you. But I need this bottle opened, and you're just in time to do it. Then you can leave."

Bitsy was the door Josiah would have to go through to get to Rose. He would do a backflip off the roof if it would win Bitsy's approval. He strode to the island and took the jar from her. "I'm honored you would ask for my help." The jar opened with one easy twist of his wrist. He smiled and handed it back.

"Don't get cocky," Bitsy said, setting the jar on the counter. "I loosened it for you."

Josiah wasn't offended by her brusque manner. Everybody knew what a *gute* and charitable woman Bitsy was, always the first to a sickbed, always baking or sewing for someone who needed a hand. She was a tough nut to crack. That was all. "I'm glad I

28

could help."

Bitsy eyed him unapologetically, as if trying to figure out why he was standing in her kitchen. "Well. I always say *denki,* so *denki.* You can go now."

Rose smiled at her *aendi* before pulling the ointment and bandages out of the drawer and setting them on the table. "Leonard Nimoy gave Josiah a bad scratch, Aendi Bitsy. I told him I'd give him a Band-Aid."

Bitsy propped her hands on her hips. "Leonard Nimoy? We haven't even had her a week, and she's already scratching people. I've half a mind to send those cats to obedience school."

Josiah followed behind Rose as she slipped a towel from the drawer, got it wet, and squirted a little soap on it. She turned before he had the chance to back away, and he found himself face-to-face with her, with only inches between them.

She caught her breath. He cleared his throat and backed away a bit. *Oy,* anyhow. He wanted to kick himself. How could he gain Rose's trust if he kept startling her?

But he liked being close, for sure and certain.

She didn't relax. "Do you want to sit down?"

"Where do you want me to sit?" He wanted to sit next to her, wherever she was going to sit.

She pointed to a chair at the table.

He knew how uncomfortable she was, and he wished he knew how to make everything all better. He'd have to settle for a re-assuring smile. Would she see the concern behind it? He sat down, rested his injured arm on the table, and stretched it out so Rose could reach it easily. She hesitated for only a moment before sitting next to him and dabbing at the scratches with her wet towel.

"Does it hurt? I don't want to hurt you."

He would rather let Leonard Nimoy scratch him again than let Rose think that she was causing him any pain. "You're very gentle. I can barely feel it."

"Josiah is a farmer," Bitsy said, still standing at the island. She skewered a pickle with her fork. "His life is pain."

Josiah chuckled. "It's not as bad as all that."

"You're at the mercy of the weather," Bitsy said.

"Not so much the weather as the grace of *Gotte*," Josiah said. "Farming is hard work, but it's taught me to trust in the Lord. He might send rain or drought or an early frost.

I've learned to surrender to His will, no matter how hard the lesson."

Bitsy nodded. "After all you've been through, I suppose you've learned that."

After all he'd been through.

Jah. The pain of his parents' deaths still felt like a fresh, untended wound. He glanced up to see Rose studying his face, her own eyes soft and misty, her expression lined with sympathy and pain. He'd lost both his parents, just like Rose had, but he had been old enough when his parents died to make some sort of sense of the whole thing. Rose had been a little girl.

"I'm sorry," Rose whispered.

"I'm sorry about your parents too."

He could see her struggling for a carefree smile. "I almost don't remember them. I was only five when they died, too little to remember much." Something even deeper than grief briefly darkened her features. "And of course, there were no photos."

Unable to bear the thought of her shouldering the sorrow all by herself, Josiah slid his hand over hers. "They'll never be forgotten as long as you carry them in your heart."

Her eyes pooled with moisture, and she sprang to her feet. "I think it's clean," she said, turning her back on him and marching to the sink with her towel.

Josiah felt so low, he could have slid underneath the crack between the door and the floor. He had made Rose cry, or at least think about crying. If Bitsy caught a glimpse of Rose's face, she'd probably point her shotgun at Josiah and kick him out of the house.

"Your *mater* had hair like Lily's, lips like Poppy's, and eyes like yours," Bitsy said. She took a big bite of her pickle, laid it on the counter, and ambled into the storage room, still talking. "She had pretty long fingers and wasn't clunky like I am."

Feeling as if there were an anvil tied around his heart, Josiah watched Rose out of the corner of his eye. She stood at the sink with her back to him and splashed water on her face. She came back to the table, and he tried to communicate an apology with just a look. She wouldn't meet his eye.

He leaned toward her. "I'm sorry, Rose," he whispered, so Bitsy in the storage room couldn't hear. "I'm sorry if I said or did anything to upset you."

She drew her brows together. "*Ach, nae. Nae.* Of course not. I was just thinking about my parents."

He didn't feel much better, but she seemed to be telling the truth. Still, he hated to think that he'd been the one to make her unhappy. *Ach, du lieva,* couldn't he do anything right?

Rose smeared ointment onto the four scratches on Josiah's arm, then covered them with two Band-Aids and a square of gauze. She wrapped several layers of medical tape around the gauze, securing it better than he secured his hay in the winter. "Do you think that will be okay?"

Josiah lifted his arm and flexed his hand. "This wouldn't get wet on a leaky boat in a hurricane. Can I come over every time I need a Band-Aid?"

She blushed and stared faithfully at the wood grain on the table.

Could he just kick himself now and get it over with? "I'm sorry. I won't tease if you don't like it."

She dared a glance at him. "It's okay."

He stared at her for a second longer than he should have before scooting his chair out and standing up. "I should go."

Bitsy seemed to shoot out from the back room. "Before you leave, Josiah Yoder, I have some things I need you to lift."

"Lift?" Rose said.

Again, Josiah tried not to act too eager. "You need me to lift something?" If Rose saw how useful he was, maybe she'd give

33

him a chance to win her heart.

Bitsy pointed to the storage room. "There's a fifty-pound bag of flour in there that I need you to dump in the flour bin."

"But, Aunt Bitsy . . ." Rose said.

Josiah jumped right in. "*Ach,* I don't mind. I'm happy to help carry the heavy stuff so you don't have to."

Rose seemed confused, but she didn't say anything else.

Bitsy took him into the storage room, where there were rows of shelves covered with jars of golden honey, dozens of bottles of peaches and cherries and spaghetti sauce, and bags of wheat and rice stacked five high. She pointed to a bag of white flour on one of the shelves. "That one."

Josiah slid the bag off the shelf and threw it across his shoulder. Fifty pounds wasn't that much. He'd hefted hay bales twice this size. "Where to?"

"Into the kitchen," Bitsy said. She led the way and directed him to set the flour on the butcher-block island. She glanced at Rose. "You've got muscles. I'll give you that, Josiah Yoder. You don't mind muscles, do you, Rose?"

Rose quickly averted her eyes as if she'd been caught staring. "I don't know what you mean."

Bitsy grunted. "They come in handy on the farm, I suppose." She opened a cupboard underneath the island and pulled a bin from one of the shelves. *"Ach,"* she said. "This is already full."

"I was trying to tell you," Rose said. "Poppy filled it last night."

Bitsy shrugged. "Back to the storage room then."

Josiah hefted the bag of flour over his shoulder and took it back to the shelf in the storage room.

Bitsy followed him with a rag in her hand. "I'll just wipe up this flour dust," she said. "You can go now, Josiah. You've overstayed your welcome."

Josiah tried not to feel dejected. He had been allowed to stay several minutes longer than in his wildest dreams. He mustn't be greedy. He went back into the kitchen. Rose seemed less composed than ever. She was fidgeting with the strand of hair again. "Before you leave, would you like a loaf of bread?" she said.

He gave her a guarded, not-too-eager half smile. "I'd like that very much."

She nodded, took a box of tinfoil out of the drawer, and tore a piece off the roll.

Bitsy emerged from the back room just as Rose wrapped Josiah's loaf of bread in the tinfoil. She squinted in Josiah's direction. "What are you doing, baby sister?"

Rose drew her brows together. "I'm sorry, Aunt Bitsy, but I'm sending some bread home with Josiah."

Bitsy gave Josiah the stink eye — for what, he didn't know, but he'd kind of been expecting it all morning. "Absolutely not."

"But, Aunt Bitsy, we have an extra loaf."

Bitsy looked as if she were ready to pounce on him. "Josiah should know the rules."

"What rules?" Josiah said.

Bitsy held up one finger. "Number one. No kissing on the porch."

Rose turned bright red. "Aunt Bitsy!"

Bitsy put her arm around Rose. "That's just for Lily and Poppy, baby sister." She glared at Josiah. "Right?"

Josiah's throat constricted. The thought of kissing on the porch probably gave Rose nightmares. How could Bitsy be so cruel as to plant that thought in her niece's head and scare her off ever wanting to talk to him again? No matter that Josiah was hoping to kiss Rose on somebody's porch, it was Rose's feelings that mattered right now. "No kissing on the porch," he finally said.

Bitsy eyed him as if she didn't believe a word he said and held up a second finger. "Number two. Paul Glick is not allowed in

36

the house." Paul Glick was Lily's ex-boyfriend, and he had a mean streak a mile long.

Josiah couldn't much blame Bitsy for that rule. Lily's fiancé, Dan Kanagy, was Josiah's best friend, and Paul Glick had made Dan's life wonderful miserable.

"Number three. Don't feed the boys. They are like stray cats. If you feed them once, they will keep coming back. I don't need another stray cat."

Josiah took a deep breath to try to clear off the wagon that seemed to have parked on his chest. "I'm sorry. I don't want any bad feelings. I won't take not even one slice."

Rose wrapped her arms around her *aendi*'s neck and leaned her head so they were touching foreheads. "Aunt Bitsy, Josiah lives all alone without a soul to cook for him."

She was defending him? He felt like singing. "It's okay. I completely respect your *aendi*'s rules. Nobody asked me to barge into your house."

Bitsy was firm as a mountain. "His sister feeds him sometimes, and he's twenty-one years old."

"Twenty-two," Josiah said. "I'll be twenty-three next week."

Bitsy nodded. "Plenty old to take care of

himself."

"I've taken care of myself for four years."

"He won't starve," Bitsy insisted.

Josiah met Bitsy's eye with a steady and earnest gaze. "And I wouldn't see Rose upset for the whole world."

She narrowed her eyes into slits. "Neither would I."

Rose was on the verge of tears. "But, Aunt Bitsy, he's an orphan. Like me."

Bitsy scrunched her lips together as a sigh rumbled deep in her throat. The sigh turned into a grunt, which came out of her mouth as a growl. She lifted her gaze to the ceiling. "You know I have a soft spot for orphans. Why does he have to be an orphan?"

Was she talking to *Gotte*? Probably, unless someone Josiah didn't know about lived upstairs.

She threw up her hands in surrender. "Fine. Give the orphan a loaf of bread if it makes you happy."

Josiah pinned Rose with a serious gaze "But only if it makes you happy."

Rose curled her lips slightly. "It does."

"It's just a loaf of bread, Josiah," Bitsy said. "You've got to promise not to take it the wrong way."

"I promise," he said, with no idea what the "wrong way" was. Anything to make

Bitsy happy. And Rose.

Rose handed the loaf to Josiah.

"You made this?" he said.

"*Jah.* It's honey wheat."

He smiled. "I think I've died and gone to heaven."

"Just so long as you do your dying somewhere besides my yard," Bitsy said. "Bees are funny about things like death."

Josiah opened the door, rested his hand on the knob, and looked at Rose. "If you ever need anything — jars to be opened or basil or fennel or new shoelaces — please let me know. I'll do whatever you need. Okay?"

"Okay," Rose said, seeming all the more embarrassed. He should probably quit talking.

He stared at the loaf of bread in his hand. Rose had freely offered it, even when her aunt had resisted. She had smiled at him in an unguarded moment. Maybe she wasn't terrified of him. Maybe she liked him okay. Maybe there was hope he could soften her up.

"You're looking at that bread as if you're contemplating scripture," Bitsy said. "Don't you have crops to get to? You shouldn't let all those muscles go to waste."

He tucked the loaf under one arm. "Sorry.

I just want you to know that I'm very grateful for the bread. Not everyone gets something from Rose Christner's kitchen."

"Oh sis yuscht," Bitsy said, wrinkling her nose in disgust. "You're taking it the wrong way. Against my better judgment, I let Rose give it to you, and now you're taking it the wrong way." She looked up to the ceiling. "Heaven help us."

CHAPTER THREE

"Leonard Nimoy," Rose said. "Leave Farrah Fawcett in peace. She's trying to take a nap."

The faint smell of leftover smoke stung Rose's nose as she sat in the honey house and tried to concentrate on her drawing. She'd opened both windows for ventilation, but the honey house was still warm and uncomfortable. She hadn't expected anything different in August.

Farrah Fawcett lounged on a little pillow in the corner while Leonard Nimoy tried to coax Farrah Fawcett to play with her. The kitten pawed at Farrah Fawcett's tail, nudged her with her nose, and finally hopped on top of the indignant cat in an attempt to get her moving.

The cats were here for company and, if Rose was honest with herself, protection. Of course, a small orange kitten and a spoiled white house cat wouldn't be much protection when it came right down to it, but having the cats around gave Rose a small measure of comfort.

This time of year, Rose usually sat outside under a tree to paint honey supers — the white boxes that made up a beehive when they were stacked on top of each other — but with all the mischief that had been happening on their farm, she didn't dare linger outdoors by herself, and she was too embarrassed to ask one of her sisters to sit with her, even if they would have gladly done it.

Nae, better to sit in the stifling honey house than to risk an accidental and terrifying meeting with a stranger who wanted to do her harm.

The trouble had started over two months ago when someone had tipped over one of their beehives in the middle of the night. Since then, whoever was bent on making mischief had ripped their laundry off the line, chopped up their chicken coop, and even taken a wheel off their buggy. Last week, they had set fire to the honey house, and it would have burned to the ground if it hadn't been for Luke and Dan and Aunt Bitsy's two industrial-sized fire extinguishers.

One corner on the outside of the honey house had been scorched and the inside smelled faintly of smoke, but at least the building was still standing. A few days ago, Luke and Poppy had brought new wood, fixed the damage to the outside, and given it a new coat of white paint.

Good as new.

If only her nerves could be fixed the same way.

Whoever was trying to scare them had scattered the chickens, worried the bees, cut off Queenie's tail, and terrified Rose out of her mind. Who could be so mean? Since the first time the troublemaker had tipped over the beehive, Rose had been able to think of almost nothing else. She'd bitten her fingernails down to nubs, and she laid awake at night long after her sisters had gone to sleep, listening for faint sounds of trouble outside her window as her heart pounded in her ears.

Even though it wasn't the Amish way, Aunt Bitsy had notified the police, but they didn't have many clues, and they couldn't do much unless they caught the vandal or vandals in the act.

Would the troublemakers try to burn down the barn next? Or hurt one of her sisters? Rose flinched as her pencil lead snapped. She'd been pressing too hard.

She wasn't much of an artist when she

was nervous.

Rose sharpened her pencil and drew the outline of a tree on the honey super. She had painted all the hives on the Honeybee Farm with flowers and vines and butterflies, but this time she wanted to try something new: a farm scene, complete with a barn and a horse. Aunt Bitsy had bought the new hive as a wedding present for Lily, and Rose had volunteered to paint it. She thought Lily might like a farm scene to remind her of the Honeybee Farm when she didn't live here anymore.

Rose tried to ignore the twinge of loneliness that always accompanied thoughts of her sisters and their weddings. It wasn't that Rose didn't want her sisters to marry — how could she not want them to be happy? — but she and Aunt Bitsy would be left alone to care for the farm and the hives. Who would go to gatherings with her or help her make Bienenstich cake or quilt with her in the evenings? Who would protect her from overeager boys or overbearing grandparents?

Rose outlined a few individual leaves poking out from the tree. Painting was one of the only times Rose felt truly at peace, even with the cats fussing at her feet. When she painted, she could forget about smoke and fire and laundry sitting in the mud. She could forget about her sins and her sorrows and not have to put on a brave face for her sisters or her aunt or the rest of the world. She liked not having to be anyone but herself, not having to meet anyone's expectations, not having to pretend to be brave.

The kitten gave up trying to coax Farrah Fawcett and sat right on her head. "Leonard Nimoy," Rose scolded. "Farrah Fawcett won't want to be your friend if you sit on her." She didn't want to dash Leonard Nimoy's hopes by telling her that Farrah Fawcett wouldn't want to be her friend no matter what. Rose got up from her stool, lifted Leonard Nimoy from Farrah Fawcett's head, and took her to the scratching post. Luke Bontrager had made the scratching post because he felt guilty for foisting Leonard Nimoy on them in the first place. Aunt Bitsy had adamantly resisted another cat.

"Play over here, Leonard Nimoy." Maybe if she scratched the post, Leonard Nimoy wouldn't scratch poor young men who came to the house — young men like Josiah Yoder who didn't deserve to be scratched, no matter how much of a worry he was.

And Josiah Yoder was definitely a worry.

He wanted something from her. She could

sense it in the way he looked at her, as if she were the only girl in the world — as if something he needed very badly were hidden upstairs under her bed. She hated feeling like she owed him something or that she was somehow responsible for his happiness. She would only disappoint him in the end, like she always did.

Rose couldn't be confident like Poppy. Poppy wasn't scared of anything, and Rose was scared of everything. Boys tended to grow impatient with how mousy she was. Lily was clever and fun, a girl everyone wanted to be around, someone who wasn't afraid to go to gatherings and talk to boys. She was never a disappointment to her sisters.

Rose was a disappointment to everyone, even herself. She hated how frightened and weak she was, how she couldn't push past her nightmares to find peace.

Josiah either wanted something from her, or he wanted to do something *for* her — make poor, orphaned Rose Christner his project. She knew she had a reputation for being weak and timid. People in the community tried to prove what *gute* Christians they were by feeling sorry for Rose and doing acts of Christian charity for her.

Rose didn't want anyone to feel sorry or

make any sort of sacrifice for her. People tended to get hurt when they tried to please Rose. She didn't want to be a burden, she didn't want to be a project, and she certainly didn't want to feel obligated to anyone.

Jah. Josiah Yoder was a worry.

She sketched an outline of a horse running past the tree. She'd paint it chestnut brown, like their horse, Queenie, and she would paint the barn red and might even paint the barn door pink.

Rose's heart skipped a beat as she heard the gravel crunch outside the open window. It skipped another beat as she saw someone pass by the window. She only caught a glimpse, but whoever it was wore a blue baseball cap and a white T-shirt, and he passed within a few feet of the honey house.

Rose's pencil slipped from her fingers as she jumped to her feet and scooped Leonard Nimoy and then Farrah Fawcett into her arms. She pressed her back against the wall and listened. What would she do if the stranger came into the honey house? Would he attack her? Would he try to burn the honey house down around her?

Panic wrapped an icy hand around her throat as she squeezed the two cats as if they were life preservers. Farrah Fawcett meowed and stuck her nose in the air as if she were quite put out that Rose had interrupted her nap. Leonard Nimoy's wide, trusting eyes seemed to be asking what all the fuss was about.

Her head throbbed with the force of her pulse.

Dear Heavenly Father, please don't let him hurt me or Farrah Fawcett or Leonard Nimoy. Make him go away. Please make him go away.

She jumped clear to the ceiling and left her skin behind when someone knocked softly on the honey house door. Was she going to die? If she screamed loud enough, would Aunt Bitsy hear her in the house?

Another knock. "Rose? Bitsy told me you were out here. Can I come in?"

"Josiah?" she called, too breathless to make much of a sound at all.

He opened the door, took a step inside, and caught sight of Rose plastered against the far wall. In an instant, his expression went from untroubled calm to cold tension. "Rose, are you all right?"

She felt so shaky, she thought she might faint. "I . . . I don't know."

Before she could draw breath, he was at her side, wrapping his hands around her arms. His touch felt warm and comfortable, like a weather-worn pair of canvas gloves. His voice was like a caress against her cheek.

"What happened? Can I help?"

She felt a tear trickle down her face. "I saw someone outside. I think he was the one who set fire to the honey house."

Josiah glanced out the window to his left. "Just now?"

She nodded.

"Which way did he go?"

"Out behind, I think."

He rubbed his hands up and down her arms. Leonard Nimoy climbed up his arm and tried to hitch a ride on his shoulder. He gently pried Leonard Nimoy off and handed the kitten back to Rose. "Should I have a look around, or do you want me to stay here?"

She almost begged him to stay, but if the stranger was going to burn down the honey house, it would be better if at least one of them got out. "I . . . you can go. But you've got to be careful. I don't want you to get hurt."

His shocking blue eyes pierced through her skull. "It's okay, Rose. I won't let anyone harm you." He kept his gaze on her as he backed away. "Lock the door behind me, okay?"

She nodded.

Farrah Fawcett wriggled out of Rose's arms and jumped to the floor. Rose kept a tight hold of Leonard Nimoy as she tiptoed to the door and turned the lock on the doorknob.

Not daring to move, she rubbed Leonard Nimoy's soft head while she listened for any sound outside. She thought about throwing the door open and making a run for the house, but she was too frightened to go out by herself with just two cats for protection. Farrah Fawcett had wasted no time in curling up on her pillow and closing her eyes.

One cat. She only had one cat for protection, and Leonard Nimoy was just a kitten. Of course, her little kitten had given Josiah a big scratch only yesterday. Rose wasn't completely defenseless. Her heart seemed to tumble over itself. She was worse than defenseless. She'd never risk Leonard Nimoy to save herself.

She stood in silence, hardly daring to breathe in case someone heard her. Tears trickled down her cheeks as the anxiety grew more and more unbearable with every passing second. She should never have let Josiah risk danger for her. How could she have been so selfish? Guilt pressed on her as if she were buried under a pile of rocks. Hadn't she learned her lesson with her parents?

Every muscle in her body pulled taut as

she heard the sound of low voices coming her way. Trying to keep herself from collapsing into a heap, she grasped the knob with her free hand, closed her eyes, and rested her forehead against the door.

Please, Heavenly Father, let it be Josiah. Let him be okay.

The knock on the door startled her even though it was as soft as a whisper. "Rose, it's Josiah. Will you let me in?"

She unlocked the door and opened it. Josiah stood there with a soft smile on his face, his eyes alight with something deep and gentle. Next to him stood a boy who couldn't have been more than sixteen, five or six inches shorter than Josiah, wearing a blue baseball cap and a white T-shirt.

Josiah reached out and took her hand as if to keep her from falling. Instead of resisting, she held on tight, just in case her knees gave out. "Rose," he said. "This is Jack Willis. He was cutting through your farm on his way home."

Jack Willis' sticky-outy ears seemed to be holding up his baseball cap, and his shaggy black hair stuck out in all directions from beneath it. "I'm really sorry. We moved here three months ago, and I figured out it was faster to catch the bus by shortcutting through your property. I should have asked first, but I didn't know if you Amish were allowed to talk to people." He jabbed his thumb in Josiah's direction. "Joe says you're allowed."

Rose's heart was still going a mile a minute. "Oh," she said, patting the moisture from her face with the edge of her apron. She didn't know why she bothered. Jack and Josiah had already seen the tears. "You . . . you startled me. That's all."

Jack had dark eyes and a friendly smile and didn't seem to think less of her for being so foolish. "I'm sorry about that. My mom tells me I'm kind of sneaky that way. Me and my folks should have introduced ourselves when we first moved in. We've met our nearest neighbors, but there are a few pastures between us and you."

Still holding Rose's hand, Josiah stepped into the honey house and tugged her to the stool. "*Cum* sit down. You're still a little shaken up."

Rose sat, and Josiah immediately let go. She felt as if he'd withdrawn his strength, but it also gave her a chance to gather some of her wits.

He didn't move far from her side. "Somebody has been playing tricks on Rose's property. Last week they set fire to this building. The three sisters are a little wary of strangers."

Jack shook his head. "I'm real sorry for cutting through without asking."

Rose tried to smile. "You didn't mean any harm." She wouldn't for the world want him to feel bad about it. She was the one who had behaved like a baby.

Jack sniffed the air. "Our house caught fire once 'cause my dad put up too many Christmas lights. I had to stand in the snow for an hour in my pajamas until the fire department let us back in. It got one wall of the garage. My mom was pretty scared. She kept hugging me and my sister." He cleared his throat and shuffled his feet. "I guess I better go. Mom's expecting me home."

Rose bit her bottom lip. "It's okay if you take the shortcut."

Josiah studied Rose's face and nodded. "I'll warn Rose's aunt Bitsy so she doesn't come after you with her shotgun."

Jack looked impressed. "Okay. Sick."

Josiah left Rose's side long enough to see Jack to the door. "If you ever see anything suspicious going on over here, will you let us know?"

"Sure." Jack scrunched his lips together. "But what do you consider suspicious?"

"Anything that doesn't look Amish enough."

Jack shrugged. "I don't really know what you mean, but I'll keep my eyes open."

"Thank you," Josiah said.

"Okay," Jack said, giving the door a solid tug. "See ya."

Josiah was back at Rose's side in an instant. He knelt on one knee next to her stool and pulled a white, expertly pressed handkerchief from his pocket. "Do you want me to walk you back to the house?"

Rose dabbed at her face with Josiah's handkerchief. It smelled like laundry fresh from the line. She'd humiliated herself with her irrational fears, and Josiah felt obligated to help her because he thought she looked helpless.

She was helpless.

And Josiah had made her his project.

She wished with all her might that she could square her shoulders and announce that she could walk herself to the house — thank you very much — without help from anyone — but she couldn't. She was terrified of things lurking in broad daylight. No matter how humiliating, she needed Josiah to walk her to the house. Josiah placed his hand over hers. *Jah.* He thought he needed to take care of her. "Rose? Are you okay?"

She pulled her hand from his and folded her arms. His eyes flashed with uncertainty.

She didn't like that look, as if she'd spoiled all his hopes and dreams. It didn't matter what she did. She always made things worse. "I'm sorry I got so scared over nothing." *Oh sis yuscht.* Tears were again dangerously close to the surface.

"It wasn't *nothing.* Someone tried to burn down the honey house last week. I would have been frightened too. You never have to apologize. I am more than glad to do what I can for you."

Jah, he felt sorry for her. *"Denki,"* was all she could say.

His gaze lit on the honey super on the table. "Is this a new hive you're painting?"

She looked down at her hands. "It's still rough. My first sketch on the super."

"The super?"

She patted the white box that held the nine frames that the bees would one day fill with honey. "Each box is called a super. We stack three or four supers on top of each other to make a hive."

"You're doing something different than flowers on this one."

"A farm scene."

"I love it," he said. He picked up one of her paintbrushes and eyed the tubes of paint sitting in a bin next to the super. "I've never seen so many different colors."

"I've probably spent too much money on paints, but I love all the different shades."

"My favorite hive is the one with the tiny pink roses. It makes me think of you." He stared at her in silence before clearing his throat. "I hope it doesn't offend you that I have a favorite. It doesn't mean I like the others less."

His blue eyes were earnest and attractive on his face framed by his dark auburn hair. The effect looked like orange-red maple leaves against a deep blue sky. She found his look unnerving and breathtaking at the same time. "The roses are my favorite too."

He ran his hand along the lines of her drawing. "This farm scene will be wonderful-*gute*. People will want to come to the farm just to see your paintings."

"*Nae.* I don't think they will."

He smiled. "I drive by your farm just to see the Honeybee sign out front. I like the butterflies."

Rose's heart beat double time at the sight of that smile. "I love monarchs."

Josiah seemed to get unreasonably excited. "Really? My sister has a butterfly garden. There are monarchs everywhere in her yard." He lowered his eyes. "Would you let me show you sometime?"

Rose's stomach could have been a butterfly garden. The thought of Josiah showing her around Suvie's yard made her giddy with anticipation and sick with anxiety. Josiah was handsome and kind and eager to please. But she dreaded being alone with him. He'd expect her to keep up a conversation and say clever things and make him laugh. She'd fail miserably, and Josiah would feel sorry for her, and she'd be humiliated yet again.

Perhaps Josiah wanted to show her the butterfly garden because he pitied the poor, painfully anxious girl who seemed to need rescuing. Josiah wanted to do his duty as a Christian.

She couldn't bear either possibility.

Maybe she'd just pretend he hadn't asked. "It wonders me if you will walk me back to the house?"

The light in his eyes dimmed but didn't go out. "I'd be glad to. Can I carry anything for you? Paints? Pencils? Cats?"

"Will you carry the paints? I will see to the cats."

Rose shepherded Farrah Fawcett off her pillow and herded her out the door. She picked up Leonard Nimoy and the scratching post and walked out of the honey house.

Josiah followed a few steps back, as if shielding her from an attack, and whistled a tune from the *Ausbund.* She relaxed a little. The whistling meant she didn't feel pressure to have a conversation with him. Her head was swimming with too many worries already.

They walked up to the porch and found a dead mouse waiting for them on the welcome mat. Rose shuddered. Josiah gave her a sympathetic smile. He must have thought she was the most pitiful girl in the whole world. He picked up the mouse by the tail and flung it off the porch.

Inside, Aunt Bitsy stood regarding the sink with a pair of sunshine-yellow rubber gloves on her hands, a plunger in her fist, and a temporary spider tattoo crawling up her neck. She turned when she heard the door open. "Josiah Yoder," she grunted. "I'm glad you're here."

Josiah grinned like Leonard Nimoy with a ball of yarn. "You are?"

Aunt Bitsy rolled her eyes. "I'm not glad to see you. I'm glad you have strong farmer's arms. My sink is clogged, and I can't press this plunger hard enough to clear it."

Josiah's grin only grew wider. "I'm happy to help." He set the bin of paints on the table and took the plunger from Aunt Bitsy. With all the force of his broad shoulders, he shoved the plunger into the sink, pumping it up and down vigorously and making water splash on the counter and the floor and Aunt Bitsy.

"Don't flood my kitchen, Josiah Yoder. I haven't made supper yet."

Josiah worked that plunger up and down for another minute, then pulled it from the sink. Both he and Aunt Bitsy eyed the drain.

"Nothing," Aunt Bitsy said. "It was no use for you to be here after all."

"I could unscrew the curved pipe thingy below the sink," Josiah said.

Aunt Bitsy narrowed her eyes. "The curved pipe thingy? Josiah Yoder, I get the feeling you don't know much about clogged sinks. I'll wait for Luke Bontrager. Much as I'm against it, he's coming to see Poppy tonight."

Josiah stood up as straight and tall as a sycamore. "I can do it. I've watched my brother-in-law unclog a sink before."

Aunt Bitsy took the plunger from Josiah. "All right then. Let's see what you can do yet."

"Do you have a bucket?"

Rose fetched the cleaning bucket from the storage room as Josiah cleared all the soap and rags and supplies from the cupboard under the sink. He turned onto his back and slid so half of his body was inside the cupboard and he was looking up at the sink from below. Rose handed him the bucket, and he set it down at his knees within easy reach.

He began unscrewing one of the washers connected to the elbow-shaped pipe.

Aunt Bitsy leaned over to watch him work. "You're going to get —"

The water trickled slowly out of the unsealed pipe for a few seconds and then in a great *woosh,* soaked Josiah and his clean blue shirt with filthy, gray dishwater. Josiah howled, sat up suddenly, and smacked his forehead against the metal pipe. Rose winced. That was going to leave a mark.

"— wet," Aunt Bitsy said.

Pressing his hand against his forehead, Josiah shot out of the cupboard as the rest of the dishwater splashed to the bottom and dribbled out onto the floor.

"Are you all right?" Rose said.

His entire upper half was soaked, and there were little bits of rice and lettuce and other food particles stuck to his navy shirt. He took his hand from his forehead, leaving a smudge of black scum. A small goose egg was already starting to form just above his eyebrow. Looking a little dazed, he attempted a grin. "Bitsy, your clog is fixed."

Aunt Bitsy's nostrils flared as if she were

60

barely keeping her patience. "What were you planning on using the bucket for?"

He squinted in Aunt Bitsy's direction and scratched his temple, leaving more sink scum. "I didn't think any water would come out."

Aunt Bitsy smirked. "It wonders me what you thought *would* come out."

Leonard Nimoy splashed her paws in the puddle on the floor as if she were playing in the rain. "Stop that!" Aunt Bitsy scolded as the kitten started lapping up scummy sink water with her tongue.

Josiah lifted Leonard Nimoy by the scruff of the neck and deposited her a few feet away from the puddle. "Do you have a towel?"

Rose raced into the storage room once again and collected four old towels they used for rags. She came back and handed them to Josiah. Instead of drying himself off, he knelt down, wiped out the cupboard, and then sopped up the water from the floor. Bitsy took one of Rose's towels to wipe the water from the back of Josiah's neck. The minute she touched him, he reared his head in surprise and smacked the back of it against the inside edge of the cupboard.

"*Oy,* anyhow," he said. He pulled his head

from inside the cupboard and scrubbed his hand along the back of it.

Aunt Bitsy snorted, which was as close to laughter as she ever got. "You're jumpy for someone so tall."

With his hand wrapped around the back of his head, Josiah looked at Aunt Bitsy out of the corner of his eye and chuckled. "I thought you were a spider."

"I didn't want you to drip."

"Is your head bleeding?" Rose said.

Josiah looked up at Rose, and his blue-eyed grin made her heart gallop. "Thanks to your aunt Bitsy, I have a bump on both the front and back of my head."

Aunt Bitsy grunted her disapproval. "Don't blame me that you're so thick."

Watching Aunt Bitsy warily out of the corner of his eye, Josiah tightened the washer back onto the pipe and finished wiping out the cupboard. It looked cleaner than when he'd started.

Though he tried to refuse her help, Rose grabbed another towel and helped him wipe the disgusting water from the floor. He crawled around on his hands and knees, trying to get every drop he'd spilled. His trousers as well as his shirt were soaked by the time they were done.

Josiah gathered up the wet towels. "Washroom?"

"I can take them," Rose said.

"I'm already wet and dirty, and I sort of stink," Josiah said. "And you smell like lavender. You'd better let me take them."

She twisted her lips into a lopsided grin and led Josiah to the washroom. He dumped the soaked towels into the sink and wiped his dirty hands on his equally dirty trousers. "I'd better go home. I need to take a shower. Or three showers. I don't know that this smell will ever wash off. Your aunt might not let me back in your house again."

"She might if our sink clogs."

He laughed. "She won't let me near that sink."

"Cum," Rose said, taking the small hand towel from the hook over the sink and running some water over it. She reached up and wiped the black scum from Josiah's forehead, being careful not to press too hard on that goose egg. He turned to stone, not taking his eyes from her face as she carefully dabbed at first his forehead, then the side of his face. A shower would be best, but at least he could ride home without looking like he'd been swimming in the sewer. "That's better," she said, rinsing out her towel and hanging it on the hook to dry.

With his unnerving gaze still glued to her face, he cleared his throat and gave her a doubtful smile. "*Denki.* I made a mess of myself." He stretched out his arm where Rose had put the bandage yesterday. "But look. I told you this wouldn't come off in a hurricane. Still as secure as ever."

Unable to withstand that piercing gaze, she lowered her eyes and stared at Josiah's boots. "*Denki* for your help at the honey house. I feel silly for letting things scare me."

"The things that have happened on your farm would scare anybody." He reached up and smoothed a thin strand of hair behind her ear. Her skin tingled where he touched her. "We're going to find out who is making all the trouble. Please try not to worry. I hate to see you so upset."

The tingling sensation traveled all the way down her spine.

And scared her to death.

If Josiah wanted her not to be upset, he would stay away.

She couldn't keep from trembling, as if she were out on a bitterly cold night. "*Denki* for fixing the sink."

Josiah took a deliberate step back. "If ever you need anything, I hope you know you can ask me." The lines around his eyes softened, and he gave her a half smile. "I should go before my shirt dries and I have to pry it off."

"*Jah*. Okay."

They went back into the kitchen. Aunt Bitsy stood at the sink with her back to them, but she turned abruptly and leaned against the counter as if she were hiding something behind her. "Are you finally leaving, Josiah Yoder?"

Josiah tugged at his shirt and smiled. "I need a shower."

Rose very nearly forgot herself and offered him a honey cookie as a thank-you for putting up with her foolishness. But then she remembered what Aunt Bitsy said about stray cats. *They come back if you feed them.* She'd be better off if he never came back again. Her heart did all sorts of dangerous leaps when Josiah Yoder was near, and he made her feel terrified and *ferhoodled* and discombobulated all at the same time.

Who needed that?

He opened the door and turned back. "*Ach*. I almost forgot the reason I came today. Keith Chidester says you take your hives to his sunflower patch to pollinate his flowers."

Rose nodded.

"He says he's never had a better crop. It wonders me if you could bring some hives to my farm. My pumpkins are blooming."

"We charge rent," Aunt Bitsy said.

Rose frowned. "*Ach,* I'm sorry. It is too late in the season to move the hives. The bees would never find their way back."

He looked as if his horse had died. "Oh, okay. I'm sorry. I had hoped . . ."

Again, she sensed that he wanted something from her, something more than beehives and pollination. She nibbled on her bottom lip. Why couldn't he leave well enough alone? For sure and certain, she'd end up disappointing him.

"Maybe we can bring them next year," Rose said.

"Of course," Josiah said, not acting enthusiastic about waiting. "Next year." He suddenly brightened as if someone had turned a light on in his head. "You could come over and help me decide where the hives will go next year. And you could see the butterfly garden at the same time."

"*Ach.* Yes. The butterfly garden," Rose said, her heart already thumping against her ribs at that horrible possibility.

He tilted his head to catch her eye. "Okay then. We'll see you soon then? Sometime soon?"

She felt her face get warm. She didn't have the heart to tell him no to his face.

66

He'd wilt like a plucked dandelion.

He didn't press her for an answer. Instead he flashed a smile, nodded to Aunt Bitsy, and closed the door behind him.

I don't know what you want from me, Josiah Yoder. I'm more frightened of your expectations than anything else.

She sighed. Things were so much easier without Josiah Yoder here trying to yank her out of her comfort zone.

Aunt Bitsy immediately rolled up her sleeves, picked up the bucket, and opened the cupboard below the sink.

"What are you doing?" Rose asked.

"Josiah Yoder wouldn't know the difference between a sink and a snake even if one bit him. The sink is still clogged. I'm going to fix it myself."

"You should have told him. He would have kept trying."

Aunt Bitsy swatted that suggestion away as she slid the bucket under the pipe. "We would have had a flood that even Noah would have envied. Besides, I didn't want to hurt his feelings."

"Didn't want to hurt his feelings? Aunt Bitsy, you told him you weren't glad to see him."

Aunt Bitsy grunted as she knelt down beside the open cupboard. "Well, I have to keep them humble or they get too confident. I don't like a boy who's too sure of himself. That's Luke Bontrager's problem." She unscrewed the washer that Josiah had loosened and then the washer on the other end of the elbow-shaped pipe. The elbow piece fell into Aunt Bitsy's bucket. Aunt Bitsy got up and ran some tap water through the elbow-shaped pipe. Water splashed from the pipe into the bucket below. She took her yellow-gloved fingers, pulled a plastic fork covered with black scum out of the elbow pipe, and held it up for Rose to see. "We should watch Dan Kanagy very closely when he's in the kitchen. All sorts of things fly when that boy does dishes."

She let water run down the sink into the bucket, then reattached the elbow pipe by tightening the washers. "Good as new," she said, "and Josiah never needs to know. We wouldn't want him to think he got a soaking for nothing." Aunt Bitsy snapped off her gloves and washed her hands at the now-unclogged sink. "Now, baby sister," she said, wiping her hands. "We need to have a talk."

Rose's heart sank. Aunt Bitsy only called her "baby sister" when it was serious. "About what?"

Aunt Bitsy motioned for Rose to sit at the

table, and she pulled a chair out next to her. That close, Rose got a good look at the spider tattoo on her neck. Aunt Bitsy loved trying out temporary tattoos. The spider had a pink bow on its head and was smiling and waving. The tattoo was friendlier than Aunt Bitsy.

"When you came in here," Aunt Bitsy said, "you looked like you'd seen a ghost. Or a zombie. But since you don't know what a zombie is, it was either you saw a ghost or Josiah did something to upset you. And if he upset you, I'm not afraid to give him a good look at my shotgun the next time he comes over."

Of course Josiah had upset her. But he didn't deserve the shotgun. "He wants something from me."

Aunt Bitsy narrowed her eyes. "What does he want?"

Rose's sigh went all the way down to her toes. "I don't know, but whatever it is, I'll be a disappointment like I always am."

Aunt Bitsy pinched Rose's earlobe between her finger and thumb. "Baby sister, you have never, not for one day, been a disappointment."

"I was in the honey house, and a strange boy passed by my window. I thought it was the one who had tried to burn it down. I couldn't even move I was so scared. Josiah chased after him and brought him back to the honey house. He was just cutting through our fields on the way home. I embarrassed myself because I was so frightened. Then I didn't dare walk back to the house by myself. I practically begged Josiah to come with me."

"It's nothing to be ashamed of," Aunt Bitsy said. "It was a frightening thing."

"Are you frightened about the troublemaker, Aunt Bitsy?"

Aunt Bitsy shook her head. "I'm annoyed."

A tear escaped from Rose's eye. "Everything frightens me. I can't even go to a gathering without one of my sisters. You all have to bend over backward because I'm too afraid to do anything."

Aunt Bitsy frowned. "You've been through some hard stuff, baby sister. No one can fault you for being cautious."

An ache grew in her heart. "All that hard stuff was my own doing, and there's nothing to keep it from happening again."

"Not your parents' death, Rosie. That wasn't your fault."

The ache in her chest spread to her arms and hands. She didn't remember much about her parents, but she remembered whose fault it was they had died. But not even Aunt Bitsy would know that. Especially not Aunt Bitsy. She'd never forgive Rose if she knew.

Aunt Bitsy's frown carved itself into her face. "Do you still blame yourself that La-Wayne Zook went to prison?"

"I separated him from his family."

"Believe me, baby sister, that was a *gute* thing."

Rose's sisters, Lily and Poppy, practically tripped into the house, giggling like two schoolgirls. Of course they were giddy. They were both head-over-heels in love. Lily had been engaged for a month. Poppy had gotten engaged just last week.

Aunt Bitsy raised an eyebrow and leaned closer to Rose. "This is what comes of giving boys food. Giggles and more giggles."

"Isn't it a beautiful day?" Poppy said as she waltzed into the house and set her basket on the island.

"It is if you want to feel cooked like a Thanksgiving turkey," Aunt Bitsy said, standing and giving Lily and Poppy each a hug. "How were deliveries?"

Lily plopped herself in Aunt Bitsy's chair at the table. "The Yutzys want more tomatoes, and they said they'd take all our zucchini."

Aunt Bitsy nudged Lily with her hip. Lily grinned, and Aunt Bitsy made a show of being quite put out that Lily had stolen her chair. She sat down on the other side of Rose. "We've got so much zucchini, I'm thinking of changing the name of our farm to Zucchini Flats. We should pay the Yutzys for taking it off our hands."

Poppy brought four glasses to the table with her good hand and went back to the fridge for the milk. "I love zucchini. And it makes delicious bread."

"Only if you're a rabbit," Aunt Bitsy said.

"Luke loves Poppy's zucchini bread," Lily said.

Aunt Bitsy grunted. "That boy is so crazy for Poppy, he'd eat sawdust if she fried it up."

Poppy beamed like a heavy-duty flashlight. "He's so adorable, I'm going to burst."

Aunt Bitsy scrunched her lips to one side of her face. "If you're going to burst, do it outside. I've already had to clean up one mess today." She pointed her finger at Lily. "And Dan's not much better. He can't come over without bringing a gift. We'll have to build another house to make room for all his stuff."

"He's trying to butter you up," Lily said, pouring milk for the four of them.

72

Aunt Bitsy looked as if she'd sucked on a lemon. "Like a Thanksgiving turkey."

"We saw Suvie Nelson in town," Poppy said.

Rose's heart skipped a beat. Suvie was Josiah's sister.

"She needs a quart of honey. I told her we could deliver it tomorrow." Poppy glanced at Rose before setting a plate of cookies on the table and sitting next to Lily. Rose didn't feel like eating. She felt guilty for not giving Josiah a cookie when she'd had the chance.

Ach, du lieva. She was as selfish as she was weak.

"You're very quiet, Rosie," Poppy said, handing her a cookie. "Is everything okay?" She frowned. "Have you been crying?"

"She had a little fright today," Aunt Bitsy said. "Josiah Yoder came over."

Rose could practically see Lily's and Poppy's ears perk up. Rose wanted to slide out of her chair and sink into the floorboards. She'd behaved like a child yet again, and her sisters would feel even more of an obligation to baby her.

"Josiah was here?" Lily smiled like it was Dan who had come instead of Josiah.

"And he scared you?" Poppy said, probably plotting revenge in her head. Poppy

73

was always ready to defend her sisters.

Rose fidgeted with one of her *kapp* strings. *"Nae.* I mean, *jah."*

Lily's brows inched together. "You know Josiah would never hurt you, don't you, Rose?"

Of course she knew. Josiah was one of the gentlest people Rose knew. "It wasn't really his fault. He wants something from me, and that makes me nervous. I wish he wouldn't come over."

"Me too," Aunt Bitsy said. "He caused a flood."

"Maybe he wants to be your friend," Lily said.

"Like as not, he wants to make me his project." Rose sighed and propped her chin in her hand. "Everybody feels sorry for me. Josiah is nice, so he wants to protect me."

Poppy smiled. "There's nothing wrong with that."

"I don't want to be anybody's project." She felt like she had a twenty-pound weight strapped around her neck. "I wish I were different. I wish I weren't afraid."

Lily took a sip of milk. "It's okay that you're timid. It's one of the things we love about you. You're our Rosie. We wouldn't have you any other way. We don't mind watching out for you."

"But wouldn't you rather not have to? Poppy broke her hand because I couldn't watch out for myself."

Fire leaped into Poppy's eyes. "That wasn't your fault. You wouldn't have been able to punch Griff Simons hard enough to get him to let go. And you're too tender-hearted to have wanted to hurt him in the first place. I was happy to smack him in the mouth for you."

"You don't give yourself enough credit," Aunt Bitsy said. "You go to gatherings with your sisters. You ride the bus every week to the animal shelter."

"Dorothy and Joann go with me. I'm not afraid of them. It's the boys that make me nervous."

"You're fine around Dan and Luke, and Luke might be the most cantankerous person you'll ever meet," Aunt Bitsy said.

Poppy's mouth fell open before she surrendered to a smile. "I know. That's why I love him so much."

Poppy's enthusiasm for Luke coaxed a smile from Rose. "I was never afraid of Dan or Luke. I knew they loved my sisters. That was a good enough reason to love them back."

Aunt Bitsy finished off her cookie. "If you want to overcome your fears, then you have to start doing things that scare you."

"Like what?"

"Like talking to boys at gatherings," Lily said. "Or baking a cake for Josiah."

Aunt Bitsy shook her head vigorously. "Do not bake a cake for Josiah. He'll take it the wrong way and never leave us alone. I am partial to a dry kitchen."

Poppy broke her cookie in half and dunked it into the milk. "You can talk to Dan and Luke because you know they're in love with your sisters. Can you pretend that all boys are in love with me and Lily?"

"All the boys *are* in love with you and Lily," Rose said.

Lily giggled. "Then it will be easy."

"It should be easy," Rose said, "but it still terrifies me."

"Then start small," Poppy said. "What would scare you only a little?"

Rose slumped her shoulders. "Going outside by myself."

"You do that all the time," Lily said. "See? You're making progress and you didn't even know it."

"Josiah invited me to Suvie's house to see her butterfly garden."

Lily's eyes sparkled merrily. "That's a good start. Suvie would love it if you went over."

"But I don't want him to feel obligated to be nice to me just to prove what a *gute* Christian he is."

"Let him feel obligated," Poppy said, waving her hand in Rose's direction. "You'll be doing him a favor. Boys like to feel needed, even if we don't need them."

Josiah was an orphan and Rose felt sorry for him, but couldn't someone with more courage help him feel needed? "I could make him a cake," she said. "If one of you would deliver it."

Lily scrunched her lips together and raised an eyebrow. "You're not seeing the big picture here, Rose. You've got to take Josiah the cake yourself."

Aunt Bitsy crinkled her nose as if there were a bad smell in the kitchen. It was probably the lingering scum from her sink. "Josiah Yoder? Surely we can do better than that. What about starting with someone less frightening, like Freeman Beiler?"

Rose giggled. "He's a thirty-nine-year-old bachelor, Aunt Bitsy. He'd get the wrong idea. Besides, Freeman is more interested in you."

Aunt Bitsy rolled her eyes and looked up at the ceiling. "Deliver us from evil and eager bachelors, Lord." She propped her elbow on the table. "You shouldn't make

Josiah a cake if you don't want him coming over. I suggest asparagus casserole."

"B, Rose wants to show him she's brave, not poison him," Poppy said.

Aunt Bitsy raised her eyebrows. "A hearty stomach flu would keep him away for weeks."

Rose liked the asparagus casserole idea, except for the part about the stomach flu. Whenever Josiah Yoder was near, a whole flock of butterflies came to life inside her stomach. She dreaded every minute of it. Asparagus casserole would scare him away right quick.

But she wouldn't make Josiah a casserole or a cake.

She was perfectly content with her quiet life on the farm with nothing but paints and cats for company. Being lonely was better than being afraid.

Neither Josiah nor any other boy was worth the anxiety.

CHAPTER FOUR

Josiah stared helplessly at the display of paint tubes. He knew absolutely nothing about oil paints. He also knew nothing about acrylic or watercolors or tempura paint. Basically, his paint knowledge was abysmal. He'd be better off getting Rose a new paintbrush.

He shifted over to his right and tried to make sense of the paintbrush selection. Wood handles, plastic handles, rounded tips, sponge brushes. The options made his head spin. Chances were he'd pick the wrong brush, and Rose would hate him forever. The way things were going, she probably hated him already.

He shook his head. He'd better not let his thoughts stray in that direction or he'd sink into the depths of despair. Besides, Rose was too kindhearted to hate anybody. Griff Simons had tried to kiss her, and Dan said she had already forgiven him.

Josiah clenched his teeth. She was a better person than he was. He tried to be forgiving in his heart, but it was hard to want mercy for anyone who hurt Rose.

He shifted back to his left and studied the paints again. He'd carried Rose's bin of paints into her house. The paints in little tubes were the ones she used. He'd buy her one of those.

How in the world would he pick a color?

"You look like a deer in the headlights," Luke Bontrager said, coming up beside him and stuffing his hands in his pockets. "Is it because of that nice bump on your forehead?"

"It's got to be perfect," Josiah said, unwilling to let Luke discourage him. Luke had courted Poppy like a bulldozer. Josiah was going for the more subtle approach with Rose.

Lord willing, "subtle" was the right way to go about it. His heart nearly leaped out of his chest just thinking about her. He loved Rose to the moon and back and as deep as the water in Lake Michigan. He wouldn't give up until she told him to go away, and even then he might hold on to his love until the day he died.

Rose was timid, but yesterday, when she had seen a stranger at the window, she had been more concerned for Josiah's safety than her own. She even cared about the cats over herself. Josiah couldn't see loving anyone else.

He pulled one of the paint tubes from the display. It was a pretty petal pink like the dress Rose had worn yesterday, the most beautiful dress Josiah had ever seen. "Do you think she'll like this color?"

Luke smirked. "Pink says, 'I love you,' for sure and certain."

Josiah pressed his lips together and nodded. If Rose suspected he loved her, he'd scare her away. He'd been careful. For four years, she hadn't suspected that his thoughts were often on her or that she was everything he hoped for. He would never forget her kindness during his *mamm*'s funeral and afterward. She had been the one who had gotten him through it all — an unexpected gift from God. "What about brown? She wants to paint a horse."

"Dull," Luke said. "She'll think you're boring. But you are boring, so it's probably a *gute* choice."

"You're not funny, Luke."

"I'm not trying to be funny. A true friend is always honest."

"A true friend would help me pick out some paint. I should have brought Dan,"

81

Josiah said.

"And I should be at Poppy's instead of wasting a perfectly good afternoon with you." Luke grinned. "Dan wouldn't have thought to send you to the Honeybee Farm with a pocketful of catnip, would he?"

Josiah didn't even turn his head. "I caught on to what you'd done as soon as the kitten started climbing my leg." He held out his arm. "You probably don't even feel guilty for these scratches, do you?"

Luke chuckled. "Not if Rose was the one who bandaged you up."

With his eyes still glued to the paint, Josiah curled one side of his mouth. "I suppose she was."

Luke hooted and hollered right in the middle of the paint aisle. "I'm not such a bad friend after all."

"Only if you help me pick a paint color. Gray is definitely out. I don't even need your opinion about that."

Luke smiled and slapped Josiah on the back. "You know I'm joking. I'm just trying to help you take this less seriously. The worry lines are piling up on your forehead next to that goose egg."

"I can't take it less seriously. I love her, Luke, and I'm fighting for every smile she gives me."

Luke grew serious and placed a firm arm on Josiah's shoulder. "Believe me, I understand. Poppy used to hate me. It was one of the worst times of my life. Regardless of what you may think, I care about you and Rose very much."

"Then help me pick a color. It might be the one thing that softens Rose up."

"Why don't you buy one of each? Then you're sure to get at least one she likes."

Josiah rubbed the whiskers on his chin as he studied the display. "I don't want to seem too eager. It's got to be natural, like I'm not sneaking up on her. What about green? That farm scene needs grass."

Luke sniffed loudly. Twice. "Green makes me think of phlegm."

Josiah resisted the urge to roll his eyes.

Luke always made him appreciate a friend like Dan Kanagy.

Rose climbed down from the buggy with the quart of honey in her hand. It was past six o'clock, and Suvie Nelson's honey was her last errand before home. Her visit to Mammi and Dawdi had taken longer than Rose had anticipated. Her grandparents had wanted to talk about Paul Glick and Poppy, and the possibility of Aunt Bitsy getting shunned. Paul Glick, Lily's ex-boyfriend, had been threatening for weeks to have Aunt Bitsy and all the Honeybee *schwesters* shunned because, he claimed, they'd cheated him out of their honey. Plain and simple, Paul was mad that Lily had chosen Dan Kanagy over him, and he wanted to make Lily miserable because of it.

Some of the people in the community were siding with Paul even though the Honeybee sisters had done nothing wrong. A few members of the district thought Aunt Bitsy was odd, too odd to belong in the community. She tinted her hair pastel colors and prayed right out loud. Some of the neighbors wouldn't have been too sad to be rid of her. Rose didn't know why people were so concerned about it. If members got shunned for being odd, there would be no one left in church to preach the sermons.

Mammi and Dawdi seemed to think that Aunt Bitsy and her nieces would be shunned any day now. Rose was concerned about the possibility of being shunned, but someone had tried to burn down their honey house last week, and Leonard Nimoy and her sharp claws were in danger of being banished from the house, and Josiah Yoder wanted to make Rose his project. She had bigger worries than Paul Glick. Lily had immediately gotten engaged to Dan after she'd broken it off with Paul, and Paul's heart was surely in pieces. Rose could forgive him for taking out his heartbreak on the Christners.

She strolled up the short sidewalk to Suvie's house and looked to the west. The sun was more than two hours from setting. She'd easily be home before dark.

Suvie Nelson was Josiah's sister and the only immediate family he had left. She and her husband, Andrew, lived a short walk from Josiah's house on the same farm that Josiah and Andrew worked together. Rose looked down the road. Her heart tumbled about in her chest like a pebble in the river. Josiah's house was close, but there wasn't any chance she'd run into him today. She was delivering honey to his sister. Surely she'd be safe.

A child was crying inside the house. Make that two children. Suvie must be having a hard day. The door opened, amplifying the sound tenfold, and Rose's lungs collapsed when Josiah, not Suvie, stood at the threshold.

Despite the fact that Josiah had a screaming baby in his arms and a screaming toddler at his feet, he smiled as if he'd just seen his first sunrise. "Rose," he said, so softly that Rose wasn't exactly sure she'd heard it over the screaming.

Suvie's two-year-old, Aaron, was clinging to Josiah's trouser leg much the way Leonard Nimoy had done two days ago. Aaron was screaming and crying at a pitch that might have summoned all the dogs in the neighborhood. His face was wet with tears, and his curly hair was matted to his head with sweat.

Baby Arie in Josiah's arms was also screaming. She would occasionally find her fingers and suck on them for a few brief seconds and then wail again. Josiah bounced her up and down, but the bouncing only seemed to make things worse. It would have made Rose motion sick.

"Is everything okay?" Rose asked, and it was probably the stupidest question Josiah had ever heard.

Josiah bounced and bounced, and his smile bounced with him. "I'm babysitting. Suvie said there was an emergency, and she and Andrew ran out of here like the house was on fire. I can't get the baby to take a bottle, and Aaron has a stinky diaper. But we're doing okay." He smiled wider, which, considering the situation, was quite an accomplishment. "It's just so nice to see you. How are the cats?"

Rose peeked around Josiah and into the

house. A strand of toilet paper stretched from under a closed door across the living room and around Josiah's ankle. A puddle of water seeped from under the closed door and looked to be spreading by the minute. In the kitchen, a pot was boiling over on the stove, and something was definitely burning. Three-year-old Alvin sat quietly on the sofa in the front room with his hands clasped in his lap as if Josiah and the babies were his entertainment for the evening.

"Hello, Alvin," Rose said.

Alvin grinned and waved at her.

Rose hesitated and looked up at the sky. Much as she wanted to be home before dark, she couldn't abandon Josiah or Suvie's poor, temporarily motherless children. Josiah might very well manage to burn down Suvie's house or at least cause a major flood before Suvie got home. Josiah seemed to have a strained relationship with water in general.

Rose pressed her lips together. Her own selfish fears didn't matter. The babies needed her. Josiah needed her. She would push aside her misgivings to help them out and deal with the consequences later.

"Would you like some help?" she said, trying valiantly to ignore the thumping of her heart against her ribs.

He looked like a dying man who'd just been granted a few more hours of life. He didn't even try to pretend he didn't need her. "I would be so grateful."

Rose gave him a half smile and marched past him into the living room. With Aaron clinging to him like a burr, Josiah shut the door and shuffled a few steps toward her.

The most urgent problem first. Rose pulled the bubbling pan from the burner and turned off the LP gas stove. She lifted the lid, and steam ascended to the ceiling. A mushy glob of what used to be noodles sat in the bottom of the pan. The bottom was burned black, the pan ruined. She'd come just in time.

Still bouncing his crying niece on his hip, Josiah twitched his lips sheepishly. "Mac and cheese," he said.

Rose tried to be encouraging. "It would have been delicious."

Still sniffling and fussing, Aaron let go of Josiah's leg and headed straight for Rose with his arms outstretched. "Hold you," he said.

Rose picked up Aaron and propped him on her hip. She pulled a tissue from the box on Suvie's kitchen cupboard and mopped up Aaron's face. He wasn't screaming anymore, but Josiah was right. He was definitely stinky. Even the dirty diaper wasn't the most pressing problem. With Aaron in her arms, Rose went to the closed door. Water was still seeping out from under it, threatening a fuzzy pink blanket on the floor. The door was locked.

Josiah seemed to notice the water for the first time. "*Ach.* It's leaking. Aaron threw something in the toilet, and it clogged. I locked the door so he couldn't throw anything else in there."

"Do you have a key?"

He grimaced. "I didn't think that far ahead."

Rose pointed to the top of the door frame. "We leave our bathroom keys on that little ledge," she said, loud enough to be heard over the screaming baby. The poor thing. She was obviously starving.

Rose was too short to reach, but Josiah was plenty tall. With the baby, he tiptoed through the puddle of water and felt along the top of the frame until he burst into a smile. "Here it is."

Rose kissed Aaron on the cheek and set him on the sofa next to Alvin. He started screaming again, but Rose needed both hands. She quickly unlocked the door, handed the key to Josiah, and splashed into the bathroom. Water trickled out of the overflowing bowl as the toilet ran and ran without shutting itself off. Rose jiggled the handle, then lifted the lid to the tank and pulled up the float. The toilet stopped humming, and the water stopped running. She opened the cupboard above the toilet and said a prayer of thanks when she found a stack of fluffy bath towels. Suvie probably wouldn't be too happy about her nice towels being used to wipe up toilet water, but she wouldn't be too happy about her living room flooding either. Rose would have wanted a dry floor.

Rose spread four towels around the toilet and sopped up the water. The fuzzy pink blanket was safe.

Josiah drew his brows together. "I didn't even notice the water. I should unclog the toilet before Suvie gets home. I did Bitsy's sink. How hard can a toilet be?"

Rose wasn't sure what Suvie would want, but under no circumstances was Josiah to get near that toilet. "We should see to the *kinner* first," she said.

He looked at her as if she were a gift left on his doorstep.

Rose eyed Aaron and Alvin, who were wrestling on the sofa. In an attempt to get on top of his brother, Alvin kicked his foot and made a nice black smudge on the wall.

"Do you know how to change a diaper?"

Josiah nodded. "*Jah.* I change Aaron's diaper all the time. I've just never had to babysit all three of them at once. It's hard."

"Of course," Rose said to reassure him. "You're doing a fine job." Surely a little white lie was harmless. She would never want to hurt his feelings.

He chuckled. "*Nae.* I'm not. But you are very kind to pretend."

Arie had found her thumb and made loud slurping noises between her upset hiccups. She was a chubby baby with kissable cheeks and peach fuzz on top of her head. The peach fuzz was a lighter version of Josiah's auburn hair, and she was adorable, even with a bright red face and a runny nose. Rose took Arie from Josiah's arms. "Is there a bottle?"

"Suvie said she wouldn't be hungry."

"She's definitely hungry," Rose said.

Josiah smoothed his hand along Arie's soft head. "There's formula, but Suvie has never been able to get her to take a bottle."

Rose gave him a warm smile. He was doing his best. "We'll have to try." A bottle and a can of formula sat on the counter, as if Suvie had expected Josiah might need it even though she'd said otherwise. Rose picked up the formula and handed the bottle to Josiah. "Fill it with four ounces of water. Warm water but not too hot."

Josiah turned on the water. "How do I know if it's too hot?"

"Test it with your elbow."

His face was a mask of concentration as he examined the bottle to find the four-ounce line and filled it with water. He tried to stick his elbow into the bottle. When he realized it wouldn't fit, he groaned and shoved his hand against his forehead.

Rose couldn't help herself. Josiah was so earnest and so eager to do a *gute* job. He hadn't counted on his elbow getting in the way. Arie was crying, Aaron stunk like a manure truck, dinner was a glob of mushy macaroni and cheese, and Josiah was trying to stick his elbow into a hole the diameter of a silver dollar. He had obviously had a very hard afternoon.

Rose started to giggle.

He looked at her and raised his eyebrows. A low chuckle rumbled in his throat. The chuckle became gut-splitting laughter. Aaron and Alvin stopped wrestling and looked at their *onkel* as if he were doing tricks for their entertainment.

He laughed until tears sprang to his eyes. "I'm sorry, Rose. For sure and certain, *Gotte* brought you here to save my niece and nephews from their onkel Josiah."

Rose laughed. "Maybe I came to save you from them."

He smiled with a soft light in his eyes. "I've never heard you laugh before."

"Really?"

"*Jah.* This is the first time."

She was probably blushing all the way to her toes. He acted as if her laughing was the greatest thing to happen to him all week. Surely she was imagining things. She lowered her eyes and studied the words on the formula can. She didn't even know what she was reading. "Do you want to try the elbow thing again?" she said.

"What should I do?"

"Stick your elbow under the running water, then, when it's the right temperature, fill the bottle."

He grinned. "Seems so simple."

He emptied the bottle, turned the water on again, and stuck his elbow under the stream of water. He filled the bottle and studied it very carefully to make sure he'd gotten just the right amount.

"Put two scoops of formula in with the water and shake it," Rose said, bouncing the baby with increased desperation. The baby's fussing would soon become screaming again.

Josiah shook the bottle, and little drops of formula flew all over the kitchen. Rose did not even comment on it. Neither did he. He simply wiped a spot of formula from his cheek and handed her the bottle. Rose sat down in the chair next to the sofa, cradled Arie in her arms, and pressed the bottle to Arie's lips. Arie clamped her gums together and arched her back as if Rose were trying to feed her a sprig of asparagus. Rose pulled the bottle away, and Arie started screaming.

Who knew such a little baby could make such a loud noise?

Rose stuck the nipple into Arie's open mouth, and Arie coughed and choked and screamed all the louder. Okay. Not a *gute* idea to trick a baby. Rose tried again. Arie would have none of it. She was hungry but wouldn't eat.

Josiah knelt beside her chair. Aaron immediately jumped on his back. "Do you want me to hold the bottle?"

"Okay. We can try it."

Josiah growled like a bear, picked up giggling Aaron, and deposited him on the sofa before coming back to Rose and taking the bottle. Rose cradled Arie while Josiah tried to press the bottle into her mouth. Arie cried as if her heart would break.

"I'm sorry," Josiah said. "I don't know

what to do."

Rose took the bottle from Josiah and stood up. She bounced up and down while cradling Arie in one arm. With the other hand, she tried again to feed Arie. Arie smacked her lips and opened her mouth. Rose kept bouncing with one arm clinging to Arie for dear life. Arie decided she liked being fed while standing. She clamped down and started sucking.

Josiah cocked an eyebrow. "That is one determined baby."

Rose smiled at him. "If she's happy, I'm happy."

"Me too."

While Rose bounced around the room and fed Arie, Josiah changed Aaron's diaper, cleaned up the ribbon of toilet paper, and led his nephews in gathering up the wet towels and putting down dry ones in their place. Once the floor was somewhat dry, the three of them played grizzly bear. Josiah made very realistic bear noises and tickled them until they begged him to stop and then begged him to do it again. Rose couldn't help but think of her own *fater.* Had he ever thrown her up in the air like that when she was little? Had he ever tickled her or read her bedtime stories? She had no memory of his loving her the way Josiah clearly loved his nephews.

It was just another way *Gotte* punished her for her selfishness. Her parents were lost to her in more ways than one.

Rose thought her arm might fall off, but she kept a determined grip on the baby while she ate. After a few minutes, Arie's eyes started to droop. Rose carefully and smoothly sat down in the chair but tried to pretend she was still standing. Arie didn't seem to notice a difference. Rose relaxed against the back of the chair while Arie finished her bottle and fell asleep.

Rose shifted Arie so the baby was snuggled against her chest and patted her back until she got a burp. She stood and looked at Josiah. "I'll put her down," she whispered and pointed up the stairs.

Josiah nodded, looked at the boys, and pressed his finger to his lips to tell them they needed to be quiet. Alvin immediately began singing a loud song, but Arie didn't even flinch. With two older brothers, she had probably learned how to sleep through anything.

Rose found the crib upstairs and tucked a light blanket around Arie's chin. There was nothing more precious than a sleeping baby, especially with two busy toddlers down-stairs. She massaged her arm while she gazed out the window. It would get dark soon. A tendril of anxiety crawled up her spine at the thought of taking the buggy out on the dark roads. She should leave before it was too late.

But there were still two hungry children and one very unsure uncle downstairs. What if Josiah tried to fix the boys something to eat and Arie woke up? Suvie only had so many pans to spare. Rose would just have to be brave for Alvin and Aaron's sake. And Josiah's sake too.

She went downstairs, where Josiah had one boy thrown over each of his shoulders and was spinning them around the room. She glanced out the window again. "Who wants pancakes?"

Josiah stopped spinning and set the boys on their feet.

"I do," squealed Alvin.

"I too," echoed Aaron.

Josiah placed his hands on his hips and studied her face. "Are you sure? You've already saved me. If you're more comfortable leaving, I understand."

Rose managed to smile past her anxiety. "We don't want the boys to start eating the furniture."

He stared at her for a few moments before nodding. "Can I help?"

"Can you crack eggs?"

"I scramble myself three eggs every morning," he said.

Because he was an orphan and cooked for himself. The thought of Josiah all alone in that big house made Rose a little sad.

"Hey," he said, leaning over to catch her eye. "Did I say something to upset you?"

She gave him a flicker of a smile. "Of course not." Could he truly read every subtlety in her face like that? "I was just thinking that you probably keep a lot of chickens busy."

"They do not like to see me coming."

Josiah scrambled eggs and tried to keep the boys from tearing down the house while Rose made her favorite whole-wheat pancake batter and set the table. The pancake batter sizzled on the griddle while Josiah swooped both boys into their booster seats and put bibs on them. They said silent grace, and then Josiah served each of the boys a pancake with syrup and cut the pancakes into bite-sized pieces.

Rose finished flipping pancakes and sat down to eat with Alvin on one side and Aaron on the other. Aaron ate three pancakes and polished off a good portion of the eggs. Alvin couldn't stop talking about his pet snake that his *mamm* made him keep in the backyard and how it ate mice and rabbits. Josiah listened with patience to Alvin's stories, and Rose did her best to understand what Aaron said. Aaron was just learning to talk, and sometimes Alvin had to interpret for him.

"These aren't just pancakes," Josiah said. "These would make an Amish *mammi* cry, they're so *gute.*"

Rose tried not to notice the darkening sky outside the kitchen window. It would be okay. Surely she would make it home this one time, and then she'd never have to go out in the dark again.

Aaron was more syrup than boy by the time he finished. Rose gave him a kiss on the top of his head. "Do you think Suvie would mind if I gave them a bath?"

"You've done so much, Rose. How could I even ask?"

She forced another reassuring smile. The boys needed her. "If you'll carry them up, I'll wash them."

Josiah grabbed a boy in each arm and practically flew up the stairs. He deposited them in the bathroom. "I'll do the dishes."

Alvin looked a little concerned about being left with a strange girl in the bathroom. "But Onkel Josiah," he said. His lip quivered slightly.

Josiah squatted next to Alvin and helped him take off his shirt. "When you have taken a bath, I will come and read you a story."

"Will you read the one about the wolf?"

"*Jah*. Take a bath first."

Rose filled the tub and washed the boys while she heard dishes and pans clattering in the kitchen. How many young men would babysit and do the dishes?

Rose helped Aaron out of the tub first and cuddled him in his fluffy towel. She dried his hair and put on his diaper. After draining the tub, she lifted Alvin into a towel, giving him a warm hug. He wiggled his arms out of his towel and hugged her back. "I love you," he said and planted a kiss on her cheek.

"I love you too," she said and kissed him right back.

Rose looked out the window again. It was almost full dark, but she couldn't leave — not until the boys were in bed and there was no danger of Josiah's starting a fire.

As soon as the boys were in their night-clothes with their teeth brushed, Josiah came tromping up the stairs. He placed a hand on Rose's arm and sent a jolt of electricity all the way to her toes. "Rose, I don't know how to . . . you are like an angel sent from heaven. You always have been."

Her heart felt lighter than air and heavy as a stone at the same time. She had watched Josiah deal so nobly, so faithfully, with the death of his parents, never questioning *Gotte,* never saying an unkind word, even in his pain, reaching out and pulling his sister through her grief.

Rose was the weak, fearful one. Josiah was the one with a *gute* and faithful heart, and yet he was looking at her as if she were indeed an angel. She didn't know what he wanted, but she knew she'd be a disappointment to him. She almost melted into a puddle of nerves and impossible expectations, but there'd been enough puddles in the house for one day. She'd have to fall apart in the privacy of her own home.

If she ever got home. It was going to be dark as pitch by the time she left.

Alvin handed Josiah the wolf book, and he sat in the rocker and cuddled the boys on his lap. Rose felt as if she were intruding on a very private moment. Maybe she should slip downstairs.

"Don't go," Josiah said.

"*Ach.* I don't mind waiting downstairs."

He studied her face with a grin playing at his lips. "Don't you want to hear the wolf story?"

"He barks at the moon," Alvin said.

Aaron clapped his hands.

Rose sat on the edge of the bed. "Then I better stay and listen."

Josiah, so mild-mannered and unassuming, turned out to be a very *gute* storyteller. He did all the voices, including a high-pitched one for the farmer's wife and a low, gravelly voice for the wolf. Rose was just as mesmerized as the boys were.

She lingered in the doorway as Josiah tucked his nephews into bed and kissed them good night. He followed Rose out the door and shut it behind him. "Suvie always tells me that bedtime is her favorite part of the day," he whispered. "Now I understand why." They stood facing each other in the hall, and Josiah seemed to get closer without even moving. "I'm sorry that you've been here hours longer than you planned. I'm hopeless as a babysitter. But . . . I'm not sorry you came. You saved me. I just hope you didn't have somewhere you had to be tonight."

She took a small step backward. Josiah seemed to fill up the whole hallway with his presence. And he smelled like fresh-cut clover. She was having trouble remembering, but it might have been her favorite smell ever. "You really were doing fine. Aaron is a handful, but Alvin is very sweet."

Josiah smiled. "Alvin is the tricky one. If he's quiet for more than three minutes, he's doing something he shouldn't." He ran his fingers through his short hair, shorter than most Amish boys wore it. "I was taking a nap on the couch last Sunday, and Alvin cut most of the hair off one side of my head. I can't believe I didn't wake up. I had to cut off the rest to even it up."

Rose curled her lips. "I wondered why it was so short. It looks nice."

"It does? Suvie says I look like a plucked chicken."

Not a plucked chicken. Josiah would have been handsome any way he wore his hair. Rose lowered her eyes. "*Nae.* You look . . . I like it."

He fingered the black-and-blue goose egg above his eyebrow. "It definitely makes the bump on my forehead stand out."

Rose frowned. "How is it feeling?"

"Better," he said with a big grin, as if it didn't hurt at all. "The one on the back of my head is bigger. At least my hair covers that."

She cracked a smile. "I'm glad you didn't have to get stitches."

They stood in awkward silence until Josiah reached out and grazed his thumb across her cheek. "A little flour," he said.

"Oh." He was too close. She couldn't even breathe — he took up so much space. He stared at her as if he could have stood there all day. She didn't have that much time. "I should get home."

They heard a sound in the other room. Josiah raised his eyebrows. "Arie's awake."

The anxiety grew in her chest like mold. She couldn't leave Josiah by himself. No matter how late it got, the children were her most important concern. She went into the baby's room and picked up Arie. She was a cute little pink bundle of chubby cheeks and thigh rolls. Rose clutched the baby to her chest. Arie needed her. She could be brave for the baby.

Josiah walked Rose down the stairs, cupping his fingers lightly over her elbow in case she tripped. He'd been too close too many times tonight. Rose was more than a little breathless.

"I hope she isn't hungry," Josiah said with an amused light in his eyes. "I don't know if I'm up to trying to feed her again."

Rose smiled. They'd have to scrub down the kitchen if Josiah made another bottle.

The front door opened, and Suvie and her husband Andrew strolled into the room. Suvie was a tall woman with fair skin and a face full of freckles. Her hair was light yellow, like Rose's, with just a tinge of red to it, and her eyes were the same brilliant blue as Josiah's. Her husband, Andrew, was also tall with chestnut-brown hair and a perpetual smile on his face. There was nothing small about Andrew, including his big, booming voice and his loud, jolly laugh, which could be heard for miles in the outdoors.

Suvie bloomed into a smile. "I saw the buggy out front and wondered who had come to call yet. How *wunderbarr* to see you, Rose."

"How are you?" Andrew said, smiling in Josiah's direction.

"I brought some honey," Rose said.

"How very kind," Suvie said. "But you know you never need an excuse to visit." She leaned toward Rose and nodded eagerly. "Have you been here long? I hope you two have been having a nice time together."

"She got here just in time," Josiah said. "She saved the house from being burned to the ground and washed away in the toilet water."

Suvie seemed untroubled by the news of fire and flood. "*Ach, vell,* it's *gute* Rose happened to come by." She reached out, and Rose handed her the baby. "How's my little pumpkin?"

Rose grinned. "Pumpkin" was a perfect name for Arie. She was chubby and solid and orange on top. "She doesn't take a bottle very well."

Suvie huffed. "She doesn't, the little stinker. I fed her right before I left. I was hoping Josiah wouldn't have any trouble with her."

"Not much trouble," Josiah said. "But I felt really bad that she screamed until Rose got here."

Suvie stuck out her bottom lip sympathetically. "I'm sorry. We had to look in on Onkel Melvin. He isn't feeling well."

Josiah narrowed his eyes. "I thought you said Aendi Linda was sick."

Suvie was busy bouncing Arie on her hip and didn't seem to hear Josiah. "How did Alvin and Aaron do?"

"They clogged the toilet. They got to bed very late, and Rose made them pancakes," Josiah said. "Whole wheat. The best I've ever tasted."

Suvie's smile seemed to double in width. "We all know what a *wunderbarr* cook Rose is."

Rose's face got warm. She didn't deserve such praise. Everybody knew how to make pancakes.

"They clogged the toilet?" Andrew said.

Josiah nodded. "We dried up the water, but it's still clogged. I will come by and help you fix it in the morning."

"No need," Andrew said, a little too quickly. "I can do it myself. You've got plenty of chores."

Rose nearly sighed in relief. Josiah should probably stay away from plumbing fixtures.

Josiah glanced at the clock on the wall. "I've got to get Rose home. She didn't plan on spending her Friday night here."

Dread pressed on Rose's chest until it became unbearably heavy. "My family will be worried," she said, wincing at how winded she sounded. It would be a sure sign of weakness if she fainted before she even made it to the buggy.

With her free arm, Suvie pulled Rose in for a hug and kissed her on the cheek. "*Denki* for saving my brother. He loves the *kinner,* but three is quite a handful." Her eyes flickered mischievously as she pulled Rose closer and whispered in her ear. "Especially if you don't have the right equipment to feed the baby."

Rose cracked a smile. Suvie often said shocking things that made the women laugh and the men turn red.

Josiah gave Arie a kiss on the cheek. "Just so you know, Suvie, you should never ask me to babysit again."

Suvie ushered them out the door. "Maybe we'll invite Rose to come too."

Josiah followed Rose down the sidewalk. The closer she got to the buggy, the harder her heart hammered against her ribs. She would be all right. She could take Queenie fast and be there in half an hour.

Josiah slid the door open, took her hand, and helped her into the buggy. To her surprise, he climbed up next to her, forcing her to slide to her right. "What . . . what are you doing?" she asked, with an embarrassingly shaky voice.

"I'm driving you home," he said, as if surprised she didn't know.

"But how will you get back?"

He picked up the reins. "I'll walk. It's not that far."

It was too much. "It's five miles."

In the dim light, she could see the determined set of his jaw. "Rose, I would never want you to have to drive home alone in the dark."

"Denki," she said, her voice cracking into a million pieces. Relief swept over her like a flood, and she turned her face from him as silent tears trickled down her cheeks.

How had he known it was just what she needed?

CHAPTER FIVE

The sun had just disappeared below the horizon when Josiah and Dan climbed out of Dan's open-air buggy and trekked up the lane. They were headed toward the barn, but Josiah's attention was squarely focused on the house, where the propane lanterns had been lit. Rose Christner was inside that house, baking bread or painting a picture or reading a book with her sisters. What he wouldn't give to be in there, sitting next to Rose, making her smile, talking about anything just so long as he could be near her.

But he wouldn't even see her tonight, even though he was achingly close. They had parked Dan's buggy on the road so Rose wouldn't know they were here. Josiah hated that he had to come under these circumstances. Why wouldn't the troublemaker leave the Christners alone?

Dan carried a heavy-duty flashlight, and

Josiah had a roll of black vinyl tucked under his elbow. Lord willing, they could fix the buggy tonight, and Rose would be none the wiser. They crept silently into the barn, where Luke stood assessing the damage with his own flashlight.

Four long slashes had been cut down the sliding door of the Christners' buggy. Josiah clenched his teeth. Rose had been sitting in that buggy with him just last Friday.

"Poppy came by this morning," Luke said, not even looking up when they came in. "They've been canning peaches all day and haven't had to use the buggy. Rose doesn't know about it, but I don't think we can keep this from her." He motioned toward the vinyl in Josiah's hand. "I'm afraid fixing this slider will take more than just a piece of vinyl."

Josiah winced. "Rose can't know about this."

"I can fix it." Luke curled his lips slightly. "I can fix anything."

Josiah wasn't in the mood for Luke's arrogance. "What else do we need? I can call a driver and go to the store. Whatever you need. Just tell me."

Luke shook his head. "It's not that easy. We can cut the new vinyl, but then we have to get the damaged piece off the frame and hammer it into place —"

"I can get whatever you need," Josiah insisted.

Luke sighed. "I need a buggy shop."

Josiah folded his arms. "Then we take it to a buggy shop."

"At eight o'clock at night?"

"Jah."

Dan walked to the other side of the buggy. "Any other damage?"

Luke shook his head. "Not that I can see."

"Let's hitch it up and take it to the buggy shop," Josiah said.

"*Ach,* look at this." Dan came from around the other side with a pocketknife in his hand. "Is this one of yours?"

Josiah and Luke looked at each other. *"Nae."*

Dan pulled the blade from the handle. "Do you think one of them dropped it?"

The knife had a rosewood handle with gold tips on either end. The dull side of the silver blade had seven raised notches. Josiah's heart jumped. "I've seen this knife before. Or one like it."

Dan frowned. "Where?"

"I can't remember. But I will."

Luke scowled. "I'd like to personally return it to its owner and have a long talk with him."

They jumped as the barn door creaked opened, and four flashlight beams pointed in their direction. Josiah squinted into the light. He couldn't make out who was behind those four flashlights, but he had a pretty good guess. His heart sank. Rose was going to be terrified, and he couldn't do anything to protect her from it.

All four flashlights lowered at the same time, and even in the dimness, Josiah recognized the hurt and uncertainty on Rose's face.

Bitsy's hair was an ethereal shade of pink tonight, and her shotgun hung from her elbow like a purse. "Surely there are better places for a meeting."

Luke slid over and stood directly in front of the slash marks, blocking them from view just in case Rose hadn't already seen them. Josiah sidled next to him. Luke wasn't such a bad friend sometimes.

"I told you it was Luke and Dan," Poppy said. "Nothing to worry about."

"But why are they here?" Rose said, her voice shaking like a match in the wind.

Josiah wanted to gather her in his arms and hold on tight, but he couldn't move without revealing the slashes on the buggy, not to mention the fact that he'd scare her if he tried to give her a hug. "I'm really sorry, Rose. We didn't mean to frighten you."

She furrowed her brow and looked as if she were going to cry. "I don't understand."

"Neither do I," Bitsy said. She gave Luke, Dan, and Josiah the stink eye. "What are you doing in our barn?"

Poppy grabbed onto Rose's elbow and tried to pull her backward. "I think we should all go in the house and have a pretzel," she said, acting as if they hadn't just caught her fiancé skulking around their property. "They're warm out of the oven."

"That sounds delicious," Luke said, not surrendering his place in front of the buggy.

Poppy forced a smile. "Rose made them."

Rose blinked several times, and even in the dimness, Josiah saw a tear slip down her cheek. That tear felt like a fist to the stomach. "Rose," he said. "It's okay. Everything is going to be okay."

"What are you hiding?" she said.

Poppy was still trying to pull her out the door. "It doesn't matter."

Rose wouldn't budge. She just stared at Josiah with that hurt, betrayed look on her face. "What have they done this time?"

Nobody needed to ask her who "they" were.

A look of desperation traveled between

Lily and Poppy, and Bitsy's stink eye got downright smelly. "Luke Bontrager, I suspect you're behind this. I told Poppy from the first that you were trouble."

"It's not his fault, B," Poppy said. "I asked him to come." She huffed in resignation and looked at Luke. "Might as well show her."

Luke and Dan scooted away from the buggy. Josiah was the last to surrender his place. He slowly moved aside, keeping his gaze glued to Rose's face. "It's not as bad as it seems. We can fix it with a hammer and a little vinyl."

Fear saturated Rose's expression, and Josiah felt sick. Sweet Rose should never be put through this. She wiped at an errant tear. "Did everybody know about this but me?"

"I didn't," Bitsy said, "and I am very put out. I brought my shotgun out here for nothing."

"We're sorry for not telling," Lily said. "We didn't want Rose to be scared, and we thought the boys could fix it before you found out."

"It was my fault," Dan said. "We should have waited until you were in bed."

"Why didn't you tell me when I saw them out the window?" Rose said.

"I got all worked up for nothing," Bitsy

114

said. "And you scared Rose to death."

Poppy rolled her eyes at Luke. "I was hoping Rose wouldn't see my fiancé sneak into the barn."

"She didn't see me," Luke protested. "It's Dan and Josiah who don't know how to sneak."

Poppy took Rose's hand and squeezed it. "We were hoping you'd stay in the house."

Tears trickled down Rose's face, but she didn't wipe them away. It was as if she wanted to pretend they weren't there. "You were going to lie to me?"

Poppy only looked mildly contrite. "But Rose, now you see the buggy, don't you wish you didn't know?"

Josiah wished Rose didn't know. He never, ever wanted her to be this upset again.

Rose slid her hand from Poppy's and wrapped her arms around her waist. "I wish it never happened. That's not the same as wishing I didn't know."

"We just want to protect you," Lily said.

Rose pursed her lips. "You're both getting married soon. You won't be here to protect me. What will happen then?"

Bitsy jiggled the shotgun in her arm. "You'll always have me, baby sister. And my trusty shotgun."

"After we're married, we'll probably be

on the Honeybee Farm more than we're not," Dan said.

"It's very hard to get rid of stray cats," Bitsy said. "Like it or not, Dan and Luke are never going to be far away."

Josiah wanted to speak up for himself. He'd be on the Honeybee Farm every day if Rose would have him. She didn't even have to ask.

To his surprise and complete dismay, Rose buried her face in her hands and let out a heart-wrenching sob. "I'm such a burden."

Josiah closed the distance between him and Rose in four long strides as if an invisible thread pulled him to her. He had no right and no reason except that he loved her better than his own soul and he couldn't bear to see her suffer. Thank the *gute* Lord that Bitsy had more sense than he did. Before he could wrap his arms around Rose, Bitsy stepped between them and raised a warning eyebrow. Josiah backed away so fast, he probably left skid marks on the cement floor.

What had he been thinking?

Bitsy looked daggers at Josiah as she put her arm around Rose. "I'll have none of that nonsense, baby sister. You're not a burden to anyone. If anyone's a burden on this farm, it's me. You girls clean my bathrooms and tend my bees and bake up a storm in my kitchen. You might as well put me in a home for all the use I am."

"That's not true," Rose said between sniffles. "You are everything to us, Aunt Bitsy, and you know it."

"If they put you in a home," Luke said, "who would take care of the cats?"

Bitsy narrowed her eyes. "It's your fault I've got three cats, Luke Bontrager. I've half a mind to leave them at your house in the middle of the night."

Luke didn't seem impressed with the threat. "I live next door. They'd find their way back, especially if Rose is here. Those cats love Rose."

"At least I'd be rid of the cats if you put me in a home."

Luke showed all his teeth when he smiled. "We'd bring them to visit every day."

"If it hadn't been for you, Rose," Poppy said. "Aunt B would have gotten rid of those cats a long time ago."

Rose didn't look happy, but she didn't look as upset as she had a few minutes ago. "That's not true. Aunt Bitsy loves those cats."

Lily patted Rose on the arm. "I can't believe you consider yourself a burden. You're a better cook than any of us. We're not half as good at the hives as you. The bees know you and would never dream of stinging you. And you can calm Queenie out of her orneriest moods. What would we do without you?"

"You can make anyone feel better, no matter how sad they are," Josiah said.

Poppy smiled at Josiah. For a moment, he didn't feel like he'd been quite so clumsy. "*Jah,*" she said. "And the chickens always lay better for you."

Rose wiped her eyes, and Josiah saw a small grin playing at her lips. "Now you're just being silly."

What else could he say to make that smile gain in strength? "You were brave enough to come out here to investigate who sneaked into your barn," he said.

Her face immediately lost any trace of happiness. *Oy,* anyhow, he shouldn't throw caution to the wind like that. "I was too frightened to be left alone in the house."

Poppy hooked her arm around Rose's neck. "I'm sorry I didn't tell you about the buggy, Rose. Please don't be mad at me."

Rose's tears returned. "Mad at you? I could never be mad at you. I'm frightened, and I wish I wasn't." She pulled a tissue from her apron pocket and dabbed at her tears. Eyeing Josiah, she nibbled on her bottom lip. "I'm sorry that you three had to come all the way out here just to protect my feelings."

"I only live next door," Luke said, with that gentleness to his voice he only used when talking to Rose.

"You don't have to apologize," Josiah said. "We wanted to help." Truth be told, he'd rather be here than anywhere else.

Rose slumped as if the weight of the world had fallen on her shoulders. "*Jah,* I'm sure everybody wants to do their Christian duty. You're all so kind, and I'm so weak."

"*Gotte* gave you many gifts," Bitsy said, a sharp scold evident in her voice, "but if He'd given you all the gifts, there wouldn't be any left for the rest of us."

Rose pressed her lips together and nodded. She obviously didn't want to argue with Bitsy. "I think I'll go to bed now," she said, as if she were almost too weary to talk. She turned around, pushed the barn door open, and walked out.

Bitsy narrowed her eyes and looked from the boys to Poppy to Lily. "You five have really done it this time."

The barn door creaked open again. Rose stood at the opening, her eyes dull with fear and sadness. "Lily, it wonders me if you would walk me to the house."

Josiah held perfectly still as Lily put her arm around her sister and they walked out of the barn together. He struggled for breath. Rose was frightened and unhappy, and he ached to make everything all better for her.

If only she'd let him.

If only he knew how.

CHAPTER SIX

Rose set the brake, slid out of the buggy, and picked up the cake in both hands as if she were holding a shield in front of her. She'd made a small cake because Josiah lived all by himself, but now she wondered if she should have made a bigger one. The coconut cake looked so insignificant sitting on the dinner plate. Much like Rose felt at this very moment.

Her pulse raced so fast she could have been a hummingbird in flight. How had she ever talked herself into thinking this was a *gute* idea? Josiah didn't need a cake. She didn't need to see the butterfly garden. They didn't need to talk ever again.

She stood up straight and tall — which wasn't all that impressive since she was only five feet three inches — but she had to talk herself into being brave. Aunt Bitsy said that if she wanted to overcome her fears, she should do things that frightened her. She'd come all this way to bring Josiah a cake. All she had to do was hand it to him and say good day. She didn't have to stay for more than two minutes.

A week ago, Rose had just about decided that she didn't need to overcome anything. She could be perfectly happy living out her days on Honeybee Farm, baking cookies and sewing quilts. But the night in the barn had changed her mind. Dan and Luke and Josiah had been willing to sacrifice sleep and time to make sure she never found out about the buggy. How selfish she was!

Her sisters suffered inconvenience after inconvenience for Rose's benefit, and soon their husbands would be pulled into it as well. She couldn't let them sacrifice themselves or their future families for her. It wasn't fair of her to ask her sisters to give over their lives to Rose's fears. She didn't deserve it. She never had.

She was more determined than ever to overcome her fear of men. And her fear of talking to people. And her fear of trouble-makers coming in the middle of the night and tipping over the honeybees. Aunt Bitsy said to pretend that she wasn't frightened and soon she would begin to believe it, but it was hard to pretend when her knees knocked against each other and her hands trembled.

None of that mattered. She had to be more courageous if she didn't want her sisters to end up resenting her.

She looked down at the cake. Josiah had come to the barn to help fix the buggy. He had driven her home one night and then walked all the way back to his own house. He'd been so concerned when he'd rescued her in the honey house too. She had embarrassed herself, but he hadn't laughed at her or even lectured her for getting all worked up over nothing. He deserved a cake for that reason alone.

She tiptoed across the grass and climbed Josiah's porch steps. The house looked like it had been painted recently and there were even some flowers growing in the bed below the window. Boys didn't usually think about flowers.

Josiah had lived alone in the white clapboard house since his *mamm* had died four years ago. Rose felt lonely just thinking about Josiah wandering through the empty rooms, longing for his parents' company. They were both orphans, but at least Rose had Aunt Bitsy and her sisters.

Josiah's sister, Suvilla, lived not a quarter mile down the road in the house her husband, Andrew, had built when they married. Suvie's three children kept her busy, and Andrew and Josiah worked Josiah's parents' farm together. Josiah and Suvie were the only two siblings left in the family. They'd lost a little brother before Rose and her family moved onto Honeybee Farm.

Everybody had problems and heartaches. Rose had to remind herself often that she was not the only one, and it was self-centered to believe she was.

She knocked softly on the door, almost afraid that someone inside would hear her. If no one answered, she could leave the cake on the porch and never have to talk to Josiah again. A breeze rustled through the big maple in Josiah's front yard, and she couldn't hear any sound of movement from the house.

She knocked again, because Poppy would want to know that she had at least tried. Then she set the cake on the mat in front of the door and skipped off the porch. She had done her duty and wouldn't have to talk to anybody. That was *gute* enough for today. She could try something extra brave next week.

Before she made it to her buggy, she halted in her tracks. Didn't Josiah have a dog? What about raccoons and ants? She'd have to come again if Josiah's cake got hauled off by a hungry fox. Besides, Josiah's porch faced south. It wouldn't take long for the frosting to melt in the sun.

Groaning, she tromped back up the steps and took her cake off the mat. She couldn't just leave it. Josiah deserved a cake, no matter how uneasy she felt talking to him.

A honey-colored, floppy-eared hound dog came bounding around the corner of the house. Rose smiled. Josiah did have a dog, and she was beautiful.

The dog gave Rose a friendly bark, skipped up the porch steps, and nudged Rose's knee with her nose. Rose balanced her cake in one hand and scratched the dog's head with her other. "Hello, pretty dog. What's your name?"

Even though she should have expected the master would follow the dog, she flinched slightly when Josiah strode around the corner. He caught sight of Rose, and his face lit up like a blinding firework, stealing her breath clean away.

"Rose," he said, as if her name were his favorite word. He took off his hat and climbed up the porch. "You came."

She couldn't look into those blue eyes without feeling light-headed, so she turned her gaze to the dog and cleared her throat. "I love her color. Like a jar of honey."

"I hope she didn't scare you."

"Of course not. She's beautiful. How old is she?"

Josiah didn't take his eyes from Rose. "She's part bloodhound, part Labrador retriever. I got her right after my *mamm* died. She's four years and a few weeks."

Much more comfortable with the dog than with Josiah, Rose handed him the cake and knelt down beside his dog. She smoothed the dog's ears between her fingers and rubbed her hand along its neck. "You pretty dog. Oh, you are the prettiest dog in the world." She glanced up at Josiah, who seemed to be having a great deal of trouble prying his gaze from her face. "What's her name?"

Josiah gave her an embarrassed smile. "Uh, Honey. I call her Honey."

Rose didn't know why her face felt warm all of a sudden. She wished he'd quit looking at her like that. "Honey? She's the perfect color." Rose pressed her cheek against Honey's neck. "My family makes honey. We're nearly related." Honey yipped her agreement and licked Rose's cheek. Josiah just stood there staring at her. Maybe she should tell him why she had come and find a polite way to leave before her heart took off down the road ahead of her.

She stood up and smoothed her hand down the front of her dress. "I'm sorry if I am bothering you. I wanted to come over now so there was no danger of it getting dark before I got home." *Ach,* she shouldn't have said that. No one needed to be reminded that in addition to all the other things she was afraid of, the dark made her anxious.

"You're not bothering me."

"I made you a cake to say thank you for being so nice the other day."

He acted as if he'd never seen anything so *wunderbarr* as the cake in his hand. "Is it coconut?"

"Pineapple coconut."

His smile couldn't have gotten any wider. "This is . . . this is . . . I don't deserve this. It was no trouble at all to unclog the sink."

Did she even want to remind him? "Um, well. It's not for the sink. It's for driving me home from your sister's and helping me at the honey house when I got so frightened about nothing." She furrowed her brow when she realized she should have made a bigger cake. Josiah had done several things in just a few short days.

"Nothing? It wasn't nothing. I mean, what I did was nothing. What you felt was understandable. It was more work to unclog the sink, and that was nothing too."

Rose would never tell him who had really unclogged the sink. "Were you able to get your shirt clean?"

He grinned, and his gaze fell to the ground. "That rice stuck like glue. I gave up and asked Suvie to wash it. She told me to let it dry and the rice would brush right off."

"Did it work?"

"*Jah.* Suvie knows how to clean anything." He opened his front door and motioned for Rose to go in. "Do you want a piece of cake?"

"*Ach, vell,* I should go."

His face fell like a soufflé in the oven. "Oh. Okay. *Denki* for the wonderful-*gute* cake."

No matter how uncomfortable she felt, how could she bear to disappoint him? "I . . . do you still want to show me the butterfly garden?"

He gave her a doubtful look. "Only if you want to see it."

"I do."

His face cracked into a smile. He disappeared into the house and came back without the cake and with a bottle of water. He handed the water to Rose. "It's wonderful hot."

He stepped off the porch and reached out

to help her down the steps. She didn't know whether to be pleased that he was concerned for her safety or embarrassed that he thought she couldn't take care of herself. She couldn't take care of herself, but she was trying to pretend. Either way, the touch of his hand sent a tendril of warmth sliding up her arm and made her feel as if she just might lose her balance. It was probably a *gute* thing she was holding on to him. But if he hadn't been touching her, she wouldn't feel so *ferhoodled.*

Nothing seemed to make sense with Josiah so close.

Honey the dog followed Rose down the steps.

"It's a little bit of a walk to Suvie's house," Josiah said. "I don't want you to get tired. Do you want to take the buggy?"

"Only a quarter mile or so. I can see her laundry hanging on the line."

"Andrew and I put up that clothesline for her. But mostly Andrew. I held the tools. I'm a better farmer than I am a fixer."

"You helped Aunt Bitsy with her sink."

"So maybe there's hope for me," he said.

They strolled along the dirt road with Honey tagging along after them. Josiah pointed out potholes and cracks that Rose was to be careful not to trip over. Her mind raced for something clever or interesting to say, but she was too nervous to think of anything. He kept glancing in her direction as they walked, but he didn't act disappointed that she wasn't chattering away.

"Are you tired?" he said, when they were about halfway through their five-minute walk. "Because we can rest if you need to."

Again, Rose didn't know whether to be pleased he took such care, or embarrassed that he thought she couldn't walk a quarter mile without a rest. It made her all the more determined to show him she wasn't a scaredy-cat and that he didn't need to make her his project. But easier said than done. "I'm fine, *denki*," she said.

Who knew being brave was so much work?

Suvie and the children were nowhere to be seen as Josiah led Rose around to the back of Suvie's olive-green house. Suvie's yard was surrounded by a white picket fence that opened up to a grape arbor at the back. Josiah led Rose around the outside of the picket fence and into a thicket of bushes and trees on the east side of the property. "Here," he said, holding out his hand. Rose hesitated as her pulse coursed like a raging river. Lily and Poppy hadn't said anything about having to hold Josiah's hand. She wouldn't do it. She couldn't do it.

Josiah tilted his head to coax her to look at him and gave her an open smile. "I don't want you to trip. The weeds get thick before we reach the clearing."

Reluctantly, Rose reached out and let him take her hand, hoping he wouldn't sense her trembling.

Josiah tugged her along the lightly worn path, occasionally looking back and smiling at her, but mostly keeping his eyes on the trail ahead. He hadn't been exaggerating. The path was rough and bumpy, and more than once Rose nearly tripped on a protruding root or fallen branch. Heedless of the thick undergrowth or the poky bushes on either side, Honey trotted beside Rose. Rose reached out and grabbed onto Honey's collar with her free hand. Honey yipped and kept walking as if she were Rose's guide dog.

It didn't take long before they reached a small clearing, where the sunlight filtered through the trees and purple flowering bushes and other plants grew in a maze pattern Rose couldn't make sense of. Josiah let go of her hand. The meadow seemed to be alive with dozens of monarch butterflies as well as honeybees flitting about the flowers.

"What do you think?" he said, eyeing her with a barely contained smile.

"It's beautiful." She stepped into the

clearing and ran her hand across the top of a purple flowering bush. "Miss Molly."

Josiah's smile grew wider. "Suvie planted all of this the first year they were married."

Rose buried her nose in a purple bloom. "Verbena. Bees like this one too."

Josiah nodded. "I don't know what most of the plants are called, but I helped Suvie plant milkweed. She says that's the most important. Look over here."

She followed him to a thick tree stump standing in the middle of the garden. He climbed on top and helped her up to stand beside him. Aunt Bitsy had told her to pretend. She did her best to pretend that she wasn't unnerved to be standing so close to Josiah Yoder. He was just showing her the butterflies. There shouldn't be anything unnerving about that. Besides, she didn't feel obligated to say anything clever. They were too busy looking at butterflies to make conversation.

Josiah pointed to the maze of butterfly bushes. "The bushes are overgrown now, but if you look close, you'll see they're planted in the shape of letters. Do you see?"

He lightly rested his hand on her back as she concentrated on the bushes. She didn't mind. He didn't want her to fall over. "A-N-D," she recited. "K —"

"It's an R," he said, winking at her. "One bush died."

"R-E-W. Andrew?"

"It was right after they got married, and Suvie was madly in love."

Rose giggled. "It's a very nice tribute to her husband."

Josiah stared at her for way too long.

"What?" she said, feeling more than a little uncomfortable. What did he want from her?

"I love it when you laugh," he said.

"Oh," she said. A pleasant shiver traveled from the top of her head to the tips of her toes. There was no other way to respond.

"Would you like to see the roses?"

"Roses too?"

Josiah jumped off the stump and helped Rose down. Honey ran circles and figure eights around them while Josiah led her to another clearing behind the butterfly garden where all sorts of roses bloomed in a variety of colors. Josiah stood back, letting Rose move among the bushes and breathe in the sweet aroma of the flowers.

"My *mamm* planted these before I was born. Roses were her favorite," he said. "And mine." He acted as if he wanted her to like them very much.

How could she not like them? Roses were the perfect flower. "I love them," she finally said when she realized he wanted her to say something. "It is one thing I remember about my *mamm*. The summer before she died, she would cut flowers from our garden every week and put them in a vase by the kitchen sink so she could smell them while she worked."

Josiah stuffed his hands into his pockets and looked at his feet. "I put roses on Mamm and Dat's graves every Sunday night. Do you think that's wrong?"

She laid a hand on his arm. The pain of losing his *mamm* still must be very fresh. It wasn't the Amish custom to decorate graves or funerals with flowers. "Of course not, if it helps you remember them."

The lines around his eyes softened. "I wish you had something to remember your parents by."

"I have my sisters and Aunt Bitsy. I don't know what I would do without them."

He studied her face. "Are you worried you'll feel alone when they marry?"

She pressed her lips together and looked at her hands. "I try not to worry about it."

"I wouldn't want you to worry."

Rose wandered among the rosebushes, and Josiah followed her wherever she went. His presence proved a greater comfort than it was a concern. She knew she wouldn't

134

come to harm as long as he was close by.

She visited all the rosebushes, sniffing at the blooms, taking in the beauty of the flowers. "I can feel your mother here," she said.

Josiah was quiet for a few seconds. "Me too."

She bent over and let one of the velvet-soft petals of a red rose caress her face. Josiah looked as if he were trying to drink her in with his eyes.

She tried not to let his look make her uneasy. "It's a beautiful garden, Josiah. My bees would love it here."

"Do you want to see my pumpkin patch?" He looked away again, as if trying not to care too much if she wanted to or not. "Or if you don't have time, it's okay."

She couldn't bear to say no to that earnest face. "*Jah,* I want to make sure my bees will have a *gute* home next spring."

They walked back to the butterfly garden, then along the path to Suvie's yard. He held her hand again, but this time, she allowed herself to savor the feel of it without worrying about his expectations or her own overwhelming fears.

When they came through the trees to Suvie's white picket fence, Suvie was out in her yard taking laundry off the line. Baby Arie lay on a blanket at her mother's feet while Alvin and Aaron chased each other around the yard. As soon as the boys saw Josiah, they bolted in his direction. He growled and hollered like a bear, scooped Alvin into his arms, and threw him into the air as Alvin squealed his delight. Rose caught her breath as the little boy flew impossibly high before Josiah caught him and deposited him safely on the ground. Josiah did the same with Aaron, except he didn't toss Aaron quite so high. Josiah put Aaron on his feet, and the boys begged to be thrown again.

"That's enough," Suvie called from her backyard. "You'll wear your uncle out."

"I'm not tired," Josiah said, grinning wide and showing off his white teeth.

"Well, I am," Suvie said. "You give me a fright when you throw them up so far. I like it better when my children are on solid ground." She waved to Rose. "So glad to see you, Rose. I was afraid you'd never come again after what Josiah put you through the other night."

"Your children are darling," Rose said. "And I could hold that baby all day long."

Suvie smiled and took a pair of trousers off the line. "I might take you up on that in the middle of the night. Aaron, stay out of the flowers."

Aaron pumped his little legs and ran to Rose. "I wanna dee," he said, pointing to Rose's water bottle.

She smiled, scooped him into her arms, and took the lid off the water bottle Josiah had given her. Aaron took a hearty drink, spilling half the water down his shirt, and handed her the bottle back. Not wanting to be left out, Alvin hiked across the lawn and reached up to Rose. "Can I have a drink too?"

"Of course," Rose said.

"I want to take the lid off by myself."

She handed him the bottle, and he unscrewed the lid and took a drink. When he'd had his fill, he turned the bottle upside down and dumped the rest of the water in the grass.

"Alvin Roy Nelson," his mother said. "Don't be naughty."

Rose giggled. "It's okay. The grass was looking a little dry right there."

Alvin stretched out his arms to Josiah. "Hold me."

Josiah picked up his nephew and put him on his shoulders. Alvin squealed again and clamped his hands around Josiah's neck.

"Josiah, so help me, if you drop him . . ." Suvie said as she pulled the line through the pulley, moving the dry clothes to within her reach.

Josiah and his sister had the same grin. "He loves it."

"*Jah,* until he falls backward and cracks his head." Suvie folded the trousers as her gaze darted from Josiah to Rose and back again. "Will you stay and eat, Rose? It's Josiah's birthday, you know, and we have a special birthday dinner planned."

Still holding Aaron in her arms, Rose snapped her head around to look at Josiah. "*Ach.* I interrupted your birthday celebration?"

He shook his head. "Interrupted? I wasn't doing anything but chores. You brought a cake and petted my dog and toured the butterfly garden. It's the best birthday I've ever had."

Josiah was unfailingly kind. He wouldn't tell her that she was a nuisance, even on his birthday. But the light behind his eyes made her think that he wasn't just being kind. She looked away and tried to stifle the smile that threatened to break out on her face. She could do nothing about the warmth traveling up her neck.

Josiah took hold of both of Alvin's hands and bent forward. Alvin did a backflip over Josiah's head, and Josiah caught him around the waist and lowered him safely to the

138

ground. He snatched Aaron from Rose's arms, flipped him upside down and back, and set him on the ground too.

Suvie clutched her heart. "Josiah Reuben Yoder, you are going to give me a seizure. Stop throwing my children around like bags of flour. Twenty-three years old today and you still act like one of the *kinner.*"

Josiah grinned at Rose and patted Alvin on the head. "Sorry, Suvie. I'm just trying to keep up my reputation as the fun uncle."

"You'll be the uncle who isn't allowed in the house for his own birthday party if you keep this up."

Josiah pointed at Rose. "She made me a pineapple coconut cake."

"It's bound to be better than the cake I made," Suvie said, folding a sheet as she took it off the line. "Alvin, don't push your brother."

Rose's stomach fell to her toes. How could she have made a cake today of all days? Suvie would think Rose was trying to outdo her. "Oh no. It couldn't possibly be better."

Suvie curled her lips upward. "Don't worry, Rose. Mine is from a box, and I don't feel at all threatened by your cake. If I got jealous every time the Honeybee sisters made a better dessert than I did, I'd have turned green by now. Josiah deserves something very special for his birthday yet. I'm glad you showed up. Aaron, don't pull Honey's ears."

"Me too," Josiah said. How was it possible that his smile melted her heart and made her nervous at the same time?

"So," Suvie said, propping her fist on her hip, "can you stay for dinner?"

Rose's face got warmer and warmer. "*Ach, vell,* I promised Aunt Bitsy I would bake bread."

"The bread can wait, can't it?" Suvie said. "Or you can always buy it at the store. That's what I do. I can't spare the time to make bread."

Josiah arched an eyebrow. "Rose will never want to come over again if you're pushy."

Suvie smirked, but there was amusement in her eyes.

Josiah placed a gentle hand on Rose's back and nudged her in the direction of his house. "I'm going to show Rose the pumpkin patch, and then I'll be over for dinner."

"Bring that cake with you," Suvie said. "We'll let the boys eat the other one. They won't know the difference."

Josiah grinned at Rose and made her feel sort of light-headed. "You'll have to imagine what it tastes like, Suvie. I'm eating it all by myself."

Alvin grabbed onto Josiah's hand. "Can I come with you?"

"Me too," Aaron said. He wrapped himself around Josiah's leg like a tendril of bindweed.

Suvie dropped the last pair of trousers into her laundry basket. "*Nae,* Alvin, Aaron. Let Josiah and Rose to themselves yet." She nodded at Rose as if she were in on a secret.

Rose's lungs tightened, and she hoped Josiah wasn't thinking the same thing Suvie was obviously thinking.

"But, Mama," Alvin whined. "I wanna see the punkins."

"*Nae,* Alvin. Not now." Suvie picked up Arie in one arm and her laundry basket in the other. "Besides, I fear for your life in Onkel Josiah's hands."

Josiah's mouth dropped open in mock indignation. "I am a very *gute* babysitter. With Rose's help."

"Okay," Suvie said. "I admit it. You are, when you're not tossing my boys like hay bales. And the boys love you. Your one mistake was leaving Aaron alone with a toy and the toilet."

"I've learned my lesson."

"*Cum,* boys," Suvie said, as she kicked the back door open and strolled inside with her baby and her basket. Alvin and Aaron

141

obediently followed their mother into the house, running and skipping as if just the ability to move was a joy in itself.

"They're very sweet," Rose said as she and Josiah ambled in the direction of his house.

Josiah nodded. "I meant what I said. I am only a *gute* babysitter with your help."

Rose couldn't look at him. "Aside from the flood and the fire, you were doing okay when I got there."

He chuckled. "It was very bad." He pointed to the field of soybeans behind his house up ahead. "The back way isn't as smooth as the road, but I can show you the fields better if we go this way. Are you tired? Would you rather go back to the house? Do you need another drink? Alvin dumped most of your water."

Rose couldn't ignore Josiah's thoughtfulness, even though it made her uncomfortable. He was being exceptionally kind to someone he'd made his project. "I'm not tired. I would be wonderful happy to see your fields. And your pumpkins."

She could tell he was trying to subdue a smile as he nodded, put his hands behind his back, and kept walking, being careful not to leave Rose behind with his long stride. Honey wagged her tail and followed along as if they were embarking on another adventure. "How many acres do you have?"

"Two hundred. When Mamm died, I took a hundred and Andrew took a hundred, but we work it like it was one farm. I have the barn and silo on my side and Andrew has the warehouse and shed on his side. I suppose it's been that way since Dat died. I was seventeen, and me and Mamm and Andrew and Suvie worked the farm together."

"You've been doing a man's work for a very long time."

He smiled sadly. "My *dat* bought this land from his *fater.* He wanted his children to work it. Andrew and I planted grass waterways and buffer strips and rotated crops. We doubled our harvest last year from the year Dat died."

"For sure and certain, he is pleased with what you've done."

Josiah lowered his head. "I give all the praise to *Gotte.* I can do nothing of myself."

"Your *mater* was a wonderful-*gute* quilter. She and Aunt Bitsy traded patterns more than once," Rose said. "Suvie seems to be much like her."

His lips curved upward. "Mamm and Suvie are almost the same person. Mamm always said what she thought and never minded meddling in someone else's business. My *mamm* never gave an inch when she thought she was right. My *dat* loved her for it."

"And you are very much like your *fater,*" Rose said. "I was only fourteen when he died, but I remember him being a very gentle, kind man."

Josiah nodded. "A *gute* quality for a deacon. I don't know if I am like him, but I hope to be. He was the most patient man I knew. One of my earliest memories of him is when he taught me how to hitch the team to the plow. I don't remember what I did wrong, but Snapper took off into the field, and it took us an hour to round him up. Dat didn't have one angry word for me. A lot of boys got the switch. My *dat* would never have laid a hand on me."

"My *dat* was like that too. At least that's how I remember him."

"I'm sure he was," Josiah said. "If he was anything like you, he was as mild as a summer's day."

If he kept looking at her like that, she would never be able to draw breath again.

Josiah took her hand and helped her hop across a deep furrow in their path. Was it a bad thing that she was looking forward to the next furrow? "We have a hundred acres of feed corn and nearly a hundred of soy-beans."

"The corn looks to be growing well yet. It's taller than you are."

He smiled. "We will get a *gute* crop this year, Lord willing. Andrew gave in and let me plant two acres of pumpkins. I am going to plant three more acres next year and maybe more the year after that. I can sell them down south for a *gute* price."

Honey led the way as they jumped over one more furrow and arrived at Josiah's pumpkin patch, which wasn't far from his house. The pumpkin plants were afire with huge yellow blossoms that were sure to attract bees by the thousands. Rose watched as a honeybee, already covered in dusty, yellow pollen, landed on the nearest pumpkin plant and crawled into the blossom.

"Look," she said, bending over to see inside. Josiah leaned his head close to hers. "It's like a gold mine for the bee." She smiled. "Look at her legs. Do you see the pollen baskets?"

"She's got a full load."

The bee's wings moved so fast they looked like they were vibrating as she took to the air and flew away. "She's going back to the hive," Rose said. "Did you know it takes two million flowers to make one pound of honey?"

He widened his eyes. "I should plant more roses."

"I never tire of watching them. They are each tiny miracles from *Gotte,* making honey, helping plants to grow, feeding the world."

She glanced at Josiah. He had his eyes on her but quickly looked away as if she were a teacher who'd caught him daydreaming during lessons. "I love honeybees," he said, before clearing his throat and standing up straight. "That's why I want some hives here. They can pollinate the pumpkins and play in Mamm's rose garden when they want a treat." He pointed to a rise of ground almost smack dab in the middle of the patch. "I thought we could put the hives right there. Is that a *gute* place?"

"*Jah.* They like the sunshine."

"How many do you think I need?"

"Two or three," Rose said, her gaze cast in the direction of the house. Birdsong wafted from the tall oak tree standing in his backyard. Closing her eyes, she fell silent and pretended she wasn't afraid of anything. A slight breeze teased an errant strand of hair from her *kapp* and tickled her cheek, and she took in the fresh air tinged with the scent of cornstalks and good black soil.

She pretended she wasn't Josiah's project. That she wasn't a burden on anyone, and that *Gotte* loved her just the way she was. It was a wonderful-*gute* feeling, even if it couldn't last.

She opened her eyes to catch Josiah staring at her again. This time, he didn't look away as his lips formed a cautious smile. "Are you okay? There's water in the house."

Even though she was his project, it was sort of sweet that Josiah kept trying to give her water. She must look dehydrated. "I should go yet."

He shook his head as if mad at himself for not thinking of that sooner. "I've been selfish to keep you so long." He pointed in the direction of his house. "The path is easier this way."

An easier path meant no hand-holding. How was it possible to feel relieved and disappointed at the same time?

The winding path led to Josiah's back door. "Do you want to come in the house for a drink before you leave?"

She let a smile escape. "*Denki.* I'm not thirsty."

His blue-eyed gaze was so intense, she thought he might be trying to see through her skull to the back of her head. "Can I . . . I have something for you," he said. "Can I

147

bring it . . . it's in the house. Can I show you? I'll bring it out."

She wasn't quite sure what he'd said, so she couldn't do anything but nod.

He opened his back door and disappeared into the house while Honey sat on her haunches and waited patiently for her master to reappear. Rose stroked Honey's head and fretted about Josiah Yoder and his endearing smile.

Josiah returned in less than a minute with a bottle of water and a small tube in his hands. He handed her the bottle of water; then he showed her what was in his other hand. "I hope this is the kind of paint you like," he said, as if he'd just sprinted a mile. His eyes were deep pools of uncertainty and doubt. "I . . . thought you could use it on your farm scene."

She felt as if she were slowly sinking, like a buggy stuck in the mud with no way out.

Blue paint.

A small gift filled with terrifying expectations and attached to all sorts of strings.

Her hands shook, and her mind raced. She couldn't accept it, but she couldn't reject it or she'd hurt his feelings. He was, after all, just trying to be a *gute* Christian to poor, helpless Rose Christner.

He studied her face, and his expression

fell. "I guess I shouldn't have."

Ach, du lieva. She had hurt his feelings. Always a disappointment. Always such a burden. "I'm . . . I'm sorry." He already knew she didn't want it. She should have just left it at that. But that look on his face felt like being stuck with a hundred pins. She forced her lips into a smile and took the tube from his hand. "It is very thoughtful of you. *Denki.* I like blue. Like your eyes."

Josiah seemed to expel all the air from his lungs. "You don't have to take this just to make me feel better." He leaned over to coax her to look him in the eye.

She lowered her gaze even farther, unable to bear to see his disappointment or his condemnation or his frustration. He'd been thoughtful enough to buy her a tube of paint, and she was being incredibly ungrateful. "It's okay, Josiah. I'll take it."

"Rose," he said. "What do you want?"

"I've already told you. It's better if I do what you want."

She could hear the frown in his voice. "It's not better for me. And for sure and certain it's not better for you."

She would not cry.

Not until she was tucked safely inside her buggy.

She wrapped her fingers around the tube

of paint. "I need to go."

He reached out and cupped his hand around hers. "Wait, Rose. Won't you talk to me?"

Not if he didn't want to see her disintegrate into a puddle of tears. She pressed her lips together and bit down on her tongue.

"But only if you want to," he said. "Not because you don't want to hurt my feelings. I promise I won't get mad or be sad." His mouth drooped. "*Ach.* Never mind. I can't promise I won't be sad, but I can promise you are always safe with me."

Safe? She felt as if she were perched on a precipice, ready to topple into the darkness. No matter what she said, he'd be disappointed or resentful. And he'd pity her or despise her. And she'd deserve it.

But maybe he'd finally leave her be.

A sob nearly escaped her lips at that thought. Why had she come today? She'd wanted to try something brave, but she'd only succeeded in further proving to Josiah that she was weak and helpless and oh so needy. She hated being this way. She hated Josiah's pity.

When she hesitated as if she was considering staying, Josiah shooed Honey out of the way and sat on the top porch step. He gazed at her expectantly. "Please, Rose. Will you

150

talk to me?"

Swallowing her tears, she sat next to him and laid both the water and the paint between them. She pulled her knees up to her chin and wrapped her arms around her legs, making sure her dress was tucked around her ankles. If only she could make herself smaller — so small that no one could see her.

Josiah's relief was palpable as he rested his elbows on his knees and looked at her. "I've been selfish. I was only thinking about what I wanted when I bought that tube of paint. I wanted to give it to you. I didn't stop to think that maybe you didn't want me to get it. I'm sorry."

"It's not your fault."

"You never asked me to come over to your house. I sort of forced myself on you and your family." He curled one side of his mouth. "And I called Suvie pushy. I'm the pushiest of all."

"There's no need to blame yourself for my weaknesses."

"I'm to blame for thinking only of myself." His blue eyes searched her face. "I want to know what you want. What you truly want, so I can do it for you." He picked up the tube of paint. "And I am pretty sure it's not blue paint."

"It doesn't matter."

He turned his whole body toward her. "To be perfectly honest, Rose, it's the only thing that matters to me."

Could she trust him with something so deep and personal? She sighed and gazed out over the pumpkin patch. "I don't want to be afraid anymore."

His gaze grew more intense, as if darkness and light were struggling inside him. "Are you . . . are you afraid of me?"

She pressed her lips together. "I'm afraid of your expectations."

"What do you mean?"

She had to look away from that piercing gaze. "You want something from me."

"What do I want?" he said, so softly she almost didn't hear him.

"I don't know. But I am terrified of meeting your expectations." She wrung her hands together. "Because I can't. No matter what you want, I'll be a disappointment to you. I am a constant disappointment to everyone."

"You have never been a disappointment to me," he said.

"Maybe not yet, but I will be. I'm timid. I don't dare talk to boys. I cry at the stupidest things. I am weak when I should be strong. Everything frightens me, but I'm too

152

terrified to change. I can't even gather up enough courage to walk back to the house by myself in broad daylight. I'll disappoint you, Josiah." The tears would not be stopped. "The burden of your expectations is too great."

"What if I just want to be your friend?"

She lifted her head and studied his face. "*Do* you just want to be my friend?"

He averted his eyes and rubbed the side of his face as if he were trying to scrub the skin off. "*Nae.* That's not what I want."

It hurt so much she nearly cried out. She swallowed the pain and nodded her head as the tears flowed down her cheeks. "I'm sorry, Josiah. I don't want to be your project."

"Rose," he said, "it's not what you think." He grazed his thumb along her cheek, wiping off a tear. "Do you remember when my *mamm* died?"

"*Jah.* It was a terrible time for the whole community."

He gave her a half smile. "The day of the funeral still seems like a dream. All those people came through the house, but I have never felt more alone. My *dat* had died two years earlier. I felt like I was drowning."

"I'm sorry," she said. She had barely known her parents. Josiah had lost the big-

153

gest part of himself when first his *dat,* then his *mamm,* died.

He looked at her with unmistakable sadness in his eyes. "You are the one thing I remember clearly from that day."

"Me?"

"You and your sisters stayed to clean up. You were sixteen, so young and so pretty. All the boys thought so."

Rose pressed her hand to her cheek. He was exaggerating. Josiah had always been nice like that.

"We knew how shy you were. You always stayed close to your sisters and never talked to any of us." He furrowed his brow. "Until that day."

She sniffed and wiped at another tear. "I remember you were crying."

"Most everyone had left, and I was just sitting there alone with a gaping hole in my heart, wondering what was to become of me. I looked up and this beautiful, shy, angelic girl was standing right in front of me. You were afraid to talk to boys, yet you put aside your own fear to comfort me."

"I couldn't let you carry all that grief by yourself."

"I knew you were uncomfortable. Your hands trembled. But you were too kind to let me suffer by myself. Do you remember what you said?"

"Nae."

He took off his hat and ran his fingers through his hair. "Maybe I remember it for what you didn't say. You didn't say any of the hurtful things that people usually say at funerals. You didn't tell me that my *mamm* was in a better place or that *Gotte* must have needed another angel." He lowered his eyes and fingered the brim of his hat. "I was so empty and so bitter, and I'm not proud of it, but I was angry at *Gotte* and the bishop and everyone in the district. It felt like they cared more about Levi Junior than they did about my *mamm.* They hardly had two words to say about my *mamm,* but they all said plenty about Levi Junior. 'Josiah, you know that Levi Junior never meant to hurt anybody.' 'Levi Junior is a *gute* boy who made a careless mistake.' 'Of course you'll be a *gute* Christian and forgive Levi Junior in your heart.' 'Your forgiveness could keep him out of jail.' " Josiah's voice cracked into a million pieces, and he covered his eyes with his free hand.

Rose's eyes stung with tears — not for herself, but for the broken-hearted young man who still wept at the memory of his *mater.* Levi Stutzman had been eighteen years old and still in *rumspringa* when he had bought a car and a cell phone. He'd been texting and driving when he hit a buggy with four Amish women inside. Josiah's *mamm* had been killed. None of the others had been seriously hurt.

Rose laid her hand on Josiah's arm. "You may have been angry, but you never said a word against Levi Junior."

"But in my heart I hated him for taking my *mamm*." He set his hat on the lower step and placed his hand over hers. "You sat with me for two hours and didn't say one word about Levi Junior. You didn't tell me I needed to forgive him and didn't make me feel guilty for hating him. You asked me about my *mamm,* and then you cried for her and let me cry with you. You wanted to talk about why people loved her, why I loved her. You wanted to hear about the quilts she made and about the time she chased the cow through the corn and about when she made a hole in the ceiling with the pressure cooker."

"You have some wonderful memories."

"I was very ungrateful. I had nineteen years of memories with my *mamm.* You had barely five," he said.

"Nineteen is not near enough either."

His eyes filled with tenderness. "You listened to me. I felt a glimmer of hope that

156

I would be all right because Rose Christner helped me see it. You'll never know what that meant to me."

She looked down at her hand, which was still comfortably sitting on his arm. It was too much to gaze into those eyes indefinitely. "No matter what happened at the funeral, everybody loved your *mater.*"

Josiah nodded. "In time, I understood that. I visited Levi Junior in prison and forgave him. He forgave himself too." She didn't pull away when he laced his fingers with hers. "I don't expect anything from you, Rose. On that day of the funeral, I just knew I wanted to spend more time with you. I guess I hoped some of your kindness and bravery would rub off on me."

Rose sighed. "I don't have any bravery to spare."

"You were sixteen and scared of boys. I had to wait until you got older so I could figure out a way to sneak up on you. So far, I haven't been doing a very *gute* job of sneaking."

"So buying me paint is your way of sneaking up on me?"

"I thought you'd like blue."

Her lips twitched slightly upward. "You probably know by now that I am not the type who likes people sneaking up on her."

157

He groaned. "I know. I've been going about it all wrong."

"I like blue so long as it doesn't come with conditions or strings attached."

He narrowed his eyes. "You're afraid you'll disappoint me?"

"I *will* disappoint you."

"So if I have no expectations, you won't be afraid of me?"

She frowned. "Well, I don't know. I don't want to feel like a project either — like you have to be nice to me because I'm pitiful."

He squeezed her hand. "Rose, you're not anyone's project, especially not mine. I promise not to expect anything from you, even an occasional birthday cake, if you promise not to be worried about disappointing me. I'll bring you paint and you can keep it or give it back without hurting my feelings. I just want to make you happy. I think you deserve to be happy." He grinned and slipped his hand out of hers. "Besides, I'm too busy to make anybody a project, but if I did, it would be Paul Glick."

"Paul Glick?"

"The worst-behaved people are usually the ones who need the most love."

Rose pursed her lips. "We definitely need to try to love and forgive Paul Glick, but I'd rather do it from a distance."

"Maybe I'll see if I have time for a project next year."

His silly grin made Rose giggle. "As long as I'm not your project, you can choose whoever you want."

His smile faded as he gazed at her. "You should always be laughing."

She took a deep breath. "I know. I cry too much."

He shook his head. "That's not what I mean. You don't want to be afraid anymore. I'm going to do everything I can to see that you aren't."

"But that's exactly what I don't want. I don't want you to sacrifice anything for me. I don't want you to go out of your way, and I for sure and certain don't want you to waste one minute thinking or worrying about me."

He rubbed the whiskers on his chin. "You might as well ask me not to breathe or eat."

"I will let you down, Josiah. I always do because I'm not brave or strong. Are you sure you want to be my friend?"

"I'll carry a supply of tissues in my pocket at all times, just in case."

He didn't seem to understand what she was trying to say. "I'm going to become tiresome."

"I don't want you to be anxious every time

we see each other. Try to remember that I have no expectations for how you should act or how you should treat me. If you get sick of me, you can tell me to leave and it won't hurt my feelings."

"And when you get sick of me?" She lowered her gaze, not wanting to see what she feared she'd see in his eyes. Better to never talk to him again than to disappoint him and watch him walk away six months from now.

"I won't."

"*Jah,* you will."

He took her hand in his once again. "I promise that I won't leave you until you tell me to go."

Her heart felt heavy and dull. She pulled her hand away. "That's too much pressure, and you're too serious."

"Friends are loyal." He stood and pulled her up with him. "No pressure and no expectations."

"When you grow tired of me, I don't expect you to stay my friend," she said.

He bowed his head as if in surrender. "I'll do whatever you want."

She wasn't quite satisfied with that answer, but she didn't know what else to say. Deep down, she didn't want to talk him out of being her friend, no matter how frightened she was of his expectations, no matter how bad it would hurt when he finally gave up on her.

And he *did* have expectations, despite what he'd said. But she had warned him. She could take a small bit of comfort in that.

He snatched the paint from the step. "So," he said, smiling doubtfully, "do you want the paint?"

She mustered her courage, just to show him how contrary she could be and maybe to test if he'd truly meant what he'd said about not caring if she took it or not. "You are very kind, but I can't accept it." She waited for his disappointment.

He smiled as if he hadn't a care in the world and stuffed the paint in his pocket. "Okay. Blue was a bad choice. I'll try a nice brown next time." His eyes sparkled with mischief.

"You will not," Rose said. "I hate having to keep refusing you."

He tapped his finger against his chin as if thinking really hard. "They have a wonderful-*gute* phlegm-green color at the craft store."

She giggled. "Sounds like something Luke Bontrager would buy."

His mouth fell open. "How did you know?"

■ ■ ■ ■

It was still broad daylight, and Rose insisted that she could drive home by herself. Josiah watched the buggy down the road until he couldn't see it anymore. Had he scared Rose away by telling her too much? He'd been so careful not to say or do anything that might upset her, but it seemed he did nothing *but* upset her.

Oy, anyhow.

He shouldn't have said anything about the funeral. Rose couldn't begin to understand what that meant to him. For her, it was just another memory she couldn't measure up to. For him, it was the day he had fallen in love with Rose Christner.

Rose had literally saved him after his mother died. She'd listened. She hadn't judged or admonished him. She hadn't urged him to offer forgiveness he wasn't ready to give. After she'd sat with him for two hours, he'd known she was the girl he wanted to marry. Rose and her sisters had brought Josiah dinner every week for three months and then once a month for a year. Every time she'd crossed his threshold, it had been like the sun rising on his soul.

After that, it had been everything he could

do to stay away from her. She was only sixteen. They both needed to grow up. But every breath he took from that moment on was focused on being worthy of Rose Christner. He'd named his dog after her. He watched her at gatherings, never daring to get too close for fear of frightening her away. He did a lot of praying in his fields and a lot of crying on his pillow. Thoughts of her were what had eventually led him to the jail to offer his forgiveness to Levi Junior.

If he lost her, he'd never forgive himself.

Josiah walked slowly back to the house. He slipped his hand in his pocket and curled his fingers around the tube of paint that Rose hadn't wanted. If he won her, it would be worth every long night and every tear ever shed.

He took off his hat, hung it on the hat stand, then pulled the paint out of his pocket. He slid a cardboard box out from under the table and dropped the paint in with the thirty other tubes he'd bought. He slumped his shoulders and stared at the paint tubes, each a different color. Maybe the store would take them back. Maybe he'd keep them. Rose might want them someday.

Either that or he could take up a new hobby.

Honey followed him into the house and jumped onto the sofa. She propped her paws on the back of the sofa, tilted her head to one side, and looked at him. Her floppy ears dangled off her head like rags, and she seemed to be smiling at him. The sofa sat in the living room with its back to the kitchen, and Honey often perched like that to watch Josiah as he made supper for himself.

Rose's pineapple coconut cake sat on the counter. *Ach.* It was his birthday. Rose had made him a cake. He pulled a fork from the drawer, speared it into the cake, and took a bite. The toasted coconut on the outside and the creamy pineapple filling on the inside made him sigh with pleasure. He'd never tasted anything quite so delicious. There was no better proof that Rose was an angel from heaven.

Rose had made him a cake. She'd come all the way from Honeybee Farm to deliver it herself. She'd laughed and smiled, and she'd liked his pumpkins. It was the best day he'd ever had.

"Happy birthday to me," he said, taking another bite.

Maybe things weren't so hopeless after all.

CHAPTER SEVEN

"Rose Christner, you must stop slouching," Mammi said. "You look like a turtle hunched over like that. You'll never get a husband if you don't make the most of everything *Gotte* has given you."

Even though she was kneading bread dough, Rose pulled her shoulders back until her shoulder blades were practically touching. Mammi had scolded her for slouching twice already today. Her back was going to kill by the time they went home.

Lily, who was mopping the kitchen floor, gave Rose a reassuring smile. Rose gave her one right back. Saturday afternoons spent at Mammi and Dawdi's were always a bit trying on Rose's nerves. Mammi seldom had a kind word to say, even to her beloved granddaughters, and Dawdi was constantly scrutinizing all of them to make sure they were behaving like proper and righteous Amish girls. Poppy usually got the brunt of

Dawdi's displeasure because she seldom behaved like a proper Amish girl, but that was one of the things Rose loved the most about her sister.

Poppy was brave and bold and didn't let anyone frighten her or push her around. Rose wished she was more like Poppy, who let Mammi's criticisms flow off her like water off a duck's back.

The Honeybee *schwesters* visited their grandparents a few times a week, and on Saturdays they spent the whole afternoon there cleaning and baking for Mammi and helping Dawdi in his garden. Mammi and Dawdi lived on two acres of land in the middle of town. Dawdi had a small garden, and Mammi grew herbs for cooking. Dawdi was eighty-one years old, worn out and bent over with age. Maybe his knobby back was the reason Mammi was so adamant that Rose stand up straight.

Rose often studied Mammi's face in hopes of catching a glimpse of her mother. Mammi was almost ten years younger than Dawdi, and she looked as young as Dawdi looked old. Her light brown hair had only a few streaks of gray, and her wrinkles congregated around her eyes and mouth, leaving the rest of her skin smooth and soft. Rose thought she was a very pretty woman. Had her *mamm* been pretty like that?

Mammi stood at the threshold to the kitchen and inspected Lily's mopping and Rose's kneading. "You didn't sweep well, Lily. You're slapping around all sorts of crumbs with your mop."

"Sorry, Mammi," Lily said. "I'll make sure there are no crumbs left when I'm done."

Lily and Rose never argued with Mammi. If she said they were wiping down walls or washing clothes the wrong way, they simply agreed with her and tried to better follow her instructions. That was probably why Poppy spent her time in the garden with Dawdi. Dawdi didn't approve of Poppy's behavior, but he would have to be blind not to see how *gute* she was with the plants. His tomatoes always grew better when Poppy tended them, even with her hand in a cast.

Keeping her shoulder blades tightly together, Rose separated the dough into pans and covered the loaves with a dishtowel to rise. Three loaves to carry Mammi and Dawdi through to next week. Maybe Josiah could use a loaf of bread to carry him through his week. She'd have to make him a loaf or two when she got home.

Mammi propped her hands on her hips. "You didn't give the kneading enough time,

Rose. It must have plenty of air or it turns out heavy as a brick."

Rose nodded. "Don't worry, Mammi. I kneaded them extra, just the way you like."

"I hope so. I won't have my bread ruined. You seem not quite yourself today."

"I do?"

"You would have forgotten the salt if I hadn't reminded you. You're usually so careful."

Rose washed the sticky dough off her hands and then set to work on the counter caked with flour. What was Mammi talking about? She wasn't distracted in the least. It was just a normal Saturday, like every other Saturday they'd spent at Mammi's. The day before had been a normal Friday, spent baking cakes and running errands and crying like a baby in front of Josiah Yoder.

She forgot about her shoulder blades and felt her face get warm. Josiah had seen her cry so many times, he probably feared she would dry up and blow away. That's probably why he kept trying to give her water.

Still, he hadn't made fun of her or run as fast as he could in the other direction. Maybe he hadn't even pitied her.

Next to her sisters and Aunt Bitsy, Josiah was probably the kindest person Rose had ever met. At the funeral, he might have felt nothing but anger and hurt, but she'd never heard him say a bitter word about Levi Junior or the bishop or anyone in the *gmayna*. She had watched him put his arm around Levi Junior's *fater* and mingle his tears with Levi's *mamm*'s. He had gone to the prison to visit Levi Junior, and although few people knew, he had helped Levi Junior's *dat* plant feed corn every year since the accident.

And he had very nice eyes, the color of a clear sky on a bright fall day.

He'd said he didn't want to be her friend. But then he'd sort of said he did. He'd said he wanted to spend more time with her in hopes some of her kindness and bravery would rub off on him.

She shook her head. He didn't know her very well if he thought she was kind or brave. In reality, she was selfish and pitiful.

What do you want, Rose?

Rose's heart flip-flopped in her chest as she scraped the dried dough from the counter with a spatula. What did she want? Josiah made her nervous, but when she wasn't busy worrying about disappointing him, she sort of liked being with him. He acted as if he was truly interested in what she had to say, and it was endearing the way he thought he could fix things when he couldn't. He was unfailingly patient with his nephews and too hard on himself when he made a mistake. She even liked the feel of his hand when he helped her cross furrows.

Ach, du lieva. Her heart felt as if it were galloping around Lily's newly mopped floor.

"Rose, you're making a mess of that apron," Mammi said.

Lily rinsed out the mop in the sink and set it on the back porch. "That's what aprons are for, Mammi."

"*Cum,* girls." Mammi tiptoed across Lily's damp floor, took Rose's hand, and tugged her in the direction of the living room.

"Don't slip, Mammi," Lily said. "The floor's wet yet."

Mammi waved her hand in the air. "Rose won't let me fall." She reached out her hand to Lily. "*Cum* and sit. Your *dawdi* wants to have a talk with you."

Rose's heart sank. Dawdi only wanted to talk when he felt compelled to call his granddaughters to repentance. Rose had heard enough from Aunt Bitsy to know that Dawdi had been a very harsh *fater.* Salome, Rose's *mamm,* had been the *"gute"* daughter, never sticking a toe out of line, embracing the *Ordnung* with all her heart. Aunt Bitsy had been the "rabble-rouser" — probably much like Poppy — and Dawdi had withheld his approval and his love.

Bitsy and Salome had loved each other fiercely, despite how their parents had treated them. Salome had watched out for Bitsy and defended her against their *fater*'s wrath. Rose had always wanted to be like her *mamm* — good, kind, and brave — even though Rose was too flawed to ever measure up.

It made Rose's heart hurt to think that Aunt Bitsy hadn't found much love in her own home. It was why she had jumped the fence and lived as an *Englischer* for twenty years. But she was so devoted to her sister that she was willing to come back to the *gmayna* and raise her nieces. It had been Salome's dying wish.

Rose said a prayer of thanks every night for Aunt Bitsy. If Bitsy hadn't loved Salome so much and hadn't wanted to honor her wishes, Rose and her sisters would have been raised by Dawdi and Mammi. She couldn't bear to imagine how much worse off they would have been.

Mammi led them into the living room and directed them to sit on the sofa. She went back into the kitchen, tiptoeing all the way. Lily raised her eyebrows at Rose and sighed. She knew a lecture was coming too, but unless they stood up and sneaked out of the house, they were stuck.

Mammi returned to the living room, carrying the plate of honey cookies that Rose and Lily had brought this afternoon. "Have a cookie," Mammi said.

"But Mammi," Lily protested, "we brought these cookies for you and Dawdi."

"Stuff and nonsense," Mammi said. "We'll get fat if we eat all these. None of you girls are fat. Yet. With all the goodies your Aunt Bitsy makes, it's a true miracle. You won't get husbands if you get fat."

Dawdi opened the front door and hobbled into the room with the help of his cane. Poppy followed close behind making sure Dawdi didn't pitch backward and fall down the porch steps. She gave Rose a resigned smirk, as if she knew what was coming as well as Rose and Lily did.

Dawdi took off his hat to reveal a full head of snowy-white hair. His unruly horseshoe beard hung down past the first two buttons of his tan work shirt. Rose had always loved that beard. It made her think of white, billowy clouds and newly fallen snow.

In the last couple of years, Dawdi had developed a wheeze in his lungs. It was especially noticeable when he breathed heavily, like after he worked in the garden and then climbed up the porch steps. He hung his hat on the hook by the door and heaved a great sigh before lowering himself to his threadbare chair that he had probably owned since he and Mammi got married. "Priscilla, sit there by your sisters," he said, motioning to the sofa.

Poppy frowned in a good-natured sort of way, folded her arms, and sat down by Rose. Lily and Poppy often placed Rose between them so she would be protected on either side. Rose looked down at her hands. They always had Rose in mind, no matter where they went or what they did. To them, it was the way they had always done things. Putting Rose's needs before their own was almost as natural as breathing. They didn't seem to resent her or even wish she were different, but Rose felt the sting of it. Her sisters sacrificed so much for her without even knowing it, and Rose had come to expect it. How selfish she had become.

Mammi handed each of the girls a cookie and sat next to Dawdi in her rocker.

"First of all," Dawdi said, "have you girls been good this week? Have you said your prayers and repented of your sins?"

All three of them nodded. "*Jah,* Dawdi," Lily said. "We have been trying to be *gute* girls."

173

Dawdi seemed pleased even though he asked that same question every week, and they always gave him the same answer. "*Gute.* I will never stop worrying about that." He scooted to the front of his chair and leaning both hands on his cane. "Now then. Have you had any more trouble on your farm since the fire?"

Poppy glanced at Lily. "They slashed the door of our buggy. Josiah and Luke took it to the shop and got it fixed."

Dawdi couldn't have frowned any harder. "Is anything being done to find out who it is? Have you seen any strangers lurking on the farm?"

Poppy squeezed Rose's hand, for sure and certain to comfort her. She was embarrassed that she needed it, but she was grateful for Poppy's firm hand. "Dan Kanagy found a pocketknife that we think one of them dropped. Josiah Yoder says Amos King sells them at the harness shop. Amos is going to make a list of all the people he remembers buying that knife. The neighbor boy who lives behind us also saw a car parked on the edge of our clover field a few nights ago. Brown and rusted, like the one that rolled my hand up in its window. He said if he sees it again, he'll get a license plate number."

Rose eyed Poppy in confusion. "I didn't know that."

"Josiah told Dan, and Dan told us," Poppy said, almost too matter-of-factly.

"Why didn't you tell me?" Rose said, even though she already knew the answer.

Poppy patted Rose's hand as if that made everything all better. "We didn't want you to be upset."

Dawdi pointed his cane at Rose. "That's right. We don't want you to be upset."

Rose lowered her eyes.

"I'm sure we will find out who is doing all the damage," Lily said. "They can't hide forever."

Dawdi sat back in his chair. "Maybe all this trouble is *Gotte*'s will. Perhaps He is trying to tell Elizabeth to repent. Sometimes He speaks in a still small voice, sometimes He speaks through earthquake and fire. You girls are being punished for your *aendi*'s sins. It is time you came to live with us and let Bitsy bear the consequences for her own choices."

Rose's chest tightened painfully. She longed to defend Aunt Bitsy, to make Dawdi see how wrong he was. But she couldn't speak.

"Dawdi," Poppy said, lifting her chin. "Was Job a wicked man?"

"*Nae*, but King David was. *Gotte* took his son as punishment for his evil deeds."

"What about Jeremiah or Paul? Did they get what they deserved?"

Dawdi scrunched his lips together like he always did when he refused to admit he was losing an argument. "I've heard talk that the deacon paid you a visit. It is a very serious thing when the deacon comes to your house. I don't wonder but Elizabeth gave him reason to shun you yet."

Dawdi never had a nice thing to say about Aunt Bitsy. They all tried to bite their tongues when Dawdi talked like that, but Poppy usually ended up in an argument with him. It did no good. Dawdi would never admit that Aunt Bitsy was one of the best Amish women who'd ever lived in the community. Lily and Poppy both grabbed on to Rose's hands at the same time. She only felt more ashamed of herself that they thought she was so weak.

"Aunt Bitsy explained everything to the deacon," Lily said. "He understands the situation and said we won't be shunned."

"That is *gute* news. We wouldn't want to be forced to shun our own closest relatives." Dawdi squinted as if trying to bring his granddaughters into focus. He never wore his glasses when he worked outside. "Now,

Lily. You broke up with Paul Glick over a month ago. I've been patient, hoping you would see the error of your ways and go back to him on your own. Paul Glick has come to visit three times since you rejected him. He still loves you and would gladly marry you if only you will humble yourself like a *gute* Amish *frau.* He's from a very *gute* family. His *dat* is a minister."

Rose felt Lily and Poppy tense beside her. She was tenser than both of them.

"A *gute* income too," Mammi said. "You are twenty-two years old, Lily. You can't reject someone as willing as Paul Glick. You might never get married."

"I've already told you," Lily said. "I don't want to marry Paul Glick."

Dawdi's squint got narrower until his eyes were mere slits on his face. "Then I'm afraid I'll have to put my foot down. You will give Paul Glick another chance or you'll not be allowed in our house again."

Mammi put her hand to her mouth. "But, Sol, who will mop my floor?"

Rose held her breath. Dawdi couldn't force Lily to do anything, especially not marry someone she didn't want to marry. It wasn't the Amish way. But the thought of Dawdi trying to force Paul on Lily made Rose ill.

To Rose's amazement, Lily seemed unruffled. Rose was shaking in her shoes, and Dawdi wasn't even talking to her.

"He doesn't treat me like a boy should treat the girl he loves. Don't you want me to marry someone who will love me like Christ loves his church?"

Not only was Lily very brave, but she spoke sense. Surely Dawdi would want his granddaughters to be treated well. Surely Mammi would want her floors mopped every week.

"Paul is from a *gute* family. *Die youngie* don't know what is *gute* for them," Dawdi said.

Lily sighed. "Dan Kanagy is from a very *gute* family too."

Dawdi smoothed his hand through his beard. "No denying that. The Glicks have had a bone to pick with the Kanagys for many years, but I've seen nothing but kindness from John Kanagy. I assume his son is the same. Are you telling me you're interested in Dan Kanagy?"

"Maybe," Lily said. Lily wanted to keep her engagement a secret until they were published in church in September.

"What if he's not interested in you? A bird in the hand is worth two in the bush," Dawdi said.

178

Still as calm as the lake in the summer, Lily stood and knelt between Dawdi's chair and Mammi's rocker. "I hate to speak ill of anyone, but Paul knew he wasn't paying me enough for our honey. I found a buyer who paid me four times as much."

Dawdi frowned. "You must have misunderstood. You're mad at Paul because he speaks the truth about your Aunt Bitsy. You should find it in your heart to forgive him."

Lily let out a slow breath and went back to her place on the sofa. "I have forgiven him, Dawdi. I just don't want to marry him."

Mammi looked as if someone had carved a line between her brows. "But what if you never get married? Do you want to end up an old *maedle* like Bitsy?"

"I'd rather be single than married to Paul," Lily said. "And you can't make me marry him. If you won't allow me in the house anymore, that is your choice, but your floors will get wonderful dirty."

Dawdi smoothed his beard, no doubt considering how dirty he was willing to let his floor get. "If we had been able to raise you, you would not be so stubborn."

Mammi worried the hem of her apron. "You're too picky, Priscilla is a tomboy, and Rose won't even talk to a boy. You'll all be

179

old *maedles,* and we'll have no posterity to carry on after we're gone."

Rose was the only one who would be an old *maedle.* Lily had Dan, and Poppy had Luke.

"Don't worry, Mammi," Poppy said. "There is still hope for us. We will all find husbands, Lord willing."

Mammi grunted her disapproval. "Rose is the only one I have hope for. She is pretty and sweet and never talks back to her grandparents."

Rose didn't dare argue with Mammi. Instead, she lowered her eyes and studied her hands. No one wanted to marry a mousy girl who startled at strange noises.

Not even Josiah Yoder.

Mammi reached out her hand. "*Cum* here, Rose."

Rose reluctantly rose to her feet and knelt down next to Mammi's rocker. Mammi took both of Rose's hands in hers. "Pull your shoulders back, *heartzly.*"

Rose did as she was told.

Mammi cupped her hand under Rose's chin. "When you have finished with the bees this fall, you will come and live with us. We will teach you how to be a *gute* and worthy Amish *frau,* and find you a godly man like Paul Glick."

Rose wanted to push Mammi's hand away and jump to her feet. She wanted to stand up to Mammi and tell her that she would never come to live with them and that if they said one more bad thing about Aunt Bitsy, she would never set foot inside their house. Someone else could make the bread.

She swallowed past the lump in her throat and tried to find her voice. It was no use. The best she could do was stare at her hands and hope that Mammi got tired of waiting for an answer. It would be better if she could shrink to the size of a mosquito and fly away. She wanted to be anywhere but here, even sitting on Josiah's back porch with tears running down her face.

Ach, how she loved her sisters. No matter how undeserving Rose was, Lily and Poppy always came to her rescue, at least they would until they were married.

"We could never spare Rose," Lily said, rising to her feet, grabbing Rose's hand, and pulling her from the floor.

"Nae," Poppy said, standing up and hooking her arm around Rose's elbow. "We would never allow Rose to leave us."

"We've got to be going now," Lily said. "Let me know if you'd rather we not come next week."

She and Poppy pulled Rose along as they

181

marched out the door and down the porch steps like three draft horses in a log-pulling contest.

Rose's steps faltered. "I left my apron."

"They can have it," Poppy said, not faltering, not looking over her shoulder, not even caring that Rose had just lost her favorite apron.

Lily gazed sympathetically at Rose. "*Oy,* anyhow. What are we going to do about Mammi and Dawdi?"

Rose was profoundly relieved and utterly ashamed at the same time. "I . . . I didn't mean for you to have to do that for me," she said. "I should have been braver." Her tears were dangerously close to spilling from her eyes. "But I just can't be brave."

Lily and Poppy practically dragged her along as they marched down the sidewalk to their buggy. "We will always protect you, Rose," Lily said.

Poppy smiled. "We don't mind. Luke says I'm always looking for a fight anyway."

"I should fight my own battles," Rose said.

Her sisters didn't even hear her. The screen door creaked open, and they turned to see Mammi with her head stuck out of the door. "Come back here," she said. "You haven't finished your cookies."

Lily smiled and waved. "We'll see you next

week, Mammi."

Mammi drew her brows together. "It's a terrible waste of food."

Rose stopped and turned around, unable to bear the thought of hurting Mammi's feelings. "We love you."

Mammi frowned and let the screen door slam behind her. Her feelings were hurt anyway.

Poppy smirked. "That was a nice thing to say, Rose, even if we'd rather love them from a distance."

Rose slumped her shoulders. "I didn't want them to feel bad."

"Don't be too worried about their feelings or they'll have you married off to Paul Glick before you can bake another loaf of bread," Poppy said.

Rose thought she might throw up.

Lily's mouth fell open. "Poppy Christner, bite your tongue. What a horrible notion."

Poppy put her arm around Rose. "I'm just teasing. You know I'm just teasing, right? I would never let Paul Glick within a hundred feet of you. I won't let him near Lily. Or Dan. Or Luke either. Luke might be tempted to break his vow of nonviolence and pop Paul in the mouth. Or I might be tempted to do it myself."

Rose's heart pounded against her chest.

"Please, Poppy. Promise me you won't ever hit Paul Glick."

"I'm teasing," Poppy said. "If I hit Paul Glick, I would be shunned and then we'd have to postpone the wedding, and Luke would probably get an ulcer."

Rose frowned. "You don't . . . you don't really think Mammi and Dawdi would try to match me up with Paul Glick, do you?"

Poppy snorted.

"Of course not," Lily said. "Despite what Dawdi hopes, Paul wouldn't lower himself to be seen with any of us. He hates us, most especially me and Dan." They climbed in the buggy, and Lily took up the reins. "I'm ashamed to say I almost married Paul." She looked around as if making sure no one was listening in on their conversation. "Paul as a boyfriend is definitely scraping the bottom of the barrel."

Rose felt reassured enough to manage a small smile. "Dan and Luke are the top of the barrel for sure and certain."

Poppy's eyes sparkled like lights reflecting off the lake at night. "If only we could find someone at the very top of the barrel for you, Rose."

Rose shuddered. "That thought scares me to death."

"You were brave enough to take a cake to

Josiah Yoder yesterday," Lily said.

Rose fidgeted with her *kapp* strings. "Aunt Bitsy said if I want to overcome my fear, I have to do something that scares me."

"And?" Poppy said, pushing her eyebrows halfway up her forehead. "Did it work?"

"Maybe it helped a little."

"You said he showed you Suvie's butterfly garden," Lily prodded. "I don't wonder that it was nice."

Poppy smiled. "And you said he was very happy about the cake."

Rose twined her fingers around one of her *kapp* strings. "He thinks I'm a better person than I am."

"Impossible," Lily said. "You're a better person than anyone could even imagine."

Rose hated it when her sisters gave her undeserved praise. "I'm not. I'm selfish and scared. Josiah tried to give me a tube of paint as a gift, and I refused it." She shook her head. "I shouldn't have told him no. I hurt his feelings something wonderful."

Poppy put her good arm around Rose. "It's not bad to keep him guessing. He'll appreciate you more if you make him work for it."

"You make it sound like I'm a chore that needs to be done. I don't want to be a burden on anybody, especially Josiah Yoder."

185

Lily turned the horse down the main street. "You're too sweet to ever purposefully hurt anybody's feelings, Rose. Don't worry about Josiah. If his feelings are hurt, it's his own fault. The most important thing is how he treats you." She cleared her throat and concentrated faithfully on the road ahead. "And . . . how he treats everybody else. It's not as if Josiah is concentrating on you specifically."

Rose furrowed her brow and bit her bottom lip. Josiah was nice to everybody. He probably gave away tubes of paint like handshakes. Her not taking one would just leave more for the next person who came to visit. She relaxed her fingers and tugged them from around her *kapp* strings. She wasn't anyone special to Josiah Yoder.

That thought made her feel considerably better.

And maybe a little sad.

CHAPTER EIGHT

"I don't know if this is such a *gute* idea," Josiah said as he and his two best friends tromped across the flagstones in front of Rose's house. "They don't know I'm coming, and I wasn't invited."

"Didn't you say you were here earlier today?" Luke said.

"*Jah.* I returned Rose's cake plate, but Rose was away visiting her grandparents. I fixed a chair and the sofa for Bitsy."

Luke looked at Josiah sideways. "You fixed a chair?"

Josiah nodded.

"With tools?" Luke said.

"I should be offended that you don't think I know how to use tools."

"You don't," Luke replied.

Josiah lifted his chin. "As it turns out, one of the chair slats was broken. There aren't tools that will fix that. I used duct tape. Bitsy was very grateful."

Luke snorted. "I'm sure she was."

"You fixed Bitsy's chair," Dan said. "She's probably wishing she had a phone so she could call and invite you for dessert. Besides, you didn't get to see Rose. That's reason enough to barge in on them."

Josiah grimaced. "What if she thinks I'm rude for coming over uninvited?"

Dan draped an arm over Josiah's shoulder. "Tell her Luke invited you. The Honeybee sisters already know he's rude. They won't blame you."

Luke rolled his eyes. "Don't be so jumpy. Rose will lose interest before she even remembers your name. And I am not rude. I'm assertive, and Poppy thinks I'm adorable."

Dan grinned. "And I used to think Poppy was such a smart girl."

Luke puffed out his chest. "The smartest. Why do you think she loves me?"

They'd been standing on the porch for nearly a minute, and Josiah wasn't altogether sure he should stay. He wanted to see Rose something wonderful, but despite what Luke thought, Josiah had to be careful. He wasn't sure he should be standing here.

Too late to reconsider. Luke knocked on the door as if he were trying to break it down. Did that boy even know what "subtle" meant?

The door opened. The lanterns inside had already been lit. The three Honeybee sisters and their Aunt Bitsy stood in the doorway, as if they had agreed to open the door together. Lily and Poppy burst into radiant smiles that put the propane lanterns to shame. Josiah's gaze immediately flew to Rose. She didn't beam like her sisters, but she did give him a tentative smile that might have meant she wasn't altogether unhappy to see him. His heart did a little jig.

The enticing smell of cooked peaches and brown sugar made his mouth water. Josiah almost wished Rose wasn't such a *gute* cook. He didn't want her to think he only came over for her cooking. He couldn't love her any more than he already did, peach crumble or no peach crumble.

Leonard Nimoy sat next to Bitsy's foot with that deceptive, wide-eyed-innocent look on her face. She didn't fool Josiah. He had some very nice scabs on his arm where Leonard had been, and he had seen the mess Leonard Nimoy had made of Bitsy's sofa.

"We hear there's peach crumble," Luke said, walking into the house without being invited. The Honeybee sisters sort of

189

scooted back to let him enter, but they didn't seem to mind. Poppy adored him, for goodness sake. She would have put up with most anything.

Bitsy frowned. "*Ach.* It's you."

Billy Idol catapulted himself into the air and landed with his claws deep in Luke's trousers. Luke pried the cat from his leg and cuddled Billy Idol in his arms. "Hello, Billy Idol," he said. "Have you been protecting my girls?"

Dan put his hand on Josiah's back and shoved him forward. "We brought Josiah too. Hope that's okay."

"I suppose he'll want to be fed," Bitsy said.

Lily's smile for Josiah was almost as wide as the one she'd given Dan. "We're wonderful happy to see you, Josiah. Rose needs to practice."

Lily was happy to see him, and she'd said something about Rose. "Practice?"

Rose's blush was about the most attractive thing Josiah had ever seen. "Lily is trying to help me get over my fears. But I'm afraid it's a lost cause."

He pinned her with an earnest gaze. "You're anything but a lost cause."

Her face got redder, but she didn't reply.

"We've got ice cream too," Poppy said, gazing at her fiancé as if he were the only boy in the world. Josiah longed for Rose to look at him like that. Mostly, he longed for her to look at him at all.

"Rose made it," Lily added.

Of course Rose had made it. If the Christner sisters had intentionally set out to torture him tonight, they couldn't have planned it any better.

Bitsy seemed resigned to the burden of having boys at her house. "Luke only gets one piece," she said, closing the door once they'd all come inside. "That boy could eat Wal-Mart out of house and home."

"I'm in the room, Bitsy," Luke said, setting Billy Idol on the window seat next to Farrah Fawcett. "You don't have to talk about me like I'm not here."

Bitsy smirked. "I wish you weren't." She looked at Josiah as if trying to figure out how he'd gotten into the house. "You fixed my chair and sofa today. I suppose you can stay. But don't get the wrong idea."

How could he get the wrong idea? He didn't even know if Rose would rather he hadn't come.

Then again, Bitsy had sort of invited him into the house for peach crumble. How could he be unhappy when he was being included in the inner circle, the one he ached to belong to. Even if he never got into their family circle, he'd get to spend at least another hour with Rose, gazing at her, hearing her voice, being driven crazy with his love for her.

He'd take any bone they threw at him and be grateful.

Luke rubbed his hands together. "Let's see this chair Josiah fixed."

Bitsy pulled it out from under the table and held out her hand as if she were introducing it. Josiah hadn't known quite how to fix the slat, but he had wanted to impress Bitsy, so he had wrapped several layers of duct tape around it. That thing wouldn't break even if Perry Glick sat on it.

Bitsy glared at Luke. She seemed to glare at him often. "Josiah did a *gute* job on it, ain't not?"

Luke's lips twitched. "Looks like he did a *gute* job."

Poppy pointed to the base of the sofa that Josiah had also covered with duct tape. "He fixed our sofa too."

Leonard Nimoy had scratched the fabric up something wonderful. He thanked the *gute* Lord for duct tape.

Bitsy looked up to the ceiling. "Dear Lord, please bless that nothing else breaks while Josiah is here."

Josiah grinned. "It's all right, Bitsy. I don't

mind fixing anything you need."

Bitsy didn't lose her no-nonsense expression. "I wouldn't want to impose."

Luke brought plates and spoons to the table. Josiah had to give Poppy credit. A few weeks ago, Luke wouldn't have lifted a finger to do kitchen chores. Now he practically clambered for a chance to help — probably to show Poppy what a *gute* catch she'd made. Poppy brought the ice cream while Rose carried the warm peach crumble to the table. Josiah took a whiff. Brown sugar and oatmeal topping sat over a pool of sliced peaches swimming in their own juices. Ice cream would make it irresistible.

Josiah found the ice-cream scoop and a spatula in the drawer. He could show them he was at least as *gute* a catch as Luke, even if he wasn't. Josiah was just a poor orphan farmer. He wasn't as *gute* a catch as anybody.

Bitsy sat at the head of the table with Lily to her right and Poppy to her left. Dan sat next to Lily and Luke sat next to Poppy. That left the chair opposite Bitsy, and Josiah was pretty sure it wasn't for him.

Dan and Lily had their heads together giggling about something, and Poppy and Luke were arguing about whether Poppy could scoop the ice cream with a broken hand.

Poppy never wanted Luke to help her with anything, and Luke got annoyed when Poppy stubbornly tried to do things that Luke was perfectly capable of doing for her.

Usually, Josiah didn't mind not being noticed. He just wanted to work the land and serve *Gotte,* but tonight, a sharp and heavy lump of coal lodged in his throat. What was he doing here? Rose deserved a bishop's son with acres and acres of land. She deserved a hundred tubes of paint and every sort of paintbrush she could think of.

"Are you all right, Josiah?"

Rose was standing closer than he had realized, looking at him with those wide, innocent eyes that always captivated him. She reached out and laid a hand on his arm. It felt as if she were pulling him back from a cliff.

"What could be better than peach crumble and ice cream with Rose Christner?"

Her smile sent his temperature to the sky. "Don't say that until you taste it." Rose nearly sat down before stopping short when she noticed there wouldn't be enough chairs. "*Ach,* Josiah, sit there," she said, motioning to the last chair.

He cleared his throat. "I should probably go. Morning comes early on the farm."

"*Nae,* Josiah," Rose said. "You fixed Aunt

Bitsy's chair. You deserve to sit. I'll stand."

Bitsy growled. "All the unselfishness in this room is giving me a headache." She pointed to the back room, where she kept her bucket for unclogging the sink. "There's folding chairs in there, Josiah. Grab one."

"We'll scoot closer together so you can sit on this side," Dan said.

Bitsy shook her finger at Dan and Lily. "Don't get fresh, and don't get any ideas."

Feeling a little less awkward, Josiah retrieved the folding chair from the back room and sat next to Dan while Rose sat at the end of the table. At least he had an excuse to be near her. Rose dished up servings of peach crumble for everyone. He was probably imagining things, but did she give him the biggest bowl?

Jah. He was imagining things. If wishes were horses, beggars would ride.

Josiah took a bite and nearly floated off his broken folding chair. "This is . . . I could live off this. It's wonderful-*gute,* Rose."

A smile played at her lips. "The peaches were very *gute* this year."

Dan popped a bite of peach crumble in his mouth. "I hear Rose helped you babysit, Josiah."

"She didn't help me babysit. She babysat.

I watched and tried not to burn down the house."

"That's not true," Rose said. "He played with his nephews, and I cooked pancakes."

"And fed the baby and gave the boys a bath and mopped up a flood," Josiah said.

"Did you try to unclog their sink?" Bitsy said.

Josiah smiled. "*Nae. That* I could have done."

Bitsy shoved her lips to one side of her face. "*Gotte* gives us all different gifts."

"You drove me home," Rose said, pinning him with a serious gaze.

If she looked at him like that every day, he'd never be sad again.

Poppy licked her spoon and gazed around the table. "We have some news," she said. "About Griff Simons."

Luke stiffened in his chair, and the muscles of his jaw twitched. Dan frowned, and Josiah's chest tightened with anger. Griff Simons had tried to kiss Rose on her way home from the animal shelter a few weeks ago. Poppy had broken her hand fighting him off. Luke had assured Dan and Josiah that Griff wouldn't attack any of the Honeybee sisters again, but that didn't stop Josiah from worrying.

"What has he done?" Luke said, looking

like a bear ready to charge.

"He has a girlfriend, and the girlfriend thinks Amish people are cute." Poppy smirked. "Her words, not mine. Griff and the girlfriend stopped us on the road when we walked home from the bus stop yesterday."

"All three of you?" Dan said.

Poppy nodded. "She wanted to meet us. Griff pretended we were his friends because he wanted to impress his girlfriend."

Josiah studied Rose's face. "Did he frighten you?"

Rose curled her lips in an attempted grin. "At first, but his girlfriend was very nice."

"Luke took a punch for Griff," Poppy said. "I don't think he was planning on bothering us again. But it's nice he has an agreeable girlfriend. He wouldn't dream of harming his pretend Amish friends."

"Let's hope he and the girlfriend have a very happy relationship for many years to come," Dan said.

Luke put his arm around Poppy and tugged her close. "I'm glad you're okay."

"Luke Bontrager, if you don't want Leonard Nimoy to use your head as a scratching post, you'd best take your arm from around my niece," Bitsy said.

Luke grinned and winked at Bitsy as if he

never took her seriously. "It's too bad your niece is so irresistible."

Bitsy's look could have shaved the fur off a fish.

Luke chuckled and took his arm from around Poppy. "Do you blame me, Bitsy?"

Bitsy nodded. "*Jah*. I do."

"We have some *gute* news too," Dan said, "about the knife I found in your barn."

Josiah glanced at Rose. "We don't need to talk about this now."

Rose bit her bottom lip and pushed the rest of her ice cream around her plate. "I . . . I want to hear what you know."

"I don't want you to be frightened."

"What I don't know frightens me the most," Rose said.

Josiah didn't think he believed that. Sometimes ignorance truly was bliss, but his opinion didn't matter. Dan had already opened his big mouth.

Dan put down his spoon. "Amos at the harness shop remembers at least three of the *Englischers* who bought that kind of pocketknife from him last month. He gave us their names and addresses. Tomorrow, Luke and Josiah and I are going to go to their houses and see if any of them have a brown car like the one that almost drove off with Poppy's hand."

Deep lines gathered around Rose's mouth. "You could get hurt."

Josiah leaned forward and gave Rose a reassuring gaze. "We're just going to look for cars."

Poppy placed her palm on the side of Luke's face, eliciting a growl from Aunt Bitsy. "I should go with you. I'm the only one who has actually seen one of their faces."

Luke shook his head. "Nope. You're not going anywhere near those houses."

"That's what you think," Poppy said.

Rose seemed to be unable to catch her breath. "So it *is* dangerous."

Josiah couldn't stand to see Rose frightened. "It's not dangerous."

Rose didn't believe him. "But then why doesn't Luke want Poppy to go?"

"All we're looking for is a brown car," he said. "If we find one, Bitsy can call the sheriff."

It felt like a jolt of lightning when Rose reached out her hand and grabbed his. "Please don't go. Any of you. There's got to be another way. Maybe they won't come back anymore. Maybe slashing the buggy is the last thing they'll ever do."

That wasn't very likely, but Josiah didn't say it. "We still want to find out who it is."

She squeezed Josiah's hand harder as her eyes pooled with tears. "I don't care if we ever catch them." She blinked, and two teardrops splashed onto the table. "I'd be sick if something bad happened to one of you."

"We'll be okay, Rose," Luke said. "We've all been baptized. You know we'll leave at the first sign of trouble."

"What if you can't leave fast enough?" Tears rolled down her face as she stared at Josiah. "Please don't go."

No matter how badly he wanted to catch the troublemakers, Josiah would have crawled to Canada and back to make Rose happy. He could certainly never refuse anything she asked.

He laid his other hand over hers so her hand was snugly sandwiched between both of his. "If you don't want me to, then I won't."

A sigh of profound relief escaped from between her lips. *"Denki."*

He wished he could sit there forever, holding Rose's hand safely within his own, but Bitsy was already eyeing him as if he had a bad smell. With great reluctance, he pulled both of his hands away, retrieved a tissue from his pocket, and handed it to Rose.

She stared at him as if he'd just saved her

cats from certain death. "You brought tissue."

"I promised I'd always have some just in case."

She sniffled and smiled. His heart fluttered like a bird in flight.

Bitsy tapped her hand on the table. "That's all fine and good that Josiah has tissues, but we still need to figure out how to catch the troublemakers. They tried to burn down my honey house. I don't take kindly to someone who likes to play with fire."

Luke looked none too happy that he wouldn't be able to search for the knife owner. He sat back and folded his arms. "Bitsy, maybe you could tell the police what we know and ask them to look."

It wasn't the Amish way to involve the police with anything, but Bitsy had lived as an *Englischer* for twenty years and she wasn't touchy about such things. Today, Josiah was secretly glad that Bitsy didn't act like a normal Amish *frau.* They needed all the help they could get to keep the Honeybee sisters safe.

"I'll call the sheriff again," Bitsy said, "but some days I wonder if he's very smart. He keeps calling me Misty, and the last time he was here, he left his badge on my counter. I pinned it on and called myself 'Officer

Baxter' for two days."

Poppy giggled. "And Farrah Fawcett still ignored you."

Rose finished wiping her tears. "You wrote three parking tickets."

Everyone laughed. Josiah studied Rose's face. She was the most beautiful girl he had ever laid eyes on, even with the constant worry lines around her eyes. He was more determined than ever to find out who was making all the trouble on the farm. Rose would not be truly happy until she felt safe. Josiah would not be truly happy until he was sure Rose was out of danger.

Despite Bitsy's protests, Luke had three helpings of peach crumble with ice cream. Josiah would have licked his plate if it weren't impolite. After dessert, they did up the dishes. Lily handed Josiah a dish towel, and he and Rose dried.

A loud knock drew everyone's attention to the door. Luke held up his hand to tell Poppy to stay where she was, but Poppy pretended she had no idea what he was trying to communicate. Dan strode to the door, and Luke and Poppy joined him there. Josiah sidled closer to Rose and positioned himself so he stood between her and whoever was on the other side.

Griff Simons, big and thick and as surly

as a bull with a burr in his rump, stood on the porch with a police officer stationed close behind him. Luke tried to nudge Poppy behind him. She wouldn't budge. Luke's scowl could have melted all the ice cream in the freezer.

Griff wasn't as tall as Josiah, and he looked even shorter because he hunched over as if he was just about ready to try to touch his toes. With his neck and arms as thick as tree trunks, he would have been a pretty *gute* match for Luke in an arm-wrestling contest. On his right forearm, he sported a tattoo of a skull with a snake coming out of its mouth.

Josiah's anger flared like his own private forest fire. Griff had tried to kiss Rose. Josiah didn't even want to contemplate what he would have done if he had been there. He glanced at Rose. Lily hooked her arm around Rose's waist, and they stood as still as stone pillars.

"Can we help you?" Luke said through clenched teeth. Josiah could tell he was trying to be as friendly as possible even though he wasn't very good at it.

The officer kept a hand on Griff's arm as he stepped forward. "Is Frau Misty here?"

Bitsy gave a low growl, one that only those nearest to her could hear, and pushed Luke and Poppy aside to get to the door. "What can I do for you, deputy?"

The deputy was a good head shorter than Griff with a pudgy face and a stomach that hung a few inches over his belt. He spoke as if he were too lazy to move his lips. "Remember when someone tried to burn down your barn a couple of weeks ago?"

"I think I remember that," Bitsy said with a straight face.

The deputy nodded. "Griff went to the emergency room that same day with second-degree burns on his arms. It looked suspicious, so the hospital reported it to us."

"I didn't do anything," Griff protested.

"You can speak when you're spoken to," the deputy said.

Griff shut his mouth. The deputy's size and demeanor weren't all that intimidating, but a badge and a gun were probably enough to keep any kid quiet, at least temporarily.

The deputy sniffed the air. "I can arrest him if you want, but I know you Amish don't like going to court. I thought I'd let you have a talk with him first."

"I appreciate that," Bitsy said, squinting in Griff's direction. "Griff Simons, you've given us quite a bit of trouble. Are you still mad at Poppy for punching you in the face?"

The deputy frowned. "Who punched him in the face? That's assault."

"Water under the bridge, deputy," Bitsy said, her gaze pinned squarely on Griff. "Did you set fire to my honey house?"

The deputy glanced up at Griff. "She means the barn. Did you try to burn down their barn?"

Bitsy didn't even correct him. "Did you set that fire, Griff?"

Griff seemed to grow smaller, as if he were ashamed he had been dragged over here in the first place. "I haven't never been on your property except when my dad brought me."

"Are you telling me the truth?" Bitsy said.

"Yeah." Griff scowled and held out his hands so they could see the fading burn marks and old scabs on his arms. No wonder he had gone to the hospital. "I burned myself when I tripped and fell into the campfire." His eyes shifted between Bitsy and the deputy.

Josiah pressed his lips together. Griff Simons was lying. But which part of his story was a lie?

"He did it, all right," the deputy said, getting worked up enough to move his lips. He drew a cigarette lighter from his pocket. "I found this in his room."

Bitsy scrunched her lips together, propped

her hands on her hips, and fell silent. They waited as she stared at Griff. "Have you had a yeast infection lately? Or the chicken pox?"

Griff slowly shook his head as if leery of being led into a trap. "No."

She looked up at the ceiling. "Lord, are You purposefully trying to annoy me? I know Your ways are not my ways, but can't our ways align with each other every once in a while?" Not taking her eyes from the ceiling, she paused as if she were waiting for an answer. After a few seconds, she threw up her hands. "He didn't do it, deputy," she said. "And now we're going to have to give him a cookie."

The deputy didn't seem to like her answer, but he didn't argue. He'd probably dealt with Amish people often enough to be familiar with their ways. "Okay, then. If you're sure."

"I'm sure," Bitsy said, seemingly irritated to have to admit it.

"Then I can go?" Griff asked, his tone a mixture of defiance and relief.

"Just a minute." Bitsy went to the cookie jar and pulled out three cookies the size of saucers. Josiah suspected the Honeybee *schwesters* always had a full cookie jar. Bitsy wrapped the three cookies in a napkin and handed them to the deputy. "Thank you for your *gute* work. We are very grateful."

The deputy acted as if she'd handed him the keys to a new car. "Thank you, Frau Misty. You know how I like your snickerdoodles."

"There's more where that came from," Bitsy said. "Whatever help you can give us is appreciated."

He nodded. "I'll keep looking for the culprits." He shoved his thumb in Griff's direction. "And I'll keep an eye on this one. He's always been a troublemaker."

The deputy turned and walked down the porch steps. Griff turned to follow him.

"Not so fast, Griff," Bitsy said. "Come in, and sit down."

Josiah's chest tightened, and for a second he wondered if he'd heard right. Lily and Rose gasped. A look of surprise passed between Luke and Dan. Poppy clenched her fists at her side, probably getting ready just in case of an attack.

Griff narrowed his eyes. Josiah didn't blame him for being wary. They could have cut the suspicion on both sides with a knife. "Why?"

Only Bitsy seemed perfectly at ease, and as grumpy as ever. "Because you need a cookie. And we need to talk."

Griff eyed Bitsy as if she were luring him into an ambush. "My girlfriend is waiting at the house."

Josiah very nearly spoke up. Griff couldn't be allowed in the house. He'd scare Rose out of her wits, and under no circumstances was Rose to be frightened. But it wasn't his place to say who was and was not welcome in the Christners' home. He clamped his mouth shut and prayed that Bitsy knew what she was doing.

Just in case, he took a step forward to create a protective perimeter around Rose.

Griff didn't seem inclined to do what Bitsy wanted. He tromped down the porch steps. "I'm not gonna sit and listen to you preach to me about hell or nothing. I didn't do nothing wrong."

Bitsy narrowed her gaze. "Why don't you come in and have a cookie and tell us how you got those burns."

A shadow passed over Griff's already-cloudy expression. "My dad don't want trouble with the police."

Bitsy folded her arms. "Then maybe we should talk about it."

To Josiah's disappointment, Griff slowly and reluctantly tromped back up the stairs and into the kitchen. Everyone gave him wide berth, as if he might suddenly decide to swing his arms and break somebody's jaw.

Bitsy pulled out a chair at the table. Josiah was kind of surprised when Griff sat down. "Do you like milk with your cookies?"

"I don't want anything," Griff said. "The deputy told my girlfriend she had to wait at the house."

"You've come this far," Bitsy said. "Might as well have a cookie."

"What kind?"

"We have chocolate chip and snicker-doodles."

"Chocolate chip," Griff said, as if he wasn't happy about admitting it.

Everyone in the room seemed rooted to the floor, unable to do anything but stare at Griff and wonder how he had gotten into the house. Bitsy poured Griff a tall glass of milk, put a whole stack of cookies on a plate, and took them to the table. She must have been expecting Griff to eat a lot of cookies. That or she planned on his being here for a long time.

"I need to text my girlfriend."

"Invite her over. There's plenty of cookies."

Griff pulled his phone from his pocket, fiddled with the screen, and then put the phone away. Bitsy handed him a napkin and leaned her hands on the table so she could look him in the eye. "How old are you, Griff?"

Griff eyed the cookies, but he didn't touch them. "Eighteen."

Her piercing gaze could have made a grizzly bear flinch. "Did your dad give you those burns?"

Griff stuck out his chin. "I told you. I tripped."

"Tripped because you were pushed?"

Griff's belligerent confidence seemed to falter, and he looked down at his hands. "My dad doesn't want no trouble with the police."

Bitsy was always doing the unexpected. She sat down next to Griff and placed her hand firmly on his arm. "You've done nothing to deserve being hurt like that."

"I got a fresh mouth," Griff said.

Luke pried his feet from the floor and sat down on the other side of Griff at the table. "A father should never strike his son."

Griff looked at Luke as if he'd just realized he was in the room. "I'm sorry my dad hit you," he mumbled.

"I'm sorry your dad hits you," Luke said.

Griff traced his finger along a crack in the table. "Why did you take a punch for me? Why should you even care?"

Luke shrugged. "I knew your dad was going to be angry if he found out you'd hit a girl. I also know what happens to you when your dad gets angry."

Griff kept his gaze on the table. "Yeah, well. Thanks."

The surprises kept coming. Poppy sat down next to Luke. "Luke wants to protect everybody. Even you."

Griff folded his arms across his chest as if he were wrapping himself in a cocoon. "I'm sorry I hit you. I got angry."

"Like your dad?" Poppy said.

He hunched over in surrender. "I shouldn't have done it." He picked up a cookie from the plate, almost as if he were simply looking for something to do with his hands. "I'm sorry I scared Rose and tried to kiss her. It was a joke. I didn't think she'd cry."

Such an explanation strained Josiah's ability to believe. The anger flared brightly inside him and immediately burned itself out. At least Griff had offered an apology. That was no small thing.

"Please don't tell Ashley what I did," Griff said. "She likes Amish people. She'd break up with me."

Josiah thought it would serve him right, but he also knew that everyone deserved

211

forgiveness. It was what the Amish taught almost every week in church. Griff had hurt Rose. Could Josiah find it in his heart to forgive him?

"I hope you can be happy," Rose said, not moving from the safety of Lily's arms. Josiah could see her hands trembling even as she spoke. Her kindness took his breath clean away.

A low rumbling seemed to shake the very foundation of the house. Griff perked up at the sound. "That's Ashley. I let her drive my truck."

A few seconds later, Ashley knocked on the door. How could someone put so much excitement into three taps?

Dan was still standing dumbly by the door, so he opened it. The girl at the door had long, jet-black hair, so shiny it seemed to sparkle in the lamplight. It cascaded over her shoulders like a waterfall and fell almost to her waist. Her hair framed her round, mousy face and her lively brown eyes.

Her earrings looked too thick to fit into the holes in her ears, and Josiah winced at the thought of distended earlobes and huge ear holes. She wore a pair of tight jeans and flip-flops bedecked with dozens of little blue beads.

"Hello," Ashley said. "Is Griff here?" She

peered into the kitchen and saw Griff sitting at the table with his back to her.

He turned and looked at her.

"Griff!" she squeaked.

Her grin was so infectious, Josiah couldn't help but smile himself.

Without waiting to be invited in, she skipped into the house and threw her arms around Griff's neck from behind. "I can't believe the police dragged you away like that. He didn't even have a warrant or anything." She looked at Bitsy. "Did you tell the police he didn't do it?"

Bitsy nodded. "*Jah.* We knew it wasn't Griff."

She squeezed her arms tighter around Griff's neck. "Oh, thank you so much. You Amish people are so nice." She bent farther and pressed her cheek to Griff's. "I told you, didn't I, Griff?"

"Yeah. You told me."

"I said, 'Griff, these Amish folks are super nice. They forgive everybody.' I said that, didn't I, Griff?"

"Yeah."

Ashley took her arms from around Griff and stood up straight. She gazed around the room as if she were in a museum. "I've never been in an Amish house before. Hi, Lily. Hi, Rose." She furrowed her brow. "Is

213

it Poppy?"

"*Jah,*" Poppy said.

"After we met the other day, I was going to remember your names. I really was."

"You did very well," Lily said.

Ashley smiled. "I was shocked when that policeman came to take Griff away. He said Griff set your barn on fire. But he didn't." She tapped Griff on the shoulder. "Show them your burns, Griff."

"I already showed them," Griff said, holding his arms out anyway.

"It could have been so much worse." Ashley's smile faded to nothing. "His dad smacks him around almost every night — especially when he's drunk. He had to get five stitches last week."

Griff seemed to fold into himself. For a boy so big, he was getting smaller and smaller. "I don't want to talk about it."

Ashley's eyes sparkled with tears. "We've got to do something. Enough is enough."

"They'd only put him on parole anyway. Nothing changes, and calling the police only makes him madder."

"Do you have to live with your dad?" Bitsy said.

"What about your mother?" In spite of his gruff exterior, Luke was always the champion for the underdog.

Griff shook his head, and Josiah thought he looked a little sheepish. "She kicked me out."

Standing behind him, Ashley laid both hands on his shoulders. "The stupid jocks were always starting fights at school. What else could he do?"

"Can we do something to stop your *dat* from picking on you?" Luke asked.

"He needs to move out," Ashley said. "But he can't live with us. Me and my mom live in a studio apartment. There isn't even enough room for a cat."

"I wish I had that problem," Bitsy muttered under her breath.

"I can't afford to live on my own," Griff said. "The government won't give me no more money."

Oy, anyhow. Every muscle in Josiah's body seized up at once. It seemed as if a thick rope pulled him in a direction he didn't really want to go, but he had to do it. Jesus said to love everyone. *I was a stranger and ye took me in.* "I live all by myself. You can stay with me," he said. His voice seemed to echo off the ceiling.

Everyone stared at him as if his ears had just fallen off. Except for Rose. The tenderness in her eyes made him feel like a bowl of mushy tapioca pudding. "He'd have a roof over his head, and he'd be away from his dad," Josiah said.

"You would do that?" Ashley said, scraping her jaw off the floor and bursting into a smile. Before Josiah even had the wherewithal to fend her off, she threw her arms around his neck and squeezed so hard she nearly choked him. Her heavy perfume stung his nose, and even though he'd never been allergic to anything before, he thought he might break out into a rash.

Unsure if it would be rude to pry her off, Josiah let Ashley hug him until she had a mind to let go. Josiah felt increasingly awkward when it seemed Ashley had nowhere else she needed to be besides attached to his neck.

To his relief, Bitsy finally said something. "You can give Josiah his windpipe back now."

Ashley giggled and released Josiah. She immediately turned to Griff and wrapped her arms around him from behind again. "I told you the Amish were nice. I mean, really nice."

Griff grimaced as if Josiah's suggestion didn't taste very good. "Who are you?"

"I'm Josiah Yoder."

"Look, Josiah, it's nice of you to offer, but you got no TV, no computers, and no air-conditioning. I'd go crazy."

"At least you wouldn't get hit," Josiah said.

"But the weirdness factor of living with some Amish guy is off the charts. I can't do it."

"But it was a really nice thing to offer," Ashley said, smoothing a lock of Griff's hair against his head.

Josiah nodded, ashamed of the relief that flooded over him. He hadn't wanted Griff to say yes, but Jesus would have wanted Josiah to open his home to a fatherless child. Josiah didn't have a father, but he was not fatherless. Griff's father was alive, but he couldn't have been less of a father if he were completely invisible.

Griff took Ashley's hand. "I've got to save up enough money to move out. Maybe join the army."

"You're not going to join the army," Ashley protested. "I would die if you got killed."

Griff finally took a bite of the cookie and drank half the glass of milk. "We've got to go. You won't tell the police about my *dat*?"

Bitsy shrugged. "That's your choice, not mine, but you'll come to us if you need help?"

Griff scooted his chair from the table and stood up. "I don't know. I usually just call Ashley."

Ashley slid her hand into Griff's back pocket and let it rest there. "If any of you ever need help, you know you can always call me or Griff. But I'm sure you already know that." She patted Griff on the chest. "I know he's been a good friend to you."

"The best," said Bitsy, without a hint of sarcasm in her voice. "Do you want some cookies for the road?"

Griff nodded and picked up the whole plate. "Thanks." He came around the butcher-block island, too close for comfort. Josiah overreacted and stepped in front of Rose just in case Griff wanted to kiss her. It was completely irrational and completely stupid, but it was his first impulse to protect Rose. If Griff noticed, he didn't show it.

"Hey, man, nothing personal about not wanting to live with you."

"I'm not offended." Relieved was a better word, but Griff need never know that.

"Does anybody have a pen?" Ashley said.

Dan retrieved a pen from the drawer. Ashley grabbed his hand and wrote something on his palm. Dan's eyes nearly popped out of his head and rolled out the door.

"Here is my cell number," Ashley said. "I know you don't have a phone, but if you borrow someone else's phone, I'd love you to call me. You're all so cute."

Ashley nudged Griff out of the house with his plate of cookies and shut the door behind her. Everyone seemed to breathe a collective sigh of relief. Josiah's neck was so tight, he feared it might never bend again.

Bitsy grunted. "He just took one of the Sunday plates. I hope he enjoys it."

"I feel sorry for him," Lily said.

Poppy frowned. "Me too."

"Don't feel too sorry," Aunt Bitsy said. "He got a very nice plate as a memento."

Luke pressed his fingers into the back of his neck. "He's in a very bad situation, but I'm wonderful glad Josiah doesn't have to live with him. Whatever made you offer?"

Josiah shook his head. "I don't know. I hate the thought of his *dat* beating up on him."

Rose was suddenly right next to him looking at him as if he'd unclogged every sink in her house. "I've never seen such kindness."

"I'm sorry his *fater* is less of a man than he should be."

Rose's blue eyes sparkled. "And you are more of a man than most will ever be. You would have made your *dat* very happy."

Josiah looked at his hands as his face got warm. "I hope so."

Dan studied the phone number Ashley had written on his hand. "I gave her the permanent marker. This is never going to come off."

Lily giggled. "At least you'll always know how to reach Griff's girlfriend."

"I can't believe you invited him into our house, B," Poppy said. "What were you thinking?"

Bitsy shrugged. "When *Gotte* tells you to do something, you do it, no questions asked. I prayed for *Gotte* to give Griff a yeast infection, and *Gotte* told me to give him a cookie. I hate it when that happens."

CHAPTER NINE

Josiah sat outside the toolshed, where there was more light to work, but all the light in the world wasn't going to help him figure out this post driver. Andrew was usually the one who fixed the farm tools, but he was at a school meeting and wouldn't be home for at least another hour. Even though Alvin was only three years old and wouldn't be in school for another three years, the entire community took an interest in the *kinner*'s education. Andrew had just as much say in whom they hired to teach as anybody.

Josiah tried to loosen the tiny screw behind the pull cord. The screwdriver slipped and tore an inch-long gash in his trouser. *Oh sis yuscht!* That was going to leave a mark. And probably a little blood. He had fixed the Honeybee sisters' sink and their chair and even one of the loose boards on their porch. Surely he could get this post driver to start before Andrew came home.

He stood up to survey the damage to his knee. Suvie would mend his trousers, and there were only a few spots of blood.

Glancing at the scabbed scratches on his arm, he thought it would be wonderful-*gute* if Rose were here to give him some first aid. Maybe he could ask her to mend his trousers. That would give him another excuse to visit her. Then again, he didn't want to make a pest of himself, and he didn't want her to think he was taking advantage of her kindness.

How he wished he could just say, "Rose, I think of you every time my heart beats. I love you down to my bones. Will you please just marry me already?"

That's what he was going to say someday.

But not today. Not unless he wanted her to lock her bedroom door and never come out.

A smile pulled at his lips. She had smiled at him more than once the other night. There was reason to hope, if only just a little. But he certainly wouldn't allow his hope to take wing. There were too many things he could do wrong before she came anywhere close to agreeing to marry him.

Or learning to trust him.

Or deciding to love him.

Oy, anyhow. His hope wilted like cornstalks in a drought. He should never think about what could go wrong.

"Josiah, you know you're not allowed to use the tools," Luke said, as he and Dan tromped over the dirt toward the toolshed.

"I'm not allowed to use your tools," Josiah said, picking up his screwdriver and trying to look like he knew how to use it. "Half of these tools are mine. Andrew says I can use whatever I want."

"It's because he's too polite to tell you to keep your hands off." Luke smoothed his fingers down the driver chuck and took a close look at what Josiah was working on.

"It won't start," Josiah said.

Luke rolled his eyes. "You're trying to fix it with a screwdriver? You should be arrested." He pulled a wrench from the toolbox and nudged Josiah aside. "Let me do this before you hurt yourself."

Josiah would have protested, but he had, in fact, already hurt himself and the post driver was no closer to working than it was before. He was humble enough to admit that Luke was better than he was with a pair of pliers.

"So," Josiah said, "did you two come for a friendly visit or did you hear the post driver crying for help?"

Luke sat down and started fiddling with

one of the driver's bolts. It was in much better hands now. "We came to tell you what we found out about the knife."

"The pocketknife in the barn?"

Dan nodded. "We went to the three addresses, but didn't see a car like the one that tried to run down Poppy."

Josiah narrowed his eyes. "Wait a minute. You went to the houses?"

"Jah."

"I promised Rose we wouldn't."

Luke pointed the wrench in Josiah's direction. "You promised Rose that *you* wouldn't. Everybody just assumed that Dan and I agreed."

"Which we didn't," Dan said. "We want to protect Poppy and Lily just as much as you want to protect Rose. No one was going to stop us from checking out those addresses."

Luke nodded. "We kept our mouths shut so Rose wouldn't be worried and Poppy wouldn't insist on coming with us. I kept it a secret so she won't be mad at me."

"You're a coward," Dan said.

Luke shrugged. "Maybe. But at least Poppy is safe."

Josiah wasn't altogether happy about it either. He had promised Rose they wouldn't go to those houses. Then again, like Poppy, she need never know. "But you didn't find out anything?"

"Nae," Dan said. "Amos only gave me three addresses. It wasn't likely that we'd find anything."

Luke tightened a bolt, yanked the pull cord, and the engine roared to life.

Josiah shook his head. "How do you do that?"

Luke flipped the wrench up in the air and caught it by the handle. "It's a gift from *Gotte.* Poppy thinks it's adorable."

Josiah rubbed his hand across his mouth to hide a smile. Luke's arrogance didn't need any more encouragement, but for sure and certain, Josiah was glad his post driver was working again.

"I'm glad Poppy finally decided to like you," Dan said. "I was starting to feel sorry for you."

Luke set the wrench in the toolbox. "We have one piece of *gute* news. The boy who cuts through the Honeybee Farm sometimes . . ."

"Jack?" Josiah said.

"*Jah,* Jack. Dan talked to him yesterday. He saw the car we're looking for and got part of their license plate before they drove away."

"He did?" Josiah said.

Dan half smiled and pressed his fingers back and forth across his forehead.

Luke pulled a piece of paper from his pocket and unfolded it. "I wrote it down. It's S."

Josiah waited for a few seconds until he realized that was all he was going to get. "S?"

"*Jah*," Luke said. "It wonders me if we should give this to the police."

Dan was still hiding behind his hand, but Josiah could hear him chuckling softly. Josiah couldn't help joining him.

Luke was sufficiently offended that both his friends were laughing. "Well, it's something."

Josiah braced a hand on Luke's shoulder. "You're right. Even the smallest thing might help us. And we've got to protect our girls yet."

Luke and Dan both sobered.

"*Jah*," Luke said. "We're not giving up."

Josiah nodded. He wouldn't give up on Rose or the license plate.

They were making progress. They had an S.

"It wonders me if Mammi and Dawdi lie awake at night thinking of ways to offend us," Poppy said as she, Lily, and Rose trudged up the porch steps after another difficult Saturday at Mammi and Dawdi's house.

Rose sighed. "I suppose they mean well."

Poppy slumped her shoulders. "Do they?"

"They love us very much," Rose said, trying to convince herself as much as she was trying to convince Poppy. "Dawdi is afraid for our souls, and Mammi is afraid we'll all be old *maedles.*"

They stopped in front of the welcome mat, where the mangled body of a mouse greeted them. *"Ach,"* Lily said. "Why can't Billy Idol leave mice on Griff Simons's porch instead of ours?"

"But he's such a dear cat," Rose said. "We would be overrun with mice if it weren't for him."

Poppy pointed to one of the floorboards on the porch. It was covered over with a thick layer of duct tape. "It looks as if Josiah has been here yet."

Rose's heart hopped like popcorn on a hot skillet. Was he still here? Had he come to see her? Why hadn't she worn the pink dress instead of this drab brown one?

Her heart pounded wildly until they opened the door. Aunt Bitsy kneaded bread at the counter, Farrah Fawcett lounged on her window seat, and Leonard Nimoy

227

chased a puff of lint around the kitchen. Josiah wasn't here, and it surprised Rose at how profoundly disappointed she felt. She took a deep breath and willed her heart to beat normally. Josiah didn't usually spend his Saturday afternoons on the Honeybee Farm. Why should today be any different?

Aunt Bitsy kneaded dough with more force and enthusiasm than anybody Rose knew, huffing and puffing as if she'd just sprinted a country mile. She was also sporting a new hair color. "You're back," she said.

"B," Poppy said. "You dyed your hair while we were gone."

"Very pretty," Lily said. "I like it. It looks like sunshine."

Aunt Bitsy raised a sticky, flour-caked hand and swatted away Lily's compliment. "The package calls it 'daisy yellow,' but now that it's on, I think it looks more like urine. I'm redoing it tonight."

"Aunt Bitsy," Rose said, "you didn't need to start the bread. I don't mind making it."

Aunt Bitsy kept up her energetic kneading. "I had a few extra minutes after my other chores. I don't mind."

Rose didn't want to seem too eager, but she had to ask. "Was . . . was Josiah here?"

Aunt Bitsy halted her kneading as if someone had turned off a switch. *"Jah."* Her

228

lips twitched upward. "Can't you see he fixed the porch?"

"What was wrong with it?"

"A floorboard was loose. He tried to hammer it down and almost broke his shin. Then he decided duct tape would work just as well."

Poppy glanced at Rose. "Oh. Well. It looks very —"

Aunt Bitsy erupted like a geyser. "Where's Luke when I need him?"

"You don't like Luke," Poppy said.

"I don't." Aunt Bitsy growled. "But I need him. Josiah Yoder wouldn't know a plunger from a potato."

Rose eyed Bitsy doubtfully. "You didn't . . . did you tell him that?"

"*Nae,* of course not." Aunt Bitsy took her butcher knife and slammed it into the bread dough twice, cutting it into three nearly identical globs. She was very accurate with that knife. "Josiah is an orphan and he's trying so hard, and I don't have the heart to hurt his feelings."

"You never care about Luke's feelings," Poppy said, tempering her words with a smile. Luke didn't seem too upset about the way Aunt Bitsy talked to him, so Poppy obviously wasn't either.

Aunt Bitsy waved her butcher knife in the

air. "That's because Luke Bontrager is too big for his britches. That boy couldn't be cut down to size with a pair of heavy-duty pruning shears." She looked at Lily. "And Dan was so eager when he first came over, I wanted to smack him upside the head. Josiah always acts like he's inches away from falling into the depths of despair. I have to be nice, even though it almost kills me." As if to emphasize her point, she motioned toward the sofa. "Even if he buries my whole sofa in duct tape."

In addition to the patch of duct tape Josiah had applied three days ago, there were two more long patches of tape on one of the sofa arms. Rose smiled. Josiah was trying his best to be thorough and conscientious.

"Leonard Nimoy is trying my patience something wonderful," Aunt Bitsy said. "The scratching post is three inches from the sofa, and she ignores it." She pinched her index finger and thumb together. "She's this close to being deported."

Rose immediately scooped Leonard Nimoy from the floor and placed a quick kiss on the top of her head. "You can't get rid of Leonard Nimoy, Aunt Bitsy. Farrah Fawcett would be devastated."

All four of them looked to the window

seat. Farrah Fawcett lifted her head and eyed them as if she were a queen surveying her subjects.

Poppy giggled. "*Jah,* Farrah Fawcett seems quite attached to Leonard Nimoy."

Rose sighed. "She wouldn't know how much she loves Leonard Nimoy until Leonard was gone. She'd have to spend all those lonely days on the window seat without Leonard Nimoy trying to sit on her head."

Aunt Bitsy washed her hands and took three pieces of cat food from the dish on the floor next to the window seat. "The only solution is to train them."

"Train the cats?" Lily said.

With the cat food in one hand, Aunt Bitsy pulled a book from the bookshelf near the sofa and showed it to them. *"Training the Best Dog Ever,"* she read from the front cover. *"A Five-Week Program Using the Power of Positive Reinforcement."*

"But they're cats," Poppy said.

"I know, but the library didn't have any books on cat training, and I figured since dogs and cats are both house pets, it should work for my cats." Aunt Bitsy scooped Farrah Fawcett from the window seat and set her down on the floor. "Rosie, bring Leonard Nimoy over here. I want to show you the trick they learned this morning."

Rose cocked her eyebrow in curiosity and set Leonard Nimoy next to Farrah Fawcett.

Aunt Bitsy pinched a piece of cat food between her fingers and held it up just out of Farrah Fawcett's reach. "Roll over, roll over, Farrah Fawcett," she said, making kissing noises with her lips and waving the cat food in a circular motion above Farrah Fawcett's head. Farrah Fawcett watched the swirling cat food for a few seconds before yawning and averting her eyes, as if such a game were beneath her. Leonard Nimoy swatted at the cat food, but it was too far over her head to reach, even when she used her hind legs to leap for it.

Aunt Bitsy lowered the cat food right in front of Farrah Fawcett's face and extended her other hand. "Shake, Farrah Fawcett. Shake."

Farrah Fawcett had obviously had enough childishness for one day. She eyed Aunt Bitsy with disdain, strolled to the bowl on the floor, and got her own cat food without having to do any tricks. Leonard Nimoy mewed and reached out her paw for the treat. Aunt Bitsy immediately grabbed Leonard Nimoy's paw and shook it. She looked at her nieces and twitched her lips. "It's slow going. I might have to send them to obedience school after the weddings."

Rose scooped up Leonard Nimoy again. "Oh, you *gute, gute* kitty. You learned how to shake hands." It never hurt to give Leonard Nimoy some encouragement. If she learned to roll over, Aunt Bitsy wouldn't dream of getting rid of her.

Aunt Bitsy deposited the few pieces of cat food back in the bowl, gave Farrah Fawcett a smirk, and washed her hands. Then she returned to her dough and started forming it into loaves. "How was Mammi and Dawdi's house today?" she said, as if she were asking about the weather. Aunt Bitsy never let on, but she knew perfectly well how visits usually went with Mammi and Dawdi.

Lily plopped herself into a chair at the table. "They tried to convince me to marry Paul. Dawdi threatened to bar me from the house again."

Poppy rolled her eyes. "If only he knew how tempting that threat is."

"I don't think they'll stop until I'm married," Lily said.

"Maybe you should just tell them you're engaged," Rose said. It might make visits to Mammi and Dawdi's more pleasant.

"Not yet. I want people to be surprised when we're published in church."

"Dan and Luke have been spending a

suspiciously large amount of time over here," Poppy said. "I think most people already suspect."

Lily smiled. "I suppose that's true."

Rose snuggled Leonard Nimoy up against her chin. "They keep insisting that I come and live with them when Poppy and Lily are married. It makes me nervous."

"You know you can't be forced to do any such thing," Aunt Bitsy said, covering her loaves with a dishtowel. "My *dat* is trying to scare you. He did it all the time when I was growing up." Unhappy and unspoken memories traveled fleetingly across her face before she huffed and pretended they hadn't been talking about anything important. "*Ach, vell.* It doesn't matter, Rose. You are an adult. I am an adult, and there's nothing Dat can do about it."

Aunt Bitsy seldom talked about her childhood, but Rose knew it hadn't been a happy one. Rose felt doubly blessed. Although she had lost her parents, she'd still grown up in the happiest of homes.

Aunt Bitsy pinched Rose's earlobes. "Try not to let him upset you. That was my problem, and it didn't solve anything."

"I wish I could be courageous and stand up to both of them," Rose said. "They shouldn't pressure Lily, and Paul should quit trying to talk them into it."

"There are different kinds of courage, and don't you forget it." Aunt Bitsy's frown sank farther into her face. "I got a letter from Wallsby today."

Rose nodded to her *aendi* as if her getting a letter from Wallsby was nothing to be upset about.

Aunt Bitsy opened the pencil drawer and pulled out a letter. The back of the envelope had five Bible stickers stuck to it. Aunt Bitsy still had a few friends in Wallsby. The Honeybee sisters had lived there with their aunt for two years after their parents had died.

Aunt Bitsy pulled the letter from the envelope — two pages filled with neat handwriting in blue ink. "Edna says the girls are fine, but she hopes the rest of her babies come one at a time."

"*Oy,* anyhow," Poppy said. "I don't think I'd survive if I had twins."

Aunt Bitsy pinned Rose with a steady gaze. "LaWayne Zook died last week."

Rose felt as if the wind had been knocked right out of her. She pressed her hand to her neck.

Poppy took Rose's hand. "*Cum.* Sit down."

Rose obeyed numbly, as if it were someone

else Poppy was talking to and not her.

Aunt Bitsy ran her fingers along the crease in her letter. "He'd been in the hospital for almost three months when he passed. Liver failure."

"From drinking?" Lily said softly. She was probably hoping Rose wouldn't hear her.

Aunt Bitsy nodded. She filled a cup at the sink, brought it to the table for Rose, and sat down next to her. "This is none of your doing, Rose."

Rose bit back a sob. "Then why do I feel so horrible?"

Poppy sat next to Lily and grabbed on to Rose's wrist, but she didn't have anything to say. Her sisters watched her with concern and pity in their eyes.

For sure and certain, they were glad *they* hadn't testified against LaWayne Zook.

Rose clasped her hands in her lap and put that unkind thought out of her head. Her sisters would have done anything for her. They never blamed her for what had happened, even though they'd been forced to move after LaWayne went to jail.

Ach! She wished she had never known Mary Beth Zook. She wished they had never moved to Wallsby. She wished her parents hadn't died. Dawdi said that wishing denied *Gotte*'s hand in their lives. Rose had learned herself that no amount of wishing or even praying would change the past.

"Now that he is dead, you don't have to be afraid of him anymore," Lily said.

Aunt Bitsy studied her face and frowned. "You still blame me for insisting you testify?"

Rose finally broke down. "I don't know. How can I blame you, Aunt Bitsy? How can I blame anyone but myself?"

The memory she had tried to bury resurfaced and left her gasping for air. She and Mary Beth had been playing dolls in the Zooks' haymow when Mary Beth's *dat* had come home. It was the middle of the day, and he had been let go from his job at the greenhouse because he often went to work intoxicated.

Rose had never seen anyone drunk before, and LaWayne's slurred speech and slow movements had frightened her. Rose and Mary Beth had been using one of the bridles in the barn as a swing for their dolls. LaWayne had yelled and cursed all the way up the ladder.

Rose clamped her eyes shut as the memory overtook her. She could still smell the pungent odor of horses and fresh-cut hay mixed with the sickly sweet scent of alcohol on LaWayne's breath. She saw the dust motes floating in the beams of sunlight that peeked through the slats of the barn and felt Mary Beth's breath against her cheek as they clutched each other and huddled behind a bale of hay. And most of all, she remembered the sounds — LaWayne's slurred, threatening words as he climbed the ladder, coming closer with every heartbeat, Mary Beth's crying, apologizing to her *dat* again and again, the sound of Rose's own whimpers as LaWayne snarled at her.

Rose flinched and rubbed her hand up and down her arm, the arm LaWayne had broken when he'd shoved her from the haymow and she'd tumbled onto a pile of straw on the barn floor. He'd been pulling Mary Beth's hair. She couldn't cower behind the hay bale and let him hurt her very best friend in the world.

What haunted her most was LaWayne's tortured expression when he realized what he had done. He'd bolted down the ladder — afraid he'd killed her — and snatched her out of the pile of straw. He had grabbed her arms and shaken her until she started breathing again. The pain in her arm had been like fire. The terror in her heart had never completely subsided.

He was the one who had carried her into the house and sent one of his boys to fetch

Aunt Bitsy. He was the one who had apologized again and again as Rose lay on Mary Beth's bed sobbing in fear and pain while she waited for Aunt Bitsy to come and get her. Mary Beth's *mater* — Rose couldn't even remember her name — had brought Rose a cool rag for her forehead. She had shushed Rose, pleading with her to stay quiet. "You won't tell anyone what happened, will you? That's a *gute* girl. Mary Beth's *dat* loses his temper sometimes, and he is very sorry. You'll be a *gute* girl and keep our secret."

Oh, how she wished she had done as she had been told.

Aunt Bitsy had clutched Rose to her bosom in the hospital and squeezed the wind right out of her. Because the thought of losing one of her girls had made her resolute, she had called the police, and they'd arrested LaWayne right there at his home, in front of his children. The bishop had insisted that LaWayne's drinking was a church matter and that the church would handle it. He'd said it was a sin to take a *fater* from his family. Aunt Bitsy had sent Rose upstairs when the bishop had come, but Poppy and Lily had pulled the bed out from the wall so all three of them could listen to the conversation through the air vent. Bitsy had been firm with the bishop and even more insistent with the police.

Rose's testimony sent LaWayne to prison for three years. The entire community had been shaken. Women refused to talk to Bitsy at *gmay* or invite her to quilting bees or canning frolics, and none of the Honeybee sisters had been allowed to play with anybody else's children. When it came time for school in the fall, the deacon had told Aunt Bitsy that her nieces were not welcome in class until they repented and let LaWayne come home.

It was then that Bitsy decided to move to Bienenstock — close to her parents, and far enough away from Wallsby that they could start over.

Aunt Bitsy wrapped her arms all the way around Rose. "Maybe my heart was full of revenge, but I would do it again if I had to. LaWayne Zook hurt my baby girl. I would have faced a whole roomful of bishops to defend you."

"But what was done was done. My arm was already broken. Enough bad things had already happened." Rose leaned her head on Aunt Bitsy's shoulder. "We should have forgiven him and let it be."

"But, baby sister, how many more times would LaWayne have hurt his own children if he hadn't gone to jail? Have you thought about the children you saved by testifying against him?"

"You didn't testify to get revenge," Lily said. "You testified to help children like Mary Beth and her brothers, even though they couldn't see it."

"But he was so sorry, and a family lost a *fater.*"

"It was his choice to throw you to the ground like that. You could have died." Aunt Bitsy shuddered. "*Gotte* gave you a soft place to land."

"I was okay."

Aunt Bitsy cupped her hand over Rose's cheek. "You weren't okay, Rosie. It's only been in the last year that you haven't had a nightmare every night." Her eyes flared with emotion. "In many ways, he stole your childhood."

"I've forgiven him."

"*Ach,* baby sister, I know you have, but it's hard to leave the damage behind, even with such a forgiving heart. I pray every day that you'll leave your fear by the side of the road, but I wish you'd never had to carry it in the first place."

Rose placed her hand over Aunt Bitsy's. "The *gute* and the bad that have happened to me have been *Gotte*'s will. I don't like being afraid, but the fear is part of who I am. I would never dare question *Gotte*'s plan." She reached into her apron pocket to find a tissue. It was empty. Where was Josiah when she needed him?

Lily snatched a tissue from the box on the counter and handed it to Rose.

"The person you haven't forgiven is yourself," Aunt Bitsy said.

Rose concentrated very hard on the wood grain in the table. "Josiah said I deserve to be happy."

"I like him more and more all the time," Aunt Bitsy said. "Even if he's used all my duct tape."

"But how can I be truly happy when I tore a man from his wife and sent him to prison? LaWayne's whole family has been affected by that choice. How can I be free of that?"

"Because LaWayne made his choices too." Aunt Bitsy leaned back in her chair. "La-Wayne had just as much opportunity to be happy as you. It's not your fault that he chose misery." Aunt Bitsy scooted out from under the table, and her chair screeched along the wood floor like a semi trying to stop at a red light. "Let's start dinner."

The sisters stood, and Lily and Poppy each gave Rose a giant hug. "I agree with Josiah," Lily said. "You deserve all the happiness in the world."

Poppy nodded. "So does Josiah. He's had his share of heartaches in his life, and he is such a *gute* boy."

"*Jah,*" Rose said. "I want Josiah to be happy. I want everybody to be happy. Even Paul Glick."

Lily giggled. "I think Paul is happiest when he gets himself worked up into a fit of righteous indignation. We've given him lots to be indignant about. He's happy."

Poppy pulled four plates from the cupboard. "What's for dinner, Aunt B?"

"We're having tacos from sunny Mexico."

"Sunny like your hair," Lily said.

Aunt Bitsy grunted her displeasure. "Bitsy Kiem and her urine-colored hair. It sounds like a grunge band. Or a Broadway musical."

Chapter Ten

Rose felt like a raccoon trying to sneak into the henhouse. With her heart beating a thousand miles a minute, she peeked around the aisle to spy on Paul Glick. He stood at the counter helping a customer, oblivious to the fact that Rose was trying to work up the courage to go over there and give him a piece of her mind.

Well, not exactly give him a piece of her mind.

After several Saturdays of being lectured to by her grandparents, Rose couldn't bear to hear Mammi and Dawdi sing Paul Glick's praises one more time. How could she stand by while they wounded Lily's feelings with their harsh words?

She had driven the buggy to the Glick Family Amish Market with every intention of going right up to Paul and giving him a talking-to about kindness and revenge and bearing false witness against his neighbors.

He must be told that he had no chance to win Lily back and that he must stop trying to convince her grandparents otherwise.

Rose was determined to talk to Paul for Lily's sake — to put his vindictive lies to rest forever. If that wasn't bravery, she didn't know what was. But the minute she had climbed out of her buggy, she had reconsidered. She wasn't brave enough to give Paul a lecture.

She sidled down the aisle and tried to spy him in the cracks between the shelves. Maybe she could buy a tub of licorice and nicely ask Paul to please stop harassing her family and find another girl to marry.

Rose picked up two tubs of licorice and took two steps toward the end of the aisle before she realized her knees were practically knocking together. Maybe she would simply give Paul a kindly smile and apologize to him for the bad feelings she'd been harboring toward him these last few weeks. Or months. In truth, she'd been harboring bad feelings for Paul for years. Should she apologize for everything? Should she tell him she just wanted him to be happy?

She turned around and tiptoed back to the middle of the aisle, where she returned the licorice to the shelf. She didn't like licorice. Why had she even thought of licorice? Biting her bottom lip and trying to keep from shaking, she picked up a tub of pretty, pastel-colored mints. Mints were nonthreatening. Who didn't feel kindly toward their fellow men when they ate pink and yellow mints?

She tiptoed back down the aisle and let out a tiny squeak. Paul Glick was standing at the counter staring in her direction and frowning so hard Rose wondered if he had a stomachache. He'd seen her. There was no turning back. Her throat constricted. She wasn't going to be able to talk to him, even if she'd wanted to, which she didn't. All she had to do was buy her cute, friendly mints and go away. It was a start. Aunt Bitsy would be proud of her courage.

Well, not really courage.

Aunt Bitsy would be proud that Rose hadn't fainted at Glick's Market — unless of course, Rose did happen to faint. At the moment, that was a very real possibility. Paul glared at her as she took halting steps to the counter. She didn't have to say a word, just show Paul her mints and give him her money.

She laid the mints on the counter and reached into her apron pocket for the five-dollar bill she knew was there. Paul narrowed his eyes as if she had dumped a hand-

246

ful of fresh manure in front of him. "I can't take your money," he said.

She wanted to ask why not, but she couldn't manage a sound. Her fist tightened around the bill in her pocket.

Paul picked up the friendly mints and shoved them toward her. There was nothing else to do but take them from his hand. "You Honeybee sisters earn money by cheating people. We don't take dirty money here at Glick's Family Market."

Rose should have known she'd be no match for Paul's nastiness. Her legs suddenly felt too weak to stand on, and even though it moved her a few inches closer to Paul, she clutched the counter to keep from collapsing into a heap. Every muscle in her body trembled, and an invisible hand seemed to clamp around her throat, cutting off whatever air might have squeezed through.

There was nothing to do but leave the mints and get out, if she could make it to the door without disintegrating into a puddle of tears and humiliation. She slid the mints onto the counter and turned to go.

"You can't just leave them here," Paul said, as if she'd committed a crime. "It makes extra work for me if I have to reshelf them. Put them back yourself."

With her stomach clenched in mortification, Rose picked up the mints. She nearly jumped out of her skin when she heard a familiar voice behind her. "Is everything okay?"

She didn't think her stomach could sink any lower. If there was one person she didn't want to witness her humiliation, it was Josiah Yoder. She opted not to turn around. Maybe he didn't know it was her from the back.

Paul was suddenly all smiles. "Josiah Yoder. I can ring those purchases up for you right now."

"Rose was here first."

Her stomach fell to the floor. It had been silly to think he didn't know it was her. *Ach, du lieva.* Why, oh why had she come? Paul's disdain was bad enough, but to be humiliated in front of Josiah Yoder was unbearable.

Paul pressed his lips together, lifted his chin, and didn't even glance at her. "She was just leaving."

Although she couldn't bear the contempt or the pity or whatever it was she was going to see on his face, Rose turned around. Josiah looked as if he were made out of stone as he stared at Paul with intense blue eyes. His face was a mask of calmness, but his eyes flashed with a hint of profound anger. She caught her breath. She'd never seen Josiah angry before.

He had a bag of chicken feed slung over his shoulder as if it weighed nothing at all, though Rose knew it had to be at least eighty pounds. In his other hand, he held a five-gallon jug and the very expensive quilt that, until one minute ago, had hung on the far wall of the store, clenching it in his fist as if he'd hurriedly snatched it off the wall. He was carrying at least six hundred dollars' worth of merchandise. "Is your cash register broken?" Josiah said.

Paul glanced at Rose. "It works fine. Rose will buy her mints at another store."

Josiah's eyes turned wintery, like ice so cold it burned to the touch. "You are a Christian, Paul Glick, and nothing in our faith justifies you treating Rose like this."

Paul glanced at the five-hundred-dollar quilt in Josiah's fist. "I think you misunderstand this situation. Let me ring up your purchases, and then we can talk about it in private. Rose and her *schwesters* don't have the understanding and wisdom we men do."

Josiah's expression was righteous and terrible at the same time. He'd never looked so handsome. "Rose is smarter and kinder than the two of us put together. There is nothing you can say to me that you can't say to her."

In spite of her distress, Rose's heart skipped. Josiah thought she was smart?

Paul folded his arms across his chest and stood with his feet firmly planted on the floor. "It is because I am a Christian that I'll not do business with her. *Gotte* commanded us not to steal. I don't sell to liars or cheaters."

Josiah laid his purchases on the counter. When Paul reached out for them, Josiah grabbed Paul's hand as if he were shaking it. Paul tried to pull away, but Josiah held fast.

Rose flinched. She would hate herself if this turned into a fight.

Josiah grasped Paul's hand with the grip of a farmer and eyed him seriously. "I know that Lily broke your heart."

"She didn't break anything," Paul muttered.

"If I lost a girl like that, I would never be whole again. But that is no reason to be cruel."

"It's not cruelty," Paul said. "It's justice. The Honeybee sisters must suffer the wrath of *Gotte.*"

"And you are not Him," Josiah said.

Paul's nostrils flared. "I am His servant."

Josiah released Paul's hand, lowered his eyes, and shook his head. "Then perhaps you don't know the Master you serve."

"Is there a problem?"

Rose didn't think her throat could get any tighter. Paul's brother, Perry, came up menacingly close behind Josiah, looking as if he'd just as soon hit somebody as shake hands. Perry was not tall, but he was twice as thick as Josiah and probably a hundred pounds heavier.

Rose nearly lost what fragile composure she had left. This was why she didn't want anyone to protect her or make her a project. She wouldn't be able to live with herself if Josiah got hurt.

Her legs shook so hard she could barely stand, but she found the strength to step between Josiah and Perry. If Perry wanted to hit someone, let it be her.

Surprise popped onto Perry's face, and he took a step back.

"Rose," Josiah said, in a voice that came from deep within his throat. "Rose, it's okay. No one is going to hurt me." He laid his warm hands gently on her shoulders.

She looked up at him, and his icy-blue gaze nearly made her melt. His fierce expression was a mixture of astonishment, pride, and determination. There was something else there too, but she didn't dare guess the secret behind his eyes.

Perry frowned. "What's going on, Paul?"

"Nothing," Paul said, dismissing his brother with a wave of his hand. "Josiah is buying this quilt."

A confused smile crept onto Perry's face. "That's nice. It's been up there for almost a year."

Josiah took Rose's hand right there in front of Paul and Perry and tugged her toward the door. "*Cum,* Rose. I know a driver who can take us to Wal-Mart."

"What about the quilt?" Paul sputtered, the panic flickering in his eyes. He obviously saw his profits walking out the door with Rose Christner.

"It's very beautiful," Josiah said. "I hope you can sell it."

Complete silence.

As soon as they emerged into the daylight, Rose pulled her hand from his and walked as quickly as she could down the street. It was a silly thing to do. She couldn't outrun Josiah, and he certainly wasn't going to just let her go like that. The tears were already trickling down her face. *Oh sis yuscht,* along with everything else, she hated for him to see her like this.

As she'd expected, he couldn't just let her go. "Rose, wait," he said, catching up to her before she'd even gone five feet.

She stopped, because it was pointless to run, and dangerous when she could barely see the sidewalk past the tears.

He pulled a handkerchief from his pocket, and the tenderness in his eyes nearly knocked her over. "Are you okay?"

A fresh wave of tears hijacked her. Josiah was so *wunderbarr,* and he had witnessed her mute humiliation. He'd seen how weak and helpless and foolish she was, and she couldn't bear it.

"It was my own fault. I never should have tried to —"

"Of course it wasn't your fault. No one deserves to be treated that way, especially not you." The anger in his voice sounded like a barely controlled fire.

"I went in there because I wanted to prove to myself I could be brave, but I should have known that Paul isn't ready to forgive yet. I'm so ashamed."

Oh, how she loved that piercing gaze, and oh, how she hated it.

"Rose, you thought Perry was going to hurt me, and you got between us. That's the bravest thing I've ever seen anyone do."

"That wasn't brave. If you were hurt for

my sake, I'd never forgive myself."

"And I'd never forgive myself if I didn't step in to help you," he said. "Would you have wanted me to stand aside and do nothing?"

She bowed her head. "*Nae,* but I wish you hadn't seen me humiliate myself."

"I came for that very reason," he said.

She snapped her head up to look at him. "You came to see me be humiliated?"

He plastered a silly grin on his face and coaxed a reluctant smile from her. "I stopped by your house to see if Bitsy needed any repairs done, and she told me you were on your way to the market. I don't trust any of the Glicks to be nice to you, so I drove over just to be sure you were okay."

"Were you really going to buy that quilt? It costs five hundred dollars."

He shook his head. "I came in, saw you standing at the counter, and grabbed the most expensive things I could find in a hurry. I wanted Paul to see that he'll lose money if he mistreats his customers, especially the Honeybee sisters." He studied her face and lost any hint of a smile. "Was that dishonest? I hope you don't think it was dishonest."

She lowered her eyes to the pavement. "I think it was very kind of you to stand up for me like that, but I wish I was brave enough that you didn't have to." To her frustration, the tears began to flow again.

He took a tissue from his pocket and handed it to her, then nudged her chin with his finger. "You never have to be brave when I'm around. I'll protect you."

"I hate thinking that you pity me and you're only my friend out of the goodness of your heart."

"We've talked about this before, Rose. You know I don't pity you."

She walked to her buggy. He followed. "You wouldn't like it if someone treated you like a baby."

He gave her a small smile. "Suvie treats me like a baby."

Rose couldn't help but smile back. "She treats you like a younger brother. If she treated you like a baby, you'd move to Indiana."

"Florida. Indiana is too cold."

She curled one side of her mouth.

He rested his chin in his hand and gazed at the sky, tapping his index finger against his cheek. "So I have to prove to you that I don't pity you or think you're a baby?"

"Even though I am."

"You aren't."

Rose dabbed at her eyes. "You just saw

me fall apart over a tub of mini mints."

He shrugged. "Who can resist the little white sprinkles?" He leaned against her buggy. "If you want to prove your bravery, come with me and we'll do something dangerous."

Rose's heart skipped a beat. Just one more reason to be ashamed. She had told Josiah that she didn't want his pity, but she couldn't bring herself to agree to anything dangerous, not even to prove herself.

Maybe he saw the doubt — or more likely, abject fear — in her expression. He reached out and took one of her *kapp* strings in his fingers. "There is an Amish market in Bonduel that sells those mini mints. I'll take you there, if you dare."

"That . . . that doesn't seem very dangerous."

"It does to someone who gets bullied at Amish markets."

"But I don't want you to feel obligated to buy anything for me," she said.

"Who said anything about buying something for you? You'll have to pay for your own mints." He winked at her. "After the market, we could take your mints to the lake and stick our toes in the water."

"That doesn't seem very dangerous either."

He grinned. "You never know what creatures are lurking in the lake. Maybe a fisherman will row by and give us a ride in his boat. Would that be dangerous enough?"

The way he was looking at her made her warm yet shivery all over. She could maybe do a boat, if it was small and wasn't a motorboat. And if they didn't go too fast. If Josiah knew how to swim so he could rescue her if she fell in. Or maybe they could stay very close to the shore so that if the boat tipped, she wouldn't go in over her head.

She nodded. "Okay."

He bloomed into a smile. "Okay?"

She nodded again, hoping to reassure herself more than him. She hadn't done so well at Glick's Family Market, but at least she'd tried. Josiah would be with her if she needed him, and his presence would lend her courage. She might even get in that boat.

As long as she had a life jacket.

Chapter Eleven

Josiah couldn't stop whistling. He whistled while he gathered eggs and made breakfast. He whistled while he mucked out the barn and milked the cow. He whistled as he hitched up Max to the courting buggy, and he whistled on the road to Rose's house. He would have to stop whistling once he got to the Honeybee Farm. He couldn't carry a tune in a bucket, and he might very well scare Rose away with his sour notes.

For the first time ever, he had allowed his hopes to run wild. Monday had quite possibly been the best day of his life. It hadn't started out that way. When he had walked into Glick's Market and seen how Paul was treating Rose, he had almost lost his composure. The temptation to chastise Paul Glick, angrily and righteously, was almost overpowering.

Thank the *gute* Lord he had kept his temper, but his instinct to protect Rose had almost made him irrational. Her tears were the sight he hated most in the whole world.

Rose had dropped her buggy off at home, and they had taken his courting buggy to the Lark Country Store in Bonduel, where the owners were much friendlier than Paul and Perry Glick. They had bought a tub of mini mints for Rose and a tub of licorice for Josiah. He liked the colorful licorice with black and yellow stripes and pink circles. Rose had crinkled her nose and stuck out her tongue when he let her taste a piece.

They had spent over an hour in the Lark Country Store, looking at books and clocks, trying on hats and aprons, and making each other laugh. Rose's laugh was probably his favorite thing in the whole world. Her laughter meant she wasn't afraid or worried. It meant she was happy. Rose deserved to be happy.

Along with their mints and licorice, they had bought graham crackers, chocolate, and marshmallows and driven to one of the camping spots near the lake. Josiah had built a fire and whittled some roasting sticks with his pocketknife. Then they had roasted marshmallows for s'mores. With Rose sitting next to him and gifting him with her smile, the s'mores were quite possibly the best thing he had ever eaten.

When they were done, Rose had made him stamp out the fire and then pour water onto the smoking coals. They didn't have a bucket for water, so Josiah had emptied all his licorice into his pockets and used the empty licorice tub to scoop water from the lake and douse the fire.

After that, they had kicked off their shoes and sat on the edge of the lake to watch the sunset. That pained, uneasy expression that Rose often wore hadn't appeared once. They had talked about his parents and her parents and how Rose loved to paint more than anything. Josiah had thought about how he loved looking at Rose more than anything. She told him about her bees and how the bees came to know her so that she didn't even have to wear gloves by the end of the season. They talked about cats and her sisters and even Paul Glick.

It never ceased to amaze Josiah how forgiving Rose was. Even after Paul had treated her so poorly, she'd still forgiven him and hoped he could learn to be happy without Lily and without the Honeybee *schwesters'* honey. She sincerely longed for him to find peace instead of worrying about profits. Josiah couldn't see that happening, but Rose believed in the goodness of everybody.

By the time he had brought her home, he had fallen more deeply in love with her than ever.

He practically leaped from his buggy and bounded across the flagstone path that led to the house. He'd raced through his chores this morning so he could spend the afternoon with Rose — maybe take her to the lake. Maybe just sit and watch her as she painted or made bread. He didn't even have an excuse to give Aunt Bitsy for his visit.

Unless being madly in love was a *gute* excuse.

Even that excuse probably wasn't *gute* enough for Bitsy.

The body of a small bird sat on the welcome mat, its feathers askew, its mouth open in what was probably its last scream. Billy Idol usually left mice on the doorstep. A bird was rarer. Josiah picked the poor creature up and carefully laid it under one of the bushes next to the porch. The sight of a dead bird would surely upset Rose.

Josiah knocked on the door, and it creaked open wide enough for Bitsy to poke the barrel of her shotgun through. Josiah gasped and took a cautious step backward. It would be *gute* if Bitsy's finger didn't slip and blow a hole through his chest. That would sort of ruin his day.

"Oh, it's you," Bitsy said, nudging the door open wider with the gun barrel. "I suppose I'm glad to see you." She set the gun down and propped it against the wall.

Josiah's eyebrows probably flew off his forehead. Bitsy's hair was no longer a lovely pastel shade of pink or blue. It was a bright, fire-engine red, as if she'd stuck her head in a can of paint and swirled it around. Not only that, but three-inch plastic skeleton earrings dangled from her ears. "Whoa, horsey!" he said, too shocked to temper his reaction. "What happened to your hair?" Quickly recovering himself, he stretched a smile across his face and pretended he hadn't done anything out of the ordinary. "I mean, that is a very nice color, Bitsy."

Bitsy seemed more annoyed than usual. "I colored it this morning," she said, stepping back so Josiah could come in. She slammed the door behind him. "I've never done it quite so dark before. I was hoping it would make me feel like Wonder Woman, but I look ridiculous. It will be gone by the time the girls get back tomorrow morning."

Josiah deflated like a flat bicycle tire. "Rose isn't here?"

Bitsy fiddled with the skeleton in her right ear. "They went to a funeral in Cashton. A van came and picked them up last night, and they'll be home tomorrow around noon."

"Oh, I'm sorry. Who died?"

"Their great-onkel Titus on their *fater*'s side. I didn't know him, and they barely knew him either, but they thought they should go. There wasn't an opportunity to let anyone know. Even Dan and Luke don't know."

Ach, vell. He wouldn't be seeing Rose today, but he should probably make the most of being here. Leonard Nimoy sidled up against Josiah's leg, so Josiah knelt down and petted her. "Is there anything you want me to fix while I'm here?"

"Nae." Bitsy's frown looked as if someone had drawn dark lines on her face to match her dark hair. "But there's something that I want you to see." She picked up her shotgun as she motioned toward the door. *"Cum* outside."

Josiah's heart felt heavy without his even knowing why. Maybe it was the way Bitsy looked at him. Maybe it was the fact that she didn't want him to fix anything. She was usually so happy when he offered to fix things around her house. Maybe it was because her knuckles were white around her shotgun. Josiah had a feeling he didn't want to know why she brought the shotgun with her.

Leonard Nimoy and even Farrah Fawcett followed them out the door. Billy Idol joined their procession as they marched across the flagstones. Josiah felt even worse. It must be serious if Farrah Fawcett could be stirred from her window seat.

Bitsy's hair was a torch leading the way as they tromped toward the back of the barn. "Please tell me it's not the chicken coop," he said. The troublemakers had destroyed the Honeybee sisters' chicken coop a few weeks ago, and Luke and Poppy had rebuilt it. Rose would be upset if they had chopped down the coop again.

Bitsy's earrings clicked softly as she shook her head.

Josiah breathed a sigh of relief. Behind the barn, the chicken coop stood straight and secure, and two or three chickens pecked at the ground at Josiah's feet. Nothing looked out of place or amiss. Maybe whatever Bitsy was concerned about had nothing to do with the troublemakers.

Farrah Fawcett padded past the chickens and found a comfortable spot beneath the chicken coop to lounge. The chickens ignored her. They'd had enough experience to know they were in no danger of being chased by the white cat. Billy Idol crouched and crept toward a large black hen scratching in the dirt. When Billy Idol got close enough, the hen squawked and flapped her wings before running around the side of the barn and out of sight. Leonard Nimoy acted as if she wanted to make friends with the chickens but was afraid she'd get pecked to death. She kept her distance.

Bitsy pressed her lips together and pointed up behind Josiah's head. Dread filled him at the look on her face. He turned around. In letters three feet high, someone had spray-painted a message on the back side of the barn.

Rose must be punished. Vengeance is mine.

"I think they put it here in hopes that Rose would see it before we painted over it, like we have the others," Bitsy said.

Josiah's blood turned to ice, and his legs could no longer support him. He felt as if he were falling from a very high place into a dark abyss. He grabbed onto the edge of the chicken coop to keep himself upright.

Bitsy rested her gun against the barn wall, took Josiah's hand, and guided him to sit on the wide edge of the chicken coop. He propped his elbows on his knees and buried his face in his hands. Bitsy bent over to make eye contact and rubbed her hand up and down his arm. Even that uncharacteristic show of sympathy didn't help. How could anything help?

"It's going to be okay, Joe."

"How . . . how can you say that? Rose is in danger. Aren't you frightened?"

She shook her head. The skeletons in her ears looked as if they were dancing on top of her shoulders. "I'm angry. Very angry. It's lucky I didn't catch the cowards painting my barn last night. I would have been tempted to shoot them, and I don't think I'd do well in prison. Orange isn't my color."

Josiah wanted to throw up. "I don't know what to do. Tell me what I should do. Why would anyone want to hurt Rose?"

Bitsy heaved a great sigh. "I think I know who has been making all the trouble."

Josiah snapped his head up. "You do?"

"Although if they really want to punish who is responsible, they should blame me, not my Rosie."

Josiah thought he might jump out of his skin. "Who are we looking for?"

"I will let Rose decide whether she wants to tell you. I think she's afraid you will reject her. So many people have let her down."

He grabbed both of Bitsy's hands. "You know I would never, ever hurt Rose, don't you?"

"*Jah.* I know," Bitsy said.

A lump grew at the back of his throat. "*Denki* for your trust in me."

"I wouldn't go that far," she said, pulling her hands from his grasp. She didn't seem like the type who liked to be touched, even in an emergency. "You've gone through three whole rolls of duct tape, and you want to take my little girl from me. The whole situation makes me a little suspicious. And a little testy."

Josiah stared at her in disbelief. "What do you mean?"

"I'm not blind, young man, and I didn't just fall off the turnip truck."

He shook his head. Nothing got past Bitsy Kiem. "Then you understand why I'm so upset."

"So am I. If Rose wants you to know who hates her this much, she'll have to tell you herself."

Josiah stood up. "I thank the *gute* Lord that she wasn't here this morning and that we still have time to paint the barn before she gets back. I'll go buy some paint. Do you have a tall ladder?"

Bitsy narrowed her eyes until they were almost closed. "I think Rose needs to see it first."

"Needs to see what?"

"This message. Rose should see it before you paint it."

A fierce, protective emotion filled Josiah's chest, as if he were a wolf guarding his den from predators. "Absolutely not."

"We've hid too many things from her."

Josiah couldn't believe what he was hearing from Rose's own aunt. "Don't you realize what this would do to her? She'd be terrified."

Bitsy folded her arms. "*Jah,* she would, but she doesn't want us to treat her like a baby. We should think about what is best for Rose."

Josiah's voice rose with his agitation. "I *am* thinking about what is best for her. Her greatest desire is to not be afraid anymore."

"We've got to tell her, Josiah. The secrets don't make her happy."

He paced frantically in front of the chicken coop. "What she doesn't know won't hurt her."

"Maybe we only think it doesn't hurt her," Bitsy said, as if she really knew. As if she should decide what was best for Rose.

Josiah's chest tightened as anger and fear squeezed the air out of his lungs. "*Nae,* Bitsy. We can't tell her. I won't allow it." He slapped his hand against the side of the barn. "I will not allow it."

"Josiah Yoder," Bitsy said, as if she were scolding a naughty schoolboy. "Your anger will not help my Rosie."

Josiah stopped pacing, backed into the barn wall, and sank to the ground, breathless and spent as if he'd just swum the length of Lake Michigan. He covered his face with his hands. "I'm sorry, Bitsy. I am not one to lose my temper like that. But don't you see? I know Rose. She'll be so frightened she won't be able to eat or sleep. She can't know. She just can't know."

Bitsy knelt on the ground in front of him, nudged his hand from his eyes, and cupped her hands on either side of his face. "You think I don't know what it will do to my little girl? You're so arrogant that you think you know her better than I do?"

He took a deep, quivering breath. "Of course I don't."

The emotion in her eyes was so intense, a weaker person might have looked away. With the skeleton earrings and the flaming-red hair, she looked fierce indeed, but Josiah held her gaze, waiting to be chastised for his arrogance.

"Do you love my Rosie?" she said.

The question stopped his heart. Maybe he couldn't imagine its ever beating again if he lost her. "*Jah.* I love her."

269

"More than Dan loves Lily? Or Luke loves Poppy?"

"No one can ever love anyone as much as I love her."

Bitsy seemed satisfied with this answer, even though all the words in the whole world were inadequate to express how he really felt. She took her hands from his face and frowned. "Then I'll let you decide."

"Decide what?"

"I'll let you decide whether to tell Rose or paint the barn and erase all the evidence. After me and her sisters, you are the one who loves Rose the best. You can decide."

He studied her face doubtfully. "Do you really mean that?"

"I really mean that, though I might regret it for the rest of my life, just like I regret this hair color. It was rash and imprudent. Don't make the same mistake."

Josiah thought he might weep with relief. He had promised Rose that he would protect her. She never need worry as long as he was around. "*Denki*, Bitsy. *Denki.* I am only thinking of Rose, you know."

"*Jah.* She's all you've thought about for a very long time."

He stood and brushed the dust off of his trousers. "I'll be back soon," he said. "I'm going to buy some paint."

■ ■ ■ ■

"I never want to go back to that paint store again," Luke said as he got out of the car. "Did you know that Wal-Mart has about two hundred different shades of red? No wonder the barn door ended up orange."

"And then pink," Dan said.

Luke, Dan, and Josiah had painted the Honeybee sisters' barn door twice in the middle of the night to cover up messages painted there by the troublemakers. The first time, the door had turned out orange. The second time, it had come out a deep shade of pink. Josiah refused to let that happen again. Rose must never suspect the back of the barn had been painted over.

He hefted the five-gallon bucket of red paint from the trunk of the car. It was probably much more than they needed, but he didn't want to risk running out. He'd gone to the phone shack down the road from the Honeybee Farm and called a driver to take him to Luke's, and then Dan's, house. They had both gladly agreed to help him paint. He hadn't expected anything less, but his friends' generosity had nearly overwhelmed him, just the same.

The driver had driven the three of them

271

into Shawano for paint. The *Englischer* at the paint store had helped Josiah carefully match the color of the Christners' barn.

Josiah paid the driver while Dan and Luke carried the paint and rollers behind the barn. Josiah grabbed the ladder from the barn and met his friends in the back. The afternoon sun beating against the side of the barn nearly blinded him. Painting would be a warm job. Not that he cared about his discomfort. It was a pleasure to do anything for Rose.

While Josiah pried the lid off the paint, Luke and Dan stood back and surveyed the big, bold letters that had been spray-painted on the side of the barn. Luke muttered something under his breath, and Dan let out a long, low whistle.

"We've got to find out who is doing this," Luke said.

Josiah's chest tightened. If he thought about it too hard, his fear and anger would render him useless to his friends or Rose. He could go home and stew about it later. Right now, they needed to concentrate on finishing the barn. Rose would be home in the morning.

"It helps knowing who they're mad at," Dan said. "We can narrow down our search."

Josiah scrubbed his hand down the side of his face. "Why would they be so mad at Rose?"

Dan looked at the ground and shuffled his feet. Luke stared straight at Josiah and folded his arms. "It's something that happened a long time ago."

"What?"

"It's Rose's to tell," Dan said, looking apologetic that he had to keep a secret from his best friend.

The pain ambushed Josiah, so intense that he had to press his palm to his chest to keep from crying out. One more reminder that he was not in the Christner family circle. One more reminder that he truly was an orphan. And Rose hadn't trusted him with her secret, whatever it was.

Maybe she would never trust him.

Another ambush. This time like a rock to the head. Rose certainly wouldn't trust him if he hid things from her. He wanted to protect Rose, the same way he wanted water or sunlight, and he couldn't bear the thought of her being upset. It was better if she never found out.

He clamped his eyes shut and tried to clear his head.

What would Rose want?

He tried hard to push that question out of

his head. It didn't matter what Rose wanted. He knew what was best. He'd seen her face when she'd discovered the slashed buggy. It would have been better if she hadn't seen it.

But she had wanted to know, all the same. *Oy,* anyhow.

Josiah threw his head back and growled like a badger. Luke and Dan stared at him. They must have thought he'd gone crazy.

He hated the very thought of Rose's terror-stricken face, but if he truly loved her, he would treat her the way she wanted to be treated. She didn't want Josiah to pity her. She didn't want anyone to keep secrets from her, no matter how painful. She wanted to be given the chance to be brave, even if she was scared to death.

He gazed at the black, hateful words on the barn wall. He pictured her face when she read them, felt her hands tremble and saw her eyes fill with tears. How could he do that to her?

He kicked the open bucket of paint at his feet. Red droplets splattered into the air. He'd have to tell her. And he hated the very thought.

"Oh sis yuscht," Luke said, jumping back to avoid the flying paint. "We've got a paint stirrer. You're going to break your toe."

Dan grabbed Josiah by the shoulder with

a firm hand. "Are you okay?"

Josiah gave up trying to destroy the bucket and gave the dirt at his feet one last hard kick. "Someone threatened Rose. I'm furious."

"We're right there with you," Dan said. "Rose isn't the only one in danger, and even if she were, we'd still feel the same way."

Josiah pressed his fingers into his forehead. "What can we do? I need something to do or I'll go crazy."

"We can paint," Dan said. "That's something."

Josiah suddenly felt as weak as a kitten. "We can't paint. Not until Rose sees it. She wouldn't want us to hide it from her."

Dan frowned. "Even if it will scare her?"

Josiah rubbed his forehead harder. "*Jah.* Even then. It's what she wants, no matter how much I don't want her to know."

"Are you sure?" Dan asked.

Josiah nodded. "When she comes home tomorrow, we'll show it to her, and then we'll paint."

Dan's lips drooped. "I'll paint with you, but you've got to promise not to kick any more paint buckets. Luke does not look good in polka dots."

Some of the specks of flying paint had landed on Luke's shirt and face. He looked like he was coming down with the chicken pox. Luke glanced down at his cream-colored shirt and groaned. "Josiah Yoder, it's a *gute* thing you're my best friend, or you'd have a mouthful of dirt right now."

Josiah just shook his head. A friend like Luke Bontrager truly made Josiah appreciate Dan Kanagy.

At least he was good for something.

CHAPTER TWELVE

Josiah, Luke, and Dan had been sitting on the porch since eleven o'clock, listening for the van that would bring the Honeybee sisters home from Cashton. Luke was whittling a stick, Dan was reading *Summer of the Monkeys,* and Josiah wasn't doing anything but worrying. Rose was going to be devastated, and he alone would be responsible.

More than once in the middle of the night, he'd considered jumping out of bed and coming to the farm to paint the barn himself. It was his love for Rose that compelled him to get up, and it was his love for Rose that ultimately kept him at home. This was what she would want, no matter how hard it was to bear.

He didn't know if it would be harder for him or her.

At three minutes before noon, a white van pulled up the lane. Josiah didn't know whether he was dreading the sight of that van or hoping for it. He wanted this to be over. He wanted the Honeybee sisters to be safe and the troublemaker to be caught so that Rose would never have to be afraid again.

Well, he supposed that wasn't all he wanted.

He wanted to marry Rose more than anything in the world. Would *Gotte* think he was being greedy?

Lily, Poppy, then Rose emerged from the van, each with a canvas bag slung over her shoulder. Josiah's heart did a double somersault. Lily and Poppy both smiled at their fiancés, but Rose positively beamed at Josiah, as if he were the most *wunderbarr* sight in the world. He wasn't sure what to make of it, but it had to be a *gute* thing. She was happy to see him. At least for another minute or so.

Someone inside the van said good-bye, and Rose waved as the van turned around and drove back the way it had come.

Dan, Luke, and Josiah walked down the porch steps in unison. Even as happy as he was to see Rose, Josiah couldn't smile. Not when he was about to shatter what little sense of security Rose had left.

"What a nice surprise," Lily said. "Are you

our welcoming committee?"

"Something like that," mumbled Luke. He took Poppy's bag and slung it over his shoulder.

Dan took Lily's bag, and Josiah reached for Rose's. Her eyes glowed with warmth as she handed it to him.

"How was the funeral?" Dan asked, glancing at Josiah. They had decided they should ease into the bad news slowly. Now Josiah was having second thoughts. Maybe they should just get it over with, like ripping a bandage from a wound. Or maybe they didn't have to say anything. They could still sneak over tonight and paint before Rose was the wiser.

His mouth felt as dry as sawdust. No matter how painful, he knew he had to tell her. And he should use the bandage method before he talked himself out of going through with it.

"Rose," Josiah said, before any of them said a word about the funeral.

It was better this way. It was better this way.

If he told himself enough times, he might start to believe it.

She looked at him with those trusting eyes. He'd worked hard to earn that trust. He couldn't betray it now.

"Rose," he said again. "There is something I need to show you. Will you come?"

They had decided that Josiah would show Rose the spray-painted barn first, and the others would come later. That way, if Rose fell apart, she wouldn't feel like she had embarrassed herself in front of everyone. Josiah had told her that he didn't mind if she cried, but he knew how unnecessarily ashamed she felt.

Bitsy had insisted he should be the one to tell Rose. Bitsy liked him, and she knew how much he loved Rose. His heart swelled. He wouldn't disappoint either of them.

Rose glanced at her sisters doubtfully while trying to pretend she had no doubts. "*Ach.* Okay. Where are we going?"

Needing to touch her, to assure her of his faithfulness, he took her hand firmly in his. He didn't even care if Bitsy was watching from the window. He needed Rose's comforting touch probably more than she needed his. He glanced at her and suddenly felt overwhelmingly sad.

Maybe she didn't need his at all.

A blush tinted her cheeks as she looked down at her hand in his, but she didn't pull away. He shouldn't hold her hand. Rose was too kind to reject him, even if she didn't want him to touch her. *Oh sis yuscht.* His heart felt as if it were breaking, and she hadn't even said a word.

She furrowed her brow. "Are you all right?"

"Will you come with me?"

She seemed to sense that he needed the solace of her hand in his. Her sisters made no objection, and Bitsy was nowhere to be seen as they strolled around to the back of the barn.

"Rose," he said softly as they got closer to the chicken coop. "Something terrible has happened."

She squeezed his hand tighter. "Aunt Bitsy?"

"*Nae. Nae.* Bitsy is fine. She's in the house making apple cake with caramel topping. Everyone is fine. It is something else." He pulled her up short. "It is something that Luke and Dan and I can paint over, and you will never have to see it. A message that the troublemakers painted on the barn. If you would rather not know, we can go back to the house right now."

He hoped against hope she would ask him to take her to the house.

She turned pale but didn't even glance behind her. "I'd like to see it."

His heart sank, and he pulled her closer and tucked her arm beneath his elbow as they walked. "I'm going to watch out for you, Rose. I don't want you to worry."

They walked the short distance around the barn. Josiah's hand shook as he turned and pointed to the ugly words that would surely upset her.

Rose must be punished. Vengeance is mine.

She turned to stone beside him as she read the message. For a moment, her face was a mask of calm indifference. And then she began to tremble. Holding on to her arm, he could feel the tremor of her deepest fears. "It's all my fault," she whispered. "All because of me."

"*Nae,* Rose. This is not your fault."

Tears pooled in her eyes. "I have gone against *Gotte,* and hurt my family." She put her hand to her mouth, as if to contain the sorrow that wanted to spill out. It didn't work. She began to sob.

Rose's pain felt like a stab to his heart. He should have known that, along with the terror, she would blame herself. Not caring about consequences, he gathered her into his arms and pressed his lips to her forehead. He didn't know if she would pull away or welcome his embrace, but he couldn't think of what else to do to stop both of them from falling into a dark place.

Instead of resisting his arms as he'd half

expected her to, Rose buried her face against his chest and cried as if her heart were breaking. He tightened his hold around her, letting his warmth mingle with hers, hoping his touch would give her comfort but drawing more strength from her than she ever could from him. If he could keep her this close to him forever, he would.

They stood almost motionless while Rose cried and Josiah's heart ached for her. "I'm getting your shirt wet," she said, almost as if that upset her as much as the painted message on the barn.

He reluctantly took one arm from around her and pulled three tissues from his pocket. "I don't mind the wet shirt."

Still in the protective circle of his arms, she wiped her nose and let out a shuddering sigh. "I didn't think I could humiliate myself any more than I already have."

"You haven't humiliated yourself. You've only proven you care deeply. If you weren't so soft, you wouldn't take things so hard. But your softness is your greatest strength. You use it to love and minister to people. I would never change that about you, not for all the dry shirts in the world."

"I'm scared," she said, as if she were confessing her worst sin to him.

The ache in his chest was nearly unbearable. "I almost wish I would have painted it over yesterday."

"Yesterday?"

"They painted it the night after you left for the funeral. Bitsy showed it to me. I wanted to paint over it before you came home."

She caught her bottom lip between her teeth. "They've left messages before, haven't they? That's why our barn door used to be orange and now it's pink."

He frowned. "It's hard to match paint color in the middle of the night."

"Were those messages for me too?"

"*Nae,* but we wanted to protect your feelings. That's why I nearly painted over this message too. You never would have known it was there."

She lifted her head to study his face. "Why didn't you?"

"Because as much as I knew it would upset you, I also knew you would want to see it. You don't want to be afraid, but you don't want to be treated like a child. It's impossible to fulfill your two greatest desires at the same time, so I chose the one I thought would make you the happiest. Now I'm not so sure."

It was as if someone lit a candle behind her eyes. "You think I am brave enough to handle the truth."

"Of course. But I hate it when you're frightened."

To his surprise, her mouth widened into a breathtaking smile. "You don't think of me like a child, do you?"

He could barely focus on her question. Her smile knocked him flat. *"Nae."*

"You don't pity me or think I'm a project."

He curled one side of his mouth. "How many times have I told you?"

"But you've never shown me before."

Pressing his lips together, he shuddered to think how close he had come to painting the barn. He would have ruined everything. Would she trust him with more? "Bitsy said that now we might know who is making the trouble on the farm. Do you know what she meant by that?"

It was as if all the anxiety and fear came flooding back. Only this time, she didn't want him close to her. She pulled away from his embrace and turned her back on him. "I did something I shouldn't have when I was a little girl, seven years old. We had to move away from Wallsby because of it."

"Do you want to tell me about it?"

She ran her hand along the rough wood of the chicken coop and glanced at him. The light in her eyes had gone completely out. "A lot of people were mad at me."

Josiah wracked his brain for anything a seven-year-old might do to make a whole community mad at her. He couldn't think of a thing. "You know that I would never be mad at you," he said softly.

"Don't say 'never.' It is a very long time."

She trusted him, but she didn't trust him enough. The pain of it felt like something hot against his skin. "I . . . you don't have to tell me anything," he said, choking on every word.

She gazed at him, and he could see something shift in her expression. Though he'd tried to mask it, she saw his hurt. She would never do anything to cause another person pain even at great expense to herself. "I was in the haymow with my friend Mary Beth."

"Rose," he said. "What do you want?"

"What?"

"Do you want my tube of paint or don't you?"

She frowned. "That makes no sense."

"While it's true I'll feel bad if you don't tell me your story, my feelings don't matter as much as yours do. This is your story, not mine." He went to her, reached out, and smoothed one of her *kapp* strings between his fingers. "What do you want?"

"If I don't tell you, you'll think I don't

286

trust you."

"Do you?"

She hesitated. "I'm afraid."

His gut clenched. "What are you afraid of?"

"That I'll be a disappointment."

He wanted to shout from the rooftops that she would never be a disappointment. But she didn't like "never." And she didn't like shouting, and she was afraid of heights. Rooftops were out.

"You'll never know the strength of my friendship until you test it."

She wrapped her arms around her waist, fell silent, and stared at the barn. He ached for her to trust him, but he wouldn't force her and he certainly didn't want the story because she felt sorry for him. Like her, he didn't want to be pitied. But he longed to be loved. *"Cum,"* he said. "Let's go back to the house. Bitsy will want to hear about your trip, and I promised her I'd fix your wobbly folding chair."

To his amazement, she reached out and took his hand. He thought his heart might forget how to beat. Gazing at him doubtfully, she bit her bottom lip. "Mary Beth and I were playing in the haymow with her *dat*'s harness. He came up the ladder and shoved me off the haymow. He had been drinking, and I broke my arm."

Josiah winced. "You broke your arm?"

"I don't think I ever recovered from that. Aunt Bitsy called the police. She'd lived among the *Englischers* for so long, it was a natural thing to do. She was furious. She really is quite terrifying when she's mad."

"I don't wonder that she is," Josiah said.

"I testified against him, and they sent him to jail."

Josiah rested his shoulder against the side of the barn. "It's not the Amish thing to do. The elders want to deal with those matters inside the church."

"*Jah.* The community didn't shun us, but they might as well have. The boys pulled my hair. Poppy got in a lot of fights. The girls wouldn't talk to any of us, even at *gmay.* We had to leave after that."

"I'm sorry."

A thin tear trickled down her cheek. "His whole family hated us. They said I'd stolen their *fater* from them, that *Gotte* would punish us for what I had done. The night before we moved out, someone dropped a note on our porch. It said, 'Vengeance is mine, saith the Lord.' That's why Aunt Bitsy thinks she knows who it is. It is a very familiar phrase."

Josiah couldn't stand that look in her eyes, as if everything in the world were bleak and dark and cold. In two long strides, he was beside her with his arms around her. "Rose, you have nothing to be ashamed of. The thought of someone hurting you makes me sick. Funny, isn't it, how the elders asked me to testify on behalf of Levi Junior, but they wanted you to stay quiet on behalf of the man who hurt you."

"You testified to help Levi Junior. My testimony only hurt LaWayne Zook."

He raised his eyebrows in a question. "I'm not so sure. If someone hurt Alvin and Aaron, I would have called the police too."

A soft moan escaped her lips. "You would?"

"Even though it's not our way. Even though *Gotte* is the final judge. Maybe it is weakness in both of us, but I can't blame you for it."

She sighed as if she had been holding her breath for a long time. *"Denki,"* she said, "for not being disappointed."

"I could never be disappointed in you."

Her lips twitched upward. "Never is a very long time."

He glanced at the black letters on the barn. "We need to find LaWayne Zook and have a talk with him."

Rose seemed to wilt in a matter of seconds. "He's dead."

"When did he die?"

Rose drew her brows together. "He died just about the time mischief started happening on our farm."

Dread filled Josiah's chest like an overflowing bathtub. He had a very strong feeling that whoever was making mischief blamed Rose for LaWayne's death. But he could never tell Rose that. She'd wither under the weight of it all. He clenched his jaw to keep a growl from escaping. Never was a long time. He had to tell her. "I think they want revenge."

She closed her eyes as if the truth were too painful to look at. "Of course they do. Someone is mad about LaWayne Zook, and I am responsible." Her voice and her fragile composure cracked like ice on a lake. "*Ach,* I wish I hadn't testified. I've hurt so many people."

She backed away when he tried to gather her in his arms, so he kept his distance and watched in wretched silence while she cried herself out. After a few minutes, she let him put his arm around her shoulders and lead her into the house.

He'd never felt so determined or so powerless.

He would find the person who hated Rose and somehow make him stop terrorizing the

Honeybee sisters. In the meantime, he would protect Rose and this farm as best he could.

But he felt powerless to give Rose new eyes, to help her see what she would not see. To show her the way to let go of years of buried guilt for things she had not done. Only *Gotte* could do that.

Would *Gotte* show him the way?

CHAPTER THIRTEEN

Rose's eyes stung like they always did after she cried. She pressed the cool towel against her face and breathed in its fresh scent. Lavender. Aunt Bitsy used lavender laundry soap because the scent was supposed to be calming. It was said to help you sleep if you sprinkled it on your sheets.

Rose stared at the bare wall in the washroom. She didn't know if she would ever be able to sleep again. Someone wanted to do her harm, and she couldn't say with certainty that she didn't deserve it. She clamped her teeth together and shoved the towel over her mouth. She would not cry again tonight. Crying in bed left her pillow wet, and it was hard to go to sleep with a stuffy nose. She'd cried enough. She wasn't a child anymore.

At least Josiah didn't think so.

She felt as if a warm blanket had been thrown over her shoulders. Josiah really did care about what she wanted. He hadn't just been pretending. With an almost-smile on her lips, she wiped her hands and set the towel near the sink.

He meant what he said. She was his friend, not his project.

Her heart fluttered like a garden of butterflies when she thought of his strong arms around her. It was there, even under the shadow of that horrible message, that she had felt safe. Josiah made her forget about guilt and shame and broken arms and dead parents. He didn't like it when she cried, and he was happy when she laughed, but he didn't try to talk her out of her feelings.

He made her feel as if life were worth living.

Her smile grew wider. She liked him — for his kindness and forgiving heart, his eagerness and thoughtful reflection. He occupied her thoughts often enough, but lately he was in her head all the time. At the funeral of Great-Uncle Titus, whom she had barely known, her mind had been in Bienenstock in a little white farmhouse where Josiah might have been scrambling eggs or petting his dog. She pictured him with his nephews and niece, playing grizzly bear or reading them a book. It made her smile when she thought of him lying on his back under the sink with water pouring from above him, or Aunt Bitsy's incredulous expression when he used duct tape to repair the propane lantern in the kitchen.

Rose giggled. Josiah was so earnest, not even Aunt Bitsy had the heart to put him down, even when his attempts to fix things were woefully inadequate. He desperately wanted to do the right thing, no matter what he tried. She loved him for that.

Or . . . what . . . she loved him for that?

Her heart flipped over and over itself, like a ball bouncing wildly down the stairs. Did she love Josiah Yoder? Her head spun even as her heart did flips. There was too much confusion. She had no answer.

Rose climbed the stairs and went into the room she shared with her sisters. Lily and Poppy were already in bed, but neither of them was asleep. The small lantern on the bedside table hissed quietly. Rose had always been comforted by that sound. It meant there was light in the house, and she need not be afraid.

She removed her *kapp* and untwisted her braid from its bun. It was going to be a very long night. Sleep would be impossible. Maybe she should ask her sisters if they could sleep with the lantern burning all night. Of course they would agree, but it was a shameful waste of kerosene.

"*Cum* and sit," Lily said, propping herself on her elbow and patting a space on her bed for Rose. "It wonders me if you are feeling better."

Rose took a deep, cleansing breath and thought of Josiah. "They probably won't come back tonight."

Lily grabbed onto Rose's hand. "Of course they won't come back tonight. Josiah, Dan, and Luke will paint the barn tomorrow, and it will be *gute* as new."

"If only it was that easy to fix everything else," Rose said. "I have put all of you in danger. I don't know how to make it better."

Poppy growled. "Whoever is causing the trouble is responsible for their own actions. No matter how angry they are, they have no cause to scare us."

Rose drew her brows together. "But I would feel responsible if anything happened to either of you."

"This isn't your fault, Rose," Poppy said. "And we will be all right."

"You broke your hand for me," Rose said. "You were not all right."

Poppy looked down at her cast and turned her arm over. "That was Griff's doing, and even he's coming around. Someone we once feared actually sat at our table and apologized."

Lily shook her head. "It's unbelievable, really."

"A miracle from *Gotte.*" Poppy reached over and squeezed Rose's braid. "I think we can expect more miracles yet. We just have to wait for them. *Gotte* will provide."

"What do we do until then?" Rose said.

Lily gave Rose a reassuring smile. "If we stick close together, we'll be okay."

If only Rose could be so sure. "You two will be gone by the end of September." She did her best to let them see she wasn't trembling. "Aunt Bitsy and I will be all alone. That's when they will come for me."

Lily sat up and threw her arms around Rose. Poppy moved to Lily's bed and also wrapped her arms around Rose. She felt like a sandwich. "*Nae, nae,* Rose," Lily said. "You must never even imagine such things."

"How will I be able to sleep in this big room all by myself? Even now, the small sounds in the middle of the night keep me awake. I don't know what I'll do."

Poppy squared her shoulders. "Then we don't get married."

"What?" Rose and Lily said at the same time.

"Not until we catch the troublemaker,"

Poppy said. "We postpone the weddings until we have found him." She pushed some errant strands of hair from Rose's face. "There's nothing more important to us than you, Rose."

Lily's eyes filled with pain, but she nodded and linked her elbow with Rose's. "She's right, Rose. We will stay with you."

Rose recoiled in alarm. "*Nae.* I won't let you sacrifice your wedding day for me."

"It would only be putting it off until you feel safe," Poppy said.

Rose frowned and shook her head. "*Nae.* I won't let you do it. Dan and Luke would hate me."

"They'd understand," Poppy said, as if she were trying to convince herself. "And even if they didn't, they'd have nothing to say about it. We're sisters first."

"*Nae,*" Rose said, more adamantly this time. "I will not have you sacrifice your happiness for me."

"We love you. We'll do anything to make you happy."

The thought of what her sisters were willing to give up pressed against her until she couldn't breathe. To her horror, she realized that everything her sisters did was to accommodate her. Their whole lives had been centered around making her happy, and she had been very willing to let them take care of her. She was so weak that they felt compelled to sacrifice everything, even Luke and Dan, for her. At heart, she was still that spoiled little five-year-old who fussed and carried on until her parents gave her what she wanted just to shut her up.

She stood so fast that she practically yanked Lily's arm out of the socket. "I don't want either of you to do anything for me. I won't have your ruined lives on my conscience too."

Poppy grabbed her hand and tried to pull her back to the bed. "That's not how we feel, Rose. We love you."

"Love should never demand such a sacrifice," she said. "I won't let you."

Lily stood up and tried to pull Rose into an embrace.

Rose resisted with everything she had in her. "I need to be alone. Please let me alone." She marched out of the room and down the stairs to the kitchen. Farrah Fawcett was curled up on the window seat. Leonard Nimoy was curled up near Farrah Fawcett's tail. She had obviously been prohibited from touching any part of her, but Leonard Nimoy always seemed to want to be close to Farrah Fawcett, just the same. Leonard was a persistent kitty. It wouldn't surprise Rose if they were best of friends in the end.

Leonard Nimoy lifted her head when Rose walked into the darkened kitchen. Trying not to disturb Farrah Fawcett, Rose scooped Leonard Nimoy onto her lap and buried her fingers in the kitten's soft orange fur. Leonard Nimoy rested her head in her paws and went back to sleep.

The cats wouldn't care if she cried her eyes out. It seemed crying was the only thing she did with regularity anymore.

With no one to see, Rose indulged in the tears. She thought about her parents and how ungrateful she was to miss them. Aunt Bitsy couldn't have been a more loving substitute. *Gotte* had been *gute* to her, even if she hadn't deserved it.

A thread of light descended the stairs. Rose cradled Leonard Nimoy in her hands and tucked her knees up to her chin to make herself smaller, but it wasn't as if Aunt Bitsy wouldn't see her.

Aunt Bitsy held her lantern aloft and gazed into the kitchen. "Rose Christner, you gave me the fright of my life."

"I'm sorry, Aunt Bitsy. I couldn't sleep."

"It's only nine o'clock. I can't imagine you've tried very hard yet."

"It wouldn't matter," Rose said.

Aunt Bitsy set the lantern on the counter. The light illuminated her light red hair. She hadn't been able to quite get all the red out this morning. "I would think, with Josiah looking out, you'd be sleeping like a baby."

"What do you mean 'with Josiah looking out'?"

In her green, fuzzy slippers with googly eyeballs on the toes, Aunt Bitsy shuffled to the window, reached over Rose, and nudged the curtain aside. "See for yourself," she said.

Rose set Leonard Nimoy on the window seat and stood up to look out the window. It was dark, but she could make out a figure in a straw hat sitting on the porch with his elbows propped on his knees gazing into the darkness.

Aunt Bitsy's lips drooped into a thoughtful frown. "He refused to leave. He's going to spend the night on the porch."

"He can't do that. He's got a farm and pumpkins."

"He says he can sleep fine, but he's only saying that to humor me."

"He . . . he can't," Rose said, the words squeezing from her throat as if she were choking. "What if someone knocks him out or slits his throat?"

"Nothing so dire is going to happen, baby

sister. Josiah wants to be here. I've given him a pillow, a blanket, and some duct tape, with my permission to fix whatever he wants."

Frustration and anger and helplessness tightened around Rose's chest. She was truly going to suffocate. "He . . . can't, Aunt Bitsy. He just can't."

She slapped the leftover tears from her face. Josiah would not see her cry. He would not be witness to her weakness one more time today. With no prayer covering or shoes and stockings, she tore herself from Aunt Bitsy's side, grabbed the lantern, and threw open the front door.

Startled, Josiah jumped to his feet and turned to look at her. His gaze settled briefly on her unkempt braid before he looked into her eyes. "Rose? Is everything okay?"

With great effort, she held back the tears and slammed the door behind her, not caring if Lily or Poppy heard it upstairs. They already knew how upset she was. "You can't do this, Josiah. I won't let you."

"Did something frighten you?"

Oh sis yuscht! She was no match for the compassion in his eyes. How would he believe anything she said if she made a fool of herself by crying? She clamped her eyes shut so she wouldn't have to look at him, almost like a childish game of hide-and-seek — *if I can't see you, you can't see me.* "This isn't right, Josiah. You have a farm to look after. You need your sleep."

She opened her eyes when he curled his fingers around her arms in that gentle touch that she had come to like too much. Why had she let him get so close to her — let him think it was okay to touch her and comfort her and save her from frightening shadows in the night? Why did those blue eyes make her want to give in to his kindness?

"I'll sleep better here knowing you're safe than at home worrying myself sick."

She pulled away from him. An ache of longing passed across his features and stabbed her right in the heart. "You wouldn't have to be here if I could take care of myself."

"You take care of yourself just fine, but someone has threatened you. I want to protect you. I *need* to protect you."

"*Nae,*" she said. "Don't you see? People get hurt when they try to protect me. And then they get disappointed."

"Not me. That will never be me."

"Never is a very long time." Since she was seven, she hadn't raised her voice in anger to another human being, but she was practically yelling at him now. "I don't want your help, Josiah. The shame is unbearable, and the fear is worse. You already know how weak I am, and when you help me, it just compounds my humiliation. But the fear is even bigger. I can't stand the thought of you getting hurt."

His eyes practically glowed with emotion. "Rose, I'd face ten Perry Glicks plus a hundred Griff Simonses for you."

She threw back her head and groaned. "But I don't want you to. I can't be responsible for you."

"I never asked you to."

"Of course you didn't, but you're too kindhearted not to want to help me."

"I'm not doing this because I'm kindhearted. I'm doing this because I'm afraid for you." He shook his head as if he hadn't wanted to admit that. "I feel powerless, and this is all I can think of to do. It's the only way I can have a little peace."

She saw the truth of his words in his eyes, but she couldn't let him make this kind of sacrifice for her. "It's too much, Josiah."

"Rose," he said. His voice was soft and tender, and she couldn't bear it. She wished she could plug her ears and never hear that voice again. "You have the purest, kindest heart I know. You would never turn away someone who needed your help, and you make me want to be a better man. I could never do too much for you."

A sob started in her throat. *Ach, du lieva.* She had to maintain control. Swallowing the tears, she paced persistently back and forth across the porch. "Why do you say things like that? You know I am not that person." She began to tremble. It was at least eighty degrees outside, and she was shivering like a leaf. "I can't do it, Josiah."

He tried to reach out to her, but she stepped back. The last thing she needed was the comfort of his touch to confuse her.

The pain in his blue eyes was one more thing to feel guilty about. "Rose, this isn't . . . I don't understand. You're so . . ." He heaved a long sigh. "You're so . . ."

Her chest ached. It was as if her parents had died all over again. "Disappointing?"

His eyes flashed with intensity, fierce and deep. "I was going to say unselfish."

"You want me to be different than I am." She turned her face from him. "And I can't meet your expectations."

He took off his hat and scrubbed his fingers through his hair. "I don't expect anything."

"Then I think you should stay away."

His eyes grew as wide as dinner plates.

"What?"

"You promised me that you would leave when I told you to go. Now I'm telling you. I don't want you sleeping on my porch. I don't want you putting yourself in danger."

"I'm not in danger —"

"You *will* get hurt, and I can't live with anything else on my conscience. I don't want you here."

"Rose," he whispered. There had never been so much pain in a single word.

"I don't want to see you anymore," she said between ragged breaths. It was the biggest lie, as well as the most profound truth, she had ever told.

"Rose," he said again. His voice sounded as if the summer had just died.

She kept her eyes glued to the line of duct tape on the porch floor. "*Denki* for trusting me enough to show me the message and for letting me cry on your shoulder and get your shirt wet, but I will be okay. I want you to go."

She couldn't look at him, so she couldn't begin to guess what he was thinking. She had warned him that she would be a disappointment. Lord willing, he finally understood why. "Okay, *jah*," he said, his words falling to the ground like stones. She heard, more than saw, him walk slowly down the steps. The gravel crunched beneath his feet as he made his way down the lane. Was he going to walk all the way home?

She almost called to him. *Take my horse. Take our buggy.* Instead, she stood motionless on the porch listening to the fading sound of his measured footsteps.

When she couldn't hear even the slightest remnant of sound, she took a deep, shuddering breath. May the *gute* Lord forgive her for hurting the gentlest soul she'd ever known. Was it possible to feel guiltier than she already did? She'd warned him about her. In time, he'd understand how blessed he was not to have the burden of Rose Christner in his life.

There was no reason now to choke back her tears. She sat down on the porch and bawled like she had the night her parents died, like a lost five-year-old with not even a doll to cling to for comfort. The tears burned her cheeks and her eyes felt raw, but it didn't stop her from crying. There would never be enough tears to fill up her ocean of pain.

It would hurt for a long time.

CHAPTER FOURTEEN

Even though there were about forty steps to making bee sting cake, it was one of Rose's favorite things to bake, partly because it took skill to see that the cake didn't fall and to make sure the cream filling turned out just right and to melt the butter without burning it. But mostly she loved making Bienenstich cake because it was something the Honeybee sisters always did together.

Poppy liked to mix the dough, and Lily always prepared the almond topping and poured it on top of the cake just before it went into the oven. Rose was the one who made the cream filling. There was a certain rhythm, almost a music, to working side by side in the kitchen with her sisters, making something delicious and beautiful to gladden someone's heart. A bee sting cake was a glorious gift to give. When someone got a bee sting cake, they knew they were special because the sisters had spent so much time on it. The effort to make the cake was part of the gift.

But ever since Rose had ordered Josiah off the porch, an air of anxiety had settled over the house. Everyone seemed weary and sad and unfriendly, even Aunt Bitsy, who seldom let anything put her in a bad mood. Well, a worse mood. Aunt Bitsy was always endearingly grumpy.

"Rose," Poppy said. "Will you cut the cake into two layers? I can't do it with my cast."

Rose cut the cake, then carefully put the top layer on a platter while Lily spread the bottom layer with cream filling. Rose and Lily together lifted the other layer on top of the cream filling. It looked beautiful and delicious at the same time. They'd been baking in the kitchen all afternoon, but there hadn't been any happy chatter or laughter like there usually was when they cooked together. Lily and Poppy tiptoed around Rose as if she were a sleeping badger. They refused to say one word about Dan or Luke, and they glanced at her out of the corners of their eyes as if they were afraid if they said anything, she would burst into tears.

Usually, when they knew Rose was upset or worried, they tried to reassure her that everything was going to be okay. Lily would never fail to give her a hug, and Poppy was always willing to punch someone if Rose needed her to — even though Rose would never have dreamed of asking.

Rose wiped a drop of cream from the plate and bit back her tears. She had never been more upset in her life, but her sisters would never know, if she could help it.

Since she had stormed out of the bedroom four nights ago, it seemed they weren't quite sure how to treat her, and it broke her heart. After Josiah had left and she had finished crying, she'd gone back into the house only to find Lily and Poppy sitting at the kitchen table with Aunt Bitsy.

She had walked right past them without a word, gone up to their room, and pretended to be asleep. They hadn't tried to get her to talk, then or since. If her sisters had decided they didn't love her anymore, she completely deserved it. She had hurt them very badly when they were only trying to be kind to her. Since she refused to let them take care of her, they didn't know what to do with her or how to fit her into their lives. The truth was, someone as selfish and spoiled as Rose *didn't* fit into their lives.

She had never felt so alone.

Rose hated herself for hurting them, but she couldn't bear to let anyone give up one more thing for her, and she couldn't bear that anyone might get hurt.

Not her sisters. Not Josiah Yoder.

The night after she had ordered him off their porch, Josiah had returned with Dan and Luke to paint the back of the barn. She had stayed shut up in the house, and he hadn't even tried to see her. She had watched him leave from one of the upstairs windows while Dan and Luke came in for ice cream. *Ach,* could anyone be crueler than she was?

She bit down on her tongue to keep the tears from flowing. She would not think about Josiah. It was hard enough to keep her composure with her sisters this close.

Lily scraped some of the extra cream from the bowl and licked it off her finger. "It's so smooth, Rose. The best you've made yet."

"Denki," Rose said, flashing Lily a half smile. Lily didn't see it because she quickly turned away to put the dirty bowl in the sink.

Aunt Bitsy came in from outside with her shotgun. She didn't venture out without it anymore, and she always took the extra precaution of taking Billy Idol with her. Billy Idol was tough, but he wasn't quite as threatening as a shotgun. Leonard Nimoy frolicked into the room as if Aunt Bitsy had

310

just taken her on a grand adventure. Billy Idol came in scowling and hissing. He would have made any watchdog proud.

Rose bit her lip. The shotgun, the somber looks, her unhappy family were all because of her. All this trouble and worry was about her. Rose's throat swelled up, and a weight the size of a buggy pressed against her chest.

What could she do? Every dream was a nightmare. Every day felt as if she were marching closer and closer to some terrible event, and she had no one to turn to. She didn't want to turn to anyone. No one must be in danger but her, but the possibility of danger was terrifying.

Aunt Bitsy rested her shotgun against the wall. "Dan and Luke must think we don't have anything better to do than entertain them."

Lily's head snapped up, and it was the first time Rose had seen her smile all day. "They're here?"

Aunt Bitsy grunted. "An hour early. Nobody likes guests an hour early. Have they forgotten their manners?"

"I don't mind if they're here early," Lily said.

Aunt Bitsy shrugged. "It just gives Luke more time to eat us out of house and home."

Poppy beamed. "I know. Isn't he adorable?"

Aunt Bitsy opened the door before they could knock.

Luke and Dan came into the room as if they were family, which they were. Both of their gazes immediately settled on Rose, disquiet gleaming in their eyes. They were friends with Josiah and no doubt fully aware of how horribly Rose had treated him. Dan and Luke were both too kind to scold Rose, but they were probably wishing they could.

"If you come early, you have to help with dinner," Aunt Bitsy said.

"I don't cook," Luke said, winking at Poppy. "It's women's work."

Aunt Bitsy didn't take Luke's bait. She was getting soft. "You eat more than your fair share, and Poppy has a broken hand. You're cooking whether you want to or not."

Although Rose felt alone and vulnerable and frightened out of her wits, she wouldn't have reconsidered Lily's suggestion of postponing the wedding for the world. Lily lit up like a propane lantern whenever Dan was near, and Poppy was like a Fourth of July fireworks show. Rose would never be the one to separate her sisters from the boys they loved, no matter how devastated she would be when they left.

312

For some silly reason, Josiah, with his dark auburn hair and blue eyes came to her mind. Seeing him was like watching the sun rise, and sometimes she felt the fireworks when he smiled at her. Was Josiah her Dan?

Not anymore. The heaviness in her chest thickened like ice on the lake in January. She would never forget the sound of his voice when she had told him to go away. It was as if he would never find happiness again. She'd been mean and adamant — for his own good. But Josiah hadn't seen it that way. She had proven a disappointment to him after all, and for sure and certain he wouldn't be coming back.

A sob tried to claw its way out of her throat, but she swallowed hard and bit her tongue. She would draw blood if she let Josiah linger in her thoughts any longer. She turned the cake plate around and around. Their Bienenstich cake looked very pretty. Maybe Poppy and Lily would want to serve it to their fiancés instead of taking it to the Millers.

"Is that cake for me?" Luke said, losing his grim look and grinning at Rose like an affectionate big brother. "You shouldn't have." He reached out to take a sample of Lily's almond topping.

"It's for Eli Miller," Poppy said, giving

Luke's hand a swat with a wooden spoon. "He had bunion surgery yesterday."

Luke's eyes widened in disgust. "Bunion surgery? Your fiancé is less important than bunion surgery?"

"*Jah*," Poppy said. "And don't you forget it."

Dan followed Lily to the sink, where they both washed their hands. "What am I making for dinner?" he said, flicking some water on Lily.

Lily let out a little squeak and threw a towel at Dan. "Rose baked a pizza crust. We're having cold chicken bacon ranch pizza."

Dan gave Rose a smile. "*Denki,* Rose. I could eat your pizza crust plain, and it would be a fine dinner."

Rose held perfectly still. If she tried to form her lips into a smile, she might just burst into tears. Lily and Poppy were as happy as she was miserable, and they were happier without her.

"*Cum,* Rose," Lily said, eyeing her doubtfully. "You spread the ranch dressing while Dan and I cut chicken."

Rose very nearly turned and ran up the stairs and fled to the safety of her room, but that would leave Luke to spread the dressing, and he wasn't even good at pouring water. For the sake of the pizza, she'd have to bite back the tears for a few minutes longer.

Poppy handed Luke some plates. He stared at them as if he had no idea what he was supposed to do. Poppy rolled her eyes, and he cracked a smile. "Okay. Fine then. I will set the table, but only because I'm hungry. Remember my willingness when you consider giving that cake to Eli Miller. I'll bet he doesn't set the table for his wife."

Poppy grinned. "He can't. He just had bunion surgery."

Rose spread the dressing, and Dan helped her sprinkle chicken and bacon and cheese while Lily made a salad. Rose set the pizza on the table and turned to see Poppy and Luke with their heads together, whispering and looking in her direction.

A shard of ice pierced her heart. *Ach, du lieva*, they were whispering about her. She didn't even belong in the family anymore.

When Luke and Poppy had gotten engaged, Rose had surrendered her place at the table to Luke and moved to the end of the table opposite Aunt Bitsy. Before today, it hadn't hurt so bad to give up her seat. Today it was as if she sat on the outer edges of everyone else's life, looking in on their happiness.

Lily put her arm around Rose. "*Cum,* Rosie. Sit by me this time."

What was wrong with her? How silly she was to feel sorry for herself. "You should sit by Dan."

"I'll have many years to sit by Dan after we're married," Lily said. "I want to sit by you."

Rose looked at the lonely chair at the end of the table. One of the slats had a strand of duct tape wrapped around it. Her heart flipped like a pancake. Josiah had fixed that chair. She gave Lily a half smile and squeezed her hand. "I don't mind."

Lily pursed her lips but didn't argue.

They sat down, Rose in her duct-taped chair, and took hands for Aunt Bitsy's prayer.

"Dear Lord," Aunt Bitsy began. "I am going to bless the food first, because I always forget. Please bless the food and make us grateful for it. Amen." She growled and bowed her head again. "Lord, I forgot all the other stuff I was going to say. We are a little nervous about people making trouble on our farm. They seem to be picking on Rose specifically, and I won't stand for that. Please will You give one of them a bladder infection and the other the measles, or whatever You see fit. And Lord, I'm still

waiting for that dose of humility for Luke
Bontrager, if You're not too busy. Amen."

Luke leaned back in his chair and smiled.
"How can I be humble when I have the
prettiest fiancée a boy could ask for?" He
nodded at Lily. "No offense to you."

"No offense taken," Lily said. "Rose and
Poppy are both far prettier than I am."

Aunt Bitsy shook her head adamantly. "All
you girls are as unique as the flowers on our
farm. The bees like them all. There isn't a
prettiest one."

Dan winked at Lily. "I am partial to lil-
ies."

Josiah had winked at Rose like that once.
She lowered her eyes and stared at her
napkin. Luke had obviously set the table.
Her napkin was crinkled and bent as if
someone had made an attempt to fold it
and given up. Her thoughts wandered down
the lane to Josiah's little house and pumpkin
patch. She had sent him away to keep him
safe, but she couldn't have felt worse about
it. She hated the thought of Josiah all alone
in that house with no one but Honey the
dog to comfort him.

Dan seemed a little sad tonight. Rose
frowned. Dan was never sad. "Josiah has a
whole garden full of roses," he said.

Rose tried to ignore the butterflies that

came to life in her stomach. She had seen the rose garden. Josiah had taken her there. Her chair creaked as she leaned back and wiped her mouth with her napkin.

Luke smirked. "I can take that chair to my shop tonight and make a new slat. Josiah shouldn't be allowed near a roll of duct tape ever again."

Rose frowned. "Please don't fix it."

Luke eyed her doubtfully. "It looks a little ragged. Are you sure?"

"Josiah has a *gute* heart and wanted to fix it, even if he didn't know how. He did the best he could." Her voice cracked, and her heart suddenly broke for Josiah and the man he was trying to be. He didn't always do it right, but he did it with great enthusiasm. "It's perfect the way it is."

Poppy gazed at Rose and pursed her lips. She nudged Luke's arm with her elbow. "Tell her, Luke."

Luke looked from Poppy to Rose to Dan, and back again.

"Tell her," Poppy insisted, between gritted teeth.

Luke was stubborn and cantankerous and arrogant, but he was always gentle with Rose. She liked that about him, even if she knew he was doing it on purpose. He was also protective and strong, and he loved

Poppy. Rose adored him for how happy he made her sister. He placed his hand on Rose's arm. "Carl Poulson drove us to Wallsby this morning. Josiah came with us."

She didn't know if her heart beat faster at the thought of Josiah or the thought of LaWayne Zook and his angry family.

"We wanted to find out about LaWayne Zook," Dan said.

There was a long pause. Everyone looked to Rose, waiting for her reaction. She fidgeted with her crinkly napkin and tried not to seem distressed. "And . . . what did you find out?"

"We met LaWayne's cousin Matthew, who told us that LaWayne's wife left Wallsby while LaWayne was in prison," Luke said.

Another pause as they stared at Rose, no doubt making sure that this information didn't make her faint. She tried to ignore the panic rising in her chest and did her best to look interested but not terrified enough to need medical attention. "Where did she go?"

"She left the church and got a divorce."

Rose held her breath so a moan would not have the chance to escape. Divorce meant excommunication and shunning.

Luke reached out and wrapped his fingers around Rose's wrist. "Do you know how many times one of his seven children was in the hospital before he pushed you, Rose?"

She shook her head.

The muscles of Luke's jaw twitched. "Twelve."

Dan leaned in, and everyone else seemed to lean in too, as if he were telling a great secret that the cats weren't allowed to hear. "Matthew's wife, Erna, and LaWayne's wife, Martha, were very close. Martha didn't want her children to grow up like that. The elders had tried several times to call LaWayne to repentance. Before she left for good, the ministers took Martha and the children out of the home twice."

"But LaWayne would not stop drinking," Luke said, his eyes flashing with anger. He did not look kindly on anyone who hurt a child. "When LaWayne went to prison, it gave Martha the opportunity to escape."

Poppy's expression was soft. "Don't you see, Rose? Because of you, Martha got her chance to leave."

"But she left the church," Rose said.

"That wasn't your fault any more than La-Wayne's drinking was," Luke said. "He died three months ago of cirrhosis."

"What is cirrhosis?" Poppy said.

"It's a liver disease from drinking alcohol," Dan said. "LaWayne couldn't stop drinking, even when he got out of prison and moved back to Wallsby. His death is no one's fault but his own."

Aunt Bitsy laced her fingers together. "But someone is mad at Rose."

Dan slumped his shoulders. "Or maybe LaWayne's death has nothing to do with what's happening on the farm."

Aunt Bitsy shook her head. "Too much of a coincidence. And coincidences are only for those who don't believe in *Gotte.*"

Rose's throat tightened. "So this is *Gotte*'s will?"

"*Nae,* baby sister. *Gotte* is leading us to the troublemakers."

"What about LaWayne's children?" Poppy said.

Luke fingered the stubble on his chin. "Matthew says they all came back for the funeral, but none of them live in Wallsby anymore."

"Maybe one of them lives too close," Aunt Bitsy said.

"Matthew said he would try to find out where all the children are scattered. At least three are still living at home with Martha."

Once again, they turned in unison to stare at Rose. She clasped her hands together so they wouldn't see the trembling. If they wanted some sort of reassurance from her that she would be all right, they wouldn't get it. There wasn't room in her heart for despair or hope. She could only feel the fear.

Dan nodded. "We will find them."

"And what will you do when they are found?" Rose said, gripping her fork until her hand stiffened.

"Luke is strong and I'm fast, and Josiah is determined," Dan said, glancing at Rose when he mentioned Josiah. She didn't even flinch. "But none of us is foolish enough to try to catch a troublemaker. We'll leave that to the sheriff."

"If he is in the mood to answer his phone," Aunt Bitsy said. "I've stopped calling him four or five times a day."

Poppy widened her eyes. "Four or five times a day?"

Aunt Bitsy huffed in irritation. "I only call him once a day now. Surely he has time to talk to me once a day. All he does is chase runaway cows and shovel roadkill off the highway."

Rose couldn't school her expression well enough to fool anybody, let alone her perceptive sisters. "It's going to be okay, Rosie," Lily said. "I promise we will not let anything happen to you."

"We all want to keep you safe," Dan said. "And I want to protect my fiancée."

322

Rose closed her eyes and willed the ache of fear to subside. "I can take care of myself." They could probably tell she was lying when she burst into tears. Lily and Poppy jumped from their seats and were immediately at Rose's side with their arms around her. She felt ashamed and relieved at the same time. "I hate being a burden."

Lily knelt next to Rose's chair and took her hand. "Rose, we've been trying to tell you. You are anything but a burden."

"But everything you do is for me."

Lily shook her head. "And everything you do is for us. You paint hives, you mop floors, you bake eats for every gathering. You were the one who always made me feel better when I got teased at school. You stay up late at night and let us talk about our boyfriends."

Dan's face lit up. "You talk about us?"

Luke laced his fingers together and put them behind his head. "Poppy thinks I'm adorable."

Aunt Bitsy snorted. "You're not even a penny's worth of adorable. Don't get cocky."

"I can't let you sacrifice your lives for me," Rose said through her tears.

Poppy smoothed a piece of hair from Rose's cheek. "Then won't you just let us be your sisters?"

"That's what I want most in the world," Rose said. She wasn't altogether sure they understood. She was sobbing pretty hard.

Lily squeezed her hand. "Then let's just be sisters and do what we've always done — stick together and take care of each other."

"We are all in the same boat," Aunt Bitsy said. "Even Luke. The hand cannot say to the foot, I have no need of thee."

Rose wiped her eyes. "I need my sisters."

"And we need you," Poppy said.

It was amazing how much heartache and loneliness could be washed away by the unconditional love of a sister. Rose was doubly blessed.

After a long, bracing hug, Lily and Poppy sat back down in their seats, and Rose regained enough composure to carry on a conversation. She needed to tell Luke and Dan how much she appreciated them. She managed a smile. "*Denki* for going to Wallsby. At least we know more than we did."

"We spent three hours there this morning," Dan said. He again glanced doubtfully from Rose to Luke to Lily. "And then we took Josiah to the hospital."

It felt as if someone with big hands had shoved Rose against a wall. "The hospital?"

Luke rolled his eyes. "He told us it was just a cold, but he kept coughing and coughing and started sweating, and then he turned pale as a ghost."

"Luke," Dan said, looking at Rose out of the corner of his eye, "we don't need all the upsetting details."

Luke grunted. "Matthew didn't want to let us in his house for fear Josiah would give his family some dread disease."

Rose scooted to the edge of her chair as if to catch the information faster. "Is . . . is he okay?"

"He's got walking pneumonia. The doctor told him to stay in bed, so of course the minute we dropped him off at home, he went to milk the cow."

"Walking pneumonia? Is it serious?"

"He's wonderful sick," Dan said. "But he'll be okay if he doesn't try to work himself to death."

Both Luke and Dan studied her face as if they could find answers there. Lily and Poppy concentrated faithfully on their dinner.

"He just . . . he's very unhappy," Dan said, as if he really didn't want to say anything but felt like he should.

Rose could think of absolutely nothing to say, and she wouldn't have been able to speak past the lump in her throat anyway. Josiah was sick — wonderful sick — Dan had said. She ached just thinking of Josiah all alone and ailing in the house where his *fater* had died.

Was it her fault he was sick?

She was fully aware that she had hurt Josiah very badly. In time, he would come to understand it had been for his own good. Maybe he already did. She had been a complete disappointment, and he was probably glad he'd gotten rid of her. "I'm very sorry to hear that," she said, mostly because she didn't know what else to say.

"I'm sure Suvie's taking *gute* care of him," Lily said.

Luke breathed out a long and plaintive sigh. "If Suvie gets sick, the *kinner* get sick. For sure and certain, she's keeping her distance."

Rose frowned. "It wonders me if the doctor gave him any medicine."

Luke shrugged. "I don't know. I wasn't really paying attention."

If she wanted to get any information, Luke was not the person to ask. He was more aggravating than a raccoon in the chimney. "Dan," she said. "Did Josiah take any cough medicine or something for his fever?"

"I don't know," Dan said. "We dropped

him off, and he said he was going to milk the cow."

"You didn't tell him he should rest?"

He shook his head. "I don't feel right about bossing him around."

Rose's agitation grew at the indifference of Josiah's two best friends. "Does he have any essential oils? What about menthol? Did you check to see if he had dry mustard on hand?"

Luke took a bite of pizza. How could he eat at a time like this? "Josiah is twenty-three years old. He can take care of himself."

If Rose had been Poppy, she would have had the courage to scold Luke for being such a dunderhead. What boy could be trusted to take care of himself when he was sick? They had no sense at all about such things.

"Besides," Luke said. "I have no patience for sick people."

Rose felt compelled to take him to task. "Your *dat* had cancer for two years."

"I suppose I used up all my sympathy on him."

Rose pressed her lips together and stopped asking questions. She wasn't going to get any satisfactory answers from her sisters' aggravating fiancés. She'd have to take matters into her own hands. She couldn't turn a blind eye to Josiah's suffering. She wouldn't have to stay long or feel obligated to explain herself.

Josiah needed help, and she would go. No matter how uncomfortable or frightening. No matter how she dreaded seeing his disdain or feeling his rejection.

No matter how much it hurt.

CHAPTER FIFTEEN

Josiah stood up straight as another fit of coughing overtook him. It felt as if a thousand shards of glass were ripping at his throat, leaving him raw and breathless. It couldn't hurt any worse if he hacked up an entire lung.

Ach, vell. It couldn't hurt any worse if he broke every bone in his body. The coughing and the fever and the headache were nothing compared to the ache in his heart that brought him to his knees even without walking pneumonia. He almost welcomed the physical pain. It helped dull what would never go away.

The hacking and the fretting had kept him up all night last night, so before the sun had come up, he'd mucked out the barn and milked the cow. Milking did not go well with a cough. He often sang to the cow to calm her down, and Flossy did not take kindly to his barking cough. She'd been so nervous, she had nearly knocked the pail over twice, and she had swished her manure-caked tail and hit Josiah in the face.

When there had been light enough to see by, he'd staggered to the pumpkin patch to do some weeding. He'd scared all the birds and the bees away, and aside from his coughing, the day seemed oddly quiet, bleak, and unfriendly. Honey sat on her haunches in the dirt, keeping watch over him as if she feared he was going to keel over and die any minute. Maybe he would.

Sweat trickled down his back, but he felt deathly cold, as if he were freezing from the inside out.

A honeybee, unconcerned by the coughing, landed on the bindweed Josiah was just about to yank out of the ground. He paused and watched as the bee stuck out its tongue and collected nectar from the small flower. Rose could have spent hours in his pumpkin patch, watching the bees play among the blossoms, delighting in the little yellow balls of pollen attached to their legs, listening to the pleasant hum of their vibrating wings.

The pain of the memory was so sudden and sharp, he doubled over. He clamped his eyes shut but still saw Rose everywhere. He saw her tenderly tugging a blossom close to her nose so she could take in its aroma. He imagined her eyes lighting up at the sight of Suvie's butterfly garden and saw her marvel at the beauty of the roses. Her smile was quite possibly the most beautiful thing he had ever seen, and her voice made his heart break just thinking about the sound of it.

He would never be able to subdue the memory of Rose, so vulnerable yet so determined, seeking the comfort of his arms in the shadow of the red barn. It was the only place he had ever wanted her, tucked safely in his embrace and close to his heart.

But it hadn't been his choice. Rose didn't want him. One word from her, and he had walked away. Turning his back on Rose was like cutting off his own hand, but it didn't matter. He would have done anything for her.

He gave her his heart and let her break it.

Josiah wrapped his arms around Honey's neck. How pathetic he was! He'd fallen hard and fast for Rose. He'd named his dog for her. He'd spent every hour of every day thinking about her. He hadn't been careful enough or patient enough. Rose's rejection had been his own fault, and that realization tortured him more than anything else.

The coughing spasms took over once more, and he pressed his fingers to the bottom of his rib cage in an attempt to contain the pain. He didn't wonder but that he would tear every muscle loose in his gut.

"Would you go lie down if I weeded your pumpkins for you?"

At the sound of her voice, his pulse became a raging river. He turned to see Rose standing at the edge of his pumpkin patch, her eyes full of anxiety, her arms curled around the handle of a large basket. She wore her rose-petal-pink dress, and she stood with her back to the morning sun. The light shining behind her made her look as if she were from another world, like an angel from the heavenly clouds come to deliver a message.

He leaped to his feet and went to her, reaching out and taking the basket from her arms. It was heavy. "Weeding is hard work," he said. "I would never want you to have to do it."

"Never is a long time," she said, her voice gravelly and low, as if she were doing her best to maintain some semblance of composure.

She didn't want to be here. That much was painfully clear. But he loved Rose well enough to know that she would go anywhere if she thought someone needed her, even someone as unworthy as Josiah Yoder. He didn't allow himself to look into her eyes. It would hurt too much, and the pain was already overflowing.

Without her basket for protection, she clasped her hands together in front of her. "I brought some chicken soup."

He glanced at her basket. "*Ach. Jah.* That is very nice." He broke into a fit of coughing.

She took a step toward him. "*Cum.* Let's get you into the house."

He hated that she felt obligated to help him when it was clear she wanted to be anywhere but here. "Rose, you are so kind, but there is no need. The doctor gave me some antibiotics, and I cough whether I'm up or down. I might as well get some work done." He lifted the basket slightly. "*Denki* for dropping this by."

Pain flashed across her face before the worry returned. She reached out and took his hand, sending a ribbon of warmth snaking all the way up his arm. "Please will you come?"

She tugged Josiah toward the house, and both he and Honey followed without a word — not that Honey had ever said anything before, but she was as silent and solemn as if Rose had asked her to keep watch.

The back door led right into the kitchen. Josiah grimaced. He'd been sick for three days. The kitchen looked as if Aaron and Alvin had been let loose to cook supper. Rose stopped just inside the door, reached up, and removed Josiah's hat. That simple action felt too intimate, as if Rose belonged in his kitchen. As if she fit in the natural flow of his life. He ached with the wish that it were so.

"Are you cold?" she said. "You're shivering."

"I . . . I don't know."

She balanced on her tiptoes and laid her hand across his forehead. While she was close, he breathed her in, savoring the scent of lavender that she always carried with her. "You're burning up." She sent him to the moon when she took his hand and pulled him to the sofa. "Lie down and take off your boots."

He didn't have the strength or the will to argue. Rose's presence made him feel as if he were on a dizzying roller coaster. There was nothing he could do but hold on tight to what was left of his shattered heart.

She took the basket from him, and he sat and removed his boots. Then he stood up with his boots in his hand.

"I'll put them away," she said.

"I don't mind."

"I do." While he laid down and tried to

get comfortable — a task made impossible by the fact that Rose was in his house — Rose put her basket on the kitchen counter and set his boots on the mat next to the front door. She hesitated, turned, and gazed at him as if she were memorizing his face. Her eyes were full of fear and worry and pain and sorrow, and his heart broke all over again. He could make it all better if only she would let him.

Ach. Of course he couldn't make it all better. He was the one responsible for it all.

She marched down the hall, came back with the navy-blue blanket from his bed, and laid it over him. "Here," she said, taking a small brown wafer from her pocket. "This is a honey lozenge. It will soothe your throat."

"Did you make it?"

"*Jah.* Honey cures just about everything."

He bolted upright when he started coughing again. It was too hard to catch his breath lying down.

"Here." She went back down the hall and came back with his pillow. He leaned forward, and she propped the pillow behind his head so he could rest in an upright position. "That will help with the coughing," she said.

But it wouldn't help with the pain. Every

time she came close, his fingers ached to lay a caress on her cheek or play with a strand of hair from under her *kapp.* He was going to drive himself crazy. How foolish he had been to think his despair couldn't get any worse.

She put her hand on his forehead again. He clenched his teeth. Despair and torture.

"You're very hot." She went to the kitchen, and he could hear her filling a glass with water. She brought the glass and two pills. "Motrin," she said. "And drink plenty of water."

He swallowed the pills and the entire glass of water just in case it would make her happy. "I didn't think I had any Motrin in the house."

She gave him a half smile. "I wasn't counting on you having anything in your cupboards. I brought it with me." She took the glass from him. "Try to sleep if you can. I will redd up."

Try to sleep? Rose was here. Sleep would be impossible.

Honey sat next to the sofa, as if keeping vigil over a dying man's bedside. Rose cupped her hand under Honey's nose and puckered her lips. "Take care of him, Honey," she said. "Come and get me if he needs anything." Honey wagged her tail.

Rose cooed and scratched Honey's head before standing up and going back into the kitchen.

The back of the sofa faced the kitchen, so Josiah couldn't see her, but he could hear her, and that was misery enough. He closed his eyes and tried to ignore the pain of losing her.

It was no use. His senses were saturated with the sound of Rose moving about his house, her feet swishing against the floor, her gentle hands folding towels, washing dishes. He held his breath with his ears attuned to her every movement. This was his fondest desire, to have Rose a part of his home, a part of his life. A part of him — the biggest part of himself, and the only part that truly mattered.

He felt her soft touch on his shoulder and opened his eyes. "Can I warm you some chicken noodle soup?" she said. "I made it this morning."

The lump in his throat was too big to speak. He merely nodded.

She smiled and nodded back.

In desperation, he grabbed her hand before she could slip away again. "Please, Rose," he said, the words coming from deep within his throat.

She hesitated and looked down at her

hand in his as if she had no idea how it had gotten there. He felt her tremble under his touch.

"Rose." He squeezed tighter. "Please don't make me stay away."

It got so still, he could feel her pulse against his fingers. "Josiah," she whispered, keeping her eyes glued to their hands. "It's for your own good."

"Like I thought hiding the truth about the barn was for your own good?"

She shook her head. "It's not the same."

With his heart banging against his chest, he rose to his feet and wrapped his hands around her arms. "Rose, do you like me? Because if you don't like me, I'll not say another word. I'll not come around ever again." He had to force the bitter words out of his mouth. The thought of never speaking to Rose again made him weak.

She wouldn't look at him. "You shouldn't be on your feet."

He nudged her chin up with his finger until she met his eye. "Rose, do you like me?"

"I do," she said, with a catch in her breath.

He thought his heart might sprout wings and fly. "Then why did you send me away?"

"I already told you. I won't let you put yourself in danger for me. I would never forgive myself if you got hurt."

"Shouldn't I be the one to decide? Like you with the barn?"

She furrowed her brow and considered his question. "You need to sit." To his absolute delight, she took both his hands and pulled him down to the sofa as she knelt on the floor at his feet.

He tried to pull her up. "Sit by me," he said.

"*Nae.* I want you to look me in the eye. I need to tell you something."

He wouldn't argue with her, though he wasn't comfortable with the thought of her kneeling at his feet. But he liked not needing an excuse to gaze at her.

A fit of coughing overtook him, and he coughed until he thought he might burst a blood vessel. He feared Rose would decide she didn't want to get his germs and run from the house before she said another word. She did stand up, but instead of bolting for the door, she filled another glass with water and brought it to him before returning to her place on the floor. The coughing finally subsided.

She clasped her hands in her lap. "You should be resting."

"I can't rest as long as you look so troubled."

The tiny creases around her eyes deepened. "I know." She settled deeper into the rag rug on Josiah's floor. "I want to tell you something I've never told anyone, not even my sisters or Aunt Bitsy."

She paused, and Josiah held his breath for fear of doing something, anything, that would make her change her mind.

"I'm only telling you because I don't want you to be sad anymore. I can't bear the thought that something I did made you unhappy. I know you want to come to my house and keep watch on my porch and be my friend, but I can't allow that. I won't let you come back, but I can at least help you understand why I said the things I said. After you hear what I have to say, you'll thank me for asking you to go."

His gut clenched. *Never, Rose. I'll never let go.*

She took a deep breath. "If you're sick of my crying, you should stop me right now, because I have never been able to think of this without tears."

Ach, du lieva. He ached to reach out and pull her into his arms. Clenching his fists, he became as immovable as a stone. "I'm sad when you cry because it means you're unhappy or frightened, and I hate to ever see you upset. But I would never tell you

340

not to cry. You feel things down into your soul. I wouldn't want you any other way."

Another deep breath, as if she were stalling for a little bit of extra time. She blinked back several tears and met his eye. "I'm the reason my parents are dead."

Because he didn't want to scare her away, Josiah remained perfectly still, even though her words sent him reeling. Rose's parents had died in a car accident, but in some way Josiah couldn't comprehend, she blamed herself.

"Rose, you were five years old."

She nodded, as if being five made her even guiltier. "I was a spoiled child. My parents and my sisters coddled me, and I thought I deserved anything I wanted. No one but my parents loved me, and I'm sure even they didn't most of the time. I wanted a Tickle Me Elmo doll for Christmas."

"I don't even know what that is."

She dabbed the moisture from her eyes. "One of my *Englisch* friends had one. It's a red, furry animal that makes laughing noises. It was all I could think about. When my *mamm* told me that she couldn't find one in any store in Shawano, I threw a fit. I fell on the floor and kicked and screamed. I held my breath until my face turned blue. I refused to eat."

Josiah stayed quiet and gazed at her, willing her to see that there was nothing but compassion behind his eyes. How often in fifteen years had she offered it to herself?

"Mamm finally convinced Dat to hire a driver to take them to Green Bay to search for a Tickle Me Elmo doll. They died in a car accident on the way home. The police returned the doll to me still in its box." She seemed to disintegrate before his eyes. Covering her face, she sobbed into her hands.

Every tear was like the twist of a knife in his heart.

"The day of the funeral, I sneaked downstairs in the middle of the night and threw the doll into Dawdi's woodstove. Then I knelt by the stove and begged *Gotte* to send my parents back. I promised Him I would never ask for anything ever again. But He didn't listen. He took my parents to punish me for my selfishness." She lifted her head and looked at him, the tears still streaming down her face. "I didn't speak for a year, fearing that if *Gotte* heard my voice, He would smite me or one of my sisters dead. Since that day, I've tried not to ask *Gotte* for anything, except to plead for the lives of my family and to beg forgiveness for my sins."

He couldn't keep his distance a second longer, even at the risk of getting her sick. Trying to stifle his coughing, he slid off the sofa, sidled next to her, and wrapped both arms around her shoulders.

To his surprise, she buried her face in the crook of his neck and let him hold her. "This isn't the reaction I was expecting from you," she said.

"Then maybe you don't know me very well," he said, his heartbeat vibrating like a bee's wings.

"But you understand why you need to stay away."

"*Nae*," he said. "I don't understand that at all."

"If you got hurt, *Gotte* would never forgive me. I killed my parents, and I am responsible for LaWayne Zook's death as well."

He pulled her closer and smoothed his hand up and down her arm. "My darling Rosie," he whispered. The words tasted like honey on his lips. For years, he had stored up dozens of sweet names he longed to call her — if only she would let him into her heart.

Now he knew why she had guarded the entrance so carefully.

He smoothed a strand of hair off her cheek. "My nephew Alvin is three years old, just two years younger than you were when your parents died. Would you blame him for anything?"

She pressed her lips together. *"Nae."*

"Now think of *Gotte,* who loved the world so much that He gave His only begotten Son to die for His people. Do you think *Gotte* would punish Alvin for a temper tantrum? Do you really believe that He would be so vindictive with one of His children? *Gotte* promised to forgive us when we repent. He asks us to forgive seventy times seven. Don't you think He would forgive us at least as often?"

She pulled away from him and furrowed her brow. "But if I hadn't thrown such a fit about a foolish doll . . ."

"Nothing we do can change *Gotte*'s plan for us. A little golden-haired five-year-old who wants a doll more than anything can't make the world spin in a different direction."

"But it did turn upside down when my parents died."

"Can you say for certain that wasn't part of His plan?" He brushed his thumb down the side of her face. Her skin was softer than silk.

For the thousandth time, he thought of the small envelope that had been sitting in the dresser drawer for weeks, and his heart stumbled over itself. Should he give it to her? Would it make her happy, or would she reject it like she had the paint? "Rose," he stammered. "I have something I want to give you."

She immediately stiffened, and the turmoil in her expression cut him like a knife.

"You don't have to accept it if you don't want, and you won't hurt my feelings."

"*Jah,* I will," she said. "I have done nothing but hurt your feelings."

"I've gotten over the paint disaster. I only cried for about two hours."

Rose lifted her gaze as a hint of a smile played at her lips. "For sure and certain, you didn't cry, but I did hurt your feelings."

"Only because I felt bad for making you uncomfortable. The last thing I want to do is make you upset, and I know you'll be honest with me if I do."

He rose to his feet, paused long enough to cough, then went into his room to retrieve the envelope. He came back and, *oh sis yuscht,* his hands shook as he sat down and handed it to her.

She clearly didn't want to take it. Maybe she didn't want to have to reject him one more time.

Reluctantly, she pulled the photo from the

envelope. A teenage girl with hair like amber honey and eyes the color of cornflowers in early summer looked into the camera, perhaps a bit uncomfortable but smiling all the same. She wore an Amish *kapp* and a black dress with a white apron.

Rose gasped and turned as white as a sheet. She stared at the photo, and Josiah couldn't even tell if she was breathing. "Where did you get this?" she whispered.

He studied her face doubtfully. "An old *Englisch* friend of your *mater*'s."

She didn't respond.

"Are you all right?" he said. "Can I get you some water?"

A soft, involuntary giggle tripped from between her lips. "*Nae. Nae,* Josiah. No water. I just need to see . . ." Almost reverently, she fingered the edges of the picture. "She had kind eyes."

"Like yours," Josiah said. "Bitsy didn't want to get your hopes up if it came to nothing. Your *mamm* had an *Englisch* friend take a photo of her on the day of her baptism. Maybe it was one last exciting thing to do before she took her vows. Maybe she wanted something to show Bitsy since Bitsy had left home by then. Your *mamm* told Bitsy about the photo, but Bitsy never saw it."

"Where was it?"

"I tracked the *Englischer* down in Milwaukee, and she sent it to me. I'm sorry I couldn't find one of your *dat*."

To his dismay, she broke into a fresh round of tears. "I don't deserve this. I don't deserve such kindness."

"Please don't say that. You deserve every *gute* thing. Remember when I told you I have no expectations? I have to admit that I do want something from you after all." He took a tissue from his pocket and dabbed the wetness from her face. "I want you to be happy."

"I don't deserve —"

"Do you think Griff Simons deserves to be happy? And Paul Glick and petty Dinah Eicher, Luke's old girlfriend?"

"*Jah.* I think everybody —"

"Everybody deserves to be happy," he said, finishing the sentence she was going to say before she thought about it too hard. "People like Paul Glick won't let themselves be happy because they're holding tight to the things that make them miserable. There's fear in letting go."

"But I can't just forget all the mistakes I've made."

"What use are you getting out of their memory now?"

She furrowed her brow. "Only heartache, I suppose."

"When I imagine you fifteen years ago, I see a little girl who felt so guilty that she never let herself grieve for her parents or for herself." He nudged her to sit up straight and traced his thumb along her cheek. "She needs to grieve, Rose."

"I know," she said. Her voice broke like glass against stone. She covered her mouth with her hand as a heart-rending sob came from the depths of her pain.

He sat silently and let her cry.

It was a full minute before she said another word. "I miss that carefree little girl."

"She's still in there."

"But she's never been the same."

"Except that she is wearing pink in my imagination. Same as you are today."

That coaxed a smile from her lips.

He cocked an eyebrow. "Are your feet falling asleep?"

A reluctant giggle. "*Jah,* they are."

He scooted around and leaned his back against the sofa, stretching his legs out in front of him. Rose did the same, sitting so that her arm was comfortably pressed against his. He thought he might burst with joy at that small gesture. "You are not a wicked girl, Rose. And you are not responsible for your parents' deaths or LaWayne Zook's drinking. LaWayne's *fater* and his *fater* before him very likely showed him the path, and he didn't know how to do anything but travel it."

"I still wish it had been different."

"I do too," he said. "I wish my *mamm* had not gone out that night. I wish I had worked harder that day in the fields so my *dat* wouldn't have had a heart attack. But why spend any more precious time wishing and grieving for something that will never be? I don't think *Gotte* would want you or me to do that. Remember how He told Lot's wife not to look back?"

Rose sniffled as a grin played at her lips. "I would rather not turn into a pillar of salt."

They gazed at each other. It was as if some sort of bridge had been crossed. His heart felt as if it would burst.

She took another look at her picture and pressed it to her chest. "I might not deserve this, but I'm keeping it. I have my *mater* again."

"Unlike a tube of paint, you really can't give it back."

Her eyes sparkled with their own light. "You were counting on that, weren't you?"

"*Jah.* I'm pushy like that." He nudged

Rose's foot with his. "I have some bad news."

She studied him with hesitant curiosity. "What is it?"

"Nothing you have told me makes me want to stay away. In truth, it makes me never want to leave your side."

Her smile grew slowly, as if she couldn't decide whether to be happy or sad about that. "I thought you would be relieved you didn't have to be my friend anymore."

"You can't be rid of me that easy," he said, erupting into an attack of coughing.

She stood up and offered her hand. "I need to make you a mustard plaster. Lie down."

He liked it when Rose Christner bossed him around. He plopped on the sofa, and Rose spread the blanket over his legs.

"Did you tell me all of this because you think I'm dying?" he said.

She grinned. "*Nae,* but you might wish you were dead after you smell my mustard plaster."

"*Oy,* anyhow. Will it make my eyes water?"

"*Jah.*" She smiled as if she were looking forward to it. "You are going to be fine as long as you stay off your feet and out of the pumpkins."

His throat constricted, and he grabbed her

hand before she could move away. "Will you let me come back to Honeybee Farm when you've cured me?"

A shadow of disquiet traveled across her face. "I suppose it should be your choice."

"*Nae,* Rose. It is only your choice."

After a little consideration, she gave him the tiniest of smiles. "We're in desperate need of some duct tape."

Even being deathly ill, he'd never felt better in his life, as if he could skip and hop and leap all around the house. "I'll bring a whole roll."

"Aunt Bitsy will be pleased."

CHAPTER SIXTEEN

Rose tucked an errant lock of hair underneath her bandanna before going outside onto the porch. The sun had set, but there was still enough light to see the barn and the honey house and even the beehives that stood near the small pond at the front of their property to her left. Crickets had begun their chirping orchestra and a whippoor-will sang his three-note song to the sky. Rose smelled the slightest tinge of autumn in the air. It was going to be a beautiful night. Dan would probably sleep better on the porch than he did within the walls of his own home.

Lily and Dan sat on the top step, holding hands and gazing into the fading light in the sky. They both turned when she came outside.

"I am to give you strict instructions that there shall be no shenanigans on the porch," Rose said in her best Aunt Bitsy voice.

Lily giggled and rested her head on Dan's shoulder. "Maybe we need to get a list from Aunt Bitsy of exactly what shenanigans are. I never know if I'm breaking the rules or not."

Dan shook his head. "*Nae*. We don't want a list. It's easier to ask forgiveness than permission, and I don't want to stop holding your hand."

Luke and Dan had decided they liked Josiah's idea of keeping guard on the Honeybee sisters' porch every night. They had taken turns every other night while Josiah was sick; then the three of them went every third night to make sure the sisters were safe. It seemed to be working. They hadn't had an incident on the farm since the ugly black words had appeared on the barn a week and a half ago. Lord willing, the troublemakers had given up, or Dan, Luke, and Josiah had scared them away. Whatever the reason, they were all beginning to feel a little better, even Rose. With Josiah close by, she could almost believe that nothing bad would ever happen to her again. She could almost believe that every *gute* thing in life was coming her way.

Rose sat next to Lily on the step. "In less than three weeks, you won't have to sleep here anymore, Dan." She smiled when she said it, even though she felt the sting of the loss as if it had already happened.

Dan and Lily would be living in Dan's *mammi*'s old house in town, and Luke and Poppy were going to stay in the *dawdi haus* attached to Luke's parents' home. They wouldn't be far, but things would never be the same.

Dan frowned. "Luke, Josiah, or I will still be here every night. We won't stop caring about you just because we're married."

"What will you do when it gets cold?"

Lily put her arm around Rose's shoulders. "We'll cross that bridge when we come to it."

"I'm hoping whoever it is will think it's too cold to make trouble. Wouldn't it be nice if they moved to Florida? Or, Lord willing, we will find out who it is before the snow comes."

Rose simply nodded. She shouldn't have brought it up. It only upset her when she thought about the possibilities. Rose slipped her hand into her apron pocket and fingered the photo of her *mater* she had kept there ever since Josiah had given it to her. At least a part of herself had been returned. She could take comfort in that. "I came out to look for Leonard Nimoy. She's not in her usual spot tormenting Farrah Fawcett."

"She followed me to the honey house earlier when I took more jars out there," Lily said. "Maybe I accidentally shut her in."

Dan leaned back on his hands. "More jars? You must be expecting to pull a lot of honey."

"The supers are heavy." Rose laced her fingers together around her knees. "It's been a *gute* year."

"I should build another honey extractor," Dan said. "It will take four or five days to pull all that honey."

Lily nodded. "Carole will buy all the honey we want to sell her, and she's paying us twenty-five cents more per pint than last time."

Paul Glick used to buy their honey for a fraction of what Carole Parker paid them. Rose felt almost rich with the amount of money that came in. "We'll have more next year with two more hives in Josiah's pumpkins. Think of all the cat food Aunt Bitsy can buy with the honey money." Or the fireworks. Aunt Bitsy was planning on setting off fireworks at the wedding, but she was keeping it a secret from Lily and Dan.

Dan grinned. "Maybe Ashley and Griff would like to help with the honey. Griff is getting to be downright friendly. I'm glad

Ashley thinks Amish people are cute."

Rose laughed. "Ashley is very sweet, Dan Kanagy. Don't say anything against her."

Dan raised his hands in surrender. "I agree with you, but it doesn't do anything for my confidence to be called cute."

Last Thursday, Rose had organized her sisters and their fiancés to help out on Josiah's farm until he was back on his feet. She wasn't quite sure how it had happened, but Ashley and Griff had shown up at Josiah's place the following Saturday to lend a hand. Griff wasn't much help in the pumpkins because he was afraid to pull up anything in case it was a pumpkin plant, but he didn't do any harm either so they didn't mind his hanging around. Ashley picked up on the milking as if she were a farmer's daughter, and she was very good at mucking out the barn, even in her flip-flops.

Rose stood and skipped down the porch steps. "I'm going to look for Leonard Nimoy in the honey house."

"I'm sorry if I accidentally shut her in there."

"It's getting dark," Dan said.

Rose pulled a small flashlight from her apron pocket. "You can see me from the porch. Keep an eye out until I come back."

"If Leonard Nimoy isn't in the honey

house, try by the chicken coop. She sometimes likes to stalk the chickens," Lily said.

"Hurry back," Dan said. "Josiah said he might come by yet."

Rose's heart jumped for joy. "He did?"

Dan grinned. "I supposed there's no 'might' about it. A team of horses couldn't do much to keep him away."

With that happy news, Rose turned and strolled down the lane. She turned on her flashlight, though she really didn't need it. It wasn't that dark yet, but she always felt a little more secure with a light and brave enough to walk to the honey house and back by herself. Of course, Dan and Lily were close by, but still, it was a big step for Rose.

The gravel crunched under her feet as she strolled to the honey house, pointing her flashlight first to one side of the lane and then the other. "Here, kitty kitty. Here, Leonard Nimoy. The cat food looks wonderful-*gute* tonight."

She opened the honey house door and stopped dead in her tracks as her heart lodged in her throat. A young man with straggly hair under a baseball cap stood in the darkened room with an empty glass jar in each hand. Broken glass lay at his feet.

Her flashlight slipped from her fingers as she backed away rapidly. Instead of finding the door, she came up against something hard and unyielding that knocked the wind out of her. The wall turned out to be another young man, not tall but not inclined to be knocked over. She gasped as he yanked her back against his chest and rammed his hand over her mouth. He pressed so hard that her teeth cut against the inside of her lips.

The one holding the jars backed all the way to the wall as if he'd been shoved, obviously as surprised to see her as she was to see him. Rose couldn't see much by the light of her dropped flashlight, but he must have been an *Englischer.* He wore a baseball cap and blue jeans. "Let's get out of here, Jethro," he hissed.

Jethro, the boy behind Rose, squeezed her tighter. She winced but didn't struggle. Terror made her limbs weak, and she couldn't do anything but stay upright. "She'll give us away."

"Then let's just run. Now. We can run faster than she can, and we have a car." As strange as it was at a time like this, the *Englischer* tiptoed over the shards of glass and set the unbroken jars gently back on the shelf. "Come on. Let's go."

"Wait a minute," Jethro said. Rose squeaked as he tore the bandanna from her hair and pressed his hand into her face so she would turn her head. "Which one are you?" he said. "Buddy, grab the flashlight."

The *Englischer* snatched Rose's flashlight from the floor and shined it in Rose's face. Jethro took his hand from her mouth and squeezed her cheeks until she winced in pain. She was too frightened to cry out, and no one at the house would hear her weak attempt anyway. He got a *gute* look at her, and she got a *gute* look at him.

Fright tore through her. It was dark, and she hadn't seen him for thirteen years, but she was fairly sure that LaWayne Zook's youngest son was the one who held her fast. Dan had said that LaWayne's wife had left the church, but Jethro wore a traditional Amish straw hat, a dark shirt, and suspenders. He couldn't have been more than seventeen or eighteen, but he was solid like LaWayne and his expression was one of pure hatred.

"Rose," he growled, slapping his hand back over her mouth. "This is the one, Buddy."

Buddy recoiled in shock, almost as if he wished Rose had not walked into the honey house. "Let's go, Jethro. We've done enough. You've had your revenge. Let's get out of here."

"We're not going until I show her what she's done. She's going to see."

"What do you mean, Jethro? You can't show her anything."

Rose thought she might pass out from the sheer force of her blood racing through her veins. She had never felt such pure terror before. How she wished she were like Poppy, who would have fought her way out of the honey house with her bare hands, or even Lily, who would have been able to struggle free and run away. But Rose was helpless, as helpless as the seven-year-old girl who had been shoved out of the hay-mow. As helpless as the five-year-old praying for *Gotte* to send her parents back.

The only thing she did well was cry, but her tears would do her no good. They never had. She was useless.

"We're taking her to Wallsby," Jethro said.

Buddy's expression flooded with confusion and panic. "Wha . . . right now?"

Jethro nodded. "I want her to see."

Buddy pressed his palm against his forehead and nearly made his hat fall off. "Are you crazy? That's kidnapping, Jethro. You're crazy." He pointed toward the door. "They're sitting out on the porch. They'll see us."

Jethro didn't hesitate. He shoved Rose

farther into the room. "We go out the window."

Buddy seemed almost more panicked than Rose was. He walked backward as he panted for air. "No, Jethro. This is crazy. We'll get arrested."

"Open the window. We can crawl out."

With his eyes flashing in alarm, Buddy opened the window on the side of the honey house away from the porch where Dan and Lily sat. Leaving the flashlight on one of the shelves, he scooted the table beneath the window, climbed onto it, and kicked out the screen. Then he went out the window feet first.

"Get up there," Jethro said, shoving Rose toward the table with his hand still over her mouth. "Don't make a sound or you'll be sorry."

Rose couldn't have made a sound if she wanted to. It was all she could do to stay upright.

Something small and orange dropped from one of the honey shelves near the window and landed on Jethro's shoulder. In his surprise, Jethro yanked his arm up and snapped Rose's head back against him. Rose heard a hiss and a growl as Leonard Nimoy dug her little claws into Jethro's skin. He momentarily released Rose and snatched the kitten from his arm. Leonard Nimoy didn't go quietly. She left eight long and bleeding claw marks.

"Don't hurt her!" Rose screamed, finally finding her voice.

Jethro set Leonard Nimoy on the ground and pressed his hand against Rose's mouth. "Shut up, Rose. Shut up."

Rose could see the kitten out of the corner of her eye as she tried to climb up the shelf again. She was preparing for another attack.

Jethro shoved Rose toward the window once more. "Get up there."

She couldn't do it. Her legs felt like jelly. For sure and certain, she'd end up in a heap.

When he saw she wouldn't move, Jethro put his mouth up against her ear. "Get up there or the next person who comes through that door is getting smacked in the head."

Terror clamped an icy hand around Rose's throat as she heard the thud of horse hooves and the crunch of buggy wheels against gravel outside. The faint sound of off-tune singing accompanied the buggy's approach. Josiah! He was coming up the lane in his courting buggy. She had to get Jethro away from here, and the only way to do that was to get out with him.

With Jethro's not-too-gentle shove, she found the strength to pull herself onto the

362

table and climb out the window. Buddy was on the other side to grab her hand and soften her landing. Jethro followed close behind.

"Stay quiet," he said, "or you'll get hurt." He hooked his arm around her waist and half dragged, half carried her across the clover field and deeper into the night.

She felt both profound relief and a sense of dread darker than she could have ever imagined.

She had saved the ones she loved most in the whole world.

Would anyone save her?

Josiah had started humming a tune the minute he'd hitched up his buggy. The humming had turned into whistling about halfway here. The whistling had turned into singing on the last mile of his journey. He had probably disturbed a lot of birds and livestock that were trying to sleep, but he was too happy to keep it to himself. He was in love with Rose Christner, and he thought maybe she loved him too. He wanted to share his *gute* news with everyone.

Thanks to Rose, he was mostly healed, but singing made him cough, so he would sing a song, take a break to cough, and then sing another one.

Because she had the kindest heart in the world, Rose had organized Bitsy and her sisters and Dan and Luke to help on Josiah's farm while he recovered. She hadn't allowed him to lift a finger for four whole days, even when he had started feeling better. He hated being down in bed like that, but Rose had cooked him dinner every night and made him a cake or a pie or some other delectable dessert to help him feel better. He'd probably gained ten pounds lying around.

Suvie, who usually took very *gute* care of him, had been noticeably absent since he'd gotten sick. He was grateful he got to spend time with Rose instead, which was probably the reason Suvie had stayed away. He'd have to thank her for her neglect.

Even Ashley and Griff had come to help with chores on Saturday. How Rose had gone from being terrified of Griff to teaching him how to weed pumpkins was a miracle. *Gotte* always knew that Griff could change. Maybe everybody else just needed to see it to believe it.

The best news of all was that Josiah had been able to track down the phone number for LaWayne's ex-wife today. She lived in Shawano, not ten miles from Bienenstock with her younger children and her new husband. Josiah planned on calling her tomorrow. Maybe this whole thing could be settled before the next *gmay.*

A thrill of anticipation traveled up his spine. He had it all planned out. As soon as Rose was out of danger, he'd buy a case of duct tape and come over every week to fix something for Bitsy. Then, after three or four months, he would ask Rose if he could court her. Then three or four months later, he'd start bringing over tubes of paint. A few months after that, he'd beg her to marry him, and Lord willing, she'd say yes. He'd be the happiest boy in the world.

It would just about kill him to go so slow — he was passionately in love, after all — but he wouldn't do anything that might jeopardize his chances with her. He loved her. Waiting another year or two would be a small price to pay if he could be with Rose forever.

Lily and Dan sat on the porch holding hands under the light of a lantern. A pang of jealousy hit him like a snowball to the chest. He wanted to sit out on the porch and hold hands with Rose something wonderful, but that wasn't in his plan until month six. *Oy,* anyhow, how could he bear to wait?

He tamped down his longing and tried to be grateful for what he did have. Rose had allowed him back onto the farm, and he would see her tonight. He was blessed indeed.

He jumped from his buggy and strode across the flagstones. "Is Rose inside?"

"*Gute* evening to you too," Dan said, looking genuinely happy to see him. He and Dan had gotten closer in the last few months, painting barn doors in the middle of the night together, keeping an eye out for troublemakers, and courting Christner *schwesters.*

"Sorry," Josiah said. "Good evening to you. Is Rose inside?"

Dan laughed. "Why waste time with your best friend when you can be with a pretty girl?"

Josiah nodded. "*Jah.* That's what I'm thinking."

Lily's eyes sparkled with amusement. "You just missed her. She went to the honey house to find Leonard Nimoy."

"By herself?"

"*Jah,*" Lily said. "She's getting braver all the time."

Wonderful-*gute.* Maybe he could move his schedule up a little. If Rose was willing to walk to the honey house by herself in the gathering darkness, maybe she'd soon be accepting tubes of paint without reservation. "I'll go get her," he said, already halfway down the lane.

"If she's not there, she was going to look behind the barn," Dan called.

Josiah frowned. The honey house was one thing. Behind the barn was quite another. It was out of sight of the house, and too many bad things had happened there. He didn't want Rose behind the barn by herself, whether she was brave enough or not.

He jogged to the honey house and opened the door. "Rose?" It was too dark to see much, but she obviously wasn't there. A twinge of urgency stuck him like a pin. She'd gone behind the barn. Picking up his pace, he covered the distance between the honey house and the barn in a matter of seconds. The chickens had already gone to roost in the coop, and Rose wasn't there. Neither was Leonard Nimoy.

His heart skipped a beat. *Don't panic. Maybe he missed her on her way back to the house.* He ran to the front of the barn and called to Dan as he crossed the flagstones. "Did she come back? Did you see her?"

Dan and Lily both stood up. "What do you mean?" Lily said.

"I can't find her."

Lily marched down the steps. "What do you mean, you can't find her? She went to the honey house not five minutes ago."

Dan grabbed the lantern from the hook on the porch, and without another word, the three of them raced to the honey house. Josiah outstripped Lily and Dan by several yards. Maybe she was in the honey house after all, and he'd somehow missed her.

He opened the door. "Rose?" Nothing but darkness and silence replied.

Dan finally caught up with the lantern and held it aloft so they could get a better look. Broken glass on the floor sparkled in the lamplight like so many fallen stars. A table had been moved to beneath the wide-open window to their left, and a small flashlight sat on it, still glowing.

Lily gasped. "That's Rose's flashlight. I don't understand. She was just here."

Josiah's heart skipped a beat when he heard a faint squeak to his left. Leonard Nimoy sat on one of the shelves shivering like the last leaf on the tree. "Leonard Nimoy!" Josiah picked up the kitten and cradled her in his arms. "Leonard Nimoy, do you know what happened to Rose?"

Leonard mewed mournfully and buried her head against Josiah's shirt.

Josiah handed the kitten to Lily and took the lantern from Dan. He shined it in the direction of the window. There was a smear of blood on the edge of the table and one on the windowsill.

Sharp, hard, icy fear stabbed Josiah in the chest. He thought he might be sick.

Dan leaned his head out the window. "They must have climbed out this way."

Dan didn't need to explain who "they" were. They wanted revenge on Rose, and now they had her.

"They can't have been gone long," Josiah said, willing his shaking legs to move. With the lantern still grasped tightly in his fist, he ran out of the honey house and tore across the fields behind it. He didn't have time to wait for Lily and Dan. Hadn't Jack Willis told him that he'd seen the troublemakers' car parked behind the Christners' property a few weeks ago?

"Dear Heavenly *Fater,*" he prayed. "I'll do anything. I'll give anything. Please don't let them hurt my Rose."

He felt like he was in one of his dreams where he ran and ran and never got anywhere. The field seemed a hundred miles long with no end in sight. He heard Dan's heavy footsteps behind him, but couldn't begin to guess if Lily had followed.

He leaped over the pasture fence, sprinted through the stand of trees that marked the edge of the Christners' property, and came to a paved road where he could see four or five houses in the gathering darkness. There were no rusty brown cars parked on the road. There were no cars at all. A hundred yards ahead, he could see taillights of a car, but he had no way to know if that was the car he was looking for or if Rose was inside.

Completely spent, he fell to his knees on the pavement and yelled his frustration to the sky. His voice echoed off the house across the street and came back to him.

Dan emerged from the trees and gazed down the road. "Oh no," he said, swiping his hand across his mouth.

Josiah clawed his way out of the depths and got to his feet. He'd be no good to Rose if he couldn't keep himself together.

"What do we do now?" Dan said.

"Where's Lily?"

"She ran to the house to tell Bitsy and Poppy."

A dark figure appeared from behind a tree across the road. Josiah held his breath and lifted the lantern higher. Whoever it was turned on his phone flashlight and shined it in Josiah's face. "Is that you, Joe?"

Josiah recognized the sticky-outy ears and the shaggy black hair before the light fell on Jack Willis's face and his wild, frightened expression.

"It's me," Josiah said. "Can you help us, Jack? They've kidnapped Rose."

Jack nodded. "I know. I saw them."

"You did? Which way?"

Jack pointed south. "But you won't catch them. They drove out of here like the police were chasing 'em."

Josiah tried to keep his head. "Did you get a license plate number or anything?"

"Remember how you told me to keep an eye out for that car?"

"Jah."

"I came outside like ten minutes ago and there it was, parked right here, right where I saw it before. It wasn't locked, so I climbed in and opened the glove box." He shoved his hand in his pocket and pulled out a crinkled piece of paper. "I copied down the registration information. I know where they live."

Josiah could have given Jack a hug. *"Ach, du lieva."*

"I got out of the car and was walking across the street when they came running through the trees. It was two of them, and the one guy was dragging an Amish girl. I could tell she didn't want to go with them, but I didn't know what to do to stop them. I was afraid they'd run me over. I'm sorry."

"You wouldn't have been able to stop

371

them," Josiah said, his gut a pit of rocks. "And you might have gotten hurt."

"I got their address," Jack said, handing Josiah the paper. "They live in Shawano, but I don't have a car to take you there."

"Can I borrow your phone?" Josiah asked. Jack handed his phone to Josiah, who handed it to Dan. "Do you remember that number?"

Dan's face briefly clouded with confusion before he caught his breath and nodded. He pressed the numbers on the screen and handed the phone to Josiah, who prayed with all his might. If she didn't answer, he didn't know what he'd do.

Finally, thankfully, a voice on the other end. "Hello?"

"Hello, Ashley?" Josiah said. "I need your help."

CHAPTER SEVENTEEN

Foam rubber protruded from several cracks in the vinyl in the backseat of Buddy's filthy car. Rose sat on one side of the backseat with her back pressed against the door, her arms clamped tightly around her waist and her feet tucked underneath her in as small a ball as possible. Jethro sat in back with her, probably to be sure she didn't decide to open the door and hurl herself out of the moving car. At this point, she was almost desperate enough to do it.

She had never in her life been able to keep herself from crying when she was upset. And even though she yearned with all her heart that she could stop, the tears slid down her cheeks like rainwater against a window. She tried her best to cry silently, but an occasional whimper came out of her mouth that made Jethro all the angrier.

"Shut up," he said, when an involuntary sob escaped her lips. "You're getting on my nerves."

Rose pulled her arms tighter around herself and tried to shrink to nothing. What was going to happen to her? Did Jethro want her dead or in pain? Was he planning on doing something unspeakable to her in the dark of the night? She shuddered down to her toes as the tears dripped down her face.

How she wished Josiah were here. He would hold her close and make everything all better. She never felt so happy as when she was with him.

They'd been in the car for nearly a half an hour, and Rose had no idea where they were taking her. For the first ten minutes of the trip, Buddy and Jethro had yelled at each other because Buddy wanted to let Rose go and Jethro wouldn't hear it. Buddy was probably about Jethro's age, but he seemed younger, anxious and unsure about everything. He was beside himself, telling Jethro that they'd get arrested for kidnapping, while Jethro yelled at Buddy to shut up and drive the car. Buddy's phone wouldn't stop ringing, and over and over again, Jethro yelled at him to turn it off.

"I can't," Buddy whined. "My mom gets really mad when I turn off my phone. She'll take it away."

Jethro glanced out the back window, as if he was sure the police were right behind them. Then he closed his eyes and massaged his forehead.

Rose pressed her lips together. Jethro's hands shook, and beads of sweat formed on his upper lip. He was nervous. *Nae,* he was frightened. She furrowed her brow. At least as frightened as she was.

How could that be?

She studied his face and tried to remember the little boy she'd known thirteen years ago. Jethro's sister Mary Beth and Rose had been seven years old, and Jethro had been two years younger. He hadn't been one of those pesky little brothers who teased or pulled hair or called his sister names. He'd had a sweet, timid disposition and always asked very nicely if he could play house with them. Rose and Mary Beth would often call upon Jethro to kill spiders or get them drinks of water. He would happily do whatever they wanted just so he could be near them. When they played with their dolls, Jethro would make believe he was the *fater* with a stick for a hunting rifle. He liked to march around the barn and pretend to shoot wild animals that meant harm to the babies inside. Mary Beth had told Rose that their *dat* had a hunting rifle, and he some-

375

times took Jethro with him on the deer hunt.

How his heart must have broken when his *dat* went to prison! No matter how cruel or abusive his *dat* had been, Jethro would have remembered the *gute* times and been devastated when his *dat* was ripped from the family.

Guilt slammed into Rose and made her cry all the harder. If it hadn't been for her, Jethro would have grown up with a *fater.*

She clamped her eyes shut and heard Josiah's voice in her head. He would not let her blame herself for LaWayne's drinking or Martha's choice to leave her husband. Because of Josiah, Rose had begun to see things differently. Maybe she wasn't responsible for the broken arm or LaWayne's uncontrollable temper or the broken family. Whatever part she had played, Josiah said *Gotte* had forgiven her. And maybe, just maybe, in a small way, she had helped save LaWayne's children from suffering at the hand of one who was supposed to love them.

She looked at Jethro again and saw that little boy, so sad, so wounded, unable to understand the consequences of his *dat*'s choices. Of course he would look for someone to blame. Of course Rose was a likely choice.

Rose wiped the tears from her face. She

couldn't be brave like Poppy or clever like Lily, but she could be kind, like her *mater* had been. Maybe she didn't want to be anyone else.

Buddy turned off the highway onto a little country road that looked as if it led to a cornfield. The road curved sharply to the left, then to the right. After a few hundred feet, Buddy stopped the car. Rose couldn't see much out the window, but she knew exactly where they were.

Buddy picked up his phone. "We can't stay here very long. My mom has called me like eight times. She's already gonna be mad."

"All right," Jethro growled. "Just give me a few minutes." With a flashlight in one hand, he got out of the car and reached in to pull Rose out his side. He grabbed her wrist and yanked hard.

"Please don't pull me," she said, in a voice of perfect calm. "I can walk. I want you to show me."

He narrowed his eyes in suspicion, but he let go of her hand and let her slide out of the car without touching her. "We'll be back soon," Jethro told Buddy, and Rose felt a small sense of relief.

He'd said "we," which meant that he probably didn't mean to murder her and leave her body in the Amish cemetery. She said a silent prayer of thanks. Bitsy and her sisters would be very sad if she died. And maybe Josiah would too. Maybe he'd miss her quite a bit. She'd miss him more than words could express.

Jethro clamped his fingers around Rose's arm and pulled her up a gentle hill to a small gravestone in the middle of the cemetery. He yanked her to a stop and shoved her to kneel on the ground in front of it. "You killed him," he said.

A few weeks ago, Rose might have agreed with him, but she didn't believe it anymore. Josiah was the best soul she had ever known, and he said she wasn't responsible.

"I'm sorry," she said. And she was. Sorry for a confused little boy. Sorry for a terrified *mater.* Sorry for a *fater* who couldn't control his temper or his addictions and left destruction in his wake.

"He was in prison for three years. Three years and my *mamm* didn't want to wait. As soon as the police took him away, she packed up our things and moved us out. She filed for divorce. She got herself excommunicated, all because you wanted revenge."

Did he really think a seven-year-old could comprehend revenge?

Jethro paced back and forth behind Rose, his voice rising in agitation with every word. "When he got out of prison, Mamm wouldn't take him back. I wanted my *dat,* and Mamm locked him out of the house. She filed a protective order against him. A protective order! Against her own husband."

"I'm sorry," was all Rose could say.

Jethro quit pacing and stationed himself to Rose's right. He folded his arms and glared at her. "Mary Beth didn't want our way of life. She's going to college. My *mamm* doesn't live Plain anymore either. I wanted to be Amish. Mamm couldn't see that salvation comes only in living a Plain life. She's going to hell. They're all going to hell." He took off his hat and ran his fingers through his hair. "Dat returned to Wallsby after prison, but the community never really accepted him because Mamm had divorced him. They couldn't understand that it was her fault. And yours. All yours, Rose Christner. The courts forced Mamm to let us visit Dat, but it wasn't the same."

He knelt down next to her and yelled in her face. "You stole my *dat* from me. He and Mamm would still be together if you hadn't testified. He would have stopped drinking. I know he would have."

Rose held her breath, expecting him to

strike her or shove her or slap her face. He didn't even touch her. She turned to face him, unable to hear anything else but her heart pounding in her ears. If Jethro wanted to punish someone for his *dat*'s death, could she muster the courage to offer herself?

"You brought me here to see your *fater*'s grave, to make me feel sorry. I am sorry. Very sorry," she said, sounding as weak as she felt.

He stood up and kicked the grass at his feet. "You should be."

"If . . . if you think it will make things right, I want you to take your revenge out on me." With trembling limbs, she stood, bowed her head, and laced her fingers together. "Strike me as many times as you think will make up for what you lost."

Her words seemed to shock him to the core. The lines on his face became hard and sharp, as if someone had slashed at him with a pocketknife. "Strike you? What are you saying?" He wrapped his arms around his head as if he were trying to protect his face. "You think I would hit you? You think I would hurt anyone like that and send myself to hell?" He paced back and forth as if he were in a cage and jabbed his finger in her direction. "I'm not like that, Rose Christner. I would never be like that."

Rose thought she might faint with relief. Did he really mean not to hurt her? She couldn't see his face well by the flashlight on the ground, but maybe there was more of that sweet little boy left than she had imagined.

She thought back to the fire behind the honey house. Aunt Bitsy had said whoever set the fire hadn't wanted to actually burn down the honey house. Why hadn't Jethro killed the chickens when he'd chopped up their chicken coop? Why had he merely cut off Queenie's tail instead of permanently docking it? She glanced at the eight scratches from Leonard Nimoy on his forearm. After the kitten had attacked him, Jethro had placed her on the ground as gently as a mother cat would have done.

Her heart started beating again for what felt like the first time in half an hour. Jethro Zook meant her no harm.

Jethro meant her no harm.

He wanted to scare her and make her sorry for what she'd done, but he didn't want to hurt her. Deep down, he had a *gute* heart. A broken, confused, *gute* heart.

Suddenly, she didn't feel frightened of him anymore, only profoundly sad for the little boy who had an image of a *fater* that had never been real — and for the *fater* who had wasted his life because he couldn't see past a bottle of alcohol.

She let the tears flow freely down her face. "*Nae.* I can see that you would never raise a hand to me. Or anyone."

"I am not . . . I am not . . ."

"Like your *fater,*" she said.

Jethro moaned like a wounded animal. "He didn't know what he was doing. No one gave him a chance."

She reached out and took his hand. "I'm so sorry."

His eyes filled with confusion, and she thought he might yank his hand from her grasp. Instead, he studied her face for a minute and then seemed to surrender whatever resistance he had left. Keeping his hand in hers, they sat down together in front of his *fater*'s gravestone, and wept.

She held on tight and let him cry. Everyone needed a chance to grieve.

Jethro pulled his hand away and clenched his fists. "He hit me, you know."

"*Jah.* I know."

"He hit all of us when he was drunk. But he could have changed if everyone had just given him a chance."

"Jethro," she whispered. "Do you think your *mater* was trying to protect you and Mary Beth and your other siblings when she left him?"

He lifted his chin and sniffed back the tears. "He would have changed. If she hadn't left, he would have changed."

"But maybe your *mamm* couldn't bear to see one more of her precious children be hurt. Maybe if it had been only her life she was choosing for, she might have stayed. But what if she didn't think it was worth sacrificing her children to give your *dat* another chance? Would you have wanted to see him hit Mary Beth one more time?"

He turned his head and stared off into the night. "*Nae*. But if he'd had another chance, he wouldn't have gone to hell. I would have taken all the beatings in the world if it meant my *dat* didn't go to hell."

"Jesus has already taken all the beatings so you don't have to." She laid a hand on his shoulder. "Aunt Bitsy was an *Englischer* for many years. She says that addictions are very hard to overcome. Jesus paid a high price for your *dat*'s soul. I don't think He would cast off something so precious without a second thought. There is hope for your *dat* as there is hope for all sinners — through Jesus."

"At the hospital right before he died, he told me he was sorry for what he'd done, but the bishop says we don't believe in deathbed repentance."

"I think *Gotte* is happy when the lost sheep come home, whether sooner or later," Rose said. "Remember the parable of the laborers in *Gotte*'s vineyard? No matter how late in the day, all laborers will receive the same reward."

To her surprise, he laid his head on her shoulder like a child might do with his mother. "I am sorry, Rose. I have held so much anger in my heart for my *dat* and my *mamm* and even myself. I blamed you because it was easier to hate you than to hate my *dat*. It is wicked to hate your parents. When my *dat* died, I punished you and your beehives and your chicken coop. Poppy almost lost her hand."

She put her arm around him. "I forgive you, and I hope you will forgive me for the pain I've caused."

He laughed bitterly. "I hurt myself by holding on to my anger. I wish it hadn't taken me thirteen years and a kidnapping to see it."

Rose patted him on the shoulder. "Who says it was a kidnapping?"

Jethro lifted his head from her shoulder. "I'm sorry for scaring you. I'm sorry for scaring your sisters and your *aendi*."

"I forgive you, Jethro."

He furrowed his brow. "They are probably worried sick about you." He stood and offered his hand. "We need to get you home."

"Those scratches look like they hurt. Maybe on the way we could find a bandage."

He glanced at his arm and frowned. "That is one brave kitten." He helped her to her feet, and when he released her hand, Rose felt the ever-present fear leave her like a shawl falling from her shoulders. She gasped in surprise.

CHAPTER EIGHTEEN

Josiah hadn't stopped praying since he'd climbed into Ashley's truck. Every word was from the deepest, most tortured part of his soul. *Lord, let Rose be all right. Bring her home to us. Please don't let them hurt her.* Josiah's own desires were the hardest thing to surrender, but if he wanted *Gotte* to hear him, he had to be willing to lose it all. *Thy will be done.*

That thought just about choked him. What if it was *Gotte*'s will that Josiah lose Rose?

He would never breathe again. Surely *Gotte* must know that.

He was crammed in the backseat of Ashley's truck with his head bowed and his arms propped on his knees, rocking back and forth in the small space because anxiety made it impossible for him to be still. If he didn't keep moving, he would explode or disintegrate. He couldn't let himself do either.

Please, Heavenly Father, help us find her. I would be lost without my Rose.

Sweat beaded on his forehead even though Ashley had the air conditioner turned up full blast. His heart crashed against his chest like violent waves on the beach, each beat more painful than the last.

Ashley, Griff, and Dan sat in the front seat. Ashley drove too slowly, Griff talked on his phone, and Dan tried to decipher the map on Ashley's phone. Since the Amish didn't use cell phones, Dan wasn't quite sure what to do to make the map bigger or make the voice louder or scroll down the page. Josiah couldn't help him. He was as useless at phones as Dan was.

"Lightly touch your finger on the screen and slide it up," Ashley said, trying to give Dan instructions while keeping an eye on the road. "No, if you touch too hard it will take you to another screen."

To his credit, Dan didn't give up. Rose needed them. He seemed determined to figure out the phone or die trying.

"The map doesn't really matter," Ashley said. "I think we're still going the right way."

"Go faster, Ashley," Griff said, half listening on his phone.

"I can't. If I get another ticket, I'll lose my license."

Josiah nearly growled in frustration, even though he knew how ungrateful he was being. If it weren't for Ashley, he would be sitting at home going insane with worry. Right now, Ashley was the answer to many prayers.

"How are you doing back there, Joe?" Ashley said.

Josiah raised his head and made eye contact with Dan. Dan's lips were drawn together in a tense frown, and he looked as pale as a snowstorm. "We're going to find her. They're not far ahead of us."

Josiah couldn't manage any kind of a reply. Dan was trying to help him feel better, but it was an impossible task. The only thing that would make him feel better was when they found that car with Rose unharmed inside.

Griff lowered the phone from his mouth. "She says go south on 110."

"I thought you said north," Ashley said. "Dan, what does the map say?"

"I don't know," Dan said, staring at the phone in complete confusion.

Griff listened to the person on the other end of the phone. "She says go south. Toward Marion."

Ashley turned left onto a small town road. They drove a few blocks before the houses thinned out and gave way to rolling farm-land.

"Three more miles," Griff said.

"On this road?"

Griff's lips drooped into a sullen frown. "She just says three miles. Everybody's talking at me at once."

Ashley patted Griff's leg. "You're doing great with the navigation."

Griff seemed to perk up. "Thanks. It's hard over the phone." It sounded like someone on the other end was screaming with excitement. "What?" Griff said. "I can't understand you." He held perfectly still and listened carefully. "Okay. I'll tell them." He pulled the phone from his ear. "She knows where they went. There's an Amish cemetery. Turn right! Turn right!" he yelled.

It didn't even feel like Ashley hit the brakes. She took the turn and her tires squealed as if they were being murdered. Even though he was buckled in, Josiah was tossed around like a pebble in the river.

When he righted himself, he trained his gaze out the window.

His heart stopped altogether. Up ahead, an old brown car with a rusted bumper was parked along the side of the road. "There it is!"

Ashley drove right up behind the car and slammed on her brakes. Dan and Griff jumped out of the truck, and Josiah practically leaped over the seat in an attempt to get out. Even being the last out of the truck, he was the first to the car. Dan handed him a flashlight, and he shone it in the window. Someone sat in the driver's seat, but it didn't look as if anyone else was in the car.

Josiah wrenched open the front door. A boy, probably just old enough to drive, sat in the driver's seat with his eyes closed and a pair of saucer-sized earphones clamped to his head. Josiah grabbed the boy's T-shirt sleeve and yanked hard.

The boy's eyes flew open, and he ripped the earphones from his head. His eyes widened in alarm as he took a good look at Josiah's face. "Whoa, man," he said, raising his hands and pressing his back against his seat. "Whoa, don't hurt me."

"Where is she?" Josiah growled. When the boy didn't immediately answer, he pulled harder on his T-shirt.

"I told him not to do it, but he wouldn't listen."

Josiah was so angry and so terrified, he thought he might burst into flames. "Where is Rose?"

The boy pointed up an incline to his left.

"He took her up there to his dad's grave."

With flashlight in hand, Josiah bolted in the direction the boy had pointed without waiting for Dan or anyone else to follow. He sprinted up the incline and didn't slow his pace even when his lungs screamed at him to slow down. He turned off his flashlight before he got to the top and slipped behind a tree.

His heart stopped as he peeked around the tree and saw a weak light about a hundred feet ahead. Rose's white-yellow hair seemed to shine in the dim light, as a beacon for all of Josiah's hopes and dreams.

She was alive!

Denki, Gotte.

The other kidnapper was with her, but he wasn't touching her. Josiah's pulse hummed with tension. If the boy knew Josiah was coming, he might try to hurt Rose or escape before Josiah could get to her. He had to separate the kidnapper from Rose before he had a chance to hurt her.

Hoping the darkness would hide his approach, Josiah ran at the boy with all his might. Lowering his shoulder, he rammed into the boy's gut, sending both of them to the ground with Josiah on top. Rose screamed. The kidnapper dropped his flashlight and grunted as he met the ground.

Josiah pressed his knee into the boy's stomach and grabbed onto the collar of his shirt with both hands.

"Run, Rose," he yelled. "Dan is down the hill." The kidnapper didn't struggle as Josiah pressed his fists into the boy's chest and yelled at him. "What have you done? What have you done?"

There was a feather-soft touch on his shoulder, so light he almost didn't notice it. "Josiah," Rose said, her voice so gentle and sweet that he melted at the sound of it. "Josiah, look at me."

He relaxed his grip on the boy's shirt and turned to see Rose standing there holding the kidnapper's flashlight. Had there ever been a more beautiful, soul-healing sight?

"You're here," she said, "and I'm safe."

Nothing else mattered. Not the boy sprawled out on the ground, not revenge, not the terror he'd put them through.

Josiah released the boy's collar and stood up. He didn't even know if she wanted him, but he couldn't hold himself back. He gathered Rose in his arms, pressed his lips to her golden hair, and wept.

Dan was suddenly there. Out of the corner of his eye, Josiah saw him help the stranger from the ground and pull him several steps away. Josiah didn't care about the kidnapper anymore. He'd let Dan handle whatever came next. Josiah had Rose. That was all that mattered.

Rose could surely sense the great, silent sobs that wracked his body and feel the wet tears that slid down his face and into her hair. She reached up and laid her hand on his cheek. "Hush," she said. "All is well. We have nothing to fear from Jethro Zook."

He wrapped his hand around her wrist and kissed her palm. "Did he hurt you?"

"*Nae,*" she said, even as he felt her trembling in his embrace. "Is Leonard Nimoy all right?"

Josiah managed a weak smile. "Bitsy has probably given her a whole bowl of cream."

"I was worried about her."

Josiah tightened an arm around her shoulder. "*Cum.* The truck is just down the hill."

Rose took his hand and clung to it as she pulled him in the other direction, toward Jethro and Dan. She laid a hand on Jethro's arm. "I hope you find the peace that *Gotte* wants to give you."

Jethro frowned. "I hope so too."

This boy had terrorized Rose for months, threatened her whole family, and had forced her to a graveyard in the middle of the night. How could she manage a kind word for him?

If Josiah lived a thousand years, he would never deserve Rose Christner.

She pulled Josiah back to LaWayne's grave. They stood in silence and looked at it. "I hope LaWayne is at peace," she said.

"Me too." Josiah wrapped his arms around her and wove his fingers into the hair at the base of her neck. "I hope you are at peace."

"*Jah.* I am." She leaned heavily against him. "I'm not afraid anymore, Josiah. I'm not afraid."

He could tell she was completely spent. He tightened his arm around her waist, but even then her steps faltered. Raw emotion made it impossible for him to say more. He tugged her close and scooped her into his arms.

After wrapping her arms around his neck, she buried her face in his shoulder and cried softly. "Take me home, Josiah. I want to go home."

CHAPTER NINETEEN

Rose tied her apron strings in a bow behind her back and tried to comprehend the sheer number of goodies on the butcher-block island. Once word got around that Rose had been kidnapped four days ago, the cakes and pies and cookies had started coming in from all the neighbors, Amish and *Englisch* alike. The Yutzy sisters had brought over a special batch of glazed donuts, Luke's *mamm* had made them a butter-scotch pie, and Ashley's mother had sent them a plate of cookies from Wal-Mart. There were at least two-dozen desserts and loaves of bread sitting on their island.

"This is getting ridiculous," Aunt Bitsy said, planting her hands on her hips. "Do they think if they get us fat we'll be harder to kidnap?"

Lily donned her own apron. "I think it shows how much everyone in the community loves Rose."

"They love all you girls," Aunt Bitsy said. "I think the only family in the *gmayna* who didn't send something over is the Glicks. They're shunning us independently."

Rose leaned against the counter. "What are we going to do with all this food?"

"Let's freeze what will freeze," Aunt Bitsy said. "We can use it for the weddings. Luke's *mamm* says we can use her freezer. And Josiah's sister, Suvie, offered her freezer as well."

Rose's heart sped up. These days, any mention of anyone or anything related to Josiah made her pay attention.

Poppy cut a little piece out of the corner of one of the cakes and popped it into her mouth. "We'll just have to let the boys eat the rest for dinner tonight."

Aunt Bitsy smirked. "Luke could eat most of it by himself."

"We should take a few things to Josiah," Rose said. "He doesn't have a wife to cook for him."

Her sisters and Aunt Bitsy seemed to take a collective pause. They stared at Rose as if waiting for her to say something else. Was her hair tumbling out of her scarf? Did she have flour on her nose? She brushed her hand across her face just to be sure.

The staring lasted a good ten seconds, and

then Lily pulled a box of food storage bags from the drawer. "We could give one of the cakes to Griff and Ashley. I never thought I'd say this in a hundred years, but I am wonderful glad Griff lives just down the lane."

"I'm grateful for Ashley," Poppy said. "That girl is the best thing that ever happened to Griff. I just hope she never realizes that she's way too good for him."

Aunt Bitsy sidled next to Lily and started stuffing freezable cookies in plastic bags. "Yesterday, after we pulled honey, Ashley asked if I would like to start an Amish cooking blog with her."

"What does that mean?" Rose asked.

Aunt Bitsy shrugged. "You write a recipe and put it on the computer. People search for Amish recipes on the Internet, and they see your recipe."

"Ashley wants your recipes?" Lily asked.

"*Jah.* She thinks we would make a *gute* cooking team."

Rose nodded her encouragement. "It sounds like it would be fun, Aunt Bitsy."

"Maybe. But I don't know if Ashley would make a very *gute* partner. She didn't even know that you can buy chocolate chips separate from the cookies. I have a sneaking suspicion she doesn't know how to boil water."

They heard a hiss from the direction of the window seat. Leonard Nimoy was pawing at Farrah Fawcett, trying to get the white cat to play with her.

Rose picked up Leonard Nimoy. "Now, Leonard Nimoy," she said, in her most precious baby voice. "You know Farrah Fawcett doesn't like to be bothered. You have your own soft bed. Don't crowd Farrah Fawcett out of her own cushion."

She placed the kitten on the soft, cuddly cat pillow that Aunt Bitsy had bought Leonard Nimoy as a reward for trying to defend Rose against Jethro Zook.

"We should buy one of those for Jack Willis," Poppy said. "If it weren't for him, we wouldn't have found Buddy's car."

Lily nodded. "Ashley and Griff deserve a pillow too. And Josiah. You should have seen him, Rose."

There was another awkward pause as Lily, Poppy, and Aunt Bitsy stared at her. What? Did they think she didn't remember who Josiah was?

Lily cleared her throat. "He was beside himself, but he still kept his head."

Rose's heart swelled three times as big. Josiah had saved her in more ways than one.

Lily had told her that when they realized Rose was missing, Josiah had raced across the field to try to find her. Jack Willis had given Josiah the information from the car's registration, and Josiah had called Ashley. Ashley had come right over in Griff's truck and had driven Josiah and Dan to Buddy's house in Shawano. When they had explained the situation to Buddy's mom, she had been so mad, Dan said he sort of feared for poor Buddy's life. Buddy's mom had been able to track down Buddy and Jethro using the GPS on Buddy's phone, and she had communicated Buddy's location over the phone to Griff, who in turn had given Ashley directions while she drove.

Poppy stuck out her lower lip in a mock pout. "I missed the whole thing."

"I'm sure Luke was happy about that," Lily said. "Even with your hand in a cast, you would have ended up in a fistfight with Jethro Zook."

"We might have to buy Buddy a pillow too," Rose said. "He didn't want anything to do with Jethro's plan to take me to the cemetery."

Aunt Bitsy picked up the box of plastic bags and shook it at no one in particular. "I'm not buying Buddy a cushion until he proves himself."

On Wednesday morning bright and early, Buddy and his mom had shown up at their door. Buddy had looked very much like a puppy that had just been whacked with a newspaper. He'd apologized five times for letting Jethro Zook talk him into all the bad things they'd done on the farm and for frightening Rose and her sisters and for being generally stupid and ignorant — the *stupid and ignorant* part had been his mom's suggestion. Rose guessed he'd gotten quite an earful the night before. Buddy's mom had taken away his cell phone and his car and told him he'd be well into his thirties before he got them back. Rose felt kind of sorry for him.

Buddy's mother had asked if there was a way Buddy could work to pay them back for the damage he had done to their farm, and that was how Buddy had ended up helping them pull honey for the last four days.

"Buddy was a wonderful-*gute* help with the honey," Rose said, feeling like she had to come to his defense. He was just a kid. With a mother like his who didn't let him get away with anything, he would learn to be a man.

Aunt Bitsy snorted. "We've simply taken on another stray cat," she said. "Come to think of it, I should have given him all three cats as his punishment. That would have been a fair trade."

Rose giggled and covered Leonard Nimoy's ears with her hands. "Aunt Bitsy! Don't ever let them hear you say that. The cats are like family."

"Well," Aunt Bitsy said. "Leonard Nimoy did try to save your life. Jethro Zook doesn't have the chicken pox, but he did end up with some *gute* scratches."

Rose frowned. "He's sorry for what he did, Aunt Bitsy. We should be sad Leonard Nimoy scratched him."

"We should be," Aunt Bitsy said. "But I'm not. Why do you think Leonard Nimoy got the pillow?"

"Buddy was a *gute* help with the honey," Lily said. "We can all admit that."

Rose clasped her hands together. "Wasn't it *wunderbarr?*"

Aunt Bitsy narrowed her eyes. "The honey?"

"*Jah,*" Rose said. "Pulling honey is my favorite time of the year."

Another long pause as the sisters stared at her. She must have something in her teeth.

The Honeybee sisters, along with Dan, Luke, and Josiah, had spent the better part of the week extracting honey from their three dozen hives. Dan had been able to come most mornings after his milking was done, and then all three boys had come every afternoon after chores on their own farms. Ashley and Griff had come and helped them finish up today, and Buddy had been here all four days.

Rose had never had a better time pulling honey, and she wasn't ashamed to admit why — at least to herself. Josiah had come Wednesday, Thursday, and Friday in the afternoon when his farm chores were done and had been so eager to help that Luke had hidden the duct tape just in case Josiah wanted to redecorate the hives.

Josiah had seemed almost giddy about learning how to use the heated scraping knfe, and he never strayed more than a few feet from Rose's side, as if she were the earth and he orbited around her.

Rose really couldn't imagine how she and her sisters had pulled the honey by themselves for so many years. In truth, she couldn't imagine how she'd done without Josiah at all. Her hand went to the nape of her neck, where the memory of Josiah's touch four nights ago still lingered.

Someone knocked on the door. Poppy snapped her head up and grinned. "Luke and Dan aren't due for another hour. I love it when they come early."

Rose was simply glad that answering the door wasn't quite the frightening adventure it used to be.

Aunt Bitsy opened the door, and Josiah stood on the porch with a can of paint in one hand and a paintbrush in the other. His dog, Honey, sat at his feet.

Josiah caught sight of Rose and bloomed into a smile that made Rose shiver all the way down to her toes. *Oy,* anyhow. She loved that smile.

"Bitsy," he said. "I didn't get to help you pull honey this morning, but I've finished my chores and I've come to paint the barn door. I thought you might want it to match the rest of the barn for the wedding."

"*Gute* idea," Aunt Bitsy said, glancing at Rose. "Do you need some help?"

He trained his gaze on Rose. "*Nae.* I don't want to bother you. I just wanted to get your approval."

Lily grabbed a donut from one of the plates and handed it to him. "Would you like a donut?"

"*Jah,* sure. *Denki.*" He smiled at Rose. She returned his smile with an eager one of her own. They stood staring at each other in silence until Josiah seemed to remember where he was. "*Ach, vell.* I won't take up any more of your time. I'll be out by the barn if you need me."

"Make sure it's the right color this time," Aunt Bitsy said before she shut the door.

This whole staring thing with Aunt Bitsy and the sisters was becoming downright unnerving. None of them said anything. They just eyed Rose as if they were waiting for something.

Rose folded her arms and returned their gaze. "Why are you looking at me like that?"

Lily glanced at Poppy, who glanced at Aunt Bitsy, who took Rose by the hand and led her to the table to sit. Rose sat down in the duct-taped chair. Poppy and Lily sat on either side of her, and Aunt Bitsy sat next to Lily.

Lily wrapped her fingers around Rose's wrist. "Rose," she said. "How do you feel about Josiah?"

Rose's heart thumped just thinking about it. During the drive home from the cemetery, she and Josiah had sat in the backseat of the truck — just the two of them — and she had fallen asleep on his shoulder. It was then that she had seen clearly what had been tucked away in her heart for a very long time. Josiah wasn't just a friend, and she wasn't just a project. She loved him so deeply that her bones ached when she wasn't with him. But what would her sisters think of such talk? "Why do you ask?" she finally said.

Poppy took her other hand. There was a sense of urgency in her eyes. "Because he loves you something wonderful."

The tears welled up without warning. *Ach,* it felt so *gute* to hear someone say it. "Do you really think so?"

"For sure and certain," Lily said breathlessly. "More than anything."

Rose blinked and a single tear plopped on the table. "And I . . . I love him more than anything too."

It was as if her sisters and Aunt Bitsy had been holding their breath, and they finally released it. Poppy squealed and threw her arms around Rose's neck, and Lily wrapped her arms around Rose's waist. Rose tried to embrace everybody, and they hugged the stuffing out of each other.

Rose's happiness, as well as her sorrow, came with tears, and she cried into Lily's neck for the pure joy of saying it out loud. "Do you think . . . do you think he loves me enough to want a future together?"

Lily nodded. "There's no doubt about that."

"Are you sure? He hasn't said a word. Maybe he hasn't made up his mind yet."

Lily frowned. "Rose, you're blind if you can't see how much that boy loves you, but he doesn't want to rush you."

"He's afraid he'll scare you away," Poppy said.

"He's terrified," Lily said. "If you say no, he'll never smile again."

Rose wanted to deny it, but Lily and Poppy told the truth. Of course Josiah was apprehensive. Rose had made no secret that his expectations frightened her, that she thought he wanted to make her a project. Every time he had done something nice for her, she had questioned his motives. She had cried one minute, avoided him the next, rejected his gifts, and ordered him off her porch. She'd given him every reason to be cautious and every reason to give up on her.

She caught her breath and covered her mouth with her hand. If Josiah gave up on her, she didn't know what she would do. "Maybe I should let him know how I feel."

"Don't ask me," Aunt Bitsy said. "If you marry him, before long you won't be able to see the house for the duct tape. We'd become a tourist attraction." She rubbed her chin. "I suppose we could make a little money out of it. I'm still deciding if this is a *gute* thing or a bad thing."

"I think you should let him know how you

feel," Lily said. "And sooner than later."

Much sooner. With her heart lodged in her throat, Rose got to her feet. "I'm scared."

Aunt Bitsy shrugged. "If you want to learn to be brave, you have to do something that scares you."

Rose wasn't very brave, but she was madly in love. How could she let Josiah go one more second without knowing that? She grabbed a chocolate chip cookie from one of the plates on the island and headed for the door.

"You're taking a cookie for protection?" Poppy asked.

"It's an excuse," Rose said.

She marched onto the porch and shut the door behind her. No doubt they would crowd around the window as soon as they thought she wasn't looking.

With galloping heart, Rose tiptoed across the flagstones to the barn, where Josiah was just pouring some red paint into the tray. He smiled. "Rose," he said, and she thought she might faint before she had a chance to say what she'd come to say. Nothing she could do was any match for that glorious smile and the sound of her name on his lips.

She held out the cookie. "You . . . you looked hungry. I brought you a treat."

"Denki." He took it from her, pulled a tissue from his pocket, and wrapped the cookie in it. "I'll save it for later."

She nearly turned on her heels and marched back into the house. How could she have a reasonable conversation when her pulse raced faster than Buddy's car and her knees knocked together like a woodpecker on a telephone pole?

"It's a wonderful sunny day to paint," she said. Thank the *gute* Lord for the weather. Without it, people wouldn't know how to start a conversation.

He gazed at her as if he didn't want to do anything else, as if he didn't have a barn door to paint before it got dark. "*Jah.* It's supposed to rain on Monday. I hope the paint will have enough time to dry."

"Aunt Bitsy bought a new pillow for Leonard Nimoy." *Oy,* anyhow. If she weren't so dreadfully, desperately nervous, she wouldn't be so tongue-tied.

"Does that mean Leonard Nimoy is officially part of the family?"

"I think so."

With a smile on his face, he stared at her for a few moments until Honey nudged her nose against his hand. He patted his dog on the head, picked up his roller, and dipped it into the paint tray. "This is the same color we used on the back. It should match."

"Josiah," she said, too loudly and with too much urgency.

He snapped his head up to look at her, and his expression immediately clouded over with concern. "Is something wrong?"

She wrung her hands. Nothing was wrong. If she wanted to learn to be brave, she had to do things that scared her — not to mention the fact that she loved him with every breath she took.

She started again. "Josiah, remember when you asked me what I truly want?"

"*Jah*," he said. "It has always been the most important question."

She clasped her hands together to keep them from trembling. "I'm ready to tell you the real answer."

He drew his brows together. "Anything, Rose. Anything you want."

"I want . . ." Her mouth felt like a piece of day-old, dry bread. She swallowed hard. "I want to marry you. What do you think about that?"

His mouth fell open, and he glanced behind him as if Rose were talking to someone else. "What do . . . what do you mean?"

Her legs started to wobble. Better get this over with right quick. "I love you something wonderful, Josiah Yoder, and I want to marry you."

For a few seconds, he didn't say a word, just stared at her as if he was trying to decide if she was teasing him. Then, in one swift movement, he crossed the distance between them, took her into his arms, and brought his lips down on hers.

It was a little sudden and completely unexpected, but she didn't let that stop her from snaking her arms around his neck and kissing him back. She'd never experienced anything as fierce as the love she felt for him at this very moment. Josiah was her sun, moon, and stars. He was the sky and the earth, the bees and hives, and his kiss sent warmth flowing through her veins like a toasty fire on a frosty night.

He pulled away, but kept his arms around her, and regarded her with those shocking blue eyes. "I'm feeling a little foggy yet," he said. "Did you just ask me to marry you?"

"I suppose I did." She gave him a hopeful smile.

He chuckled. "It would have taken me months to work up the courage."

"Aunt Bitsy says if you want to learn to be brave, you have to do something that scares you."

"Your Aunt Bitsy is the wisest woman I

know." It was as if he was compelled to be as close to her as possible. He cupped her chin in his hand and brushed his thumb against her bottom lip. She felt the vibration of his touch all the way to her toes. Lightning struck when he kissed her again. *Ach, du lieva.* Even though she was still standing, he'd knocked her off her feet.

Honey barked and jumped up and down, then ran around and around them as if she were on a carousel.

Holding on tight to Josiah so she wouldn't fall over, she tried to catch her breath between giggles. "Do you want to think about it for a few days?"

He growled. "Think about it? I've thought of nothing else for four years. I want to marry you with every bone in my body. Is that *gute* enough?"

"It will do," she said. "How do you feel about a triple wedding?"

There was a catch in his breath when he spoke. "Does that mean I can marry you in two weeks?"

She nodded.

He threw his head back and whooped to the sky. Lifting her off the ground, he twirled her around and around until he nearly ran into the barn. She took it as a yes.

Breathlessly, he set her on her feet and kissed her again. "My Rosie," he said, cupping her face in his hands. "I love you like no man ever loved a woman. *Gotte* is *gute*." He brought his lips down on hers one more time and made her heart do a very clumsy somersault.

This was the way she wanted to feel for the rest of her life.

A loud and forceful voice startled them out of their kiss. "Josiah Yoder, do I need to remind you of the rules?"

Without disentangling themselves, they looked in the direction of the house. Aunt Bitsy stood on the porch, leaning on her shotgun like a cane and scowling in Josiah's direction as if she were thinking of shooting him. With the kitten tattoo on her neck, she looked quite intimidating.

Josiah was too ecstatic to be intimidated. "Before you get mad . . ."

"Too late," Aunt Bitsy said.

"I just want to point out that we are kissing well away from the porch."

Rose tried to hide a smile behind her hand.

Bitsy didn't think it was funny. "I'm talking the spirit of the law rather than the letter of the law, young man."

Rose couldn't help a wide grin. "Aunt

Bitsy, it's a matter of safety. If he lets go of me, I'll fall over."

Aunt Bitsy gave Rose the stink eye. "Then have him bring you into the house so you can sit down."

Aunt Bitsy had never given her the stink eye before. Getting the stink eye felt like some sort of graduation. It meant Aunt Bitsy wasn't going to treat her like a baby anymore. The stink eye was reserved for grown-ups and unapologetic fiancés.

Josiah winked at Rose. "I'm sure there's a place to sit behind the barn. Let's go find it." He tightened his arm around her waist and tugged her with him.

No doubt Aunt Bitsy was glaring at them as they walked away.

How long before she'd start shooting things?

CHAPTER TWENTY

Aunt Bitsy swung open the door to the Honeybee sisters' room and the doorknob banged against the wall behind it. "Well, girls," she said. "I've taught the cats a new trick."

Rose sat on her bed putting on her brand-new wedding stockings. Wedding stockings weren't any different from ordinary stockings except that she would be wearing them on the day she was joined for life to the boy she loved. The butterflies in her stomach had been eaten by a flock of sparrows, and the sparrows were making quite a fuss. As excited as she was, she couldn't concentrate on anything. Had Aunt Bitsy said something about cats?

Aunt Bitsy strolled into the bedroom — without the cats — and shut the door behind her. Her hair was a light shade of green to match her mint-green dress. She wasn't sporting any temporary tattoos that

Rose could see, but she was wearing a sparkly pair of earrings.

"I love your hair today," Lily said, checking her black wedding *kapp* in the small hand mirror — the only mirror in the whole house.

"It's symbolic," Aunt Bitsy said. "Green means life and spring and new beginnings." She squeezed Lily's earlobe affectionately. "Today is the most important day of your lives. I thought green would be *gute* karma."

Rose didn't know what *gute* karma was, but she hoped it would be a truly blessed day.

With only two weeks to prepare, Rose had decided not to sew a new dress for the wedding. She wore her pink dress, the one she had been wearing on the day she was kidnapped — the day Josiah had come to her rescue in Ashley's truck. The day he had taken her in his arms and made her feel safe and cherished. The day she had finally surrendered her heart. It wasn't an old dress, and Josiah lit up like a room full of propane lanterns whenever she wore it.

Poppy had chosen a royal-blue fabric for her wedding dress. It made her eyes look like bright summer leaves dancing above a serene blue lake. Lily wore a yellow dress that accented her hair. Rose didn't mind that she was the plainest sister. Josiah thought she was pretty, and he was the only one who mattered.

The flock of sparrows became a whole herd of stampeding cattle. Would she be able to get through her own wedding without passing out?

Aunt Bitsy clapped her hands together. "Would you like to see the new trick I have taught the cats?"

Rose grinned. "Of course. It will be our first wedding present."

Poppy picked an errant thread from her sleeve. "So they are learning some tricks?"

One corner of Aunt Bitsy's mouth curled upward. "More or less."

She walked out of the room, and Rose could hear her going down the hall to her bedroom. She must have corralled the cats in there. She came back with all three of the cats in her arms. Farrah Fawcett looked as irritated as she always did at the indignity of being carried by a human being. Billy Idol hissed as if he were in the arms of a murderer. Leonard Nimoy looked eager, as if her whole life was an amazing adventure. "Shut the door, Lily," Bitsy said, "so they won't try to escape."

As soon as Lily shut the door, Bitsy put all three cats on the floor. It was only then that Rose noticed that each cat had something tied to its collar. Farrah Fawcett was dragging something along behind her, like a leash that had lost the person on the other end.

Bitsy pulled a kitty treat from her apron pocket. "Sit, Farrah Fawcett," she said, holding the treat just out of reach of Farrah Fawcett's paws. Farrah Fawcett watched the treat with absolutely no interest, jumped up onto Lily's bed, and settled in for a nap. Whatever that leash thing was, it still dangled from her collar.

Bitsy grunted. "I should have said 'lie down.' At least then you might have been impressed." She unhooked the leash from Farrah Fawcett's collar and detached what turned out to be a plastic bag. She reached in the plastic bag and pulled out a beautiful white organdy apron. A wedding apron.

Aunt Bitsy held the apron up to Lily. "This is the apron your mother wore on her wedding day."

Lily gasped. "For me?"

"She would have wanted you to have it."

Lily lovingly fingered the stitches along the hem and shoulders. "She made this?"

Aunt Bitsy nodded. "Uh-huh. She was always more patient than I was with such things."

Lily put it on and smoothed it over her yellow dress. "It's beautiful," she said, blinking back tears pooling in her eyes.

Aunt Bitsy patted her cheek. "Just like the bride wearing it." She pulled the same kitty treat from her pocket. "Come here, Billy Idol."

Billy Idol had crawled under Rose's bed, probably to better defend himself in case of attack. Aunt Bitsy got down on her hands and knees and peered under the bed. "Billy Idol, come here now."

The sisters watched curiously to see what kind of trick Aunt Bitsy had in store, but Billy Idol didn't budge.

Aunt Bitsy blew a strand of green hair out of her face. "Where's Luke when you need him? He's the only one Billy Idol will listen to." She finally put the kitty treat on the floor and stepped away from the bed. Billy Idol tiptoed out from under the bed and sniffed at the kitty treat as if it might be poisoned. Aunt Bitsy wasted no time grabbing Billy Idol by the scruff of the neck and untying the small plastic bag tied to his collar. Aunt Bitsy smirked. "You should have seen me try to get that on him. This is for you, Poppy," she said, pulling a black wedding *kapp* from the bag and pressing her fingers along the seams to reshape it.

418

Poppy's eyes misted up just as Lily's had. "Is it my *mater*'s?"

Bitsy nodded. "For her wedding day." She handed it to Poppy and pinched Poppy's ears for good measure.

Poppy held the *kapp* to her face and breathed in, and a thousand memories glowed in her eyes. "I remember her smile," Poppy said, her voice shaking with emotion. "She was always smiling, even when I was naughty. Thanks to Josiah, I've got something to remember her by."

Rose had made two copies of their *mater*'s photo and given one to each of her sisters.

"She loved you very much," Aunt Bitsy said. She dabbed at what might have been moisture in her eyes. "She was the kindest, gentlest person I've ever known."

"Denki," Poppy said, giving Aunt Bitsy a hug. "I'll cherish it forever."

Aunt Bitsy squared her shoulders and cleared her throat. "Now for Rose. Leonard Nimoy has been waiting very patiently." She untied the small bag from Leonard Nimoy's collar and gave the kitten two treats. Leonard Nimoy was delighted.

From the bag, Aunt Bitsy pulled a white handkerchief with beautiful lace tatting along the edges. "Your *mamm* made this for her wedding, but I never saw her without it in her waistband or tucked up her sleeve until the day she died. She kept it to remind her of her love for your *fater,* even during the times when they were cross with each other."

Rose took the hanky and wiped the tears that were falling down her cheeks. "*Denki,* Aunt Bitsy. I couldn't have asked for anything more beautiful."

Aunt Bitsy held her hands out to Rose and Lily. In turn, Rose and Lily each took one of Poppy's hands. They stood in a circle, silently holding hands and savoring a moment that would never come again.

How far they had all come in one summer!

Lily looked like the radiant sunshine in her yellow dress. Paul Glick had beaten her down for so many years that Rose had feared they would never get her back. But Dan had shown Lily what real love could be, and she had blossomed like a flower in the springtime.

Luke had taught Poppy how to forgive and how to need another person without losing herself. She adored him, and he adored her. Poppy deserved to be adored.

Rose's heart swelled with joy almost too big to contain. Josiah had taken her gently by the hand and helped her make peace with her past and not fear her future. She loved him as if he were her own soul.

Gotte *is* gute.

Rose looked at Aunt Bitsy. Tears streamed unchecked down her cheeks. She had never seen Aunt Bitsy cry before. "I loved your *mater* so much," Aunt Bitsy said. "I hope she's not disappointed in how I raised you. I wish she could have been here to do it herself."

"Oh, Aunt B," Lily sighed.

Rose wiped her eyes. "If Mamm were here, she would thank you a thousand times for what you did for her little girls."

Poppy giggled through her tears. "I think we turned out very well."

The three sisters hugged Aunt Bitsy all at once. Aunt Bitsy embraced them right back in a tangled four-way hug. They disintegrated into a flood of tears and laughter, the perfect bittersweet beginning to a perfect day.

"We'd better stop," Aunt Bitsy said. "Or you'll none of you look fit to be married."

They all jumped when someone rapped forcefully on the door. Mammi Sarah burst into the room without waiting to be invited. All three cats darted from the room as if it were on fire. "Elizabeth," Mammi said, obviously righteously indignant about something. But then, Mammi's main personality trait was righteous indignation. "Elizabeth, you have got to get that girl out of my kitchen, or I quit. She's ruining the celery."

"What girl are you talking about, Mamm?"

"The one with canning lids in her earlobes."

"Ashley?"

The lines on Mammi's forehead piled up. "She doesn't know how to dice. Her fingernails are too long. She can't even hold a stalk of celery properly, and when I tried to correct her, she told me it was okay because she writes a cooking plog and she knows what she's doing. I don't care what a cooking plog is. That girl has got to go."

Lily leaned over and planted a kiss on Mammi's cheek. Mammi's lips puckered like a prune. "*Denki* for being in charge of the cooking today. We couldn't have a wedding without you, Mammi."

"Don't I know it," Mammi said. "And two weeks' notice was all I got — for three weddings." She pointed to Aunt Bitsy. "This is your fault, Elizabeth. You could have at least put a bug in my ear so I had more time to plan. I scoured three counties to find enough celery."

Rose cocked an eyebrow. Just how much celery was Mammi cooking down there?

"We're sorry, Mammi," Lily said. "We wanted it to be a surprise."

"Surprise?" Mammi said. "It was more like a heart attack. I had you pegged to marry Paul Glick."

Lily took Mammi's hands. "But you like Dan Kanagy, don't you?" Despite everything, Lily still wanted Mammi's approval. Rose felt the same way.

Mammi shrugged and pulled her hands from Lily's. She had never been comfortable with shows of affection. "Paul Glick is richer than Dan Kanagy, but there's no shame in working a dairy farm. It's *gute,* honest work. And Paul Glick is a bit chubby. I suppose if I was your age, I'd rather have looks than money, but I hope you don't come to regret it. Beauty fades, but money never does." She eyed Rose. "I wish you would have told me about Josiah. I was working out a way to get Paul Glick and you alone at the house."

Rose's throat tightened up. Just one more reason among several that she was glad she was marrying Josiah.

"But I like Josiah Yoder," Mammi said. "Even with that unfortunate red hair, he is quite handsome, and he owns several acres of land. It's always *gute* to marry someone with land."

"*Denki,* Mammi. I'm glad you approve. I love him very much."

Mammi looked at Poppy with her always-critical eye. "I never thought I'd see the day when you'd be somebody's bride, Poppy, especially not Luke Bontrager's. Even though the Lord looks on the heart, anyone with eyes can see how handsome he is. He could have had any girl in town. Why he picked you instead of Rose, I'll never know."

Aunt Bitsy frowned with her whole body, but Poppy didn't even flinch. "*Denki,* Mammi," Poppy said. "Luke is very handsome. I don't know why he picked me either."

Mammi clicked her tongue. "Well, stuff and nonsense, Poppy. You're pretty enough for Luke Bontrager, but I don't expect he knows about your temper yet. Best keep it a secret until after the wedding."

Nobody could ruffle Poppy's feathers on the happiest day of her life, not even Mammi Sarah. She smiled, and Rose could tell she wasn't even faking it. "Seeing as I'm getting married in less than three hours, I think my secret is safe."

Mammi stepped back, folded her arms, and surveyed each of her granddaughters. "You'll all do well enough. Be sure you speak up when taking your vows, and don't slouch, especially you, Rose. But don't be proud. Keep your eyes downcast until the bishop asks you to speak."

"We will, Mammi," Rose said. There was nothing else to do but agree with their *mammi,* who meant well but didn't know how to express her love.

Mammi nodded as if all was well. "Now, Elizabeth," she said. "What are you going to do about that girl downstairs?"

"Can she wash dishes?" Lily said.

Mammi smirked. "*Nae.* She just had her fingernails done."

"I'll be down soon, Mamm," Aunt Bitsy said. "Can you abide her for five more minutes yet?"

"I'll do what I can," Mammi said, wagging her finger at Aunt Bitsy. "But if your wedding celery is ruined, it's on your head."

"I take full responsibility," Aunt Bitsy said.

Mammi marched out the door, and they could hear her determined steps on the stairs. They paused and listened to the activity downstairs as relatives and friends bustled around the kitchen making last-minute preparations for the wedding meal. Mammi Sarah started yelling instructions before she even made it to the bottom of the stairs.

Lily giggled. "It wonders me if Ashley or

Mammi will win."

Aunt Bitsy cracked a smile. "I don't know, but I'd like to watch."

"I'm rooting for Ashley," Poppy said.

There was a light tap on the door, and Poppy opened it. Hannah Yutzy stood in the doorway with a wide smile and a piece of folded paper. "Luke asked me to give this to you," she said. "I teased him that I didn't think the groom should be passing notes to the bride right before the wedding, but he said it would be okay." She giggled. "The guests are coming. It's almost time."

"*Denki,* Hannah," Poppy said. She shut the door, unfolded the note, and started reading. "Oh, no," she said, glancing at Lily.

"What is it?"

She sat down on the bed and cradled her forehead in her hands. "Luke says he's caught wind of something that Paul Glick has planned for the wedding."

"Paul?" Lily said. "What does that mean?"

"Luke says Paul has learned a secret about Aunt Bitsy, and he plans to make a scene and demand Aunt Bitsy be shunned right before Lily is supposed to say her vows."

"He thinks he's going to stop the wedding," Aunt Bitsy murmured.

Lily sank to the bed. "I don't understand. How could he do something so cruel?"

Rose reached out and grabbed Lily's hand. "There must be some mistake. Not even Paul would try to ruin a wedding."

Deep lines etched themselves into Lily's face. "*Jah*, he would."

Aunt Bitsy growled and looked up at the ceiling. She seemed more irritated than upset. "Heavenly *Fater*, don't you think a bladder infection could have prevented all this?"

Poppy stood up and ripped the note into tiny pieces. "Aunt Bitsy doesn't have any secrets that people don't already know about. Everyone has seen the hair and the earrings and the tattoos. Paul is vindictive and wants to make a scene. That's all."

"It's my fault," Lily said. "I should have handled it differently. I should have sold him our honey for the lower price."

Aunt Bitsy shook her head. "Don't blame yourself for this. Paul has a chip on his shoulder the size of a house, not to mention a nasty streak when he doesn't get his way." Her lips drooped into a frown as she sat on the bed next to Lily and motioned for Rose and Poppy to sit next to them. "I was going to tell you after the weddings, but now's as good a time as any." She patted Lily's hand. "Paul, for all his grand indignation, will never be able to get me shunned. Not in a thousand years."

"But he said . . ."

Aunt Bitsy raised her hand to halt all objections. "I know I wear earrings and try out an occasional tattoo, but I will never be shunned."

"How can you be sure?"

For the first time since Rose had known her, Aunt Bitsy seemed unsure of herself. She glanced at all her nieces and folded and unfolded her arms. "I am not Amish."

"What do you mean you're not Amish, B?" Poppy said. "Of course you're Amish."

Aunt Bitsy shook her head. "I left home when I was sixteen. I never got baptized. I promised your *mamm* I would raise you Amish, but that didn't mean I had to convert."

Rose sat in stunned silence. That explained why Aunt Bitsy always seemed to be deathly ill two times a year for communion. Nonmembers weren't allowed.

"But," Poppy said, "everybody thinks you're Amish."

Aunt Bitsy sighed out all the air in her lungs. "I understand how much this hurts you. If you're mad and would rather I not come to your wedding, I understand. I want you to know that I never lied to you, but I made you believe something that wasn't real. The bishop and I agreed it would be better for you girls if everyone assumed I was Amish. I'm pretty good at being a proper Amish woman. I'm only eccentric in the privacy of my own home."

Poppy's jaw sat on the floor next to Rose's. "We didn't know."

"I didn't want you to love me any less."

"Love you less?" Rose said. "Aunt Bitsy, this only makes us love you more."

Poppy nodded. "You gave up your whole life for us, and we'd cancel the wedding if you weren't allowed to come."

"Dan and Luke and Josiah might have something to say about that." Bitsy nearly smiled, then seemed to remember her old self. She folded her arms and harrumphed her indignation. "Now that's all settled, we need to figure out what to do about Paul. I don't care if he tells everyone at the wedding I haven't been baptized, but I will not let him ruin your wedding day, even if I have to get my shotgun."

"The shotgun would definitely ruin the wedding day."

"We need to show Paul forgiveness," Rose said.

Poppy grunted her disgust. "We can work on that after the wedding. How do we get rid of him today?"

Lily wrapped her arms around her waist. "If I knew that, I would have been rid of him years ago."

Poppy studied the pile of shredded paper in her hand. "B, do we still have that bottle of valerian root?"

"You coming down with something?"

"I have an idea, but we're going to need some help." A smile slowly grew on Poppy's lips. "We need Ashley."

CHAPTER TWENTY-ONE

Josiah leaned in close and whispered in Rose's ear. "This is the happiest day of my life." Then, to be proper, he pulled away before anyone noticed.

"The best day of mine too," she said. Lord willing, there would be many happy days to come.

"Time to go," Aunt Bitsy said.

All twenty-four of them stepped outside.

Josiah held an umbrella over Rose's head as they walked from the house to the barn, where the wedding was to take place. A slight drizzle had started early this morning, turning into a downpour by the time the wedding started. Cars, buggies, and vans lined the lane, which was dotted with ruts and mud puddles. Lord willing, no one would step in a puddle or get stuck in the mud.

Rose didn't mind the rain. It made the air smell fresh and kept the honeybees in their hives instead of out among the guests. Still, she couldn't be completely happy, not even with Josiah so close, smiling at her like that and smelling like new leather. She couldn't relax until she knew Paul Glick would not harm her family today. They were hanging their hopes on Ashley, the girl who couldn't cut celery and thought Griff Simons was a *gute* catch.

Two hours of singing and sermons had already taken place by the time the brides and grooms and their attendants were summoned to the services. Rose and her sisters and their fiancés had moved the buggy and the horse and everything else out of the barn, and swept and washed until the floor was as clean as the one in the kitchen. Wedding guests sat on benches, the men and women facing each other.

Rose's heart thumped madly as Josiah opened the door to the barn. He held it open for everyone — Mammi and Aunt Bitsy, Dan and Lily, Luke and Poppy, the eight boys and eight girls they'd chosen as their attendants, and Rose.

Rose and her sisters sat in the center of the rows of benches facing Dan, Luke, and Josiah. Water dripped rhythmically from the ceiling and made a small puddle directly between Rose and Josiah. Rose's heart thrilled at the very sight of Josiah sitting opposite her, keeping his eyes downcast in a show of humility and reverence. She loved everything about him. How could she bear to wait even five minutes longer to be his wife?

Since the wedding was in the barn, Honey and the cats were allowed to attend. Honey sat on her haunches just beyond the rows of benches, behaving like a very proper dog at a very solemn event. Farrah Fawcett had climbed up to the haymow and was observing proceedings from above. Or maybe she wasn't watching at all. She looked to be asleep. Billy Idol stood right by the outside door, as if to make a quick escape if he needed to. Leonard Nimoy chased a grasshopper around the perimeter of the barn.

The bishop smiled and paused until everyone was seated. Before he could even draw breath, Paul, sitting three rows back, shot to his feet and scowled in Lily's direction. "I have something to say," he said, raising his voice as if he were rebuking the wind and the waves.

Rose thought she might be sick.

From a bench at the back where the *Englischers* sat, someone coughed violently. His coughs echoed off the ceiling of the barn and were so loud, Paul couldn't make himself heard above the racket.

Rose's face felt like it was on fire as she saw Ashley's head pop up from behind the men. She was wearing a skin-tight, bright red dress and impossibly tall shoes. She stood up, smiled sheepishly, and made an announcement to the whole group. Rose was absolutely stunned by her courage. "I'm so sorry. I'm so sorry. I'll take him and get him a drink or something."

Paul sank back into his seat as if he'd decided the polite thing to do was to let the sick man leave before making his big announcement.

Ashley pulled Griff — who seemed to be trying to hack up a boulder — from the bench and tugged him toward the center of the benches as if she wasn't altogether sure how to actually get out of the barn. The gold chain around her neck jangled cheerily as she snaked among the rows of Amish men. Ashley pulled a bottle from her purse and unscrewed the lid. "I just need to give him some cough medicine," she said.

Some neighbors, trying to be helpful, pointed in the right direction as Ashley led Griff between two rows of Amish men. When she was directly behind Paul Glick, she tripped over her own feet. Paul shouted in surprise as the bottle with no lid tumbled over his shoulder, spilling liquid the color of root beer down his white shirt and making a puddle in his lap.

"Oh my goodness," Ashley said as Paul jumped to his feet. The brown liquid dribbled down his legs and dripped onto the barn floor. Ashley was a very *gute* actress. She looked positively horrified. "I'm so sorry."

"Look what you've done," Paul yelled, not caring about the solemnity of a wedding ceremony. "I'm all wet."

Paul's brother Perry crinkled his nose and leaned away from Paul. Soon men in front and behind and to the side made faces and held their noses in disgust. Paul was not only dripping brown liquid, but he smelled like an outhouse in the middle of July.

"Paul," Perry whispered in a voice loud enough for everyone to hear, "you've got to get out of here. You stink to high heaven."

Ashley and Griff covered their noses. They probably hadn't expected quite that bad of a smell. "I'm really sorry," Ashley said.

Andrew Nelson, Josiah's brother-in-law, was in front of Paul. He stood up and turned around. "Paul, I think you'll need to go home and change," he said in his booming voice that most people found hard to ignore.

Paul lifted his chin. "I'm not leaving until I've said what I have to say."

"You need to go," Freeman Beiler said. "Six people are trying to get married, and you smell like a dead body."

"There's something you need to know about the Honeybee *schwesters* and their aunt," Paul said.

Andrew sighed deeply and shook his head. "We've heard the rumors, Paul. And we don't put stock in any of them."

"That's because Rose Christner is going to be your sister-in-law."

Andrew and Freeman took Paul by the sleeves and quickly escorted him and his ripe smell out of the barn. "What am I supposed to do out here?" she heard him say as they left him standing in the rain and shut the door behind him.

Rose felt a momentary twinge of guilt. She hadn't wanted Paul to be humiliated, but as Poppy had said, he had brought it upon himself with his uncontrollable anger. Rose would of course confess the whole thing to him after her honeymoon trip and beg for his forgiveness. Until then, the rest of them might as well enjoy the wedding.

Surely, nothing like this had ever happened at a wedding or even *gmay* for that matter. Someone in the back chuckled quietly. The laughter seemed to be as contagious as yawning, and soon more than a few people were trying to hide their mirth behind their hands.

Luke's brother Matthew, one of the attendants, pulled a wad of napkins out of one pocket. He stepped back to Paul's row and wiped up the liquid that had dribbled onto the floor and the bench. From his other pocket, he pulled a small pack of disinfectant wipes and swabbed down the whole area. He'd obviously been warned to be prepared.

The bishop waited patiently while Matthew finished cleaning. Ashley and Griff, who hadn't moved since Ashley had spilled her bottle, watched Matthew wipe up, then stepped around the benches and went back to their seats. Griff's cough seemed to have cured itself.

Rose glanced furtively at Josiah. He was looking right at her with a barely contained smile. He winked and lowered his eyes to the ground.

Once Paul was gone, Rose finally felt free to be totally, utterly, and wildly happy. The bishop was unruffled by the interruptions and recited the high German as if he'd been born speaking it. Lily and Dan were married first, followed by Poppy and Luke, then

Rose and Josiah. The rain tapped on the roof as they took their vows, and Rose thought that the dim, cozy barn in the pouring rain couldn't have been a more beautiful setting in which to pledge her love to Josiah.

After the service was over, they opened the barn doors, and the rain gave way to a drizzle. Men carried the benches to the large canopy that Aunt Bitsy had rented to house the wedding supper. Rose and her sisters had baked cakes for the centerpieces, with blue-and-yellow plates set at each table.

Josiah stayed close to Rose as they left the barn. Their hands brushed once, but handholding wasn't proper in public, even for the bride and groom. What Rose really wanted to do was throw her arms around Josiah and let him kiss her to the moon. From the look on his face, he wanted to do the same.

Aunt Bitsy followed Rose and Josiah out of the barn. She gave Rose a hug and patted Josiah's arm. "*Gute* job," she said.

Josiah bent over and gave Aunt Bitsy a kiss on the cheek. She turned red as a beet.

Luke and Poppy joined them, both looking so happy they might have been floating off the ground. Dan and Lily were right behind Luke and Poppy.

"It was a wonderful-*gute* wedding," Dan said. "It's as if all the happiness in the world is right here on the Honeybee Farm today."

Luke grinned like Billy Idol with a mouse between his teeth. "My favorite part was Paul's face as they closed the door on him."

Poppy cuffed him on the shoulder. "Wasn't your favorite part when we got married?"

He chuckled and gave Poppy a swift kiss on the cheek. If anybody saw him, nobody made a fuss about it. "Paul's face was my second-favorite part."

"Paul probably won't give up," Aunt Bitsy said. "But at least he didn't get a chance to ruin the wedding."

Ashley's gold jewelry tinkled as she pushed herself into their little circle with Griff in tow. She gave Rose and her sisters a hug. "No offense, but that was the longest, boringest wedding I have ever been to. Somebody should really tell those guys they don't need to talk so long. Nobody was even listening."

Josiah gave Griff a firm pat on the shoulder. "You are a wonderful-*gute* cougher."

Griff smiled and shuffled his feet. "I used to fake sick so I didn't have to go to school."

Ashley hooked her arm around Griff's elbow. "Wasn't he amazing? His coughing

439

shut that guy right up."

Lily patted Ashley's arm. "Thank you for what you did. You are a true friend."

Ashley flipped her hair out of her eyes. "Don't mention it. Anything for my homies."

"Are we 'homies'?" Dan asked.

"Yep." She smiled and pulled her phone from her purse. "I have to show you something. Look, Bitsy. Our Amish food blog already has three followers. My mom, Griff's dad, and somebody named Marvin from Florida. Isn't that amazing?"

"I feel like a celebrity," Aunt Bitsy said. She wasn't smiling, but she wasn't frowning either.

"We should go sit down," Josiah said. "We're the newlyweds."

Rose and her sisters and their husbands sat at the head table with three new beehives as their backdrop. Aunt Bitsy had bought the hives as wedding presents, and Rose had finished painting them last week. Lily's beehive featured the farm scene with a running horse and a pink barn door. Poppy's beehive was a garden full of bright red tomatoes. Rose had saved her most cherished design for her own beehive. Was that selfish?

Nae. A painting of a butterfly garden

meant more to her than it could to either of her sisters. They wouldn't mind.

The day after they had gotten engaged, Josiah had brought her a whole box of paints with tubes of every imaginable color. She had scolded him for such an extravagant gift, but he had refused to take it back, saying that a boy wildly in love couldn't be expected to do anything rational. Using Josiah's paints, Rose had painted the hive with dozens of monarch butterflies flitting amongst a sea of purple flowers. The picture would always remind her of her unbounded happiness and the gentle boy who had taken her by the hand and given her wings.

Mammi Sarah had the food ready to go as soon as they sat down. The attendants passed the bowls and platters down each table, and people served themselves.

They served roasted chicken with celery stuffing, plus mashed potatoes, coleslaw, cooked celery, buttered noodles, and a Bienenstich cake because, Lord willing, life was going to be very sweet. Even the celery turned out just right. Ashley wasn't as bad as Mammi had said.

After supper, the clouds dispersed and *die youngie* played volleyball and croquet while the old folks caught up with people they hadn't seen for months. Rose and Josiah visited with friends and relatives and held hands under the table when no one was looking. Rose would have been perfectly content to never let go of Josiah's hand again.

After games and visiting, Mammi Sarah had dinner ready. There was more eating, more visiting, and a little more secret hand-holding while Honey and the cats played at their feet.

When the sun set, Aunt Bitsy handed out pens. The blue pens had Luke and Poppy's names on them. Lily and Dan's were yellow, and Rose and Josiah's were pink. Aunt Bitsy also gave everyone a little bag of M&M's that said R&J, P&L, or L&D on each little M&M. Rose thought it was a shame to eat something so cute.

The big event was, of course, the fireworks. Luke's brothers, Matthew and Mark, stood on the little wooden bridge that spanned the even smaller pond and lit every kind of firework imaginable. Aunt Bitsy's Amish neighbors were sufficiently impressed, and Dan and Lily were sufficiently surprised.

Dan didn't seem to mind them one little bit.

Immediately after the fireworks, Mammi and Dawdi came storming across the lawn to where Aunt Bitsy and Rose and her sisters were sitting. Rose groaned inwardly. She should have known Mammi and Dawdi would not approve of fireworks. She didn't think she could stand one more lecture from either of her grandparents.

"Elizabeth," Dawdi said. "Where did you get those fireworks?"

"The librarian helped me order them online."

Mammi burst into a smile. "They were much better than the fireworks at Yost Shirk's wedding." She leaned closer to Aunt Bitsy. "No one should ever skimp on the fireworks. Cheap fireworks mean a cheap wedding, and no one wants to start out life like that."

"*Denki*, Mamm," Aunt Bitsy said. She seemed almost more pleased about Mammi's praise than she had been about the weddings. Something so rare was that much more valuable.

Mammi hugged each of her granddaughters before she and Dawdi climbed into their buggy and drove away.

Luke's brothers hung propane lanterns around the canopy for those who wanted to stay out even later. Soon most everyone else went home, and Rose and her sisters and their husbands, Aunt Bitsy, and the cats and

443

Honey were almost the only ones left. They all sat together at a long table, too tired to move.

Rose rested her head on Josiah's shoulder until she nearly fell asleep. He put his arm around her. "*Cum,* Rose Yoder. Let's go home."

"Only if you stay with me forever."

"I promise," he said. He smiled and kissed her tenderly on the lips.

"It's time for us to go too," Lily said.

"We'll help you put out the lanterns," Dan said.

Aunt Bitsy waved away his suggestion. "You go. I don't mind putting it all away."

Buddy's mom, with Buddy in tow, marched across the lawn. They hadn't come to the wedding, but Aunt Bitsy had invited them for fireworks. Rose was surprised that they had lingered. Buddy's mom carried an oversized purse, and Buddy carried an equally large canvas bag.

"Bitsy," Buddy's mom said, "we know it's late and we've overstayed our welcome, but Buddy wants to thank you for how kind you've been to him."

She cleared her throat, which sounded more like a threat than a prompt, and Buddy stepped forward. "I want to thank you for how kind you've been to me," he said, glancing at his mom to make sure he got it right.

"And he has a present for you," his mom said.

Aunt Bitsy made a face. "I don't need a present. I just want Buddy to stay out of trouble. *Gotte* tends to give troublemakers all sorts of dread diseases." She looked up at the sky. "Or at least that's what should happen."

"All the same," his mom said, "we wanted to give you something."

With his mom's prodding, Buddy reached into his canvas bag and pulled out a light and dark brown striped cat with caramel-colored eyes. "I know you like cats," he said. "My mom and me got this one at the pet store. It's a girl."

"Ach, du lieva," Rose said, already formulating a plan to convince Aunt Bitsy to keep her. She reached out and took the cat from Buddy. "Look how pretty she is, Aunt Bitsy. And what a wonderful-*gute* playmate for Leonard Nimoy."

"Baby sister, don't even try," Aunt Bitsy said, with a look that would have peeled the paint off their bright red barn door. "I will not take another stray cat, no matter how cute you think she is."

Lily reached down and lifted Leonard

Nimoy onto the table. Rose put the new cat next to her. The two cats sniffed at each other, and then Leonard Nimoy lifted her paws and nudged them against the new cat. The new cat, in turn, lifted her paws, and the two cats seemed to be playing patty-cake.

"Look, Aunt B," Lily said. "They like each other."

Josiah winked at Rose. "Leonard Nimoy really does need a friend. Farrah Fawcett completely ignores her, and Billy Idol is a bad influence."

Rose heard a soft growl come from deep within Aunt Bitsy's throat. She sat in silence staring at that cat like someone who wanted to stop the sunset but didn't know how. After a few seconds of silence, she leaned her elbows on the table, scrunched her lips together, and massaged her temples as if a very bad headache was starting. "It's time to put me in a home," she said.

Luke chuckled. "We'll bring them to visit every day."

Aunt Bitsy lifted her head and gave Luke the stink eye. "Because of you, Luke Bontrager, I am now the town's eccentric cat lady."

"Does that mean we can keep her?" Rose said.

"Fine," Aunt Bitsy said through gritted teeth. "But only because I don't have the energy to fight about it tonight."

"What are you going to name her, B?"

Aunt Bitsy raised an eyebrow. "Everyone can see she's the spitting image of Sigourney Weaver. I loved her in *Aliens.*"

RECIPES

BLENDER WHOLE-WHEAT PANCAKES

Note from Rose: I got this recipe from an *Englisch* friend who makes these pancakes in a blender. That way, you don't have to grind the wheat separately. Since we Amish don't use electricity, I have included the blender recipe first and the non-electric recipe second.

Ingredients

1 1/2 cups buttermilk

1 cup whole-wheat kernels OR if you aren't using a blender, 1 1/2 cups whole-wheat flour

3 Tablespoons cornmeal

2 eggs

1 Tablespoon honey

1/2 teaspoon salt

1/2 teaspoon baking soda

1 Tablespoon Rumford baking powder (This brand makes a difference. Without it, add

another Tablespoon of cornmeal.)

In the Blender
Step 1: Have a hot griddle greased and ready.

Step 2: Put the buttermilk in the blender and turn the blender to the highest speed. Slowly pour the whole-wheat kernels into the blender. It will sound like popcorn popping. Blend until the popping sound is gone. Add cornmeal, eggs, honey, and salt.

Step 3: After mixing well, add baking soda and baking powder and blend for 20 seconds. The batter will rise fast!

By Hand
Step 1: Have a hot griddle greased and ready.

Step 2: In a medium mixing bowl, mix the buttermilk and whole-wheat flour. Add cornmeal, eggs, honey, and salt.

Step 3: After mixing well, add baking soda and baking powder and mix for 20 seconds. The batter will rise fast!

Makes about twelve pancakes.

PINEAPPLE COCONUT CAKE

Note from Rose: You can use an electric beater if you're not Amish. We use a hand beater. It is good exercise. You can toast the coconut for the topping if you want. Josiah likes it toasted and it looks beautiful on the cake, but it is also easy to burn. Aunt Bitsy does not like the smell of burned coconut.

Cake

2 cups all-purpose flour, sifted
1 Tablespoon baking powder
1 teaspoon salt
1/2 cup unsalted butter, room temperature
2 cups sugar
1 1/4 cups coconut milk
1 1/2 teaspoons coconut extract
5 egg whites

Preheat oven to 350 degrees.

Mix flour, baking powder, and salt together in a bowl. Place the butter in a separate mixing bowl and beat with a hand beater or on medium speed with an electric mixer for 1 minute. Add sugar and beat for another minute. Add coconut milk and coconut extract to butter mixture and mix well. While beating, gradually add flour mixture into the butter mixture and beat for 2 minutes.

In another bowl, beat egg whites until stiff peaks form. Fold the egg whites into the batter and stir to mix well.

Grease and line two 8-inch cake pans and divide batter evenly between them. Bake at 350 degrees for 23–28 minutes until a toothpick inserted in the center of the cake comes out clean. Remove the pans from the oven and place on a cooling rack for 5–10 minutes to cool before removing cake from the pans.

Pineapple Filling
(Make the filling while the cake is baking so they both have time to cool.)

1 20-ounce can crushed pineapple
2/3 cup sugar
2 Tablespoons cornstarch

In a saucepan combine all ingredients over medium heat. Cook, stirring frequently until mixture gets a glossy look (about 5 to 7 minutes). Cool.

Frosting
4 oz. of cream cheese, softened
1 Tablespoon coconut milk
1 cup powdered sugar

1/2 teaspoon coconut extract
1 12-ounce container whipped topping

Beat cream cheese in a bowl until smooth. Add coconut milk, powdered sugar, and coconut extract. Mix well and then fold the whipped topping into the mixture.

To assemble, cut both cakes open, making four 8-inch rounds. This is a little tricky, so use a sharp bread knife and cut carefully! On top of one, place half the pineapple filling and top with a cake layer. Next add a layer of frosting, then a cake layer. Place remaining pineapple mixture on the cake and top with the last cake layer. Frost the sides and top of the cake. Sprinkle with coconut.

This is best when refrigerated for at least 4 hours.

To Toast Coconut
Place about 1/4 cup of coconut flakes in a large skillet. Cook over medium heat, stirring frequently, until the flakes are mostly golden brown. If the coconut is sweetened it tends to brown faster so, it will take less time.

PEACH CRUMBLE

Note from Rose: This recipe is also delicious with apples. Same directions but you might need to cook it about 5 minutes longer to make sure the apples are tender. Can't be beat served with ice cream.

Ingredients

4 or 5 medium peaches
2 teaspoons cinnamon
1 1/2 cups quick oatmeal
1 1/2 cups firmly packed brown sugar
1 teaspoon salt
1 cup flour
1 cup butter, softened

Preheat oven to 350 degrees. Peel, pit, and slice peaches. Place peaches evenly in 9″ × 13″ ungreased baking dish. In a separate bowl, combine cinnamon, oatmeal, brown sugar, salt, and flour. Cut in the butter. Sprinkle the oatmeal mixture over the peaches. Bake at 350 degrees for 30 to 40 minutes until peaches are tender. Makes 10 servings.

HONEY LOZENGES

Note from Rose: This recipe basically uses honey and herbal tea. You can use just about any kind of herbal tea you want. Some of my favorites are *Echinacea* — immune system, *eucalyptus,* or *camphor* — relieve congestion, and *licorice* — chest and throat soother. I made Josiah peppermint-honey lozenges. Peppermint is an expectorant and a decongestant.

Ingredients
2 cups water
5 herbal tea bags
Honey
Powdered sugar

Steep the tea bags in boiling water for 15 minutes.

Pour powdered sugar into a pie tin and smooth evenly with your hand. Make evenly spaced indentations in the powdered sugar with your thumb or a teaspoon. Set aside.

Add honey to the herbal tea using the following ratio: 1 part tea to 1 1/4 parts honey. In other words, if you have 1 cup of tea, add 1 1/4 cups of honey. 2 cups of tea, 2 1/2 cups of honey, and so on.

Using a candy thermometer, heat the honey and tea mixture in a saucepan over medium high heat. Stir until honey is completely combined with the tea. Bring to a boil and DO NOT STIR AGAIN. Wash away crystals from the side of your pan with a damp brush or cloth. Once candy reaches 300 degrees, remove from heat.

Pour the liquid into the pie tin in the indentations made in the powdered sugar. Allow the lozenges to harden completely. If it's rainy or humid out this may take longer. You can put it in the fridge to speed the process.